A freelance writer for fifteen years, Carl Huberman lives quietly in Cheshire with his wife and family, four cats and his conspiracy theories.

His first novel, *Eminent Domain*, was greeted as 'a potent mixture of sex, violence and intrigue . . . a real page-turner' (*Midweek*).

Also by Carl Huberman

EMINENT DOMAIN

CARL HUBERMAN

Firefall Taken

PAN BOOKS

First published 1998 by Pan Books

an imprint of Macmillan Publishers Ltd
25 Eccleston Place, London SW1W 9NF
and Basingstoke

Associated companies throughout the world

ISBN 0 330 34722 5

9 8 7 6 5 4 3 2 1

A CIP catalogue record for this book is available from the British Library.

Typeset by SetSystems Ltd, Saffron Walden, Essex
Printed and bound in Great Britain by
Mackays of Chatham plc, Chatham, Kent

Better a thousand enemies outside your house than one inside.

ARABIC PROVERB

For Alistair Bell

It was still dark as the black Mack truck pulled to a halt off US Highway 287. A short man in a dark grey suit emerged from a door in the side of its long trailer, and walked back towards three dark green cars that had parked up behind it.

The man waved the driver out of the first car, then slid into the back seat and, locking the doors, opened up the laptop computer he had been carrying and plugged it into the Plymouth Gran Fury's built-in relay system. As he waited for the scrambled connection to be completed, he looked out on the early Wyoming morning.

Dawn was some time off, but already he could detect a greying of the darkness. The sight pleased him because, if everything went according to plan, the Thursday that was about to break would be the most important day of his life – and this time he would get it right.

The screen on the computer brightened into life and he found himself looking at a young man in a dark suit and sunglasses, sitting in a grey, featureless room.

'Hello, James,' said the man in the car. 'Are we on track?'

'One hundred per cent, sir.'

'So the farmer talked?'

'Like he was on Oprah.*'*

'Have you got all the names?'

'Every one. Even with three fingers cut off, he couldn't think of any more.'

'Good. And now?'

'He's dead. Terrible accident involving fresh cement.'

'Fine. And our man with the matches?'

'On his way. Saw him off myself at Casper airport.'

'James, how soon can you get to Worthing?'

The young man seemed surprised by this question but didn't query his employer. 'Two hours.'

'Do it, James. I might have another job for you. Contingencies.'

'Yes, sir, Mr Hartsby.'

Hartsby switched off the laptop and sat back and let out a long, satisfied sigh.

Every hour of every day for the last four years had been leading up to what was about to transpire. Four years of cunning, duplicity, and ruthless ambition: par for the course for Hartsby, but he had a secret even his most loyal staff knew nothing about – and today he was going to master that secret. Then, task accomplished, he would be invincible: stronger than the heads of the FBI or the CIA, or even the President himself. It was a daunting prospect, but, possessed of his special knowledge and the cool, calculating ego that had served him so well throughout his life, Hartsby knew he was up to the job.

He stepped out of the car just as a beat-up VW van trundled past. He saw several sets of trained fingers hovering over concealed holsters, but the vehicle drove on by without incident. Walking back to the trailer, he noticed the VW's ragged bumper sticker.

TODAY IS THE FIRST DAY OF THE REST OF YOUR LIFE.

Hartsby couldn't help smiling as he added an AGAIN to the slogan. If only they knew – if only all *the suckers knew.*

Thursday 4 September
Today
5:00 a.m.

One

The white Ford Contour police cruiser had pulled off the road, the driver's door, bearing the red fireball logo of Firefall Sheriff's Department, lying wide open. Country music was wafting out, its twanging guitars and sob-story vocals providing suitable backing for Sheriff's Deputy C. M. Entwistle as he danced in the headlight beams.

He was finding it difficult to keep time and every so often he would stutter to a halt, curse, then pick up the tempo again and try a few more steps. He and Carol had been invited to a big Thanksgiving party in San Francisco and he was determined that he would learn how to line-dance. He had previously been quite content to reach the age of thirty-seven unable to do anything on a dance floor other than cross it to the bar, but he was determined that Carol would have a good time, and if that meant looking like an arrhythmic cowpoke then so be it.

The song ended and he realized what a fool he must look, stuck out in the middle of Wyoming at five in the morning. He was also beginning to feel the cold so he got back into his car – and just in time.

Another police cruiser pulled in behind his own and a bear of a man eased himself out, his red face and thinning grey hair a battered tribute to raw weather and whiskey.

'Hi, Ed,' said Entwistle, unsure if the other man had seen his display.

'Hi, Entwistle,' said Sheriff Rickenbacker.

Entwistle liked Rickenbacker, respected him as a lawman and a friend. He had been Sheriff of Firefall for thirty-three years, and only ill health was likely to see him off.

'S'pose you saw?' he mumbled.

'Saw and heard,' said Rickenbacker. 'Had complaints from Dave at KFLL; said you was drowning out his broadcasts.'

They both laughed.

'Everything OK?' said Entwistle. He himself was on duty tonight, not Ed, and he wondered if something was wrong.

Rickenbacker leaned against Entwistle's car, eased open his straining jacket, pulled out some Camels, and lit up.

'Couldn't sleep. Bed gets kinda empty these days . . .'

Rickenbacker's wife, Tammy, had died of cancer fifteen months before, and her death had hit him hard. A silence fell between them, punctuated only by Willie Nelson's muted croaking and Rickenbacker's wheezy breathing.

'Should lay off the cigarettes, Ed,' said Entwistle.

'And the booze and the barbecue and the sodas and the poker . . . Seems one day they'll recommend we don't do anything we enjoy, then we'll just up and die of boredom.'

'Keeping fit can be fun,' said Entwistle, his own body in good condition, thanks to his daily workouts.

'Try doing it without endorphins, Entwistle. See how much "fun" it is then.'

'Least it's a natural high,' said Entwistle as he watched the man savour a lungful of smoke before releasing it.

'So's Gannet Peak,' said Rickenbacker. 'Doesn't mean you have to go climb it every goddam day.'

Entwistle laughed, then they fell silent, Rickenbacker quickly finishing his cigarette and, as was his habit, spitting in his hand and grinding the butt out in his huge palm. Then he walked back to his car and opened the door.

'Think I'll go finish up some paperwork. You OK to handle any calls?'

'Sure. Ain't like there's gonna be aliens landing.'

They both looked up at the star-studded blackness above them. Even after his four years in Firefall, Entwistle hadn't got used to how *big* a country sky was compared to the snippets a city lets you see between its high-rises.

'Martians might liven up the town,' said Rickenbacker.

'God pissed off, smoking crack, holding a sackful of thunderbolts couldn't liven up Firefall,' replied Entwistle.

Rickenbacker laughed, then climbed into his cruiser and reversed out onto the highway and drove off.

Entwistle got into his own car and turned up the heater. Ed had seemed more down than usual. He wondered if it might be an anniversary; he himself always got the glooms on 8 February, the date his father died.

He pulled out his wallet and looked at his pictures: his father and mother's twentieth anniversary; Niles Dennis, his SFPD partner, sitting on the hood of their black-and-white; and a holiday snap of Carol wrapped up well against the Aspen cold. Not a lot to show after half a life, he reflected bitterly. These were the people he had loved more than any others, and two of them had died before their time. He could imagine how Ed felt with all his love being focused into one person who'd had to endure a slow, painful death. At least Entwistle's father and Niles had died quickly.

He shook himself – what had brought this on? – and, putting his wallet away, he drove off. It was a quarter after five. He reckoned to call back at the Department in half an hour, grab a coffee, listen to Rickenbacker bitching about his pension, then catch up on his own paperwork. Seven would see him relieved, then two days off to enjoy.

But as he was cresting the rise on Taft Road and could see Firefall through the trees, nestling in its odd little valley like an electric oasis, the radio hissed into life. 'Entwistle, you there? Come back,' said Rickenbacker.

'What is it, Ed?'

'Got a call from Napier's Farm. He thinks there's someone on the property,' explained Rickenbacker. 'Get out there now. No sirens or lights in case you disturb them.'

'OK, Ed. ETA Napier's, oh-five mins.'

He slammed on his brakes, did a three-point turn, and headed back along Taft Road.

Bill Napier was not one to be rattled by anyone, let alone someone stupid enough to be found on his property at dawn. Hell, just one look at Bill Napier was enough to make the weaker element shit; the man even scared

Entwistle, and they were supposedly on the same side. And with the mood that man had been in the last few months because of the drought, like as not there'd be a body to be tagged by the time Entwistle got there.

Entwistle checked the shotgun racked up between him and the passenger seat. There was little call for armed response in Firefall but at night, with unknown circumstances, he'd rather be armed and look a fool than be unarmed and dead.

He reached the gate to the Napier Farm inside four minutes and slid to a halt. The house was in darkness. Odd? Easing the car up the quarter-mile dirt track, his senses alert to any movement, he slowed as he reached the big wide barn standing to the left of the house. It looked locked, its padlock glinting in the first rays of light from the east. What on earth would anyone steal from a farm like this?

Entwistle brought the car to a halt, unclipped the pump-action shotgun, checked it was loaded, then stepped out of the vehicle into the chill morning.

Walking sideways towards the house itself, his eyes scanned the barn and the space in between where Napier usually parked his Ford pick-up, but which was now empty. Why wasn't there a light on? Unless . . . unless whoever was out here had already got into the house. Entwistle spun round and stared out over the fields.

Orange light was fringing the trees to his right like flames, throwing long shadows that did nothing to improve his nerves. He wondered if he should have grabbed his flashlight. He looked back at his Contour, its door invitingly open. Yes, the flashlight made sense.

He gave the house and barn one last look, then trotted back to the car and slid the flashlight out of its holder in the passenger footwell. Standing up, he eased the door shut and stepped towards the barn to check the padlock.

It was as he hefted the heavy lock in his hand, and found that it wasn't closed, that he noticed the faintest of lights inside the barn. Peering into the gloom he was surprised to see several low, wide vehicles. Damned if they didn't look like A. M. Hummers. But just as he swung the flashlight up, he felt cold metal touch his neck.

'Lose the weapon, now,' insisted a quiet male voice.

Entwistle didn't respond, and the man pushed the gun hard into his neck.

'I won't ask again.'

Entwistle dropped his shotgun and a hand removed his .38.

'Turn around.'

Entwistle slowly turned, fearing the worst, to see a hooded man brandishing his rifle an inch from his face. Only the eyes and mouth were visible in the weak light.

'Good decision,' the man said.

Entwistle was about to reply when he felt a crack on the back of his head – and as he fell forward he noticed for the first time that the man with the rifle was dressed all in black save for a large number 14 on his chest.

Two

How the hell had he gotten himself into this?

Greg Henley felt along the narrow wooden ledge with his foot, found nothing solid, and quickly retrieved his bare toes. He was trapped up there, and had no alternative but to wait out the inquisition taking place in Summer Campbell's bedroom. He tried to make himself comfortable but his partly engorged penis was in danger of catching on a nail. Why hadn't he grabbed some clothes?

He could hear Summer's father, Hal Campbell, ranting at her inside, his questioning switching from the strange noises heard from her room, to her current progress at school, to her deplorable choice in fashion. Would that guy ever give the poor girl a break?

Greg had been all for standing his ground when they had heard Summer's father come charging upstairs, but Summer had persuaded him that getting into an argument with her parent while sporting an erection that seconds earlier had been halfway down his daughter's throat was not the best basis for a reasoned conversation. Add to that the fact that Greg wasn't supposed to be anywhere near Firefall, let alone in the Campbells' house, and that her father kept one of the biggest gun collections in the county, and a quick dash for the open window and his current precarious hold on the guttering, twenty feet above the backyard, had finally seemed the best option. Now if only the bastard would get out of her room, so Greg could climb back inside.

'And don't think you'll ever be seeing that damn Henley boy again, girl!' Hal was shouting. 'From what I hear, they have him fixed for a programme set to fry his nigger head.'

'What do you mean?' He could hear Summer's trembling voice.

'Like he's two short of a six-pack, and they're out to give him some suds where it counts.'

'That's not funny, Daddy.'

You can say that again, thought Greg, recalling his first, and if he had his way only, bout of electro-shock therapy.

'Would be funny if I could be there to watch that peckerhead jerking all over the place when they zapped him,' chided Campbell.

Summer burst into tears and Greg could feel his own rage rising. He had been taught techniques to control himself, but what was the point, WHAT WAS THE FUCKING POINT, when bastards like Summer's ASSHOLE of a father spouted such evil, vindictive SHIT?

'You can cry all you like, girl, but just you get used to him not being around. And now you keep quiet,' he yelled. 'It's near enough 5 a.m., and I've a helluva day ahead . . .'

Summer kept blubbing.

'Understand?' demanded Campbell.

Greg so much wanted to march in and smash the man's stupid face in.

'Yes, Daddy.' More tears.

Greg heard Campbell leave the room, the door close, and heavy footfalls retreat down the stairs, no doubt taking Campbell down to his den where he could run some of his porno loops and get his rocks off.

Summer continued sobbing, though sounding rather forced now, until she deemed it safe to approach the window and help Greg climb back inside. Unfortunately, she decided to push the sash up just as Greg manoeuvred himself into a position to lift it himself – and the sudden absence of a frame to hold on to caused him to overbalance. In horror, Summer saw Greg begin to arc backwards, his arms flapping, his eyes seeming as wide as his mouth, and she grabbed for the part of him she could.

His scream as his penis was stretched to twice its normal length woke up every household within three blocks before he broke loose and plummeted backwards into the Campbells' backyard.

Greg was lucky, for large and patriotic rhododendron bushes saved him, their pink, white, and blue flowery profusion helping break his fall and cushioning the jarring impact. But even as he blinked away his disbelief and felt pain in parts of his body he didn't even know he possessed, he heard bellowing begin inside the house and realized his predicament had just turned from bad to worse.

'You OK?' hissed Summer, careful not to raise her voice as lights popped on in nearby houses.

Greg found himself unable to speak. He didn't even

want to speak. He didn't want to do much of anything, in fact. Winded, stunned, his back a mass of pain and his penis on fire, he instead concentrated on getting himself out of sight of her rampaging father.

Luckily, Campbell chose to charge back upstairs to Summer's bedroom rather than come straight out through the lounge, so Greg was allowed vital seconds to crab across the lawn and into some bushes.

He had just entered their deep shadow when Hal appeared at Summer's window to scan his backyard. His voice let loose a twisted flow of incoherent oaths and threats. He then ducked back into her room, Summer at first pleading ignorance but then shutting up once her father discovered Greg's discarded clothes. And then all hell broke loose.

What could be heard above the din was an all too clear promise that Campbell's shotgun was about to 'solve this problem once and for all!'

'But you can't, Daddy!'

'Just watch me, girl. If that nigger kid's still hiding on my property, I'm gonna blast him off it!'

Anger continued to well in Greg like a roused dog, and he fought to control it. THE BASTARD, THE BASTARD. But he knew that if he gave in to his rage he would be lost. So instead he got to his knees and edged further into the shadows. Dawn was on its way and he had better move quickly. He finally reached the fence and hauled himself over, picking up splinters. Shit! Falling face forward into loose soil, he struggled to orientate himself.

No way could he run away from this stark naked; he needed somewhere to hide. Where in hell was he, anyway? Obviously the Blacketts' backyard. Could he break in and find himself some clothes? No, better to stay outside and . . .

The Blacketts' tree house! He and Summer had made out there a couple of times when they knew the family was on vacation. He skipped across the lawn to the base of the tree – just as the Campbells' back door crashed open, the furious man continuing to broadcast his murderous intentions to the town.

Shit, the ladder had gone. Greg jumped for the lowest branch. Thank God for his weight training.

Swinging his right leg over, he pulled himself up onto the wide limb, careful not to put any pressure on his groin. Then, crouching, he clambered along its length until he was able to scramble into the tree house.

The wooden hut was about six feet square, its one open side facing the Blackett house. Turning round, Greg hunched low and stared out. It offered him a good vantage point to watch Campbell's flashlight jerking its away around his property, his shotgun glinting in the beam as he turned it this way and then that. If the lunatic so much as caught a glimpse of him he'd just keep blasting away until the tree house disintegrated.

So, breathing deeply and counting up to ten like Dr Derby had instructed him, Greg lay flat on his back and hoped Campbell's squall would blow itself out before he decided to clamber over his neighbour's fence or start looking skywards.

How long he lay there, tensed up and expectant, he didn't know, but eventually he started feeling dizzy.

It may have been the delayed shock of his recent fall,

or the fact that he hadn't slept in thirty-six hours and had walked all of ten miles to get back to Firefall. Whatever the reason, and despite his perilous predicament, Greg found himself falling asleep.

Three

MY HOME TOWN *by Alice Kerrick, aged 10*

Firefall is a nice place to live. Its full of freindly folks like the sign says and when the tourists arent about its quiet too. School is fine. There's lots to do specally round the Hole with the swimming and Uncle Art's Fun Pier. Outside Firefall the hills are interesting too. We live on Circle Four, near Hoover and my dad works in the bank and mom works in the Firefall Tourist Office. My best friends all come from Firefall. If the drilling rig is still there come winter we wont be skating like we usually do because the riggers will shout at us. They always do. Mom says such an ugly thing there in the middle of the Hole is hitting the tourist trade. Who wants to go see a hole with an oil rig in it? Dad says thats nothing just see when they strike oil and house prices fall thru the floor. I hope they dont because I dont want to leave. I like Firefall.

MY HOME TONW *by Chris Becker 10*

Firefall is borring! Just a big hole ful of water and all thos stupid tooris and theer stupid kweschuns! Always parkin in the wrong placce and asking stupid kweshuns!! I jus wish anuhter big meteryte wood com and smahs the place to peezes but not befor wev movd out! OK swimmin in the Hole is fun but theers nuhtin in winter!!! Just stopid skatin wihc is for girls. And if you dont want to go swimmin what can you do!!! Firfall is so booooooooring!!!!! Im glad they bitl that rig. May be now theyll shut up the hole town and then we gets to live somehwre else.

Hellation! Maribeth Hamilton put down Chris Becker's essay and sighed. That was one child who was not going to make it in life. She had been a teacher for seven years and had seen enough children move on from her school in Firefall to Penniston High to spot those who would ease on through to further fruitful education, and those who would slip on down to the unemployment lines. It wasn't that they were all as dumb as Chris Becker, or dyslexic like Chris Becker, or, to be honest, as hard working as Chris Becker – his essay must have taken some time to get onto paper – but ultimately what was the use? His father was a drunken oaf, his mother a mattress, his home possibly the most run-down house in the one run-down part of Firefall. A background like that breeds fighters or losers but Chris, weedy and asthmatic, was a born loser. The best she could hope to do was keep him out of bad company, but even that could only be feasible during school hours.

As for Alice Kerrick, she was by far the brightest of the twenty-one pupils in her year. She was also pretty and personable and looked destined for college and a career, rather than the jobs most girls in Firefall settled for. (Mind you, Maribeth was one to talk; teaching for her was merely a way of earning a respectable living until she could have children of her own – but to do that she would have to marry Mr Right.)

She slipped the essays back in her schoolbag and stared down at the black shorts on the motel carpet. Ben Angelis had *not* turned out to be Mr Right, hadn't even been Mr Considerate. A fellow teacher, Angelis was an ex-jock who had wrecked his leg – and thus his career – at some college frat party. He had retained the looks and build but, unfortunately, also the ego. He was a good teacher, the boys especially adoring him, but he remained at heart a macho meathead, convinced women found him irresistible. He also possessed the imagination of a football and the staying power of the average time-out.

It had taken the man six months to persuade Maribeth to spend a night with him out at the Indian Summer Motel. (It was vital that no one learned of their tryst, because Firefall was a close community, and its three thousand inhabitants – four thousand on sunny summer days when tourists flocked in to see the Hole – could spread a story faster than a summer breeze and so jeopardize her reputation.)

Never mind my reputation, she thought; *just look at the bed sheets.* The man had actually managed to come before she even got her legs open. Now, no matter how sexy Maribeth hoped she looked – stripped she was slim but not skinny, very pale, her body well proportioned but stretched to suit her six-foot-one-inch frame, with thick red hair whenever she allowed it to grow – she didn't think she merited an eruption over the bed whilst still not out of her skimpies.

OK, so he had recovered, but even when his unimaginative efforts had satisfied him a second time he had then rolled over and fallen asleep. Maribeth was used to disappointment, and was certainly a close friend of frustration, but she wasn't keen on excessive sweat and snoring, and was damned if she would put up with them all night, so she had firmly kicked him out and sent him home. He had tried hard to show disappointment but, on top of all his other failings, Angelis wasn't much of an actor. Plainly he, too, had decided that he and Maribeth were not destined to become an item and so his early departure was welcomed by both of them.

Fine by me, thought Maribeth as she shut the door on him and took a much needed shower, then tried to get some sleep at last. But she was restless and angry and needed some distraction, and because the damned TV wasn't working she had eventually succumbed to opening her schoolbag – they had left together straight after the PTA meeting the night before – and was working her way through her sixth grade's essays, nodding off now and again.

She suddenly found herself staring at the strip of light showing through above the bathroom door. Despite the anger still bubbling inside her, she found herself calming down. All she could see was this warm glow emanating from the bathroom, as the rest of the bed, the room, the *world*, became a black place that didn't matter. She could hear herself thinking it was odd and speculating that she was hypnotizing herself – and it was that thought that broke the spell.

She shook her head, the strip of light now burned on

her vision. Hellation, she needed some sleep. She looked at her watch and found that it was 5:58 a.m. She was still wide awake, bored and frustrated.

She collapsed back on the bed and stared up at the ceiling, wondering how many other bored women had stared up at those same cracks and peeling paper while some ingrate man jumped their bones. She suddenly sat up, feeling very grubby. It's OK to enjoy a sly poke away from prying eyes, but when your partner makes you feel as if you're just another addition to his collection of football trading cards – *No. 23, Maribeth Hamilton, 29, schoolteacher, single, unattached, own apartment, keen but not much of a mover* – self-disgust cannot be far away. Suddenly the room smelled excessively of sex, and the sheets looked just a touch too grey. What were the odds there wasn't one bona fide married couple in the whole damn place?

So Maribeth rose and pulled on her dark blue top and skirt, slipped on her pumps, grabbed her coat and schoolbag. She felt a twinge of guilt. She was a normal, red-blooded woman, she enjoyed sex, but there had to be some better way to obtain it – and certainly a better man. She pulled the door open, flipped off the light, and fumbled her way along the veranda. Then she remembered she had arrived here in Angelis's Cougar; her own Nova was parked up at the school.

She was stranded!

Maribeth walked over to the motel's reception office, intent on demanding that the manager call her a cab. But getting picked up here at this time would be as good as putting an ad in the *Firefall Comet*. Hellation with wings!

A country upbringing had taught Maribeth there was

little to be afraid of in the night, so she decided to walk back to town by the shortest route, down through the woods via the Apsey Firetrail. It would still take her the best part of two hours but with luck she would get back to her apartment before anyone spotted her and wondered what she was doing out so early. Even as she stepped out into the open parking lot, the chill night air made a successful grab for her lower limbs. *Hellation on a stick!* So, wrapping her coat around herself and hugging her chest, Maribeth headed for the highway, anger her only companion.

Four

Del Collingwood woke early. He usually did these days, his wife's snoring keeping him ever on the edge of alertness. It wasn't the snorts and snuffles that disturbed him, but their occasional absence. Like alarms in nuclear-power plants that *stop* to signify danger, so his wife's sudden silences would prick at the edge of his slumber and force him awake, his own breath held as he waited to hear her breathing or detect movement from the body next to his.

And so he lay there in the dark, listening anxiously for his wife's next exhalation. Deep inside, where he hardly ever dared to venture, he knew he would be pleased for her if one morning he awoke to find her still and silent for ever. Not that he didn't love Gloria – he would die for the woman if that meant her Alzheimer's would recede – but to have to watch someone he loved so much slide into premature senility and vegetation was intolerable. How many doctors he had shouted at he couldn't recall, but all had professed to be as helpless as Del now felt. As if from some irreversible cancer, his wife's mind was being slowly destroyed, until even her most basic motor functions would fail her. What pain she had suffered originally had been in realizing in her lucid moments that she was slowly going insane. Twice she had tried to take her own life, and both times Del had prevented her, his medical training holding her safe until the paramedics arrived. But had it really been worth the effort?

He felt her shift beside him now. Torn between relief and frustration, he forced himself up and into the bathroom, there to quietly weep away his guilt and terror. For he knew that once his wife passed away and her suffering ended, his own would truly begin. Thirty-six years they had been married, and not once had either strayed. Their love for one another was as sincere as when they had become engaged at age eighteen in Des Moines. Since then they had together been through a lot of traumas, travelled many miles, and put on too much weight, yet through all of it they had always been there for one another. But now, with his wife's rapid mental decline, only one of them was truly here any more, as the girl he had married – and grown old with – slowly disappeared.

He splashed water on his face and checked his watch on the cabinet shelf: 7:10 a.m. Little point now in getting back to bed. He would go into the kitchen and catch up on some paperwork at the breakfast table. Nurse Bentley wouldn't be here until eight o'clock, the time he normally left for his office.

He showered, ventured quietly back into the bedroom, and dressed, checking on Gloria with ritualistic trepidation. She was still asleep, free to enjoy whatever pleasant fantasies he hoped her disease left her. Her waking hours veered from childish pleasures to nightmarish terrors, with an occasional heart-stopping look or phrase to signify that somewhere in the deteriorating mush that had once been such a sharp mind there struggled the personality of the original owner. Like a drowning woman, she could sometimes thrust her head above encroaching water and shout for help. But Del was now too far away to rescue her.

He adjusted her pillow, wiped drool from her cheek, and kissed her lightly on the forehead. She had lost so much weight, too; her life's ambition now finally realized at too much cost. He caught sight of his own large-framed physique in the wardrobe mirror and couldn't help feeling vaguely guilty. He was a well-proportioned six foot two and although middle age was taking its toll on his waistline, not least because he now lived on takeaways and snack foods, he was still in good shape for his age.

Gently closing the bedroom door on her, he made his way to the kitchen and the workload he had deposited on the table the night before. Fighting the urge to toast a couple of Pop Tarts, he instead settled for fixing a bowl of cereal, then sat himself down.

Del Collingwood had been an FBI agent for thirty-one years, and much as he enjoyed his job and took pride in his work he had been greatly looking forward to his retirement in just three years' time. His career with the Bureau had never been spectacular, most of it having been served in out-of-the-way offices, working on small-potatoes cases or in doing the most mind-numbing follow-up work. True, he had been involved in the famous Unabomber case, but only to check on licence plates. And, yes, he had been in New York when the World Trade Center was hit, but only to interview maintenance crews in the building. Even Waco was on his CV, but *after* the incident, and then only to help man the phones in the press office following that particular PR disaster. His career had taken an inexplicable turn for the worse five years ago, when he had become embroiled in a seemingly innocent suicide case on a college campus.

An old friend from his Des Moines days had become dean of a small science college in Coly, Nebraska, near to Del's current field office. A member of his staff, a Dr Birtles, who was an astrophysicist working on a government contract, had killed himself. Wanting to avoid any scandal, the Dean had asked Del if the FBI could handle the investigation, as he had no faith in the local Sheriff's Department – and anyway, as Birtles' laboratory was funded with government money, it could be said that the suicide had taken place on federal property. Satisfied that he was within his rights, Del had agreed to intervene. However, what had seemed a simple favour to a friend became a nightmare as his investigations began to turn up anomalies.

For one, the cord the man had used to hang himself was nylon climbing rope available only from specialist stores; yet the suicide victim had weighed two hundred and eighty pounds and would have had trouble even climbing stairs, let alone rock faces. For another, he had shown no signs of depression and, indeed, had been visibly excited about a 'remarkable breakthrough' in his theoretical work on time. It was also apparent that some of his papers and computer files were missing. But as soon as Del raised the possibility of foul play, and had shown interest in the dead man's lost research, the shutters had come down, his FBI superiors had ordered him out, and his old friend the Dean had become suddenly 'unavailable'.

The very next day Del had been transferred to Atlanta – and assigned to clearing up unsolved bank robberies that were close to reaching their statute of limitations.

Since then his career had remained on hold until, last May, Del's conscientiousness and professionalism had finally been acknowledged, and he was entrusted with his own small office in Worthing, Wyoming. He had never figured out why the death of some obscure scientist should have almost ruined twenty-six years of dedicated service; but obviously he must have trodden on someone's toes . . .

He now had four agents on his staff, besides two secretaries, and he intended remaining here until his retirement. Though he and Gloria were used to constantly moving around and shifting home, each of them had begun to feel their years and longed now to settle down. Worthing had seemed a quiet, decent town in a quiet, decent state, and with no close family ties there was no reason they could not enjoy a well-deserved retirement there. *But what was there to look forward to now?*

While the Bureau's health plan covered treatment for Gloria's Alzheimer's, it didn't provide a cure. And the two of them had decided it was better if she could stay at home with nursing care, rather than languishing in some faceless institution. 'In sickness and in health' they had pledged and, God-fearing Baptists both, they meant it.

Del forced his mind off the misery of his wife's condition and concentrated instead on his work. His current caseload consisted of a stolen-car ring, the kidnapping by a couple of college students of their tutor which might or might not have taken place because all involved had been high on drugs at the time, a hijacking of a truckload of cigarettes, two missing children, both runaways from bad homes, who were no doubt half a continent away by now, and a bungled bank robbery.

He doubted half of them would be solved satisfactorily, and that at least one of the children would never turn up. He closed the file on the young girl's 10 × 8 photograph, and stared into his soggy Cheerios. He had never been able to father children and so had deprived Gloria of the family she so much wanted, though she would not countenance artificial insemination or adoption. '*God made us what we are. We stay the way God made us.*' But there were times, when he had caught her wrapped up in play with her sister's children and grandchildren, that he couldn't help wishing that God had been a bit more generous to them. Then again, He hadn't been sparing in the love department, for if ever a man had been happy in his marriage it had been Del – despite all the crap his job at the Bureau had meant for Gloria. (Nineteen homes over the years, not to say the countless nights away from each other, the vacations cut short or cancelled at a moment's notice . . .)

Del pushed away the mushy Cheerios. He had tuned the radio to an oldies station and, as Johnny Mathis finished singing, a time-check informed him it was 7:50. Good heavens, he had been sitting there for forty minutes. As he cleared away his cereal and began packing away case files into his briefcase the telephone rang.

Oh, hell, don't say this is the nurse ringing in sick.

'Special Agent Collingwood?' said an unfamiliar male voice. 'We have a situation in a town near you called Firefall.'

Del knew the place, had been there once but had never gone back. Just some big hole filled with water, which was surrounded by tacky souvenir shops. It lay about forty miles south.

'What kind of situation?'

'A serious situation. As you're the nearest Special Agent, I want you there as soon as possible. I'll brief you on the way. Your car will be there to collect you in two minutes.'

Del put the receiver back on the wall, finished filling his briefcase, then re-entered the bedroom. Thankfully Gloria was still asleep. As he tied on his holster and secured the snub-nose .38, he prayed that Nurse Bentley would arrive on time. At least she had her own key. He stroked his wife's greasy hair and wrote a note asking for it to be washed. He knew Gloria would be ashamed to see her hair in its present state.

He headed through the kitchen to the back door, then down three flights of stairs to the parking area where Agent Calthorpe was already waiting with the car.

They had been driving south for a couple of minutes before Del realized he didn't even know who had phoned him.

Five

It was the aching of his bladder that woke Greg, and it took several more disorientated and agonizing minutes before he surrendered to his need and felt urine bathing his stomach and thighs as he let go while lying on his front. The relief was welcome, the smell less so, and when he was sure this action hadn't been noticed he crept slowly forward on his knees and peered out of the tree house.

A sky of pink was now turning blue, dawn approaching on its irreversible path. He sat up, his back still hurting, and edged forward again for a clearer view. He had half expected to find Campbell still angrily stalking the open area of surrounding gardens, but instead he spotted a hooded man dressed entirely in black and sporting a large white number 47 on his back. This figure was pointing a gun at Campbell, who was standing with his hands above his head. Summer then suddenly made an appearance outside the back door, and Greg almost yelled out to warn her. But, realizing he was still totally naked, he bit his tongue and awaited developments.

Glancing over to his left he noticed that the people next door were in a similar predicament. An anonymous armed man, this time sporting a number 15 on both chest and back, was ushering them from their side door and out onto the road in front, where two others (numbers 28 and 40) were signalling with automatic weapons towards a waiting truck, and watched as their various captives climbed aboard.

Looking back towards Hal Campbell's garden, Greg saw 47 urging Summer on behind her father. He grasped the wooden frame of the tree house, feeling its brittle wood crackling under the pressure. *Don't hurt her, you fucker!*

Having delivered his captives safely to the truck, number 15 proceeded back towards the approaching Campbells, where 47 handed over responsibility for both father and daughter. What was going on?

Suddenly the dry wood being tortured by Greg's fingers snapped like a gunshot. Number 47 spun round and stared across to the Blacketts' garden. He clearly had not yet pinpointed the source of the noise, so Greg edged carefully back out of sight. He heard them speak.

'Hear that sound?'

'What sound?'

'You must be deaf. I'll check it out.'

Damn, that meant one of them was coming over, and whatever these assholes were up to they would probably be much more efficient at search and destroy than old man Campbell was. For the first time Greg felt real fear.

He pressed down on his belly and, ignoring the rough wood, wormed forward again until he could glimpse the garden fence and 47 climbing over it, his movements betraying his natural athleticism. Who *were* these guys? The approaching man crouched down and scanned the lawn along the sight of his rifle. Greg ducked back. Shit, this one was a pro all right. Then Greg heard the truck drive off, and silence reigned again.

Easing his head up, he saw that the hooded man was surveying the rear of the Blackett house as he crept backwards. He might feel satisfied that the garden was empty and just move off. But then he turned and looked upwards, focusing the eyeholes in his black ski-mask on the tree house.

Greg dodged back, cursing silently.

'You there in the tree house, come out!'

Greg didn't move, didn't even dare breathe.

'I'll give you five, then I'll fire.'

Greg saw no reason to assume he was bluffing, and when he heard the rifle being cocked he answered immediately.

'OK, OK, I'm gonna come down.'

'Nice and slow now.'

'Don't worry,' muttered Greg, as a splinter raked his palm. 'I ain't rushing.'

Carefully he rose to his knees and sat upright. Gazing down, he could see the rifle was pointing straight at his face.

'What you doing there?' said the man.

'I was hiding.'

'You naked, boy?'

Greg tried to stand up, but had to stoop below the roof, only five feet high. 'Seems that way.'

'Stupid asshole. Just get down here.'

Greg stepped right to the edge of the wooden platform. It was over ten feet off the ground, and too high to jump. So he turned round and gently eased himself over the edge until hanging in space. He knew before he landed it was going to hurt because his legs had developed cramp in the confines of the tree house, but he wasn't prepared for just how much pain would blast up his calves.

Yelping in agony, he rolled over, and rubbed at his shins and arches.

'Get up, boy!' growled the man in black.

Through the pain Greg tried to respond, but his feet remained in agony.

'You busted something?' asked 47.

Greg shook his head, then changed his mind. 'Yeah, I think so. Ankle, might be twisted, might be broke . . .'

'Asshole. You was a dog, I'd shoot you.'

'I was a dog I wouldn't be up in no fucking tree!'

'Can you stand up?'

Greg didn't need much effort to prove he couldn't. God, it hurt.

'Better crawl, then, son.'

Greg glared up at the man, and saw the white flesh ringing the eyes.

'I ain't your son. What the fuck's going on?'

'You'll find out once you can get your ass out there to the street and onto the truck.'

The man jabbed the rifle at him, and Greg rolled onto his back, unconcerned about his nakedness. 'Hey man, look at me. What am I gonna do? I need some help.'

The hooded man managed a snort, then moved nearer. Aiming the rifle at Greg's head with one hand, he offered him the other. Greg took hold of his wrist and started to heave himself up until – at the precise moment he was upright – he tugged hard with all his weight.

Knocked off balance, number 47 stumbled, his rifle sticking fast into the soil.

The two men stared at each other for an instant, then Greg lanced his middle finger into his opponent's eye. Before the other man could even yell, Greg had brought a knee up into his jaw, breaking teeth and knocking him out.

Though still finding it difficult to stand, he grabbed at his unconscious assailant's wrists and hauled him out of sight beneath a tree. There he pulled the unconscious man's hood off, but didn't recognize him. Nor was he carrying any identification.

Who *were* these guys?

Greg looked down at his own scratched and naked body. Well, at least he could now solve one of his problems – and then maybe find out where the bastards had taken Summer.

Six

Maribeth was nearing the outskirts of town, her progress slower than she had hoped thanks to a torn pump. She was now walking barefoot, grateful the trail was carpeted in dry, dead foliage that was springy to walk on and only occasionally offered a sharp surface.

She had followed the firetrail almost the whole of its length over Musky Hill and had decided to enter the town along Nancy Road, a dead-end lane that contained half a dozen houses. If she then followed Circle Six she might get home without being seen; it was being seen coming back into town at this early hour that would cause the tongues to wag – and being a single woman of her age, and with her looks, the gossips had enough ammunition already without her foolishly adding to it. And as she proceeded, she began to speculate again on the scarce availability of eligible men in Firefall.

Most men of her age were married or divorced or confirmed bachelors – making all of them unlikely candidates. (She was no adulteress; she couldn't bring herself to wholly trust a man who had failed at marriage so soon; and any thirty-year-old who lived on his own had to have personal reasons above and beyond the expense of buying a double bed.) There were few men she knew in town that she fancied, anyway. A couple of the police deputies maybe, Gil Brackhouse and that Entwistle guy, but she only knew them to nod to, or to wheedle out of writing her a parking ticket. There was also Sonny Johnson, who ran the Dayville's, but he seemed to be eating too much of his stock recently, judging by his expanding waistline. Then there was Mike Howell at the TV repair shop – but there were rumours about his dubious video collection. Of course, there was always Paul Brochard at the animal shelter where she helped out two nights a week, but despite any hints she had dropped to the thirty-something widower, he had not made any moves. Maybe she should come on stronger . . .

She found herself suddenly right on the outskirts of town, with only some undergrowth between her and the end of Nancy Road.

That was when she heard the voices.

This in itself did not give her cause for alarm, but there was something odd about these voices. This was not the intimate tone of parting lovers, or the banter of early-morning hunters, or even the blurry lingo of the vagrants who sometimes hung around town like discarded socks.

On a cautious impulse, she edged into some bushes as the voices approached her. There were at least two of them, both male, and she preferred not to take the risk of being spotted. Firefall was a quiet town, but even Eden contained its snake.

'We've got all the other roads covered now. Only here and Clark Road left,' said one voice.

'You think it'll work?' said the second, nervously.

'Sure – as long as everyone plays his part.'

They seemed to have halted, and Maribeth heard a match flare.

'Thought we weren't allowed to smoke.'

'Who's to know?'

'Remember what he said: we're all of us being watched. Any fuck-ups and we're out of it.'

'OK, so you're watching me?'

There came no answer.

'Come on, what's the harm?'

Still no answer.

'Shit!'

A cigarette butt came flying past Maribeth's ear and landed in the long grass, instantly starting to smoulder. Maribeth extended one bare foot and placed it firmly over the glowing stub, gritting her teeth at the sudden sharp pain.

The two men meanwhile moved away.

Maribeth raised her aching foot and rubbed soothingly at the red scorch mark. *Hellation!* Then, giving them a couple of minutes more, she peered out at the rough track where the road ended. Whoever they were, they were now out of sight.

Now what was all that about?

Firefall was not the sort of place for carrying out military exercises, and there were no militia nuts in town that she knew of. Oh, there were those boys who enjoyed paintball battles, but they were just morons. These two had sounded like something more serious. What had they said? 'Got the roads covered'? So only this one and Clark were still open?

Why were they closing the roads?

Firefall's only claim to fame and how it received its name stemmed from one and the same event. About six hundred years ago, according to geologists as well as local Indian legend, a meteorite had impacted on Musky Hill, excavating a large deep hole in the centre of a gently sloping oval crater. Over the years this hole had filled up with water to form an almost perfectly circular lake which was called, imaginatively, 'the Hole'. Because of its distinctive shape, and its supposed origin, a tourist industry had grown up in the early years of the twentieth century. There were now upwards of a hundred thousand visitors a year – though most of them dropped by for only a couple of hours before moving on. After all, a lake was just a lake, whatever had caused it.

Gradually a town had grown up, fanning out from the water's edge. It was laid out like a wheel, with roads like spokes radiating from the lake front, which transected a number of ring roads that spread out in widening circles to the rim of the valley. These latter major roads were called Circle One, Circle Two, Circle Three . . . and so on up to Circle Six. The seven major spokes that linked them were all named after American presidents. Four of them – Wilson, Harding, Coolidge, Hoover – ended where they touched the outer ring road at Circle Six, but three – Taft, Roosevelt, and McKinley – ran on out of town heading west, north, and south respectively. The latter two routes continued on in opposite directions to become part of US Highway 287. The only other exits from town were random dirt-tracks and firetrails, for the surrounding countryside was heavily wooded hillside in all directions. Thinking about it now, Firefall could be cut off effectively from the rest of the country if only US Highway 287 and Taft Road were blocked to traffic. And as each was no more than a two-lane blacktop, a couple of large trucks might suffice to do this. But why would anyone want to try?

She couldn't even speculate. The best thing was to contact the Sheriff. Let Ed Rickenbacker himself figure it out. Braving another quick survey of Nancy Road, she was shocked to see some new activity. Three hooded men dressed entirely in black (wearing large numbers front and back – 7, 78, and 22), and each holding a rifle or machine-gun, were in the process of herding a group of people, mostly in their nightclothes, along the road towards the truck she recognized as belonging to Phil McAllum. Except that Phil clearly wasn't driving it, for yet another hooded figure sat behind the steering wheel.

Now Maribeth was not normally prone to panic, but events were unfolding here that no amount of logical analysis could explain. Maybe there had been some major incident involving dangerous chemicals, so the army was moving everyone out to safety. Except shouldn't those men be wearing army uniforms – and protective masks rather than just hoods? But their only identifying marks seemed to be those large numbers, front and back. It was the sheer sinister menace of the scene unfolding that kept her silent and hidden in the bushes as they continued to clear the road methodically of all its residents.

After just ten minutes the truck was fully loaded and driven away. On foot, the hooded figures followed it out of sight.

Pausing a couple more minutes to make sure, Maribeth dashed across the road to the house that stood nearest.

Its front door was unlocked, unthinkable normally, and a radio was playing somewhere inside. Once inside, she called out quietly, her inbred courtesy demanding she make her presence known. When no one replied, she ventured into the kitchen. Grabbing a cloth, she pulled a smoking skillet from the electric stove and switched it off. They must have left in a hell of a hurry.

Next a quick tour of the house, running upstairs to find all the bedrooms and the bathroom empty. Back down to the lounge, where she picked up the telephone. The line was dead. Next she switched on the television for news of some local incident, but found nothing unusual referred to on the national channels.

The local TV station, Firefall Cable, was off the air, so she tuned into KFLL, the local radio station, but was rewarded only with light music playing unconcernedly.

Proceeding into the garage, she found a Neon lacking a radio, and was about to head for the house next door when she spotted a black-clad figure at an upper-storey window nearby, who seemed to be staring down at her. Maribeth ducked behind a couple of trash cans, unsure whether she had actually been noticed and unwilling to risk another peep.

Instead she crawled round to the front of the house. But when she heard shouting in the distance and a slamming door, she upped and dashed across the road, throwing herself through a hedge and straight into a pile of hawthorn cuttings, whose still-sharp thorns pricked her skin and caught in her clothes.

At the sound of fast-approaching boots she rolled about frantically to extricate herself but succeeded only in entangling herself further. Lying on her back, her heart pounding, she held her breath and listened.

At least two sets of boots began stamping around in the house she had just vacated, then a voice suggested they search the nearby undergrowth. *Hellation in a hard hat!*

She blinked her eyes open to find some way of escape – and found herself gazing directly at a vicious thorn barely two inches from her eyeball. Its evilly curved barb seemed eager to stab her blind at the slightest movement. Despite her panic to escape, she accepted she was temporarily trapped and waited for the inevitable.

'Could have sworn I saw her down here,' said one male voice.

'Sure this is the right house?' another replied.

'Yeah, I'm positive.'

'Well, she ain't here now, and it's not like one stray bitch is going to make a difference.'

'Hell . . . OK, forget it. Just some girl we missed on the sweep. Knew we should have carried checklists of all the residents.'

'Waste of time. You know the orders: gather up all we can, get them stowed away fast, and then continue the patrol. So let's go patrol.'

Amid further mutterings, the footsteps gradually receded to the far end of Nancy Street – till all she could hear was the birds twittering, and a breeze stirring the trees above her. And her heart still pounding with the rhythm of fear.

Maribeth carefully opened her eyes again to examine the menacing barb. It made her flinch. Lying totally still, she was safe, but she couldn't stay wrapped up in a bush for ever. She just had to get out of here and see what was going on. What would have happened by now to her pupils at school?

She worked her right hand up in front of her face, and prayed she wouldn't cry out as she grasped the goddam thorn. She finally closed her hand around it and pushed it forcefully away from her face. She could feel it dig sharply into her palm, then the sickening moment as it pierced the flesh before sinking a full half-inch into her hand. But at least she was able to shift the branch to one side.

The pain was excruciating and she began to sob. Even when she tried to pull her hand free of it, the thorn remained resolutely snared in her bloody palm. Only a vicious tug and a bitten lip succeeded in getting rid of it – allowing her to escape her thorny prison.

Manoeuvring through the tangled branches, she could now see the road beyond and began crawling towards it. It felt as if a hundred fishing hooks had snagged in her clothing, and she was grateful for her shortish hair. But after a tiring battle, suddenly she was free.

Blinking through streaming eyes, Maribeth loped back across the road and lunged face-down onto the front lawn of the house she had checked out earlier. She felt reasonably certain she was out of sight of the other residences because of the low hedges separating each property. There she lay, crying with relief and pain and terror, unconcerned that she was reacting like a foolish girl.

It was some minutes before she could summon the strength to crawl into the house in front of her. Making her way upstairs to the bathroom, she began to survey the damage.

Her right hand was deeply cut in several places – indeed there seemed to be no part of her body that had not suffered cuts and scratches – so after she had showered and towelled herself dry it took a good fifteen minutes to dab at every minor wound she could reach with Betadine, each new application creasing her face in agony. In the first-aid kit she found enough plasters and dressings to deal with her worst wounds, particularly those in her aching palm.

While she was dabbing away, she found her eyes drawn to a small vanity mirror which reflected the neon light shining behind her. The mirror's surface seemed completely filled with white light – and gradually this transfixed her until her dabbing slowed and ceased.

The sting of the iodine retreated, her pounding heart slowed, her whole body began to feel strangely refreshed. She wanted only to keep staring at the light . . . however futile that seemed in her present predicament. Then somehow she finally tore her gaze away from the mirror.

Instead she ran herself a glass of water and downed a double dose of aspirin. She then removed her hard contact lenses, rinsed them thoroughly, and put them back in. Time to get dressed again, this time in jeans and a blouse and some boots taken from a bedroom wardrobe.

Heading downstairs, she tried the telephone and found the line was still dead. She picked up a transistor radio tuned to KFLL, and heard with horror a man's voice talking slowly.

'*—inside. There is no need to worry. Please stay inside and all will be well. There are armed men on the street who will not harm you, but should there be any resistance they will* *not hesitate to open fire. Treat the men in black with respect, obey any orders, and you will not be harmed. I repeat, you will not be harmed if you do exactly what you are told. Resist or disobey, and you will suffer the consequences. Keep tuned to this station for further developments.'*

There was a pause and then the same voice started again.

'*People of Firefall, do not be alarmed. Your town has been taken over. Stay inside. There is no need to worry. Please stay inside and all will be well. There are . . .*'

Maribeth realized the voice was merely repeating itself, probably on a tape loop, so she turned to the television, carefully keeping out of sight of any windows. She tuned it to Firefall Cable, but the screen was now blank except for a caption.

**STAY INSIDE. YOU WILL NOT BE HARMED.
OBEY ALL ORDERS.**

Well, that seemed clear enough. The male voices she had heard outside earlier – at least three or four different ones – had sounded plainly American. No Russians or Arabs here. So who exactly were they? And where were the police, or the FBI, or the army, or whoever else was supposed to save them?

Hellation on overtime! What if the army did come pouring into town and started shooting? How many innocent people could get killed or injured in the crossfire? It could all so easily turn into a bloodbath. She rushed back to the front door and cautiously peered out at the thickly wooded hills that ringed the town.

They could be up there even now, making their plans, picking their targets. Or worse, she realized, there could be more of those hooded men in black looking down at Firefall with binoculars, watching out for residents who hadn't been rounded up yet. She slumped back against the wall, the myriad pinpricks of pain in her back making her wince. Bleakly she pondered what she might do.

Maribeth was no heroine, had never used a gun in anger, and she had no idea how many of the intruders were out there – or what their intentions might be. Perhaps it was some large-scale robbery, but what could be so valuable in Firefall that they would go to all this trouble? And why round up the population? Where could they detain such a sizeable number of people? The Town Hall perhaps – except it was currently being rebuilt. How about the hospital . . . maybe even the Fun Pier, or the Memorial Park . . .

Or else her own school! Its assembly hall could hold five hundred, each classroom sixty or more with one man guarding them. They could confine half the town's population in the schoolrooms and the yard outside, with maybe only a dozen armed men. But why imprison half the town anyway?

Hostages! That was it. They were taking them all as hostages.

Entering the kitchen, she stared at the wall clock. It read 7:53. That couldn't be right. She could have sworn it had been showing that same time when she first came into the house. She checked her watch: 5:58. Hellation, she'd managed to break the damn thing. She checked the timer on the stove. Also 7:53.

Maybe she was mistaken. But no, the second hand of the wall clock had definitely stopped. So, maybe there had been a power outage.

She stepped into the lounge. The timer on the video recorder was flashing 88:88. *Another* malfunction? Annoyed, Maribeth grabbed the radio and flipped the dial. She moved through some country music, then a talk show, a Pepsi commercial, Van Halen . . . at last a time-check. It was 8:22. OK, that seemed more like it. Now, she did not know how long these hooded types had been in Firefall, but by now some of her young pupils must have set off for school – in which case they might be already frightened stiff. Right, she had no alternative!

Somehow she needed to get through to her school and her pupils.

Seven

Sheriff's Deputy Entwistle came round slowly, the warm red fug he was swimming in slowly turning to a musty blackness that caught in his throat, dust tickling his nose and itching his eyes. He was lying face-down in dry straw, and felt a sneezing jag coming on. He tried to fight it but with his hands tied behind his back he had no way of grabbing his nose. Soon he was sneezing like a train, a regular stream of nasal explosions making him cough and gag and his eyes water. He began to roll about, trying to get himself onto his back so he could gasp relatively clean air, but the straw beneath him was uneven and suddenly he found himself rolling and unable to check his momentum until he was in mid-air, unsupported and falling through an open trapdoor.

He landed heavily on his back, his hands crushed together. As pain shot up his arms and pounded into his kidneys he found a light shining in his eyes and had to blink away tears. Damn, that was bright. He turned his head to the side and found himself staring at the front wheel of his police cruiser. Then edging his eyes back towards the bright light he found, instead of the flashlight of a captor, a hole in the wall of the barn and early-morning light lancing directly at his face like a laser beam. He took stock of his situation.

His feet were free, but his hands were tight behind his back and he was gagged, something filling his mouth. He rolled up against the Contour and using the wheel at his back levered himself to his knees. He wondered if he would be able to ease his wrists over his feet, but after a couple of attempts found his wrists were tied too tight. Finally he got to his feet and laid his head and shoulders on the hood of the car, before standing fully erect.

Something odd was going on and he had to warn Rickenbacker about it, if it wasn't already too late. However, judging by the angle of the sun, he must have been out for a couple of hours or more: time enough for whatever those jokers had been planning to have taken place. First he tried the door to his car, but it was locked. And even if he could get in, he could see broken plastic on his seat – they had smashed the radio. So, how to get out of the barn?

The big doors were locked, probably that damn padlock, maybe even a beam. He walked the perimeter of the inside, shaking sweat off his face as it trickled into his eyes. He hoped it was just sweat and not blood; they had given him some crack across his head. One slow walk round the edge of the barn showed it to be empty, the only signs of recent use the oil stains on the floor. He leaned back onto the trunk of the Contour. It would have been so easy just to drive out through the doors. He looked back at where the light pierced the skin of the building.

Peering through the slats he could see Napier's Farm sitting silent to the left, fields stretching away to the tree line on the right – and still no sign of Napier. Either the old coot had been disposed of or he had been one of the hooded men, but if he was, why the hell had they left a deputy trussed up on his property?

Entwistle leaned against the wall, and felt it had some give. It was his only hope, so he kept shoving against it, then began to shoulder-charge it. Anger soon took over and he began kicking at it like a madman until there was a loud crack and one of the vertical boards snapped – and suddenly there was a gap wide enough for him to squeeze through.

Outside in the farmyard he fell to his knees and sucked in clean air, his face plastered with sweat and dust. Then, somewhat revived, he got back to his feet and trotted over to the farmhouse, his hands still tied behind his back, his mouth still gagged. Stepping onto the porch he paused and looked around the farm. He couldn't hear anything out of the ordinary, nor see anything to arouse his suspicion. Everything was as it had appeared when he had arrived – but look where that had landed him.

He shouldered the front door and it opened with a creak. Either the house was empty or Napier was unconscious. Or worse. As Entwistle was still gagged, he couldn't call out, so his first priority was to find something to cut his bonds. Easier said than done. The logical place was the kitchen, to see if any knives were available.

The kitchen proved empty of people but full of signs of occupancy, with half a dozen coffee mugs, some still full, on the table, and the remains of sandwiches on most surfaces. There had been quite a few people here for breakfast. Entwistle couldn't help wondering if one of them had been Napier – and what had happened to him after the food had been prepared.

He scanned all surfaces but could see no sharp knife that he might use to cut his bonds, so he walked back through the hall and into the lounge. He noticed the clock read 7:36. God, he had been out for over two hours!

There were clothes scattered about, most of them workaday garments – jeans, sweatshirts, shoes. Looked like the men had changed in here before setting off. He kicked some clothing about but found nothing he could use. Looking upstairs would be pointless, so he found the cellar door, expecting Napier would have tools in the basement. Flipping the light switch by the door with his nose, Entwistle turned his back to the door, wrestled with the knob to turn it, pulled the door wide, and stared down the steps. He could smell fresh earth – and for some reason that worried him.

Carefully edging his way down the steep steps one at a time – if he were to trip, chances were he would break his neck – he waited until he was at the bottom before taking his eyes off his feet.

It was a large cellar, converted into a workshop, the smell of fresh earth not quite overpowering that of sawdust and oil. Scanning the four walls he saw old tools and mechanical bric-a-brac, workbenches, boxes, an old motorcycle in pieces, baling wire, a chainsaw, an amount of raw lumber and then, to the right under the stairs he had descended, a large freshly dug hole, with broken cement flooring in pieces by its side under a pile of damp earth.

Steeling himself for the worst, Entwistle stared down

into the hole. It was about six feet long, three feet wide, and quite deep. Grave size.

He was able to see the bottom of the hole. No corpse. Well, that was something. No, not really, he thought. Graves tend to be dug for bodies and the fact it was unoccupied didn't render it useless. For all he knew they might be planning to use it when they returned. But if that was the case, why hadn't they killed Entwistle when he was discovered?

The puzzle did nothing to alleviate his anxiety and instead he walked the perimeter of the cellar, desperate now to find something sharp. Finally he saw an old two-handed pit-saw, large and purposeful, propped up in one corner, fully eight feet high. He knelt in front of it, assuring himself it wouldn't topple over him. Old and rusty, its teeth were at least two inches long and dull with age, but it was all he could find. Turning himself round he positioned his feet on either side of the end handle and shuffled back until his arms made contact with the blade. Aware of the pit-saw's weight and that it could crash down on top of him, its length comprising little more than several dozen knives fashioned from a heavy piece of steel, he eased his wrists back until a tooth caught on the knot between his hands. Once it had snagged a single strand of rope, he began to work his wrists back and forth, praying the tooth was actually cutting into the rope.

Sweat was soon streaming into his eyes, making him blink until eventually he had to clamp them shut, his world suddenly a dark, quiet place that consisted of the pain in his knees and shoulders and the slight fretting sound as the tines of an aged saw attempted to part brand-new rope. He soon lost track of time, his efforts punctuated by explosive gasps as he had to halt and lean forward to relax his shoulder muscles. But the desperation of his situation soon made him resume his torturous exertions. How long it took him he didn't know, but after what seemed the hundredth pause to jerk at the rope to see if there was any play he felt it snap. Then it was a couple of minutes of eager fumbling and finger-bending and the ropes were off his wrists and he was pulling frantically at the gag in his mouth with his numb hands. Tossing the sodden rag aside he dragged in dry air, almost whooping with relief, but his joy was short-lived as he reconsidered his predicament.

His first priority was to search the house to see if Napier was around, next find a weapon, then find some way of communicating with Sheriff Rickenbacker.

Running up the stairs he dashed into the lounge and grabbed the phone, but it was dead. He started to toss the clothes about, hoping to find a clue to his attackers' identity other than their pedestrian choice of dress. All pockets were empty, no name labels, nothing recognizable, so he ventured upstairs – after collecting a large bread knife from a drawer in the kitchen.

The house had four bedrooms: two were completely empty, since Napier lived on his own; one contained a double bed, another a single bed. All were innocent-looking, the double bed showing recent occupation by just one person, the other made up neatly. Looking through drawers and wardrobes revealed nothing that any single farmer wouldn't own. There were no signs of violence, nothing untoward, and this led Entwistle to the conclusion that Napier might well have been a willing accomplice – which was pretty stupid if they intended Entwistle to live, because he could point the finger at the farm's owner.

The only remaining room was the attic. Snagging the handle to the ladder strapped to the upper hall ceiling, he pulled it down so as to climb into the deep triangular void. He jumped when something brushed his face, but realized it was a light cord. Pulling it, he was able to see better. He didn't know what he might have been expecting to find, but it certainly wasn't as disturbing as the sight that now confronted him.

The attic contained a large table, maybe ten feet square, on top of which was an elaborate model. Crudely made from old cereal boxes and toy cars and household objects, it was still clearly enough a model of the town of Firefall. True, all the roads were flat whereas Firefall was set in a bowl, but otherwise the layout was accurate, if not to scale. Entwistle walked around the low table, taking in this strange creation. What was it for? It wasn't detailed enough to be a labour of love, so it plainly had another purpose.

Roads were named, and there were numbered cards distributed about the town, some in groups of twos or threes on the three main roads leading into town and around the town's main features: the Town Hall, the KFLL radio and the cable TV station, the oil rig, the Sheriff's Department, the telephone exchange, the school, the surgery, and St Mary's Church.

Now Deputy Entwistle wasn't a fool. He had moved to Firefall three years before, after a bad shooting in San Francisco had killed his partner and taken out the best part of his own left knee. It was enough for the SFPD to pension him off, but not enough for Firefall to refuse his services as an experienced city policeman hampered only by a knee that played up in bad weather. (His retirement had been due more to the City's fiscal policies than to his lack of mobility, but he was damned if he would fight his case against such ungrateful employers.) So Entwistle had applied for jobs elsewhere, and taken the best of those offered: deputy in Firefall, Wyoming, with every chance that long service would allow him to run for Sheriff.

So he was now employing a mind that had eleven years' hard-core experience in San Francisco, rather than that of some yokel who merely had a hankering for a uniform and for toting a handgun in public. And, as best he could see, this was a plan for a siege: first seize the most important locations in the town, then hold the centres of communication, and use the rig and the spire of St Mary's to offer commanding views of the whole community.

The numbers on the cards probably referred to the men involved; the one who had knocked him out had sported the number 14 on his chest. Counting up these numbers he reached thirty, but there might well be others – these just being the key players. What the hell was going on? Why all this in a no-place spot like Firefall?

Entwistle went back down the stairs to the hall. He checked the time by the kitchen clock – 7:36; damn thing was broken – and found a radio and tuned into KFLL. Burt Bacharach tried to soothe him. He failed.

He next tried the television, discovered Napier didn't have cable, flicked through channels and found nothing unusual. Maybe no one outside knew yet. Entwistle had two choices: get in his car and drive to the nearest working telephone and call the authorities; or try to get back into town and see what he could do against thirty armed ... thirty armed what? Terrorists seemed too clean a word; maybe criminals was better.

He picked up a hammer from under the kitchen sink and headed out to his car, still undecided what alternative was best. Probably a combination of both: go call for help, then get back on into town.

Entwistle stepped into the barn through the gap he had made earlier, smashed his side window and climbed into the Contour, then hot-wired the engine, his keys long gone. He couldn't help noticing that his car clock also read 7:36. Odd. He backed up as far as he could in the confines of the barn, then, buckling up his seat belt, he revved hard, dropped the clutch, and let the car sprint for the doors. Whilst they presented less of an obstacle than he had expected, a newly arrived vehicle driving towards Napier's farmhouse did.

Entwistle's cruiser ploughed into the side of the black Sunfire and shunted it a good twenty feet sideways before both cars came to a rest in a cloud of dust. Shaken but unhurt, Entwistle struggled out from behind his deployed airbag, and rushed to the other vehicle to find its driver lying sprawled across the front seats.

The driver's door was fused to his cruiser's radiator grille, so he had to haul open the Sunfire's passenger door in order to check the other man's condition. The angle of the crash, and the fact that he hadn't been wearing a seat belt, meant the impact had thrown him sideways and forwards, the sudden change in momentum as he slammed into the dashboard snapping his neck. The man was obviously dead.

Entwistle's initial horror was soon joined by outraged disbelief that so much could go so wrong in so short a time. But worse was to come. He pulled the man's body out of the car. He then searched him thoroughly and, leaning back against the car, studied the sum contents of the dead man's pockets.

A Colt .38, six hundred and eighty dollars, a driver's licence in the name of Richard H. Pendleton from Milwaukee, a Hertz car rental agreement from Casper airport, and a piece of paper with the address of Napier's Farm. This revealed who he was, but there was no other evidence of his life or livelihood. Despite his sense of shock, Entwistle was still a cop, and he smelled a rat. All this man had on him was the minimum to get him food, lodging, and transport.

Entwistle popped the trunk. *Well, well, well.* Three one-gallon cans of gasoline, firelighters, and rags. He walked back to the dead driver and rolled him over.

It was unremarkable: just an ordinary man in his forties. Entwistle knelt down and studied him. All his own hair, expensive cut, though his clothes were cheap, the labels chainstore. He next checked the fingers. Smooth; he obviously did not work with his hands. Then he spotted something else.

Pulling up the man's left sleeve, he found a band of pink skin that started midway along the back of his hand and ran twelve inches up his hairless forearm. A burn scar.

Entwistle stared at the watch. A cheap Casio digital, its figures flashing 88:88. Jesus, what were the odds on three timepieces failing at the same time? *But that doesn't matter a whole lot right now, does it?*

Instead he checked the signature on the dead man's driver's licence: left-sloping, tight, controlled. Then he looked at the handwritten address of Napier's Farm: big, loopy, straight-up but extravagant. Even if the name on the licence was false, the signature would have to be genuine so he could duplicate it when signing for the rented car. And Entwistle's elementary knowledge of graphology told him that the dead man had been self-possessed, introverted, used to keeping out of the public eye, while the writer of the farm's address was more voluble, a boastful creature, probably with some authority and used to wielding it.

'Correct me if I'm wrong,' Entwistle said out loud, 'but I would say that you, Mr Pendleton, are a professional arsonist hired by the writer of this address to burn down this farm and anyone in it, no doubt to erase all evidence of occupation by our friends with the numbers – including that model upstairs in the attic. But why, my dead friend, why?'

Mr Pendleton was not forthcoming.

Eight

'Special Agent Collingwood, my name is Hartsby, ACA,' said the voice on Del's car phone. 'I will be in charge of this operation, but you will be my liaison on the ground. People will take orders from you, understand? Hostage Rescue are tied up with a hijacking at Dulles and the siege in Sacramento, and Cheyenne SWAT were shot to pieces in a botched bank robbery in Laramie two days ago. You are the highest-ranking agent I can get for the next two hours and if those bastards hold true to their noon deadline, no one will be able to get here from Washington in time to assume on-site control.'

Del didn't like the way this was panning out. It was one thing to have high-profile work dumped on his lap, but quite another to be playing power games even before he had got to the scene.

They had been driving for almost thirty minutes, lights and siren full on, and he had just had a recording of the terrorists' demands patched through to the TV in the car.

At 8:00 a.m. precisely, a hooded figure had appeared on Firefall Cable TV and had been simultaneously broadcast on KFLL radio, his voice disguised electronically.

'This message is addressed to the long-suffering people of Firefall, to the state legislature of Wyoming, and the presidents of Ultracom Oil and the United States of America. Today we have taken control of Firefall and are making a series of demands. I will read out these demands once and once only. There will be no further communication other than for those in Cheyenne, Washington, DC and Dallas, Texas, to confirm that our demands are to be met.

'One: we demand that in the interests of the environment and the people of Firefall, and communities like her throughout the world, that Ultracom desist immediately from oil exploration and remove their rig and give written assurances that they will never again attempt to explore for oil in this area.

'Two: all businesses that have suffered this last year because of the downturn in trade caused by the Ultracom exploration will be fully compensated.

'Three: in order to help our struggle against the polluters of the earth in all countries, a sum of one hundred million dollars will be deposited in an offshore bank account for use by our associates worldwide to further the cause of living in harmony with the environment.

'Four: a sum of ten million dollars in used non-sequential twenty-, fifty-, and one-hundred dollar bills will be dropped at a designated point in Firefall by helicopter.

'Five: if any of these demands are not met, or any attempt is made to enter the town without our permission by anyone whosoever, by any means whatsoever, the Ultracom rig will be blown up and hostages will die.

Repeat, the rig will be destroyed and hostages will die. They will be selected entirely at random – man, woman, or child, young or old – and they will be shot in public every ten minutes commencing at 9 a.m. We regret having to do this, but believe the greater good will ultimately be served by the sacrifice of the few – and those few need not be sacrificed at all if the government accedes to our demands.

'Those are the terms. They are completely non-negotiable – the world is watching. I will expect a telephone call at five minutes to nine detailing your response. Until then no further communication will be permitted.'

Del found himself sweating and wound his window down to catch a breeze. This was no bank siege nor some nail bomb in a trash can; this was *big*. If it all went wrong, it wouldn't only be an oil rig that blew up; Del's career would be in pieces and irreparable. Which was why he was even more suspicious when this Hartsby guy told him he was to be in charge on the ground and to take the flak.

'Surely there will be lines of communication?' Del questioned Hartsby, three decades of Bureau politics making him painfully aware that he would need to cover his back.

'True, and you will listen to them, but ultimately the decisions on the ground will be down to you and me, and relayed through you.'

'Pardon my ignorance, Mr Hartsby, but if you're in charge why aren't you giving the orders direct?'

'Let us say my presence isn't necessary. There is a lot more at stake than the fate of an oil rig and some Treasury dollars, but for now you needn't concern yourself with that. Suffice to say I work for a branch of government that gives me jurisdiction over yours. Check with your immediate superiors if you wish.'

'I will.'

'Very well. I'll call you back in five minutes and we can get on with the job at hand.'

Del didn't call his superiors. Instead he contacted an old friend of his at Quantico, a personnel officer called Elmore Fuller, who was a soon-to-retire old hand like Del. If anyone knew who Hartsby was, Fuller would.

'Emile Hartsby?' said the familiar singsong voice. 'Oh, Del, I *am* sorry. If you've pulled him on your case you'd better watch your toes – and your ass and your back, come to that.'

'Who does he work for?'

'Who doesn't he work for . . . Nominally, he's ACA.'

'ACA? The Anomalous Configuration Audit?'

'The same. Something to do with weapons, I think.'

Del had heard of the ACA but had never worked with them. Best he knew they were computer nerds who collated information on weapon use in the police and armed forces; something to do with monitoring real performance as against controlled testing in order to get the best value for money for the government and state purchasing agencies. He'd had to fill in a form one time when he blew out the side of a child molester's VW van with a Streetsweeper shotgun. Didn't need much research to say *that* gun worked. So when Fuller said 'weapons' it just made Hartsby's involvement in the crisis at Firefall even more puzzling.

'Weapons, you say? What kind of weapons?'

'Stuff even I can't find out about,' said Fuller.

'But what's a bunch of terrorists got to—'

'Unbelievable!'

'What?'

'Your call's being monitored.'

'By who?'

'Three guesses. Speak to you soon, Del. Just remember I said Hartsby was a wonderful guy, the envy of all of us here in Virginia.'

Del put the telephone down. Surely not?

It rang immediately. It was Hartsby.

'Strange choice of confirmation, but I trust it suffices.'

'Yes . . . sir,' managed Del.

'Good. I've already arranged for as many local police and state troopers as possible to rendezvous on the three routes into town. Tell your driver to head for the north road. I'm inbound on a chopper, maybe an hour behind. Keep in touch.'

'Yes, sir.'

Del replaced the phone, realizing how sweaty his hands had become. Nerves, but what he couldn't tell was whether it was brought on by the situation or by his run-in with Hartsby. Didn't matter much; if he screwed up he could kiss goodbye to carrying on working until his official retirement.

Up until Gloria had become ill he had been planning on retiring early and kicking back, but now that was all so much fantasy. With Gloria gone, it would be better to be occupied; work his way through the grief (assuming there was going to be another side to it). But mess this up and he'd be sacrificed, no questions asked. It wasn't as if he had enemies in the Bureau, just that he didn't have that many friends. But, even more than going out on a bad note, he didn't want it to be at the cost of innocent lives. Personal screw-ups he could live with (and did so); but people getting killed he couldn't tolerate.

'How long before we're there, Calthorpe?'

The driver checked a map on his lap.

'Twenty minutes.'

'Make it ten.'

Most times the rush to a crime scene was exhilarating, but this time it filled him with dread. He hadn't even arrived to assess the scene and already he had Washington on his back watching his every move. No time to massage figures, or brighten up a gloomy report: what they saw would be what he did. Sometimes he just wished he could stay in bed.

He called home to check the nurse had arrived but there was no answer. Perhaps she was in the bathroom with Gloria – he'd had the phone turned down because it sometimes frightened her. But if Nurse Bentley wasn't there . . .

He realized there was nothing he could do so he forced himself to concentrate on the crisis in Firefall. He checked the clock on the car dashboard. It showed 7:58.

'Calthorpe, what's wrong with the clock?'

Calthorpe punched at its setting buttons, but the digital display stayed obstinately at 7:58.

'Sorry, sir. It's broken,' he announced.

'OK, what's the right time, then?'

'It's . . . oh . . .'

'What?'

Calthorpe showed him his watch. It also read 7:58.

So both the dashboard clock and the wristwatch had stopped at the very moment Del had entered the car.

'Dial up a time-check,' said Del, feeling oddly disturbed by this coincidence.

'It's 8:33, sir,' Calthorpe said, putting down his mobile phone.

Del mumbled his thanks. A stickler for punctuality, he now felt even more uneasy about where he was heading. For some reason he couldn't help thinking this was some kind of omen.

Nine

If someone had told Entwistle that one day he would be trying to save three thousand people from the clutches of a bunch of terrorists while armed only with a .38 taken from a dead arsonist and riding a bicycle he would, quite rightly, have scoffed. But as he now rode along Taft Road towards Firefall, he knew that however foolhardy his proposed action, and however foolish he might look, there was little practical alternative.

The bicycle had been the only means of transport on Napier's Farm since he had totalled his cruiser and Pendleton's Sunfire. He knew that Firefall was closer than the next farm with a telephone, and he had also decided that whatever had happened would have been noticed by now, so he would be better trying to help his people, for that was how he now regarded those who lived in Firefall.

He knew small towns had a reputation for being unwelcoming to outsiders, but he and the town seemed to have fallen in love at first sight, and now more than ever he could see himself becoming Sheriff in the not too distant future. (But he couldn't help wondering what had happened to Sheriff Rickenbacker and the other deputies – and had to assume that, at the very least, they had been captured. He didn't dare think of anything worse as he knew that most of them wouldn't have given up without a struggle.)

Apart from his sense of duty and his concern for the town at large, there was also Carol. The flu bug had hit harder than either of them had expected, and there was still some way to go before her recovery was one hundred per cent. This time of the morning Carol would probably still be asleep, but that was small consolation with these men stomping around town.

Entwistle pulled out the notes he had made and saw he was very close to a roadblock, so he wheeled the bicycle off the road then edged forward, crouching low, until he could see the words NO FURTHER painted on the road, and, parked a hundred yards down the highway, one of the green Hummers he had originally seen in the barn. A man sat on top of it, cradling a rifle.

Entwistle sank back onto the verge, out of sight. Now what? He could try skirting the men and their vehicle, cross through the woods on the right or through the field on the left, but both routes would delay him. Besides, the Hummer looked a pretty secure way to travel. If only he could work out a way to surprise those guarding it and the road.

He had to believe that they were still reluctant to kill, otherwise he would have been eliminated in the barn. It was a risk – a big risk – but he would have to take it. So, after a couple of small preparations, he walked out into the middle of the road, hands clasped behind his head in surrender, and started to walk towards the Hummer.

The man on top spotted him almost immediately and called to someone else. Soon there were two men training their rifles on him from the top of the Hummer. These boys are not officer material, thought Entwistle. Standing up there like that, without any inkling of who might be backing up the stranger walking towards them down the road, they could be picked off before they even heard the shot. So when they both shouted at him to halt he carried on walking over their makeshift stop sign.

He had covered half the distance before they shouted again for him to halt and the sound of cocking rifles finally slowed him. They had rifles and could shoot him at any moment, so why didn't they? He was banking on there being a reason.

Twenty-five yards away he could see wide eyes staring at him from under black hoods. Number 32 stood up, his weapon trained on Entwistle's chest.

'Take one more step, motherfucker, and I'll blow you away!'

Entwistle stopped, hands still clasped behind his head.

'Don't want no trouble, boys,' he said.

'Who are you?'

They're not local, then. Entwistle had turned his uniform shirt inside out and left his jacket back by the bicycle, but anyone in town would have recognized his tall, wiry frame, long handsome face and shock of blond hair.

'Car broke down. Looking for gas. Saw you. Thought it better to be careful—'

The other man, number 11, jumped off the Hummer and walked briskly towards him.

'Shut the fuck up! Get down on your knees.'

Strike one, thought Entwistle: the man's scared. Bending his knees until they touched blacktop, he ignored the slight pain and was careful to keep his hands behind his head, his back straight.

Number 11 advanced to within six feet of him, the barrel of his Browning Rimfire rifle aimed at Entwistle's head.

'Name?'

'Pendleton,' offered Entwistle by way of a test.

'Pendleton who?'

Strike two: they didn't know the arsonist. 'Pendleton Smith. Out of Wichita. Travelling . . . What is this? Army?'

The man stepped closer, but not close enough. Come on, you dumb fuck, just a couple more feet . . .

'Shut up! Down on your front.'

'Can't do that,' said Entwistle, squinting up at the man and his gun.

'Why not?'

'Ask him,' he said, nodding at 32.

The man looked back over his shoulder.

Strike three, dummy.

'Drop the rifle!' barked Entwistle, the .38 revolver he had been clasping behind his neck now trained on 11's face; the man was perfectly positioned to shield him from any gunfire from 32.

The man's eyes widened in shock.

'I'll blow your fucking brains out before you can even twitch that finger. Now drop it!' shouted Entwistle.

Their eyes locked, but Entwistle stared the man down, the rifle soon clattering to the ground.

'Now get your hands behind your head and turn round.'

Picking up the Rimfire and careful to keep his

prisoner between himself and the anxious man on the Hummer, he put his .38 to the man's head and ordered him forward.

'You on the Hummer! Drop the rifle or I shoot you both!'

Number 32 shouted, 'No way, man. You're mine!'

'Drop the fucking gun!' urged 11. 'Do it or he'll shoot.'

'He won't!'

'He will. He fucking will! And I ain't dying for you or him or any fucker.'

'I can take him!' yelled 32.

Entwistle stabbed his revolver into the first man's skull. 'And I can take him – and you!'

'Drop the fucking gun . . . please,' said 32.

It was the whine of a loser. Neither of these two were professionals, either in the military or criminal world. Then he saw the other man's rifle hit the ground.

'Now follow it, and lie face-down.'

Two minutes later he had both men tied up and sitting back to back beside the Hummer, their hoods off, their frightened sweaty faces shining in the morning light. Entwistle waved the .38 about, aware of the smell of urine permeating the air.

'Now, before the both of you poop your pants, how's about you give me the low-down on what's going down in Firefall.'

Number 11 was anxious to talk, but 32 was still displaying some bravado, so Entwistle clipped the latter across the head with the gun butt, drawing blood on his brow.

'You were saying?' he said to 11.

Both men were young, early twenties: looked like they might even be college students, probably jocks. It would certainly account for the lack of brains.

'We was hired,' said 11. 'Told nothing but what we were to do. "Need to know". Everyone the same.'

'Everyone?'

'The others.'

'How many?'

'We saw . . . twelve, fifteen. That's all.'

Entwistle nodded, and ran the barrel of the gun under 32's chin.

'Do you concur?'

'W-what?'

'Agree.'

'Yes, yes. We were told to put on this gear, come out here with the Hummer, stop anyone coming past.'

'How?'

'How what?' said 11, keen to please.

'How stop them? Stop me?'

'Show them the rifles, spin a bullshit story about the army, anything to get them to go away.'

'And if they didn't?'

'Fire in the air.'

'In the air?'

'We were ordered not to shoot anyone, just fire in the air.'

'Not much of a strategy if SWAT was coming.'

'They reckoned no one would get here before—'

Number 32 elbowed 11 in the ribs to shut him up.

'Whoa there, boy, seems like we'd just got to an interesting part. Now don't you go spoiling my fun.'

Number 11 began to speak again but 32 rammed him once more in the side with his elbows.

'I've just had about enough of you, boy,' said Entwistle.

'I ain't your boy.'

'Good – because I don't believe in abusing kids.'

He slapped the gun against the side of 32's head and the man fell unconscious, sprawled across the road beside the astonished 11, who not only voided his bowels but began burbling manically. It was five minutes before Entwistle was able to make any sense of what the youth was telling him.

They didn't have any means of communication; instead they had been told to tune into KFLL and take their orders from there. That was odd. The terrified youngster was able to give him some idea of the scale of the assault on Firefall, but not a clue as to its leaders or the true strength of the terrorists' numbers – though, looking at his two captives, 'terrorist' seemed too flattering a description. And while he couldn't buy into the bullshit the boy had been spouting about the environment and wanting to close down Ultracom's rig, the ransom demand made sense. (Damned eyesore and a potential knife in the ribs to the town's economy the rig might be, but this action was out of all proportion, not least the level of organization behind it.)

Eventually he discovered these two saps were being paid five grand *after the event* to guard this road until the whole operation ended, at noon – if the stupid bastards lived that long. (Inside an hour of the outside world knowing what was going on in this part of the state, the place would look like a rerun of Operation Desert Storm – and then these two might just as well be Iraqi terrorists with the kind of treatment they'd be receiving.)

Dragging the unconscious 32 and the blubbering 11 off the road and rolling them into a dry ditch, Entwistle climbed into the Hummer and familiarized himself with the controls. At any other time he would have looked forward to trying out the vehicle, but this was one journey he had no illusions about enjoying. Turning on the transistor radio taped to the top of the dashboard, he swung the Hummer east and began the short drive towards Firefall.

He checked the dashboard clock: 8:17. That was more like it.

Ten

With increasing dismay, Del Collingwood listened again to the taped message from the captors of Firefall. He was as aware as the two dozen state troopers and federal marshals standing by their cars that official policy was one of containment and negotiation and never accession. They might persuade Ultracom to make some kind of vague promise, they might even drop the captors a bag containing cash, but the rest was just nonsense. And yet these people had threatened to kill hostages . . .

Del walked to the head of the line of police cars parked one mile north of the town. There were white cars, grey cars, beige cars, red cars. Every police force within a hundred-and-fifty-mile radius was sending men, and more were arriving all the time; the road was beginning to resemble a parking lot. Add to that the myriad flashing reds and blues and oranges that scarred his view of the town through the tree line and the irritating jabber of a dozen police radios intruding on his thoughts, and Del was feeling increasingly agitated. He reached into his pocket for a Snickers bar. Whenever he was nervous he tended to eat, which meant they were going to have to lay on a lunchcart.

'Call for you, Special Agent Collingwood,' shouted Calthorpe from back at Del's own car.

Del nodded and began trotting back there as fast as he could, then realized he was making a spectacle of himself and instead adopted an authoritative stride that got him there almost as quickly but without breaking into a sweat and looking a fool.

'Collingwood? This is Hartsby,' said the voice on the car phone. 'I'm about ten minutes away in a chopper. I trust you heard their ludicrous demands.'

'Yes, sir.'

'Your office got any info on these jokers?'

'No. They've come out of the blue, sir.'

'I'm getting my own people on to it, but we too seem to be at a loss. Usually there are rumours but this is, as you say, out of the blue. Naturally we will not be giving in to their demands.'

'That could present a problem at nine o'clock.'

'We'll cross that bridge when we come to it.'

'Might I suggest that we at least—'

'You can suggest all you like, Collingwood, but you'll do as I say. We'll talk further once I've landed.'

You mean you'll talk and I'll listen, thought Del replacing the receiver. Well, at least that got him off the hook, but that wasn't the point, was it? He had joined the FBI, and pursued his career against all the odds, in the simple belief that law and order should be maintained and that the protection of the innocent was of paramount importance. Yet here was Hartsby quite blithely content to let people die rather than make an attempt at appeasement. And even if Hartsby's own position changed after someone did die, that was still one innocent victim dead who might otherwise have been spared.

He unwrapped his Snickers bar and stared at it, aware of a dozen pairs of eyes watching him enquiringly.

'It would appear that we will not be negotiating . . .'

There was a ripple of concern, and he held his hand up.

'I agree with you. Although our official stance is not to give in to terrorism, obviously we must leave room for manoeuvre. I only hope Mr Hartsby has some heart. Now I'd like some of you men positioned further back up the road, maybe a mile or so, ready to intercept any newspeople or sightseers. Take no shit: turn them away and make it clear to them that you represent an exclusion zone. Anyone inside that line better be a cop, or they'll be deemed a terrorist and dealt with accordingly. Scare their asses. I also want choppers overhead with marksmen. Keep them out of sight of the town, but make your presence very clear to anyone else airborne. And if they fail to respond to warnings, invoke the authority of the FBI and national security. I want this town locked down and all extraneous personnel kept out of harm's way. Couple of hours from now this place will be CNN's lead item, and then all hell breaks loose.'

Damn, that was true. It was one thing to hijack an airliner or hole up in some farm, but to take an entire town hostage . . . Del threw the Snickers away and walked back to the head of the line of cars.

Leaning back on the hood of a highway patrol car, he borrowed the trooper's field glasses and focused them two hundred yards down the road on the Hummer parked broadside across US 283, north of the town. Behind the vehicle he could see at least two men with high-powered rifles aimed at him. Midway between the police units and the ex-army vehicle, a white line had been painted on the road and the words NO FURTHER painted above it, its meaning clear. There was little doubt there were marksmen supporting Del who could take out both men crouching behind the Hummer, but then what? The vehicle might be wired to explode when approached; the terrorists in the town might execute some hostages in response; and, as he switched his view to the trees on the left and right of the Hummer, Del knew there could be countless men secreted in the foliage and training their weapons on him and the police. That sent a shiver through him but he resisted the temptation to retreat.

He had done some reading on militia groups, and while most of them tended to boast a hard-core membership of a dozen or so men, and were able to call on the support of perhaps twice that number again when a show of strength was required, there were none that were sufficiently well organized or funded that they could undertake the capture of a town. He had soon noted that the men bore large numbers on their uniforms, and subsequent reports from other roads leading into Firefall where the same stand-off scenario was being enacted had produced a collection of numbers, the highest of which had been 84. Now that might well be a bluff, but if it wasn't then a minimum of eighty-four well-disciplined and motivated men could make a serious difference in just such a surprise attack. Which was all the more reason to take their threats seriously.

How many times in the past had the authorities in general, and the Bureau in particular, not taken their adversaries seriously, and suffered the consequences? How many agents were killed at Waco? And how many innocents also paid the ultimate price of official intransigence or plain incompetence?

And that, at root, was what mattered here: not an oil rig, or cash, or some meaningless set of digits in a computerized account – for who would notice a hundred million dollars when they spent twenty times that much on a stealth bomber that was too expensive to actually use in combat? No, what mattered here were the people of Firefall, the innocent victims of what was either a fanatical environmentalist group or old-fashioned criminals. Whatever Hartsby had planned, Del was not going to be railroaded into becoming the patsy for some gung-ho foul-up.

He looked up and saw helicopters circling. There were five or six of them but only two identifiable as police choppers. He ordered that their identities be checked and soon a couple were flying off, the media blackout sustaining its impetus.

One helicopter, however, came in to land. A dark blue Huey, its rotors whipping up dust as it settled to the right of the road. Immediately a man stepped out and walked briskly across the field towards the parked police cars. He was short, a little over five foot two, but well built enough to provide an authority his height might have otherwise denied him. He was dressed in a dark grey suit, buttoned up the front, a bright yellow tie providing the only colour. His face was forgettable, his thinning grey hair seemingly soldered in place to judge by the way the whirlwind about him hardly dislodged it. But his eyes were something else. Dark brown, almost black, they roved over the assembled policemen until they homed in on Del, and then he marched straight up to him, hand extended, his strangely compelling eyes fixed on Del's.

'Special Agent Collingwood? Pleasure to meet you. Emile Hartsby. I call you Collingwood, you call me Mr Hartsby – that way no one thinks we're dating. You got a sitrep?'

Del was slightly taken aback, not least by the bone-crunching grasp of the man's handshake. If firmness of grip was supposed to be an indicator of its owner's status, Hartsby was in line to become President. And if a wrist-watch was any indicator of wealth, Hartsby must be extremely well off. That costly gold number he wore was definitely not government issue.

'Nothing new to report,' said Del. 'You know their demands—'

Hartsby glanced at his expensive watch. 'Eighteen minutes to their deadline.'

Del breathed a sigh of relief. The failure of the timepieces earlier must have been a simple coincidence after all.

'We've had no useful contact with anyone in the town,' Del continued. 'All telephone lines are down, CB and radios are jammed. We're trying mobile phones but when we get through to any working numbers the owners sound panicked or can't supply information. Plus the terrorists have a good scanning set-up: all messages are intercepted and interrupted. They threaten the phone owners and they hang up.'

'Don't blame them. All exits covered?'

'The three main roads, yes. There isn't a vehicle on the west road into the town, but the "no further" message is there, and with the heavy cover provided by trees we're not risking an approach yet. And all the back trails should have our people on them inside fifteen minutes.'

'No one goes in except on your specific order. Whatever they see, whatever those fuckers do, we sit still.'

'You're anticipating that they'll execute hostages?'

'Bet your lunch on it – which would seem to be quite a big bet in your case.'

Del was stunned at his impertinence. 'That's a bit—'

'Personal? Sure it is. Not a lot you can do about it, though, is there?'

A large black truck with trailer was pulling off the highway amid another cloud of dust, its lack of markings betraying its importance.

'Looks like our comtruck's arrived,' said Hartsby.

Del watched him walk towards the giant Mack and trailer, still amazed at the man's comments. But then he realized that Hartsby had managed to sidetrack him from his warning that hostages would soon be dying. Del trotted after him and caught up with him as he stepped into the neon-lit interior of the truck's trailer.

Del's paranoia about the failed timepieces was finally laid to rest when he spotted an impressive array of digital clocks inside, each dutifully counting out the seconds. After all, ten synchronized clocks could not be wrong!

Satisfied, he switched his full attention back to the crisis.

'You're not going to agree to their demands?' he began.

'Of course *you're* not,' said Hartsby. 'You're one tough motherfucker, Collingwood. You're not about to give in to these pinko terrorist scumbags.'

The man proceeded to walk the length of the trailer, a dark corridor lit only by the buttons and screens of a series of computer consoles and video monitors that ran along either side. Manned by a dozen men all in short-sleeved white shirts and dark trousers, with microphones and earpieces strapped to their heads, it looked like a Houston launch-control roadshow.

Del struggled to keep up with him as he quickly took in the information supplied by the multiple screens.

'I would at least offer to talk—'

'Talk?' snorted Hartsby. 'Leave talk to Letterman. They've told us what they want. We can't give it to them. You know that.'

'Yes, but at least we—'

The man spun around and stabbed a finger at Del's stomach. He was at least twelve inches shorter but the determination in his eyes more than made up for their difference in height.

'We are not giving them any money, period. We are not stopping Ultracom exploring for oil, period. And we sure as hell ain't letting them blow up that rig, period and double exclamation mark. So anything you say to them is at best a lie, at worst a waste of breath. Talk all you want but you cannot offer them anything. Clear?'

'At least we might be able to stall them!'

'Then stall away,' said Hartsby, already looking back at a video screen, the subject apparently closed. 'You're in charge.'

'I really don't think—'

'Let's establish a few pertinent facts, Agent Collingwood. Number one, you're not here to think but to do. To be specific, to do what I tell you, understand? It's your badge I want, not your brain, not your input.'

Del was finding it hard to contain his temper. 'Just so I'm real clear on this: *you're* the one in charge?'

'I'm so in charge I eclipse the sun.'

'Do I salute or bow?'

'You fucking *curtsy*, Collingwood.'

'With my build?' Del said, harking back to Hartsby's previous insults about his weight.

Hartsby stared at Del. There was dead silence in the trailer. Even the computers seemed to have stilled their clicking and chattering in anticipation of a fit of apoplexy from Hartsby, but then the man let a smile spoil his aggressive posture.

'I must congratulate the FBI, Agent Collingwood. They got your profile down to a T, but the show's over now. Let's get to work. For reasons I can't go into, the one thing we cannot afford is for the terrorists to blow up that oil rig. There is a lot more at stake than Ultracom's steelwork or the threat of polluting what the locals colourfully refer to as the Hole. In fact the consequences of that rig's destruction outweigh all other considerations.'

'*All* other considerations?'

'Whatever, yes. Now, let's save that rig.'

'Don't you mean save those hostages?'

Hartsby didn't reply.

Though Del had rudimentary training in hostage negotiation, this situation was totally off the scale. He began to explain that Hostage Rescue could use a telephone just as easily as he could, but Hartsby wouldn't listen.

'You're here on the spot, able to react at a moment's notice,' countered Hartsby. 'With this comtruck you'll have direct feeds from a dozen cameras trained on the town, spy mikes zeroed on any activity we can find, recon drones at ten thousand feet with infra-red, plus whatever the satellite can give us.'

'A satellite? How in hell did you get that up there at such short notice?'

'Luck. Firefall is on a couple of standard orbits.'

Luck, my ass, thought Del, but realized that there was no other plausible explanation.

'Do I have your authority to offer them *anything*?'

Hartsby shook his head and sighed impatiently, as if Del was a child demanding an extra helping of French fries. 'The cash, yes, but stall.'

'Is anyone from Ultracom coming?'

'I am authorized by them to negotiate on their behalf.'

'Meaning Ultracom hasn't got any say?'

'Very astute, Collingwood. Now do your job.'

One minute later Del was talking to the terrorists' leader, a man who would only identify himself as number 38. Their conversation was to the point.

'We're looking into all your demands,' said Del. 'I can say that there may be leeway on the money, and

Ultracom are promising an answer soon. So things look like they're moving. What I would like is a—'

'Stop wasting my time. If you can't come on this line and say yes to all our demands inside the next ... eight minutes, a hostage will die. So stop fucking me around.'

The line went dead.

Del nodded to the agent next to him in the trailer and the number was instantly redialled.

Number 38 answered. 'One word, FBI man. What is it?'

'Please—'

'Wrong.'

The phone went dead. Del looked up at Hartsby, who smiled.

'Don't say I didn't warn you.'

Del was incensed. 'You've made me responsible for the lives of those people in Firefall, and yet you know I can't do anything to help them!'

'That's about it, yes.'

'Well, in that case might I respectfully ask to be relieved of this duty.'

'Request denied, but noted. Now carry on.'

'Carry on what?' Del said, close to losing his temper.

'Watching,' was Hartsby's disturbing reply.

Hartsby's gaze followed Collingwood as the angered agent walked away. Hartsby didn't feel any sympathy for the man; or for any of them, in fact. They were all just names on a casualty list.

Over the years Hartsby had been forced to trust certain people with knowledge of his find, not least because he himself wasn't a scientist. But once they had discovered too much, they were retired – permanently. So far, his secret was safe, but the scale of this current operation was making him jittery.

It wasn't the human lives lost, the property destroyed, or the reputations ruined that bothered him, but the fact that if things did start going wrong four years' work would be down the drain, so he would have to begin all over again. And it *would* take another four years. But the prize was so enormous it was worth the risk – and so far everything was working out just fine.

He looked at his watch, to find it had stopped. He shook it, then put it to his ear, but the second hand resolutely refused to budge. Damn, this was bad, because it could mean—

He grabbed a passing state trooper by the elbow. 'Got the time?' he demanded.

The startled cop flashed him his wristwatch, a digital which showed the seconds counting: 35 . . . 36 . . . 37 . . .

As Hartsby stalked back to the trailer, he unstrapped his Rolex and tossed it into a ditch. Five thousand dollars, and the damn thing stops today of all days. But his anger quickly dissipated. At least a faulty watch didn't spell the disaster he had feared. And what did he need one for anyway, when he had all the time in the world?

Eleven

There was something odd about all this, thought Entwistle, almost laughing out loud, given the repeating message on the radio. He slowed the Hummer to a halt and let it idle as he scanned the first street he had reached in Firefall.

Neither of the men he had overpowered had a walkie-talkie or mobile phone and the Hummer had only the cheap radio. In any big operation, communication was vital; how else would those in charge keep their men informed of changes in plan? He checked around the interior of the vehicle, but there were no written instructions either. From what 11 had told him, they had been recruited a week before by someone they hadn't met since, then told where to report and that as long as they did exactly as they were ordered they would be picked up as the entire team retreated up the road. This was, of course, patent nonsense.

With an incident of this size, even if it was only a bank robbery, they wouldn't get a hundred yards before they were pounced on by a couple of states' worth of armed cops. Committing robberies or hijackings is easy – any fool with a gun can do it. It's getting away that's the hard part.

He pulled over to the kerb and stepped out, surveying the street in front of him. It was deserted. No, more than that: it was *empty*. There were no kids playing, no one out walking, no traffic. He checked the dashboard clock. Still 8:17. Damned army surplus trucks.

Entwistle walked over to the nearest house. It was the Linsomes': a middle-aged couple with a brace of pretty teenage daughters who broke the hearts of a dozen tourist boys every summer.

The front door was open, the house empty, cooling coffee cups on the breakfast table. The carriage clock on the mantelpiece read 8:25. A clock that worked! He had been thinking that there might be some kind of electromagnetic interference, but was happy now to believe it was just a weird coincidence. He picked up the wall phone, got a dead signal, left it swinging. There was a transistor radio tuned into a country station. Picking it up, he flipped the dial to KFLL and listened to the same message about the town being taken hostage.

Returning to the Hummer, he settled in the driver's seat and checked his revolver. So now what? All he had left was the element of surprise. Tough buggers that the vehicles were, if anyone started shooting at him he wouldn't last long. However, because there were no radios, those in charge wouldn't know their roadblock had been removed – which might provide a route for police reinforcements. So should he just sit and wait, see who turned up?

No, be logical. Firefall was probably home to three or four thousand people. Rounding up that many people was impractical, and the radio was urging people to stay inside. If he could just find some people indoors who could back him up ... But first he needed to complete his disguise. He needed to find a terrorist with unsoiled clothing; then with the hood and jacket and the Hummer he would be right at home, and without radios chances were anyone he encountered would never discover he was an impostor.

He slowly eased the Hummer forward, his eyes scanning through the narrow windshield, eager to spy a likely victim. He had covered a hundred yards and was turning onto Circle Five when he spotted one such character hovering by the gate of a house. He wheeled the vehicle across the road and mounted the sidewalk, killing his speed sufficiently so that the Hummer wouldn't look as if it was about to run the man down.

For his part the man just stared at the Hummer, apparently unsure whether to wait or go. Maybe these saps knew more than it appeared, and this guy's evident wariness was precisely because he knew the Hummer shouldn't be around at this time. The Hummer came to a halt and Entwistle pushed open the door. Keeping back out of sight, he pointed his .38 at the man in black: number 47.

'Drop your weapon,' he ordered.

Number 47 raised his rifle and aimed it at the open door.

'Drop yours, asshole!'

Entwistle considered his options and decided he hadn't got any. He let the gun fall to the sidewalk with a clatter. So much for Plan A.

'Now get out!' urged 47, picking up the revolver.

Again Entwistle didn't have much choice. He eased himself out and stood erect, his hands by his side.

'Deputy Entwistle?' said 47.

Bastard knows me, thought Entwistle. Must be a Firefallian. 'What of it?'

'Come over here. Now!' The man waved his gun and eased back onto the driveway of the house.

Entwistle was reluctant to follow but still had no say in the matter. Only when out of sight of the road did 47 reveal his reason for stepping back out of view.

He removed his hood; he was a black youth. Hell, it was Greg Henley! The little psycho Entwistle had put away nine months before, after he had gone berserk in Uncle Art's Fun Pier.

'How'd you get—?' started Greg, but a fist filled his mouth and in a flash he was on his back, his head being pounded by a succession of expertly aimed punches.

'You fuck!' hissed Entwistle. 'You're in on this! I might have guessed! What's it about? *What's it all about?*'

Greg was near to passing out, the sudden assault having cracked his head on the driveway, but he managed to aim a knee at the Deputy's groin and watched as the man's eyes bugged out, his punching halted. Greg then grabbed the side of his attacker's neck and heaved him over into the bushes where, after a mad scramble, Greg found himself kneeling over the groaning policeman, the man's own revolver cocked and held to Entwistle's ear.

'Any more of that shit and you and me ain't on the same side.'

'Same side?' wheezed Entwistle. *Oh, God, my balls . . .* 'You little shit. You and your pals—'

The gun poked harder into his ear. 'I took out one of their guys, and dressed up in his gear – seemed safest thing to do. So what's your story, driving round like nothing's happened?'

'Luck. I got two on a roadblock. I took—'

'No shit. Two of them . . . Well, the odds are turning.'

'You're joking.'

'Yeah. God knows how many there are, but I'm 47.'

'And I decked 32 and 11.'

Greg stood up and helped Entwistle to his feet, though the Deputy couldn't stand upright and instead remained bent over, breathing hard through gritted teeth, his scrotum about to explode.

'Sorry about that,' said Greg, wiping his bloody nose.

'We're even now,' said Entwistle, looking up at the boy. 'How come you're here anyway? I thought they had you—'

'Locked up tight? So did they.'

Greg peeked out round the hedge, checked the coast was still clear, then he explained. 'Whatever *you* think I might be, Deputy Entwistle, all I've got is a bad temper. And I resent having my brain zapped just because I like expressing my opinion.'

'That what you call it?' Entwistle tried to stand up but felt sick and squatted down again. 'Two and a half thousand dollars' worth of damage? Kids traumatized?'

'Traumatized? They were *loving* it!'

'Because you lost?'

'I overreacted. Tough day. I was "expressing my anger".'

'Well, you must have had a lot of tough days, you mad sonofabitch. That was the fourth time I had to take you in. That's why we got the court judgement.'

'But I never hit anyone, did I?'

Entwistle tried to laugh but his guts hurt too much.

'Hey, *you* were beating the crap out of *me*!' said Greg. 'Remember when you took me in? Did I fight back?'

'No.' That much was true and, if he was honest, Entwistle had felt guilty ever since about pounding on the boy. But he had been so out of it, screaming like a lunatic, kicking and thrashing . . .

'So you just decided to leave the hospital?' said Entwistle, cupping his crotch extremely carefully.

'Yes, I came back to see Summer Campbell, see if we were still friends. She'd never visited me.'

'Her father wouldn't let her.'

'He seemed to have a lot to do with my being put there.'

Again he was right. Hal Campbell *had* taken against the boy, though there probably wasn't a parent in town who disagreed with him. And it wasn't even as if Mrs Henley objected: she'd long since endured enough of her son's tantrums.

Entwistle finally stood up straight, his face still scrunched in pain. 'Let's say we call a truce. Looks like we're the only ones in town looking for a fight.'

'You can say that again. I've been walking around for half an hour. Anyone here sees me they freaks and runs in their house, or just freezes and waits for me to walk by.'

'You didn't let them know who you are?'

'And have them make exactly the same assumption you did? Where in hell would that get me? Besides, any one of the real bad guys could be watching and if he saw I wasn't one of them . . .? Speaking of which' – he put his hood back on – 'what do you know about all this?'

'Only what the two morons on Taft told me, and what I heard on the radio. Eco-terrorism, I think they call it.'

'Heavy shit for a bunch of nature freaks.'

'Damn right. Whatever those two on the roadblock were told, this isn't about saving the whale.'

'So what now?' asked Greg, adjusting his mask's mouth hole.

'We go find me a uniform. So get in the Hummer,' said Entwistle. 'You're all dressed up so you drive and I'll keep out of sight. When you see one on his own, pull up and we'll take it from there.'

'You mean we mug him?'

'More like we get to "express our anger".'

They both managed a laugh.

Twelve

Until she was sure what the takeover of Firefall was about, and just how serious the invaders were about their threats, Maribeth saw nothing to be gained from bravado. Coming out into the open to be rounded up like the others made no sense. She didn't arm herself, as she knew she would never have the nerve to use a weapon and it would only make matters worse if she was picked up: better to be a sneaky mouse than the avenging rat. All of which posed an obvious dilemma: how was she to get across town to her school?

She had left the house on Nancy Road, and keeping to front verandas she made her way up to the end of the road where it intersected with Harding. From there she could get a good view straight down to the lakeside half a mile away in the centre of town. She could see four men in black and no one else; she only hoped the other residents were hiding inside.

Working her way through half a dozen front yards, she paused outside a run-down two-storey affair while two men crossed the road to talk to each other a couple of blocks away, their big numbers 29 and 55 clear to see. With the streets so empty, any movement on her part would be easily spotted and her efforts wasted.

She leaned back against a window and debated whether she should cross the road and get over to Coolidge, where she hoped there might be fewer men because there were fewer houses. But even one man was a danger. That's how terror worked, didn't it: by terrorizing. It was obvious when you considered it, thought Maribeth, but to see it in action . . . A few armed men, threats on the radio and TV, and everyone staying indoors *terrorized*. And if she had any common sense she would join them. She wondered if instead of trying to cross Harding she might carry on by using the backyards to one of the lower Circles.

She turned to glance through the window of the house she was hiding beside, and found a large pair of eyes staring at her. She screamed; couldn't help it. *Hellation on a stick!*

The wide eyes jumped out of sight, equally startled. Had they belonged to one of the armed men? What should she do? Where could she run? She heard a shout up the street. Why didn't she just give up now and save all the pain?

The eyes returned. She could see now that they belonged to a young boy, perhaps eight years old. She was too frightened to recognize him, but then a woman came into view beside him who beckoned Maribeth inside.

There was the sound of running footsteps further up the street. They must have heard her startled cry. She only had seconds. Keeping her back to the wooden wall of the house, she edged to the front door, which was now being held open by yet another, older woman.

'Come in, my dear. Hurry,' she urged.

Once she was in the hallway, the woman carefully closed the flyscreen, then bolted the inner door.

'Under the stairs. Under the stairs,' urged the younger woman, who was obviously the mother of the boy. 'It's Miss Hamilton, isn't it?'

Maribeth could only nod; if she tried to speak, she would probably throw up. She slid into the closet and let the two women pile clothes and sports gear on top of her, smothering her in old linen and dusty leather. Then they shut the door.

Maribeth could barely breathe, such was the tension she felt. As she didn't know what the armed men were capable of, she could only imagine the worst – and the worst was the fate that would befall the other two women if they were found to have hidden a fugitive. They could be hauled away from the boy, or shot, or . . .

She felt tempted to push off the load of junk on top of her, to go into the hallway and give herself up – but then she heard a hammering on the front door.

'You inside!' shouted a man's voice. 'What was that scream?'

There was a pause then someone unbolted the front door and light crept under the closet door.

'I cut myself . . . see. It was the shock. And it hurt like a sonofagun,' said the older woman.

'What were you doing?'

'Carrying on normal, like we was told. Fixing lunch.'

'At this time?'

'You a cook? You know how long a slow roast takes? You looked at this house? See servants and fillet steak and gold cutlery? Do you, boy? Do you?'

'Look, just shut up and keep it quiet, or else.'

'Or else what? You gonna shoot us?'

'Just let them give us the orders, old lady. Just let them give the orders.'

The screen door slammed, and as feet crossed the veranda onto the path Maribeth let out the breath she seemed to have been holding since she had first yelled in fright. Then light flooded her claustrophobic world and two sets of hands pulled her out and ushered her into the back kitchen, where she was sat down and plied with strong coffee. It was as her cup was being filled that she saw the handkerchief wrapped around the old woman's scrawny hand.

'How did you—'

'Had to have a story, so I cut myself.'

Maribeth was astounded. 'But you shouldn't—'

'So who was the screamer, then? Come on, my dear, if *you're* brave enough to be running about the streets, what's a little cut to these old cut-up hands?' She showed Maribeth her other hand, which was covered in scars.

''S what gardening does to you, so what's another nick?'

Maribeth thanked her again, then hugged the cup of coffee, lost for words. Although it was a hot day, she felt surprisingly cold.

The boy stared at Maribeth, his eyes wide with wonder. Thank heavens the little lad couldn't understand just how dangerous their situation might be.

'It's Jimmy Whelan, isn't it?' she finally remembered. He was in the year above her own class. 'Why aren't you in school?'

His mother tousled the boy's hair. 'Good thing he ain't. He's got chickenpox. Leastways, getting over it.'

'Did you see any other children going off to school?'

The boy nodded, clearly in awe of their sudden visitor. His mother patted his behind and told him to go off and play, the apparition of a schoolteacher in his own house too strong a wonder to contemplate.

'It was like a normal day until about 8:10, when they came down the street,' said Mrs Whelan. 'They didn't knock at every door, but they used megaphones loud enough for everyone to hear.'

'What did they say?'

'Keep indoors, don't cause trouble, watch TV, listen to the radio. Hell, that sounds like most days to me! But I switched the radio off; it was scaring the boy.'

'Didn't anyone challenge those men when they first turned up?'

'Some did, yes,' said Mrs Whelan senior as she ran her cut hand under the tap. 'Most got shown the gun, got shouted at. Two they hauled away.'

'Who did they take?'

'Some young feller from down the street, never seen him before. And Gerry Rankin. Put him in his own car and drove off down Harding towards the Hole.'

Gerry Rankin didn't strike Maribeth as the kind of man who would cause trouble. A meeker, milder soul she had yet to meet in town – which made it even sadder that his business had all but collapsed recently. He owned one of the two boating concessions on the Hole: Rankin's Rowboats was a collection of large, elegant, hand-painted family boats designed for lazing on the water. They even boasted small tables for picnics on board. But while people can still mess around on pedalos and canoes because they're fun, pleasure boating isn't such a pleasure when that ugly rig is always in view. A couple of times she had seen the man near to tears while locking up his yard down on Circle One and Roosevelt, more than half his boats never having seen water the whole summer. Maybe all this was the final straw that had made the poor man snap; got him shouting at the wrong person at the wrong time. She only hoped he had turned all apologetic and they had then simply put him somewhere out of harm's way.

'So what were *you* fixing to do, Miss Hamilton?' asked Mrs Whelan.

'Call me Maribeth, please.'

'Right. I'm Joan and this is Jo-Ellen, my momma.'

'What I was trying to do was to get over to the school. I guessed some of the children would have made it there, and they might be alone and frightened.'

The grandmother sat down opposite her and took hold of her hand. 'That's a wonderful thing to do, and so brave.'

Maribeth patted the old woman's good hand in return. 'You were the brave one. You didn't know what they might do to you if they found me. For all you know, I could have just killed one of them.'

They all swapped uneasy smiles.

'So what now?' said the grandmother.

'I keep trying.'

The mother nodded. 'I ain't about to argue with you, my dear. Just I got the boy and mother to look after—'

'I'm doing it for the children and, if I'm honest, because I . . . well, because I want to find out more. To see what's happening. *Do* something.'

'Well, I wish you the best of luck, and don't let me go hearing no gunfire. Just you get to them kids safe and sound.'

There wasn't any more Maribeth could say. Her children needed her support. For however young or boisterous or unworldly they were, and whatever the risks to herself, they were still her friends. So she bade the two women farewell and began the slow but safer progress of following the hill down to the Hole via the backyards of the houses on Harding Street.

Half an hour later, and running with perspiration, Maribeth flopped down against the garden wall of a house on the corner of Harding and Circle One. For most of her journey she had been able to make her way across private gardens, unworried about the eyes of the town's invaders, her only watchers being whichever of the scared inhabitants trapped inside their houses had the nerve to look out. A couple of times they had ventured to their back doors and beckoned her in but she had refused, knowing that the nearer she got to her goal the more severely her resolve would be tested. She was now approximately halfway there.

On the other side of the wall was a crossroads, with the Town Hall on the opposite corner. But she had already sneaked a look over the top and spotted a dozen armed men grouped around a pair of trucks parked to the side of the building's main entrance, its small forecourt empty except for a video camera mounted on a tripod.

The Town Hall itself was fronted by three storeys of administrative offices, the multi-windowed front boasting a large central double door atop a wide rise of shallow steps. Built in the early days of the century, it had always been too grand for such a small town. Over its rear loomed the blue arm of a large piledriver crane, erected to help build an extension that would eventually incorporate the Sheriff's Department and the Fire House, whose existing buildings were to be sold off for tourist development.

This close to the Town Hall she knew she had come too far, but she had never summoned up the nerve to try and cross Harding higher up the hill. In backyards she felt safe, but it was now obvious that she would have to make her way back to Circle Two before attempting a crossing. As she pondered her retreat, she heard a commotion from outside the Town Hall, and edging along the wall she peered over the top.

All the armed men were gathered in a semicircle behind the video camera, which was now being manned by the short, nervous figure of Dave Gantry from KFLL, the poor man having to stand on a box to use his viewfinder.

The doors of the Town Hall suddenly opened and two hooded men, 14 and 25, came out supporting a pathetic figure whose feet were dragging. At first she couldn't recognize who it was, but then they turned him to face number 38, standing on the Hall steps, and on the back of the prisoner's jacket she spotted the logo of Rankin's Rowboats.

Number 38 began to speak, directing his words at the camera behind Rankin and the two men holding him upright.

'It is now nine o'clock' – Maribeth looked up quickly at the Town Hall clock. It was indeed 9:00 a.m. – 'and there has been no response concerning our demands. As a consequence, penalties must now be exacted.'

He walked down the shallow steps, waved the two supporting guards away, and let Rankin fall to his knees, his head hung low, his body seemingly liquid. Then 38 drew a pistol, aiming it at the man's back, and fired once.

The explosion was enormous in the silence, and rumbled across the town like thunder. Rankin slumped forward.

The executioner nodded to the two guards, who dragged the corpse back into the Town Hall. Number 38 approached the camera – Gantry was bent double, throwing up.

'In ten minutes you will witness another death, and again blood will be on the hands of the government. You have therefore ten minutes to accede to our demands.'

He walked calmly back up the steps into the Town Hall, the twin doors closing silently behind him.

Maribeth collapsed onto her knees, her bladder emptying. They had killed Gerry Rankin right there outside the Town Hall, in front of everyone. *Executed* him. This was *real* – and in ten minutes they would kill another hostage. Suddenly all her hopes and delusions had been blasted away as easily as Rankin's life.

Thirteen

Hartsby was sequestered in a soundproof booth at the rear of the comtruck.

'Is your scrambler on, Dr Kapek?' he said into the small microphone attached to his earphones.

'Yes, Mr Hartsby,' came back a raspy voice with an East European accent.

'Good. Is the facility ready?' asked Hartsby, as he watched events in Firefall unfolding on a small video monitor in front of him.

'Yes.'

'And you finished the shielding?'

'Last night. It was tight. The specifications left by Douglas were—'

'Is it up and running and ready to receive?' said Hartsby impatiently

'Yes.'

'That's all I need to know. And your staff are fully briefed?'

The man sounded flustered. 'They know as much as I do.'

'That's enough.'

'When will we find—?'

'When I'm ready to tell you! Believe me, Kapek, it'll be worth the wait and you'll understand the secrecy. And remember, whatever happens, no one touches it. Clear?'

'The handling rig might—'

'The handling rig will handle it, period. No screw-ups, Kapek – none. Believe me, you don't want to know the consequences.'

Hartsby couldn't help remembering the late Professor Douglas and his sudden unexpected suicide, following a face-to-face meeting where he had voiced misgivings about their work. Some people are just too smart for their own good.

'I'll get back to you nearer the time,' Hartsby finished, taking off his earphones and unplugging the jack from the console in front of him.

He ran his fingers over the video screen and smiled, then switched that off as well. The pieces were coming together very satisfactorily. As long as everything would keep on track . . .

He exited the small booth and walked the length of the trailer to find Del Collingwood. The FBI agent was visibly shaking as he stared at a monitor.

'They just killed someone. You saw it. They shot that poor bastard.'

'All the more reason not to deal with them,' said Hartsby, seeming as unruffled as Del was appalled.

'*What?*' Del didn't know which was more horrifying: the execution he had just witnessed or the icy attitude of Hartsby.

'They warned us what they would do if we failed to

cooperate,' said Hartsby, picking at his thumbnail. 'They've proven their point. We have proven ours.'

'And in ten minutes you let them shoot another hostage? And another one ten minutes after that?'

'Yes, if they choose to execute them.'

'But we can stop them. We *have* to stop them.'

'And take that first step down the rocky slope—'

'The rocky slope? These are people's *lives* we're talking about. In case you've forgotten, our job is to protect the innocent.'

'It might say that on *your* job résumé—'

Del lashed out at him, but Hartsby sidestepped the blow and watched as Del clattered into a computer desk.

'Collingwood, I won't bore you with the consequences had you struck me.'

Del spun round, his face twisted in fury. 'Fuck the consequences to me! I'm concerned about those poor bastards in Firefall!'

'As are we all,' said Hartsby, sweeping his hand around the room.

Blank faces stared back, not one of them showing an emotion.

'Are you all fucking robots? How many people have to die before you—'

'Collingwood!' shouted Hartsby. 'Shut up. You're an FBI agent, not an old woman. Sacrifices need to be made. Circumstances dictate that we—'

Del grabbed the telephone receiver and punched the redial button. Number 38 came on the line.

'Ready to say yes?' said a calm voice.

Del stared at Hartsby, who simply stared back.

'You're in charge,' Hartsby said, then walked out of the trailer.

'You ... you've proven your point. There's no need to kill—' Del spoke into the phone.

The line went dead.

Del stood with the receiver in his hand, uncertain what to do. He knew he should call up and agree to all the man's demands – that was the human thing to do – but as a federal agent he was obliged to toe the party line of no concessions, no promises.

Finally he threw down the receiver and stormed out after Hartsby. Crashing down the trailer's steps, he paused at the bottom, unable to spot the man. Then there was a cough behind him and he turned to see him smoking a cigarette as he leant against one of the comtruck's large wheels.

'And you told him what?'

'You know damn well what I told him,' said Del, near to tears.

'So all that was just a waste of energy.'

'You wouldn't understand.'

'On the contrary, I understand very well.'

'What about that poor man's wife? His kids? His friends?'

'Not an issue.'

'Not an issue?'

'There is a bigger picture here, Collingwood, one I'm not obliged to tell you about and one I choose not to burden you with. Suffice to say that my actions have a logic that is not only valid, but also vital to national security.'

'What's more vital than protecting our people? That *is* national security. Fail to protect our citizens and there's no nation to be secure about!'

'There's a bigger picture.'

Hartsby started towards the ring of police cars. Another helicopter was landing to their right, and a man in a suit hopped out of it and ran over carrying a laptop computer. Hartsby took it and waved him back to the helicopter.

Del grabbed Hartsby by the shoulders and spun him round.

'In five minutes they'll execute another hostage, and you say I can't offer them *anything*?'

'You can offer them anything you like, Collingwood, but when you fail to deliver I fear the consequences for those held in the town will be even greater.'

'If we only—'

'Give in once, you give in all along the line.' Hartsby let out a sigh. 'OK, go back inside, dial up Mr 38, offer him the works: the money, the environmental shit, the fucking moon, see how far it gets you.'

'I will.'

Del dashed up the steps into the trailer, dialled up the number in Firefall, and waited for 38 to come on line.

'Yes?' The voice was as steely cold as before.

Del hesitated, aware of everyone watching him. All his life he had obeyed orders, however distasteful. From spying on student groups to following adulterous senators to working on state's evidence deals with murderers, he had done as he was told. But this was something else.

'Yes?' repeated 38.

Del slowly let the receiver return to its cradle, his body shaking, his face running with sweat.

Hartsby came up behind him, and clapped a hand on his shoulder. 'You are one loyal motherfucker,' he said.

Del spun round. 'I have never felt more disloyal in my life.'

Hartsby raised his palms in appeasement.

Del continued, 'Now my loyalty isn't to you or the Bureau, but to those people in Firefall. Get yourself another man. I resign.'

Fourteen

Finding one lone invader turned out to be harder than Entwistle or Greg had anticipated. They drove around the edge of Firefall following Circle Six and then Circle Five, encountering men in twos and threes but none on his own. Some of the men stood on corners, watching all four approaches to their positions, while others were patrolling streets on the lookout for stray townspeople.

Greg had to keep up a running description of all he could see while Entwistle stayed out of sight in the passenger footwell. He sensed the kid's anger but this time was not surprised at its target. He'd always had the boy down as a troublemaker whose bouts of temper or violence would one day land him in big trouble on some assault charge, maybe even a murder rap. His father had long since deserted the boy and his mother, and he had become notorious for disruptive behaviour. A high-school drop-out – and the school grateful to see the back of him – Greg had hung around town like a bad smell, trying his hand at this job or that but always ending his employment with a fit of temper or destruction. It wasn't enough to say he had a bad temper: the boy seemed almost psychotic. No wonder Hal Campbell had wanted him well away from his daughter. (The fact that Campbell was not best disposed towards coloureds did nothing to alleviate their mutual antagonism.)

The last time Greg had been in town he had taken Summer Campbell to the Fun Pier, knowing her father was out on the lake fishing, so likely to spot them. It had been an act of wilful stupidity on his part that the girl didn't deserve. Better the two combatants had met somewhere isolated at dawn to slug it out, but instead several video machines and a candy stall had been demolished while horrified tourists stared on.

So bad was the boy's outburst on this occasion that Sheriff Rickenbacker had had him tested for drugs, but found nothing incriminating; just an evil temper and a knack for losing it. Well, they could both sure do with that mean spirit now, but it would need to be harnessed, otherwise – if Greg let loose the way he had in the past – the intruders might just shoot the kid like a mad dog, and take his new handler down with him.

'Looks like we got one,' said Greg after ten minutes of cruising. 'He's standing on his own outside Madson's grocery store, smoking like a schoolkid – you know, like he shouldn't be.'

'Should be able to catch him, then.'

'He's dropped it. Shit, he's seen us. I'm stopping.'

'OK, but try and keep him talking. And watch out for his gun.'

The Hummer stopped and Greg leaned through his window. 'How's it going?' he asked.

Number 66 walked towards the Hummer as Entwistle slowly cracked open his door. 'Fine, and you?' said 66 nervously.

'Just checking out everyone's position.'

Number 66 was plainly relieved that his smoking had not been remarked upon. 'It's getting near nine.'

Greg wondered what was so special about nine. Neither he nor Entwistle had heard anything except the loop message on KFLL radio.

'Hey, you couldn't spare us one of those butts, could you?' said Greg.

'What . . . sure, sure.'

As the man lowered his rifle and reached into his back pocket, Entwistle bounded round the front of the Hummer and charged, barrelling him back through the shop door. Greg then leaped out of the vehicle and followed them inside the store.

Number 66 had come to rest on his backside just inside the door, which Greg then slammed behind them.

Entwistle spoke for the first time. 'Anyone else here?'

Their target shook his head.

'Right, off with this.' Entwistle pulled off the concealing hood. 'I know you,' he said.

Greg lifted up the terrified man's head. 'It's Duke Manners. Owns the crazy golf.'

'So it is. Looks like you've got a story to tell us, Duke.'

Duke chose instead to throw up over his lap.

They hustled the still retching Manners to the back of the shop, with Entwistle's .38 in his gut.

'Talk, you fuck, and talk good.'

'I . . . It wasn't my idea.'

'Obviously. So whose was it?'

'I don't know. I don't know who's in charge . . .

Taylor Ash got me into this. Said it was the best way to make back the money we were losing.' The man then fainted.

'Do you believe the calibre of criminals today?' said Entwistle.

'Here, this'll bring him round.'

Greg grabbed a can of Dr Pepper, shook it, then opened it so as to spray up Manners' nose. The guy reacted instantly, spluttering and gagging like he had been held underwater for ten minutes. Then, once they had settled him, he began to tell them what little he knew.

If the situation hadn't been so serious, Entwistle would have laughed.

According to Manners, the whole town was being held to ransom by a mixed gang that included Taylor Ash, a local blowhard who owned an autoshop on Circle Three. He had a reputation for overcharging on shoddy work, and his business had been lame for years. It seemed he had been persuaded to hook up with these terrorists in the hope of getting a share of the cash. And Manners, like the fool he'd always been, had joined him. But it was all operating on a 'need to know' basis and Manners needed to know very little.

Just as he finished his scanty version of events, they heard a single shot.

Greg glanced at the clock behind the counter: 9:00 a.m.

'What was that?' Entwistle turned back to their prisoner.

'Think they just shot a hostage,' said Manners.

'They *what*?'

Manners vomited yet again.

'I'd be puking, if I were you. If that's a hostage, we're talking accessory to murder.'

They quickly tied the blubbering man up tight. Entwistle debated whether to steal his clothes, but their fouled condition made the decision for him. Then they quickly walked outside and climbed back in the Hummer.

'What now?' asked Greg.

'I wish to God I knew. However many fools there are like Duke Manners involved in this, if they've just shot a hostage, it's now serious, serious shit.'

As if in answer, the transistor radio's repeating message was cut off. There was a brief pause, then, '*You were warned*,' intoned a voice. '*One man is dead and another will die in ten minutes from now unless we receive confirmation that all our demands will be met by noon today*.'

Entwistle swore. They had only just started to fight back, and already they had lost.

Fifteen

Barely able to see because of her tears, Maribeth fumbled her way along the garden wall to the house directly across from the Town Hall, her mind spinning with what she had witnessed.

No more than twenty yards from her, a man she knew, an innocent man, had been executed. And they could have picked anyone . . . even herself, had she been caught.

She reached the back door of the house and rapped gently, praying that whoever was home would prove as accommodating as the Whelans. There was no reply. She eventually tried the handle, and the door opened a crack. She gently eased it wider, convinced her movements could be heard beyond the wall, and that any second masked heads would pop up and order her to freeze. Slipping inside, she locked the door, and working her way through the house found it empty. She spotted a letter on the hall table, addressed to a Mrs Frine. Now where did Maribeth know that name from? She could not quite recall.

Stepping into the lounge, she discovered that the television had been left on. But it was tuned to static, the screen unusually bright in the darkened room. Maribeth found she couldn't pull her eyes from the white square.

Her mind became suffused with the light and a feeling of relief washed over her, as if all the problems outside had been swept away and she was safe.

She slowly walked further into the room, all the time her eyes locked on the TV screen. She felt its warmth: it was a friend there to help her. She wanted to touch it and embrace it but, as she moved towards it, her foot caught on a rug and she tripped and stumbled. As she righted herself, she realized that the television provided a distraction she could ill afford and so, averting her eyes, she flicked it off. *Hellation in a high hat*, wasn't there enough strangeness going on without her getting so easily distracted by lights?

Staying well away from the windows, she made her way upstairs to the bathroom, and saw to the mess she had made of herself. She badly needed a new pair of jeans, so ventured into one of the bedrooms – except it wasn't a bedroom but a sewing-room. Three sewing machines, racks of clothes in plastic covers, shelves crammed with rolls of fabrics, a pinboard festooned with pages from fashion magazines. *That's* who Mrs Frine was: the dressmaker who made a lot of the Prom gowns for the girl students, and fancy-dress costumes for the Christmas dance. Not pausing to speculate as to the woman's whereabouts, Maribeth hunted around for some suitable trousers.

There was a small radio standing by one of the sewing machines, with a pair of earphones. Slipping these on, she tuned it to KFLL. The same message was still repeating over and over. A quick glance at the clock on the wall confirmed that in three minutes' time they would be executing another hostage. Surely the government would act soon, would say something, *anything*, to make them stop the bloodshed.

At last she found a suitable pair of charcoal jeans and slipped them on, though wondering why she even bothered. It was plain these masked intruders meant serious business, and if she was caught out on the streets they would doubtless execute her as a lesson to the others. And did she really think she possessed enough guile to make it all the way to her school? The futility of her mission made her legs go weak.

Then she was startled by another shot, and yelped involuntarily. This can't be happening, not here in Firefall.

With shaking hands she slipped the earphones back on, just as the loop was replaced by an announcer.

'*A second hostage has now been executed. The blood of both of them is on the hands of the authorities. How long this situation will continue is entirely up to them, but I remind you that every ten minutes another hostage will be executed until our demands are met.*'

The previous tape loop then started again.

Maribeth hurled the earphones across the room in disgust, the tiny radio smashing to the floor. Sudden rage boiled up inside her at her impotence, but at least she had found a safe haven here in Mrs Frine's house. Yes, and every ten minutes she would hear another person die in the street outside . . .

And then she spotted the large dressmaker's scissors.

No, that was silly! It couldn't possibly work. But, then again, she couldn't just sit there and hope to be rescued. Whatever the risk, she must do something *positive.* So she picked up the scissors, eyeing their sharpness. They would do for the job she intended.

Maribeth began working as speedily as possible, but even so she heard two more executions take place outside before she had finished. It was all she could do to keep her hands steady. After twenty minutes of frantic activity, the task was completed to her satisfaction. She slipped on her handiwork and checked herself in the mirror. Not bad, apart from the swell of her breasts, but there was little she could do about that. She hadn't noticed any females amongst the masked intruders as yet, but that did not mean there weren't any.

As Maribeth left the room, she realized something was missing from her makeshift get-up.

Black trainers, black jeans, black sweatshirt with a giant number 9 sewn onto both back and front (she didn't possess the time or the patience to make this a double digit) and finally the hood mask made up of several socks sewn together. Seen from a distance it might do, as long as she did not encounter the real number 9. But what about a weapon? They all carried guns.

She searched through the rest of the house. If by chance Mrs Frine had a son, as like as not he would own a toy gun. Yes, thank God, he did. Grabbing what resembled a semi-automatic rifle, she found its lightness a disturbing reminder that it was just a toy. Bracing herself, she slipped downstairs.

Pausing in the hallway, she glanced at the clock placed next to the telephone. The time it revealed was 9:03, but its second hand was resolutely frozen.

Another one stopped – hellation!

On an impulse she stepped back into the kitchen. There she found both clocks had also stopped at 9:03 – precisely the time she had first entered the house. Decidedly unnerved by this, she bolted back to the door and out into the front yard.

The front of the house itself was set back, so that the wall bordering the garden gave her the cover she needed. Taking a deep breath, she set off up the hill towards Circle Two, the toy rifle slung across her back. It was naturally smaller than the real thing, but from a distance might still look like a genuine weapon.

She had covered just a hundred yards when another shot sounded. Instinctively she dropped to her knees, the heat inside her patchwork 'uniform' making it difficult to think straight. Wiping sweat from her brow, she realized it must be 9:40 – the fifth execution. *Hellation without end . . .* Maribeth turned to glance back down the hill, but was now unable to see the Town Hall or the murderous activity outside it.

Suddenly she was up and running, all caution cast to the wind as she responded to the driving need simply to *get away*.

Dashing across Harding, she sped along the side of a house at the corner of Circle Two. Then she stopped to regain her breath, convinced that her pathetic flight must have been noticed, and that a dozen hardened terrorists would be charging up the street behind her, fingers squeezing on triggers. Daring to peep round the corner of the house, she found the street was totally empty. OK, she had made it! But now what?

She could not appear to be skulking purposelessly; now disguised as one of the intruders, she had to act like one. So, with a pounding heart and legs still reluctant to respond, she launched herself unsteadily onto the sidewalk and began to march purposefully along Circle Two.

Another three minutes brought her to the corner of Hazel Road, and once more came the sound of a distant shot. She did not need a watch to tell her the government had failed again to capitulate to the intruders' ultimatum. She could only hope the authorities were using the time already elapsed to formulate some kind of rescue strategy – in which case she'd best not get caught in the open wearing enemy garb.

The road ahead of her was unnervingly quiet, like it would have been at dawn, four hours before: rows of parked cars, empty sidewalks, houses with blank windows. No movement except . . . Uh-oh, there was a black-hooded figure further up the hill, only a hundred yards away. She saw him wave to her, so she waved back – then crossed the road, ignoring his shouts.

Once out of sight, she began to run, but after a minute had to stop to get her breath back. Just as she was about to set off again, there came a yell from behind her.

'Hey, number 9, hold up there!'

Maribeth turned to witness number 31 trotting towards her. *Oh, hellation in spades!*

It was too late to run so she stood her ground, hoping this would put him at ease while . . . While she what? Shot him with a *ratatat* sound effect? Oh why did she ever think she could get away with this nonsense?

He reached her, now as breathless as she was. 'Hey

. . . how's it going? Gets lonely out here . . . waiting for orders.'

Maribeth didn't know what to say – so didn't.

'Where you meant to be patrolling?' he gasped, holding his side.

Still Maribeth could not respond, her mind a whirl.

'Hey . . . you got *tits.*'

'And you ain't got brains,' she managed at last, kicking him hard in the crotch. 'Pardon my grammar,' she added.

As he crumpled to the ground with a loud yelp, she kicked him fiercely in the side of the head, which knocked his skull against a fire hydrant.

As she remembered from her self-defence classes, the cardinal rule is: 'Don't stop until it's finished.' She had to make sure he was totally incapacitated, so she carried on kicking him until he lay still.

She then knelt and wrestled the gun from his fingers and, rolling him onto his back, pulled off his mask. She found he was a man in his thirties, red-faced and sweaty. She did not recognize him, but then why should she? Hoisting the much-needed rifle over her shoulder, she continued her anxious progress along Circle Two. She was now only four blocks across and one block up from her destination. With luck she might just make it.

Suddenly a shot rang out to her left, and the window of a red Grand Am parked right next to her imploded.

Sixteen

'We can't go round the whole town beating them up one by one,' argued Entwistle. 'We need a plan.'

'You're in charge,' Greg reminded him.

Entwistle didn't want to admit that he hadn't a clue what to do next. They could hunt out some means of communicating with the outside world – radio, mobile phone, CB – but the outside world already knew what was happening and didn't seem to give a damn.

As he wiped the sweat from his face, he could smell vomit on his cuff. Damn that Duke Manners. The last time he had smelled vomit, he had been holding Carol's head over the toilet bowl after she'd eaten a bad chilli dog at the State Fair. It wasn't a memory he wanted to dwell on, but the image of a toilet kept recurring. Why?

'I've got an idea that might give us an edge, but we need to get to Carol's first,' said Entwistle. 'It's quiet there: give us time to think. We can hide the Hummer in her backyard.'

They had been parked up behind the grocery store for several minutes, but soon Greg was heading up Roosevelt until they reached Circle Five, where Entwistle directed him onto Brent Road. At the end of this short thoroughfare, Entwistle pointed out a driveway that passed along the side of a single-storey house and continued into a paved backyard. Stepping out, he headed to the back door and unlocked it quickly.

'You live here?' said Greg.

From the outside the house looked nothing very special, just one of six identical buildings on a suburban street, but inside it looked tastefully furnished, smartly decorated, and welcomingly cool.

'It's Carol's place actually but, yes, I suppose I live here. Have done for three months. Impressive, eh?'

He preceded Greg into the lounge with its three large sofas, colourful throw-rugs on the varnished floorboards, modern art on the walls, a giant-screen television and the priciest-looking sound system Greg had ever seen.

Entwistle could not prevent his eye from falling on the mantel clock. It said 9:33, which was correct. Well, some good news!

The whole room offered such a calming blend of greys and lime greens that all Greg wanted was to sink into the nearest sofa.

'Neat,' he commented at last.

'I wouldn't say that in front of her,' warned Entwistle. '"Neat" isn't one of her favourite expressions.'

Greg grinned. 'Is she home?'

'She'll be in bed. She's had flu all week.'

Greg wandered slowly around the room while Entwistle padded down the hallway to one of the bedrooms beyond.

It was indeed an impressive house, and Greg wondered exactly who lived here. He did not recall anyone in

Firefall called Carol except the Humberts' daughter, who was only fifteen, and Jim Howlett's wife who must be in her forties – and women sporting beehive hairdos like hers don't inhabit elegant homes like this one. Could be a newcomer, of course – Greg had been out of circulation for nearly a year.

Whatever, Entwistle was a good-looking guy, so why wouldn't he land himself a classy girlfriend – obviously one with money too.

'Greg, can you come through here?'

He followed Entwistle's voice and found himself entering an all-white bedroom, the shades drawn and an air-conditioner humming gently at the window. A portable television with the sound turned down provided the room's only touch of colour.

Entwistle was sitting on the side of the double bed, checking the woman's pulse.

'Oh,' said Greg, in some confusion. 'You're Carol Glass.'

'I presume from your reaction he didn't explain about me,' she said throatily.

'I assumed he meant his girlfriend,' Greg stammered.

Carol shook her head and gave Entwistle a glare. 'Some mothers' sons are proud of them.'

Greg vaguely recalled how Mrs Entwistle had arrived in Firefall to visit her son the cop a couple of years ago, but had decided to stay when she met – and subsequently married – Frank Glass, proprietor of the Glasshouse. It was considered the best restaurant in town, and fronted the Hole itself, on the opposite side from Uncle Art's less elegant Fun Pier. The place had such a good reputation that people would travel fifty miles and more to dine there. What Greg had not known was that seven months ago Frank Glass had died after a stroke, and Entwistle had moved in for a while to help his mother get over her grief.

Carol Glass was a natural blonde in her early sixties, attractive in the way of a beautiful woman who has let herself age naturally, and, despite her current illness, she still seemed alert, and clearly combative.

'So you live with your mother?' said Greg, intrigued.

'And you never did?' said Carol.

'Yeah, but I ain't old like Entwistle here.'

'Careful, you,' warned Carol. 'Because if Entwistle here's old, that makes me ancient and, ill or no, I don't take kindly to insults.'

'Hey, hey, I'm sorry.'

Entwistle merely smirked at Greg's discomfiture.

'Well, it's nice to meet you.' Her tone changed. 'Look, what the hell is going on out there, and why is *he* dressed liked *them*?' She pointed first at Greg and then at the television.

While Entwistle fiddled with doses of medicine for his mother, he tried to explain what had happened, and what he and Greg had been doing.

'I'm glad someone's doing something, at least,' growled Carol. 'When I watched that first execution I couldn't believe my eyes. First Gerry Rankin, then Stefano Bacal . . . and someone who looked like Alan Schmidt was killed just now. It's unbelievable . . .' Words failed her.

'There's been no further word of a settlement?'

'Three dead and *still* nothing. You wonder if the

authorities are even watching. It's only money they want, for God's sake!'

Entwistle was equally baffled. 'You'd think they'd make some sort of placatory offer . . . Big question is, what do *we* do next?'

'You're going to try something, I presume,' said Carol, looking worried.

'Don't worry about me. I can handle myself.' He fluffed up her pillows. 'You still got those blueprints, Mom – for the extension work?'

'There in the study, rolled up behind the desk. But why?'

Entwistle began to explain after he had fetched the blueprints back into her room. 'OK, Greg. The Glasshouse needs extending. Business has been pretty good despite that damned rig.'

'But pretty good does not a fortune make.' Since Carol had inherited the restaurant from her late husband, she had become even more determined that it thrive and expand.

Entwistle continued, 'Anyway, the new extension needed plumbing, because it had to include a restroom. Well, these blueprints show how the existing sewers serve the restaurant and the area round the Hole, and here' – he unfurled a large white chart – 'is a photocopy of the sewer system for the whole town. There was some debate over lack of pressure and how, if the system was loaded up any more, they'd have to install another pumping station, and that Mom would have to pay for it. That's when the lawyers came in.'

'And so nothing gets done,' she said. 'I bring people into this godforsaken tourist trap – quality people, cash-endowed people who patronize their motels—'

'Save that for the council, Mom,' interrupted Entwistle. 'So we have here a plan of the town's sewers. The system shadows the road layout, thus allowing easy access when they need to dig. So we got storm drains running under the Circles, and stepped drainage down the Presidents, with sizeable feeders most other places.'

'So?' said Greg.

'So,' said Entwistle, 'with these plans we got ourselves our own private subway! No need for the Hummer, or the disguises. We can move about freely.'

'Great,' Greg muttered without enthusiasm. 'Move freely where?'

Carol raised her eyebrows. 'A very good question.'

'Shut up, Carol,' said Entwistle. 'I don't see any point in pussyfooting around. We need all the help we can get and we need to hit them where it hurts.'

'This sounds ominous.'

'We go here.'

Greg studied the map. 'Aw, fuck . . . Sorry, Mrs Glass.'

'And we get *there* by following the sewer from here, downhill all the way.'

'That just about describes it,' said Greg.

'Summer Campbell might well be there,' suggested Entwistle.

'Dirty trick, Entwistle. Dirty trick.'

Their banter was interrupted by Entwistle's mother turning up the volume of the television set, so the sound of a gunshot filled the room.

That must be the 9:40 hostage, thought Entwistle, but the bedside clock showed 9:33. Entwistle stared at it, willing its hands to move, but its mechanism seemed as good as jammed.

'What is it?' asked Carol, puzzled by her son's sudden stillness.

'This clock working?'

'Yes, fine,' she said. 'Why?'

'It's just that clocks keep stopping everywhere ... whenever I go near them.'

He knew that sounded stupid – and was not surprised to receive a scornful laugh from both Greg and Carol. But the coincidence worried him.

'Got your watch handy, Mom?' he asked.

'Sure.' She ferreted in her bedside cabinet and pulled out her wristwatch.

'See,' she said, holding it up. 'It's 9:33.'

'Yes,' said Entwistle, peering closely. 'But it's also stopped – and at the same time as your clock over there and the one in the lounge. That was the time we came into the house.'

Now looking puzzled, his mother verified that the second hand on her watch had indeed stopped moving round its black diamond-studded dial. Entwistle meanwhile rolled up the crucial map and stuffed it down the front of his shirt.

Carol grabbed his hand. 'Please be careful.'

'Ain't I always?' said Entwistle, squeezing her shoulder in return.

As the Sheriff's Deputy followed him back into the lounge, Greg pointed to the other man's uniform trousers.

'You could do with some sort of disguise if you're aiming to pop up behind enemy lines.'

'Like the *Dirty Dozen*?'

'More like *Dirty Dancing*,' said Greg forlornly.

Entwistle returned to Carol's bedroom and a heated conversation ensued. Finally he re-emerged wearing a black Armani sweatshirt over an immaculate pair of black 501s. He pulled a black ski-mask from his pocket.

'*Voilà*,' he said.

'Not the paint, *please*,' protested Carol from the bedroom.

'Paint?' Greg looked puzzled.

Entwistle led him into the utility room beside the kitchen and opened a tin of white gloss paint. Handing a brush to Greg, he told him to paint the figure 32 on both his front and back.

Three minutes later the expensive sweatshirt was ruined and his disguise was complete. Two minutes after that, they were driving back along Brent Road, each armed with a Marlin autoloader rifle and a Browning automatic pistol from Entwistle's own collection.

'You a gun nut?' said Greg, fingering the cold pistol.

'It's a tool. Carpenters got saws, doctors got scalpels, cops have guns.'

'If I knew my doctor collected scalpels I wouldn't be his patient for long.'

'If you were my patient I'd make a point of it!'

Entwistle wheeled the Hummer onto Circle Five.

Greg spoke up. 'What was all that with the clocks?'

'Just like I said: they seem to just stop whenever I turn up someplace. The clock on this dashboard – that shows when I climbed into this tank. The clocks at Carol's house – they stopped the moment we arrived.'

'Spooky, but it has to be just a coincidence.'

'If you believe in such coincidences.'

'What else could it be?'

Entwistle shrugged. He couldn't think of an answer. Instead he concentrated on his plan.

'Right, we need to get ourselves down into that storm drain on Harding. Looks like it's over on the north corner there.'

'You really think this is such a good idea?'

'I can drop you off any time. And I won't think any less—'

'I doubt you could anyway,' said Greg. 'No, I'll come along, but don't get us into any shooting shit.'

Entwistle didn't waste his breath by lying.

Seventeen

'Ain't no fuckin' women in this fuckin' operation! I'm gonna get you, whoever you are, bitch. Maybe have me some fun too!'

The man's voice was harsh, his accent Southern. He had already taken three shots at Maribeth, hitting the Grand Am each time, his aim apparently spoiled by his headgear.

Maribeth had dived to the sidewalk, with no other cover available, her mind panicked beyond reason. All she could hear was the man's anger and his boots covering the distance between them on the gritty blacktop.

'Fuckin' masks! Fuckin' weather! Hooo, baby, are you ever gonna feel me—'

He fired another shot and one of the car tyres exploded with a bang.

Maribeth screamed. The man laughed.

She was face-down on the sidewalk, winded and terrified. Looking ahead, all she could see was open sidewalk and road. To her right was a second-hand furniture shop, but its door was gated and locked. She braved a glance under the car, saw the man's feet now halfway across the road.

He paused; there was a click, then a curse.

'Fuckin' rifle! Fuck it all . . .'

She saw his weapon hit the road and clatter away. It must have jammed. Then she saw him start towards her again. What was she to do?

Ten seconds later he rounded the rear of the Grand Am.

'No women in this fuckin' outfit – and I'm gonna strip you out of yours, and see just how big your titties—'

He was now gaping down at Maribeth, who had rolled over onto her back and was staring up at him.

'My, my, my,' said number 67, pulling off his mask to reveal an ugly red face with a scar across the right cheek, a cold glint in his eyes. 'They never said nothing about R 'n' R when I signed up, but it looks—'

'Come near and I'll shoot you.'

He eyed the rifle pointing at his chest and raised both hands and pistol in mock horror. 'Can fuck me dead meat as easy as live meat,' he sneered.

'Not if you're dead yourself.'

'You gonna shoot me, then, little lady? Well, stop wasting time and do it,' he dared.

Maribeth fired once, and the man's jaw erupted a scarlet jet splattering over the car's rear window.

Dropping his revolver, he grabbed for his neck and staggered back, a strange rattle issuing from what was left of his voice-box. Then he turned and fell heavily onto his knees, both hands now clutching at the frantic pump of his neck, blood shooting inches beyond his shoulder and onto the car's rear fender, red on red. Then he slowly subsided, as if falling asleep, and slumped onto his left side, his big hands scrabbling by his sides like disobedient puppies.

Maribeth stared at the dying man, her body frozen. *She* had pulled the trigger and shot him. She had *killed* someone. Never mind that he was a terrorist and a potential rapist: one second he had been living and breathing and now he wasn't – *and all because she had put a bullet into him.*

She let the rifle fall onto the sidewalk beside her, then rolled over and retched into the gutter, her racking coughs tossing up dust into her face, which made her cough even more.

Hellation, hellation, hellation, what have I done? Why hadn't she just stayed in the motel till morning? Who cared what people would think or say? She had just killed a man because she was worried about her reputation!

A hand touched her shoulder.

She screamed and started to flail about, trying to squirm her way under the Grand Am. He wasn't dead and he had come to get her!

'Get up!' hissed a voice. 'Get up quick, before—'

Maribeth went insane then, lashing out with feet and hands, twisting this way and that, shrieking with terror. She could hear another, different voice, uttering curses, and then felt hands grabbing her ankles and slowly but surely dragging her out from under the car, the edge of the kerb rucking her sweater over her stomach. As soon as her head was clear of the vehicle's underside she was rolled over and found two of the hooded men pulling at her legs and arms.

'No, no!' she shouted.

'You stupid bitch!' she heard. 'Shut the fuck up!'

Maribeth was not going to succumb without a fight. She launched a kick at one of them, connecting solidly with his knee. He yelped behind his mask.

'That's it!' he growled and punched her on the jaw.

Everything seemed to roll to one side then, as if the world had slipped off its pedestal.

As unconsciousness claimed her, the last sound she heard was a voice saying: 'With friends like these, who needs fucking enemies?'

Eighteen

Maribeth was woken up by something cold and lumpy being pressed to her jaw. She started to object, but a hand pressed down on her shoulder and a finger was put to her lips.

'Will you please hush up,' said the blond man above her.

Glancing to her left, she found a coloured boy holding a bag of Bird's Eye frozen peas to her face.

'I'm sorry we had to hit you but—'

'That man – I shot him!'

The blond man nodded. 'It was self-defence, so no worries. Any idea who he was?'

'Just one of those killers—' She suddenly spotted their own black gear and the numbers 47 and 32 on their chests.

He saw the terrified look of recognition come into her eyes, and shook his head. 'I'm Deputy Entwistle, Firefall Sheriff's Department. This here's Greg Henley. He's been helping me.'

She tried to sit up, but her jaw ached and her head buzzed. She now recognized the Deputy; had always thought him a bit of a dish, though every time they met he had handed her a parking ticket. She wasn't so sure she recognized the boy, but his name rang a bell. She finally managed to sit up and brush the icy food pack from her face, but as a painful throbbing made its presence felt she pressed the frozen peas back to her face.

'Well, you're clearly not one of them either, so best thing would be if we pool our knowledge, see where we are, where we should go,' said Entwistle.

She shook her head vigorously despite the pain. 'Wherever we are I'm staying here. Done my heroine bit.'

'What *were* you doing?'

'I teach up at the school, so I—'

'You're Ms Hamilton, May, Merry . . .?' said Entwistle.

'Maribeth. I was trying to get over there to look after my children.'

'Stupid but brave. And you were interrupted?'

'Apparently there are no women involved in this thing. So I . . . stood out.'

'And then some . . .' Entwistle reddened and gave her a weak grin. 'Sorry.'

'Where are we, anyway?' she asked, glancing sideways.

'A basement on Keeble. The first place we found open and available when we were trying to get off the street. That shooting's bound to have attracted attention, so the place'll soon be swarming with the bastards.'

Maribeth stood up on shaky feet and looked about her. It was a small cellar, crammed with junk and cartons. By the steps was a large deep-freeze, its door open so the white light inside provided the only illumination.

'Is it safe down here?'

'The door's locked from the inside now. It looks no different from any other empty house, I should imagine.'

'Greg Henley,' she said, eyeing the boy, now she remembered. 'Weren't you locked up for . . .?'

'He's got a temper,' grinned Entwistle. 'Bit like you.'

'Yeah, but *I* never shot no one,' said Greg.

Maribeth's face fell and she began to cry.

'You're one incredible asshole, Greg,' said Entwistle, putting his arm around Maribeth to comfort her. She felt wonderfully warm. 'A lot's happened, and there's sure to be a lot to come, so best just to not think about it.'

She looked up at him, tears streaking her face. 'But I killed him. Shot him in the neck. Blood everywhere.'

Entwistle decided to let her weep her fill, so he sat her down and made sure she was comfortable on the broken rocking chair, then pulled Greg over to the freezer.

'She may not be any help to us now, after a shock like that . . . Just watch your mouth, kid. We'll find out everything we can from her, and then we're out of here.'

'Who's this "we", kimosabe? I've had it with the hero shit too, like the lady. Now one of them's dead, they'll be shooting anyone they meet. This place looks as good as any to hide in.'

'Greg, for a violent kid you sure are chickenshit.'

'Hey, it's a temper thing.'

'And these assholes running round our town doesn't make you want to kick their butts?'

'Course I do, man. Just I don't wanna get killed doing it! And let's drop this "my town" shit. This town was pleased enough to be rid of me, so I don't owe it nothing.'

Maribeth suddenly spoke up from her chair. 'So what's your plan?'

Entwistle went over and offered her his hand to pull her to her feet. She was really tall; another plus, maybe. 'Want a drink?'

She nodded and he handed her a popsicle from the freezer.

Lemon: it tasted delicious. But even as the chill of the popsicle helped cool the burning pain in her damaged hand, she couldn't help noticing that the freezer door didn't close properly.

As it slowly swung open again it provided a white rectangle of light in the dark cellar. And though the two men were talking to her, Maribeth found their voices fading, the cellar disappearing as the same light filled her eyes and then her mind. The light was all: if only she trusted this light, then all the murders, the blood, and the horrors would disappear and everything would be right again.

Then she felt a hand shaking her, and she blinked as the rescuing light was blotted out by someone moving to stand in front of her.

'You OK?' asked the Deputy.

'Yes, have you found that . . .?'

She trailed off. What could she say to him? *Have you stared at any lights lately?* It might just be a symptom of concussion; but why had the same thing been happening all morning?

'So what can you tell us we don't already know?' said Greg, realizing that any action was probably better than doing nothing. Besides, he wanted to find out what had happened to Summer, and babysitting a freezer full of food wasn't going to get him any answers.

Maribeth told them her story as best she could remember, even revealing why she had happened to be out of town. Mention of Angelis drew an odd look from Entwistle, which she tried to ignore; why was his opinion suddenly of interest to her?

The cop was nodding as she finished. 'Confirms what we've found, too. One: they haven't got good communications – no radios, nothing. Two: they don't even all know each other, so they read each other by their numbers; that gives us an edge. Three: this whole operation required inside information.'

'You mean someone from Firefall?'

'Yes. They know far too much about the town, its layout, the administrative set-up. We already know Duke Manners and Taylor Ash were involved. Could be other lowlifes, too. And how did they decide the ones to round up? Someone who lives here is behind it all.'

'Like who?' said Greg. 'There's some fucked-up dudes in town, I agree, but no one I can think of with the brains for this.'

Entwistle leaned back against the freezer and sucked on another popsicle. 'You're right, but there's something more. They were planning to torch Napier's Farm, maybe with me inside it. And they hired a professional from outside to do that. Why not do it themselves?'

'What were you doing out at Napier's Farm, anyway?' said Maribeth, trying to keep her mind off her recent nightmare.

'I got a call . . . so they must have *wanted* me there.'

Maribeth agreed. 'You were on duty, so you could have messed up their plan – got a message out too soon.'

'But whoever left me there knew the place was going to be torched. Why didn't they kill me there and then?'

Good question, thought Maribeth. 'No reason, unless . . .'

Both men looked at her expectantly.

'Nothing. It's silly.'

'Nothing's silly any more,' said Greg.

'Unless there are people involved who didn't think there was going to be any killing.'

'And if they had killed me then, that would have upset them?'

'Maybe. You said the ones you've met so far are amateurs. Maybe they'd only agreed to come on board if there wasn't any violence.'

'But that's ludicrous! They've shot six innocent people so far. Number seven coming up. It can't be more than a couple of minutes.'

Suddenly he ran to the stairs. 'Come on, we need to *see* that execution.'

'What?'

He pushed-pulled himself up into the kitchen, beckoning them to follow. Keeping low and out of sight they made their way into the lounge and near to the television. Checking first that no one was out in the backyard, Entwistle tugged the drapes closed, then switched on the TV set and tuned into Firefall Cable.

'Let's get the video running.'

'You wanna sell this to *Hard Copy*?' Greg looked amazed.

'No, I want to check this carefully. Something's not right.'

'They're shooting those poor people!' said Maribeth, tossing the pack of frozen peas at him in disgust. 'Of course something's not right!'

'No, it's more than that. Find me a tape, now!'

Both Maribeth and Entwistle noticed simultaneously that the time on the video recorder was flashing 88:88, as if its internal clock had been disconnected. The only other clock in the room had also stopped, its large red second hand pointing towards the open door like a warning.

Entwistle was too concerned about the executions to voice his fears. For her part, Maribeth was still too shook up by the shooting and the blow to her head to try and make much sense of it. Besides, what on earth could she say that would not make her sound a fool?

After several frantic seconds Greg located a videotape, slotted it home, and set it to record. Then the three of them stood and watched in horror as someone they all knew – Sheriff Ed Rickenbacker – was made to kneel, then shot in the back. As he slumped forward onto the ground, his body was dragged back inside the Town Hall building, while the leader, number 38, wagged an admonishing finger at the camera.

'There are over three thousand inhabitants in Firefall. How many more will die before you realize you've no choice? Accede to our demands now.'

Maribeth collapsed, trembling. Greg turned away,

hiding his head. Breathing heavily, Entwistle refused to take his eyes from the screen.

'That was Ed,' was all he could say. 'They shot Ed Rickenbacker.'

Greg looked back. 'I hated that bastard, but . . .' He stopped.

They all watched 38 go back inside then the screen reverted to its overfamiliar caption.

'Right, rewind,' ordered Entwistle.

'You sick fuck,' said Greg.

'Must we?' pleaded Maribeth, her own murder already beginning to play over in her mind like a taunting phantom.

'*They're* the sick fucks!' said Entwistle. 'But there's something bugging me. Now just replay it!'

Greg did as instructed. Four times.

'I've seen enough,' he said finally.

'We all knew him,' said Entwistle, 'but maybe not as well as we thought. But what . . .?' He squatted down and stroked the screen, static crackling at his fingertips. 'There's something odd . . . Look, Greg, they're shooting hostages, so that hopefully they'll soon be given what they want. Though it's taking our side a damn long time to agree to whatever that is.' He stood and paced back and forth. 'Now, I've seen people getting shot and *this* don't look right. Why in the back? I've seen two executed now, and both were shot in the back.'

'The head's messy. Bound to be gross.'

'*Exactly*. You want to scare people into taking you seriously, you do it the whole way. Hell, they're even executing them on live TV! So why shoot them in the back?'

'Does it matter?' said Maribeth, unable to contain her

annoyance any longer, her initially favourable impression of the Deputy souring by the minute.

'Please, listen,' pleaded Entwistle. 'Greg, imagine you're making a movie. You want to kill one of your actors, blow him away. You want it convincing, so what do you do?'

'Special effects: blood everywhere.'

Blood everywhere. Maribeth tried to blot out the memory.

'No, that close, death would be instantaneous, so they wouldn't bleed much. Play the tape again, *after* he's shot.'

They watched again as Rickenbacker slumped forwards, then the two guards grabbed him under the arms and dragged him back up the steps ... his body falling sideways, their hands hauling it roughly into the shadows.

'Play that last bit again,' said Entwistle. 'The bit on the steps where they ... there! *Pause* it. Now look.'

'Guy's dead. So what?'

Entwistle jumped across the room and spun Greg around, poking a finger into his back. 'Right! That close, the bullet would go straight through you and leave a hole *and* blood. Now look at Rickenbacker's shirt. Bullet in the back point-blank, and ...?'

'No exit wound?'

'So they didn't shoot him! He isn't dead.'

'How, then? Blanks?'

Maribeth turned to stare up at them.

'Better than blanks. Blanks can still mess you up. In the movies they also use a trick gun; its discharge comes out the side of the barrel, not the end. You get the bang and the flash, but nothing comes out the end.'

'So they faked his execution?'

'Yeah. Maybe the others too.'

'But why?'

'I don't think it's to save them a guilty conscience, do you?'

Entwistle ran the tape once again. 'But when they drop him on the steps, he doesn't even flinch. That guy's acting.'

Maribeth had forced herself to watch the man falling onto the steps. 'Maybe he's scared. Maybe they've ordered him to act.'

'Maybe, maybe, yes, but wouldn't he have tried *something*? Ed's a tough mother, for all his years. For an amateur he's giving a pro's performance. Remember the guys in Vietnam, the prisoners who had their confessions taped?'

Greg looked at him as if to say, 'What's Vietnam?' and Maribeth's expression was no more comprehending.

'OK, so the Viet Cong filmed these guys confessing their sins but, even though they were under threat of death, they still managed to give little signs of defiance with their fingers. They positioned their fingers to give us messages, the brave bastards. Well, I *know* Ed, and if he was forced to act he would have done something like that.'

That sounded like childish logic, he knew, but he had to retain some hope.

Maribeth touched Entwistle's arm. 'There is another alternative,' she said reluctantly.

'What's that?' he sighed, still staring at a frozen frame of Sheriff Rickenbacker just before he was shot.

'You're not going to like it.'

Nineteen

Agent Calthorpe came up to where Del sat on the verge of the highway, head in hands.

'Hartsby wants to see you.'

'Surprise, surprise,' said Del without looking up. 'Tell me, Calthorpe, what do you know about Hartsby and ACA?'

'Only what I've heard. I was talking to the comtruck driver, he gave me a "for instance". The government buys fifty thousand shotguns a year for the armed forces and federal agencies. They run a standard test to choose which makes. The Anomalous Configuration Audit then get reports on the use of these shotguns from all recipients, which they analyse. Obviously any gun submitted for test is going to be A1 perfect, but the line-produced model may not be. So every misfire, fault, and jam in the field is logged. End of the year if they find that another make of shotgun costing a hundred dollars less is more reliable, the government can change brand – and thus saves itself five million dollars. Carry that through on all weapons from penknives to tanks to bombers, and you're looking at a lot of potential savings.'

'And a lot of information – and a lot of pressure from interested parties to get good results.'

'Or a lot of pressure from Hartsby . . .'

'Bribes?'

'Favours. That's why the guy's so powerful. Through the ACA he has a finger in every branch of the armed forces and law enforcement – CIA, FBI, Secret Service, DEA, AFT, Treasury, you name it – *and* in every weapons manufacturer. And if the Audit's remit is expanded into other supply areas – vehicles, computer gear – Hartsby becomes . . .'

'God? So why is he in charge here?'

'God moves in mysterious ways.'

Del laughed, and Calthorpe joined him, both in desperate need of emotional release.

'So what would you do, knowing all that?'

'I'm not in a position . . .'

Del looked up at him. They had worked together for two years, and Del didn't even know if he had children.

'If I ordered you to do something you knew to be wrong – so wrong it would cost innocent lives – what would you do?'

'My duty.'

'Without question?'

Calthorpe paused. 'I have to trust in the judgement of my superiors, however I may feel personally.'

'And you trust your superiors?'

'Of course not! Law enforcement is no different from any other business. It isn't always the best that get to the top, but those who know how to play the game.'

Del smiled. He wished he had got to know Calthorpe better. 'So it's all a game?'

'Everything's a game, sir. That's just about the only thing I've learned that gets me through.'

'Even when people's lives are at stake?' said Del.

'Yes. But we didn't set the rules, did we? And one of the rules is there's nothing you can do about the rules.'

'Meaning nothing I do will get me out of this?'

Calthorpe sat down. 'Sir, I can't say I've ever admired you. You're conscientious but . . . I'm sorry, I'm speaking out of turn.'

'No, no, speak freely. So I'm "conscientious but . . ."?'

'But you don't know how to play the game. You have friends in the Bureau, but you don't have *contacts*. There are plenty of agents in higher positions less honest or dedicated than you.'

'Some comfort.'

'It's all us good guys have, I'm afraid.'

'And you?'

'Can I still be truthful? The difference between you and me, regardless of our abilities, is that I wouldn't have got myself into this position. You're here because you can be dumped on.'

'You're my assistant. You'll be tarred with the same brush.'

'I doubt it. I'm only doing what I'm told. So I can blame you.'

'Whereas while I'm also doing what I'm told, I can't point at anyone else?'

'Exactly. I don't envy you.'

'No one ever has, Calthorpe. So what would you do?'

Calthorpe stared at the ground. 'You're being

screwed, sir. Everyone can see that. Best you can do is choose the position.'

Del laughed. 'Colourful, but I see your point.'

'To use your phrase: walk away and you're tarred; stay on the case, you get tarred but at least you've got some say.'

'Meaning?'

'Meaning you might just make a difference.'

'Might just make a difference? Not a lot after twenty-six years in the Bureau – and with lives at stake.'

Calthorpe stood up. 'It's all you've got, sir.'

He held out his hand and Del took it and pulled himself upright. 'Where *is* the little shit?'

'In the comtruck.'

'Do yourself a favour, Calthorpe. Stay away from me.'

'I intend to. Sorry, sir.'

Del shook his hand. 'Don't be sorry for knowing the rules. I only wish *I* did.'

'They make a difference, sir,' said Calthorpe, walking away.

Del made his way across the highway, weaving through the numerous police cars and their idling crews. It was always the same in major situations: an inordinate amount of manpower sat just waiting for action. It always looked like overreaction and, to be truthful, usually was. Del had always wondered what happened to the crime rate when it became obvious to everyone that the police were all tied up elsewhere. Looking up the highway, and at the police vehicles stretching almost out of sight, chances were the ordinary criminals in Wyoming and neighbouring states would think Christmas had come early.

Just as Del reached the comtruck, Hartsby came walking down the steps, a mobile phone in his hand. 'Call for you.'

'Number 38?'

'No. The Deputy Director of the FBI.'

'What?'

Hartsby handed him the phone and walked away.

Del stared at the instrument for a few moments, then raised it to his face.

'Hello? Special Agent Collingwood.'

'Ah, Collingwood. This is Mortimer Crane, Deputy Director. Good to speak to you. Is that prick Hartsby out of earshot?'

'Yes, sir.'

'Good. Believe me, son, no matter how much you loathe that insect, there are many of us here on the Hill who loathe him a whole lot more. I understand that you're unhappy that you can't negotiate with these people?'

'Too damn right. People have been shot—'

'Goes with the territory, son.'

'You know I'm—'

'Being railroaded? Too damn right, and I'll be doing what I can to protect you, but I have to be honest and tell you that batting against Hartsby is a pretty pointless exercise. Believe me, I've tried it. Right or wrong, the ACA has mucho muscle. Even the Director checks under his bed to see if Emile's hiding there.'

'But what about negotiations?'

'Given their drastic actions so far, I've persuaded Hartsby to offer them everything. My best guess is that cash is their main priority, and we're getting it together now. It's unlikely to get to you before 2 p.m., so you'll have to stall. Naturally they'll not get away with it. We've also arranged a complete news blackout which gives us some room for manoeuvre, but with CNN and Sky all over the place this won't stay quiet for long.'

'But what if they kill more hostages meanwhile?'

'That's what bad guys do, Collingwood.'

Del didn't know what to say to this. 'Can I put it on record that—'

'Son, the only record there'll be of this conversation is the one Hartsby's little weasels are making in his comtruck even as we speak. The only reason I'm talking plain to you is that I've already got that dwarf as an enemy.'

'There's nothing else to be said, then, sir.'

'I'm afraid there isn't. Good luck.'

The line went dead and, on cue, Hartsby was at his side. Del couldn't help reflecting that the last thing anyone seemed interested in was the fate of the hostages in Firefall. It really was all a game to these people.

'Ready to get on board again, Collingwood?'

Del turned to look down at the man, desperately wanting to punch him. And the smile playing on Hartsby's lips told him that, as always, he knew this.

'Yes, sir,' said Del. 'I can offer them everything?'

'Yes.'

'About time.'

Hartsby didn't respond, and Del couldn't help but reflect that the one thing Deputy Director Crane didn't try was to persuade Hartsby to do anything he didn't want to do anyway.

A man appeared at the door of the trailer. 'Sir, we've got activity.'

Hartsby bounded up the steps, and Del followed him into the truck. There he found him watching a video monitor where three red specks were moving about on a background composed of pink blocks. Del soon understood that this was an infra-red satellite shot of an intersection in Firefall; the three blips were human beings.

'They got out of that vehicle,' said the operator, pointing out a shape.

'So?' said Del.

'So there shouldn't *be* vehicle activity,' said Hartsby.

'Why not?'

Hartsby ignored the question. Then they watched the three dots disappear, one after the other.

'They've gone underground,' commented another operative.

'The sewers?' suggested Hartsby.

'Who are those people?' said Del.

'How in hell should I know?' muttered Hartsby, deep in thought. 'Give me a schematic of the town sewers.'

Seconds later an adjacent screen showed them a blueprint.

'Now show me where they were . . . Right, and how they got there . . . OK, now show me all salient points of exit.'

'Salient points?' asked Del.

Hartsby heaved a big sigh of impatience. 'You go down into the sewers, you're either hiding or you're proceeding somewhere else – which means you have to eventually come *out* of the sewer.'

One of the operatives spoke up. 'There's a direct line following Harding to the Town Hall.'

'Exit points?' asked Hartsby.

'Two out front, one behind.'

'Get me 38,' said Hartsby.

Ten seconds later he was speaking directly to the terrorist leader. Before replacing the receiver, he said three words: 'Watch your back.'

Del stared at him, astonished.

Hartsby shook his head. 'Don't even try to understand, Collingwood. You don't even know the game, let alone the rules.'

Del remembered his earlier conversation with Calthorpe.

'You bastard, you've got me bugged.'

'Yes.' Hartsby smiled. 'Annoying, isn't it?'

Twenty

'That's just so much goddam bullshit,' said Entwistle.

'Hey, I don't know the man like you do,' said Maribeth, 'but it *is* an explanation.'

The three of them had left the basement and made their way to the corner of Harding and Circle Three, Maribeth's dead assailant oddly failing to attract any attention so far.

Greg had found a crow-iron, so getting the drain cover up was simple enough. Then they had clambered down its narrow ladder. Entwistle took the rear and replaced the heavy metal cover. All the while he kept mulling over what Maribeth had said earlier in the basement: the reason that Rickenbacker hadn't been killed was because he was in on the plot.

Even as they found their bearings in the fetid darkness, removing scratchy masks from hot faces, he kept trying to dislodge these doubts.

'That man is as honest as the day is long,' he burst out at last, his voice echoing. 'He couldn't hide anything like that from me.'

'Oh, like he'd broadcast it on KFLL,' said Greg.

'OK, Ed may be guilty, but let's not throw the switch

just yet. First we see what we can do to stop all this shit.'

He unfurled a blueprint, then got Greg and Maribeth to each hold a corner of it up against the curved brick wall while he shone his flashlight onto it.

'They're extending the Town Hall, remember? You must have seen the piledriver, the diggers, all the bricks and stuff. The back of the building is a mess: a construction site. And the drains come up right in the middle of what's serving as a builders' compound. There should be enough cover there for us to see what we're up against.'

'I don't know . . .' began Maribeth.

'"If in doubt, don't," my old man used to say,' said Entwistle. 'Your safest bet would be to stay down here, and wait to see what the government decides to do.'

Both Greg and Maribeth looked up and down the storm drain as Entwistle played the flashlight beam about its walls. Despite the smell and the damp, it was tempting.

'No,' said Greg at last, 'if Summer's there, I'm there.'

'OK, but don't go losing that temper of yours at the wrong moment. How about you, Maribeth?'

She thought again of the man she had shot; and decided she would rather be with those who had helped her than face alone the dead man's associates. 'As long as we're careful,' she heard herself saying. Never had she been so unsure of the correctness of a choice, but never so certain that it was preferable to the alternatives. Whatever lay ahead, at least she was doing something positive. They set off.

The drain was a circular tube, six feet in diameter, with a flattened bottom, so they were all able to walk almost erect. It sloped at an angle of twenty degrees, but every hundred yards or so came a drop of about ten feet, which produced a mini-waterfall – and a concomitant increase in foul odours. There was little water in the drain, just a couple of inches of it, but come heavy rain they wouldn't have been able to cope with the current generated by a larger volume. At each ten-foot drop there was a ladder to aid their descent, and one at a time they edged their way down to the lower level, their progress lit only by Entwistle's single flashlight.

After ten minutes he called a halt in order to re-examine the map.

'That was step number five, so we must be under the Town Hall. The inspection access should be on our right.'

They quickly located a manhole high up, set off to one side of the main drain. There a narrow ladder rose a good twenty feet towards several hazy spots of light.

'I'll go first,' said Entwistle, handing Greg the flashlight. 'Anything goes wrong, you two hurry back the way we came and take the first turn right. That should lead you along Circle Two. Then get out and hide somewhere.'

There was reluctant nodding, then Entwistle mounted the lower rungs and climbed carefully up to the top. There he paused to pull on his ski-mask.

The manhole cover contained four small airholes through which he could just discern some blue sky. Damn, he couldn't even decipher which way he would be facing as he climbed out. He paused to try and orientate himself. They had headed due south but he was now facing west, so he would find himself looking at the rear of the Town Hall. OK. He pushed up hard with his palms and after some initial resistance found the heavy lid begin to shift. Prising it clear of its lip, he eased it to its left and let it gently touch the ground, then carefully edged his head out into the daylight.

The builders' compound around him seemed empty of people; just piles of bricks and sand and tiles and wood, with scaffolding assembled up one half of the Town Hall's three-storey rear façade. Parked to his left, like some giant child's toy, was an old red bulldozer with a large scraper blade and a wide tow bar at its rear. Also a yellow mechanical digger and a large crawling crane assembled for piledriving, its hundred-and-fifty-foot-high arm almost vertical – pointing to the heavens as if to remind Entwistle where his only source of help might lie. There were not many windows on this side of the building, and all those on the lower two floors contained frosted safety glass.

He turned round to scan in every direction. It seemed the hooded men were not too worried about guarding this rear approach, probably because to reach this far would mean getting round the entire flank of the Town Hall, their headquarters. Good. More fools they.

He pulled himself out of the drain, and beckoned the others to follow. 'Get your masks on,' he hissed.

A minute later they were crouched behind the red bulldozer, shielded from sight of the huge building, a low wall to their backs and beyond that a grassy slope leading down to the edge of the Hole.

'What now?' whispered Maribeth.

'I was afraid you'd ask that,' muttered Entwistle. 'OK, what have we got? Now we know the rear's undefended, we could get some more people up through the drains.'

'Yeah,' said Greg, 'but look at the windows. A couple of sharpshooters up there, we wouldn't stand a chance.'

There was a long pause as Greg and Maribeth stared at Entwistle, who finally offered them a weak smile.

'All right, all right, but you both agreed it was worth a go. So now we go back and work out some other—'

He stopped as a look of horror passed over his companions' faces, and he slowly turned around.

'Now, I may be mistaken but I do believe you three aren't on our side.'

Entwistle saw four men – numbers 77, 52, 30, and 3 – training machine-guns on the three of them. At the centre of the group stood number 38, unarmed but looking no less threatening.

'You're right,' said Entwistle. 'We—'

'Just drop your weapons and follow me. Failure to comply will render you extinct.'

Greg and Maribeth dropped their guns immediately. Only Entwistle hesitated.

'You've done your duty, boy. But any more bravado and it'll be your last.'

Entwistle slowly dropped both his weapons.

'Good. Now, get those masks off.'

All three tugged them off, revealing faces red and sweaty, and somewhat relieved to find fresh air on their skin again.

'Deputy Entwistle I recognize – but not you two,' said 38 enquiringly.

'I'm Maribeth Hamilton. I teach at the junior high.'

The man nodded. 'And you?'

'Greg Henley, asshole.'

38 stepped forward and slapped Greg once across the face. 'Now move, all of you.'

He moved aside as the three were guided through the Town Hall's unprepossessing rear entrance, and were led down an adjacent corridor to a room, from the smell of it, located near the kitchens. A door was unbolted and they were pushed inside. The door slammed shut behind them, the bolts sliding back in place.

'Well, that went well,' said Entwistle.

'Shut up,' said Greg, his insides boiling.

'Yes, shut up,' said Maribeth, scarcely able to believe the mess she had got herself in. 'I don't know why . . .' But she fell silent as she took in their surroundings.

It was clearly an office, not very large, with a bare wooden floor and a single waist-high frosted window directly opposite the only door. All its furniture had been removed except for a forlorn grey metal filing cabinet in one corner and a large desk pushed up against one wall. But it was the other occupants of the room that seized her attention.

There were seven of them, all male, and all sitting against the left-hand wall staring blankly at the newcomers. The one nearest to her was Sheriff Rickenbacker, his face bruised and bloody, his eyes puffing up.

Entwistle walked over and knelt down to examine his boss's injuries. He had obviously received a beating recently, a couple of his head wounds were bleeding still.

'What happened, Ed? What's going on? We saw you shot, and we guessed it was all faked. But why the pretence?'

Rickenbacker stared up at him with bloodshot eyes, then after a moment answered through broken teeth:

'They would hardly kill their own leader.'

Twenty-one

Entwistle realized that he recognized every man in the room – had dealt with them all at one time or another – and was shocked to realize that they too must be part of the mysterious conspiracy.

One was Clayton Stick, the owner of Firefall Coffees, a souvenir-cum-coffee shop that catered for the upper end of the market. He was also the town's mayor. There was Stefano Bacal, owner of the Geological Museum, and volunteer fire chief. Then Alan Schmidt, owner of the Comet Pizza Parlour and a councilman. Gerry Rankin, owner of Rankin's Rowboats. Wolfgang Klein of Klein Construction, who were the biggest contractors in the county. And Herman Lury, owner of Firefall Heaven, a tacky souvenir shop and burger bar. Each man was middle-aged or older, and all were more or less respected in Firefall as entrepreneurs and public officials.

As Maribeth knelt down to tend to the Sheriff, Entwistle stood for a moment shaking his head. 'You're *all* in on this?' he said at last.

Obviously they were, since at least three of them had been 'executed' in the same way as Rickenbacker but were now crouching and squirming with guilt. None tried to voice an excuse or an explanation; maybe the recent attack on Rickenbacker had silenced them. Judging by spots of blood on the floor, his beating had taken place right in front of them.

He looked over at Greg, who was standing silently, his fists clenching, his body tense, like an athlete waiting for the start gun. Entwistle reached out and patted him on the shoulder. 'Hey, Greg, you still with us?'

The boy turned to face him. 'Nothing I ever did's as bad as the stunt this lot have pulled. I've been locked up in a psycho ward, had drugs pumped into me, electricity shot through my fucking brain . . . I've been accused of all kinds of shit, been despised, pointed at, blamed unfairly, hauled up in court . . . while these fuckers, these *bastards*, have sat there raking in the cash, and all the while planning to shit on everyone.'

He leaned over Clayton Stick – the squat balding Mayor shying back as if expecting a blow.

'You're the mayor of this fucking town and you're now screwing everyone who ever voted for you, who ever paid for one of your stinking espressos . . .'

Greg then spat at him, hitting the man square on his shiny dome. Entwistle grabbed at the boy's arm, but Greg shook him off and stomped to the far side of the room.

Entwistle squatted beside Stick and whispered: 'We get out of this, the leash comes off that boy and as God is my witness, there won't be no witnesses. Understand that, you piece of shit?'

Herman Lury seemed about to say something, but the look on Entwistle's face shut him up, and instead he stared down at his knees.

'I ain't about to apologize for this,' wheezed Rickenbacker, his face still gaunt with pain. 'We're all in on it, and if we make it out of here we'll all be paying the price.'

'You promised it'd be fine,' snarled Lury.

A couple of others, Bacal and Schmidt, roused themselves to express similar anger.

'Shut the fuck up, all of you,' said Entwistle. 'Just tell me what's happening here.'

'It's just like they're announcing: Firefall's being held to ransom for cash.'

'What about that oil rig stuff?'

Rickenbacker almost laughed, but it hurt so much he stopped. He coughed instead, and blood spotted his lips.

'Shit . . .' he continued. 'That's just a cover. You've seen the way this town's been since Ultracom started their drilling. They fucked up what looks the town ever had . . . and now they're in danger of polluting the Hole. Well, two months back, on 4 July, I got told some bad news by an Ultracom rigger I'd picked up for drunk driving. Seemed their geological survey revealed the Hole wasn't caused by a meteor at all. It was just a damn sink hole; the roof fell in on some underground river, and the whole damned thing filled up with water. Sorta puts an end to all the souvenirs, don't it?'

'To say nothing of the town's reputation,' said Maribeth, thinking of the seemingly endless variety of tat forced on gullible tourists by several of the men in this very room. From Comet Burgers to Talking Meteorites to 'Authentic Moon Dust – Just Don't Tell NASA'. All that would become just the junk it really was if Rickenbacker's story was true.

'But worse than that: the guy thought they were near

to actually striking oil. The core samples they'd recently sent back to Dallas had got everyone real excited. That might sound good for the local economy – lots of towns make money out of natural resources and even if it stops the tourists, there's plenty more money to be made with oil. But I also found out they'd already sewn up land rights all along Roosevelt, with a little help from Stick and Schmidt here – enough to give them unrestricted access and a route for a pipeline. They'd just pump out the cash along with the oil and to hell with our town. Firefall was *doomed.* We all were. But all of us here had more to lose than most.'

'You don't own a business,' said Entwistle, still shocked by his superior's treachery.

'No, but I ain't got a retirement fund either. Made some bad choices. And Tammy's medical bills were so damn high. Haven't got a pot to piss in now, never mind a condo to cry in. And that after thirty-nine goddam years serving this town as Deputy and Sheriff. All I got is a strip of land out near Robbins. Good times it'd be money in the bank, but Firefall the way it's heading . . .'

Rankin the rowboat owner chipped in. 'My business is down forty-five per cent on last year. If it gets any worse I've had it – and how do you sell a boat business that hasn't got any customers?'

Bacal also piped up. 'My takings are down by a half, and that's with a permanent goddam sale in the souvenir shop.'

'And beating out my prices, you bastard,' said Lury.

'Hey, business is business—'

'You got the museum, all I got's souvenirs. I can't make a cent in—'

'WILL YOU ALL SHUT UP, YOU MOTHERFUCKERS!' exploded Greg, heartily sick of their griping. Three of the bastards had had him arrested in the last couple of years.

'Hey, hey,' said Entwistle, 'calm down. *Everyone* calm down. Finish your story, Ed.'

'The rig worker and some of us were mulling this over one night, over some beers. Too many beers, it seems now. Someone had seen a movie . . . we started surmising, shooting it about . . . and came up with this dumb-ass plan. Hold the whole town to ransom for cash. But there were a few drawbacks.'

'Like you're Sheriff of the said town!' said Maribeth.

'Oh, don't give me that moral crap. Been serving the law all my life and it's got me *nothing*. I just want my share – I earned it. But we needed to get organized, get some funding, and work out an escape plan. We knew we'd have to leave afterwards, and never come back – but what's there to come back to?'

'So how come you're all in here?' sneered Greg, pleased by the pain this brought to the man's face.

'Because of trust. Entwistle, how many times we pulled in guys on the say-so of others? Get two guys together, one'll squeal. Law of nature. Someone knew someone who knew . . . Well, the rig guy knew this number 38 – don't know his real name – who agreed to help organize it. Thought the plan would work, did it for a half-share. He pays his people, we split the rest.'

'What about the hundred million?' asked Greg.

'Aw, we were never gonna get that. Just electronic money: press a button it vanishes. No, we were after the ten mill in cash. Air-dropped in – and we'd get away with that.'

'Lot of people involved here,' said Entwistle. 'Not much left after you've—'

'Hey, five mill split seven ways? Sure as hell'd keep me happy the rest of my days.'

'And all the others?'

'Who cares? They're criminals – and who are they going to complain to?'

'And you're *not* criminals?' said Maribeth.

'No, we're a deserving cause.'

'So this is a *charitable* event!' exploded Maribeth.

Entwistle was beyond worrying about the morality of Rickenbacker's plan. As a professional law officer, he was more interested in the operational details.

'So why the executions?'

'Number 38's idea. Said it'd speed up the process – the quicker it's resolved, the less time the feds have a chance to stop us. By 1:00 p.m. today we'd be vanished.'

'How?'

'Doesn't matter now.'

'This 38,' interrupted Greg, happy the Sheriff had been double-crossed, 'he's decided he wants the whole ten million?'

'Something like that. We're amateurs, he's saying – and amateurs don't get paid.'

'Hoist on your own petard,' said Maribeth, pleased there was some justice in the world, however twisted.

'Whatever.'

Just then the door opened and two armed men – 77 and 52 – entered, with 38 close behind. They grabbed Clayton Stick and began to drag him out.

As Entwistle moved to stop them, 38 fired a single shot into the ceiling. 'Shut up, all of you. It's time for another execution.'

'Haven't they responded yet?' said Rickenbacker.

'Yes, but there's too many ifs and maybes. And we want yes, yes, yes.' Then to Stick he said: 'Just do what was agreed.'

They dragged the man out and the room fell silent.

'More play-acting?' said Entwistle.

Rickenbacker shrugged.

A minute later they heard a shot, which made everyone jump even though it was expected. Then there was scuffling outside, the door was flung open, and Stick was sent sprawling face-down on the floor.

Hands grabbed at him and rolled him over. There was a hole in his forehead; blood streaked his face. Real blood from a real bullet hole. They gaped up at 38.

'If a hick deputy can guess what we were pretending, so can the FBI,' he explained. 'So from now on it's real. And in another ten minutes, if we ain't had word . . .' He left his threat hanging in the air, as effective as a guillotine blade.

Greg, Entwistle, and Maribeth glanced at each other, then around the room. Of all those confined there, they were the only ones who hadn't yet been 'executed'.

Which meant one of the three of them would have to be next.

Twenty-two

There occurred a glitch on the bank of monitors in the comtruck trailer, and Hartsby found himself staring up at the bright squares. For a few seconds he was mesmerized, as the sight reminded him of how his elaborate subterfuge had started years before.

He remembered the cold, claustrophobic darkness of the Kentucky mine shaft, the horror of impending disaster, and the black terror that drove him to embrace that strange compelling light. And then the unutterable wonder of realizing what the object actually was, and what it meant to him – and why *today* was so vital. Because soon he would be in control at last, able to do as he wished with his prize. And, oh, the plans he had for it . . .

He found himself shivering at the prospect of it all, then suddenly felt self-conscious at his public daydreaming. He hurried away from the video screens and out onto the steps of the trailer. Breathing in hard to steady the hammering of his heart, he looked up at the wide blue sky – and could not help smiling in anticipation of his triumph. But to ensure that everything would come about, it was time to move up a gear.

He came upon Collingwood leaning against a Highway Patrol car.

'Follow me,' he said, leading Del to the rear of the comtruck then across a field to a small hedge that shielded them from the array of police cruisers and ambulances.

'What is it now?' asked Del.

'Time for a few home truths. I chose you to handle this assignment because I believed your sense of duty would lead you to obey my orders.'

'Duty seems to be a very elastic term today. But when my orders seem contrary to the public good, to the ethics and standards expected—'

'Jesus, save me the lecture! Instead, be constructive. Tell me what's wrong with this operation.'

'You.'

'And stay off the personal insults, OK.'

'OK . . . So far, six hostages have been executed. You seem to be very well informed as to what is going on in the town, and yet our only means of communication are a telephone and whatever they show us on TV. And you've already said that the least of your concerns is the town: that the rig is of paramount importance. And yet here's the paradox: if you think so goddam much of that oil rig, why aren't you conceding what these bastards want, in case they blow the damn thing up?'

'If I told you, you wouldn't believe me. As I say, national security is at stake here, and it has absolutely nothing to do with a bunch of assholes wearing numbered shirts or "the environment".'

Del wouldn't be swayed. 'You possess satellite pictures within an hour of the town being taken. This comtruck just happens to be in the area. You, coincidentally, have a plan of the town's sewers. *And* you still don't seem overly concerned about the hostages being shot. Yet you've now warned the terrorist leader that there are people—'

'Do you want amateurs running loose in Firefall, taking independent action?'

'No. But—'

'But nothing. That satellite? It's been over the town for a month. Ultracom have been using it for geological surveys; it's convenient, but it's not sinister. The truck was already over at Laramie helping clean up the aftermath of that bank raid. Sewers? The truck's computers can plug into any federal computer in the country. It's called "modern technology". As for the hostages, you're free to negotiate now.'

'But why now? Why not an hour ago?'

'You dithered.'

'I dithered? I was obeying—'

'*You're* in charge. *You're* responsible.'

'I'm not carrying ... Deputy Director Crane knows what you're doing.'

'Deputy Director Crane will deny all knowledge of my involvement, as will everyone here who has seen me. Remember your little discussion with Calthorpe about playing the game? Everyone here plays by the rules. *My* rules. All those people in the truck? If I told them they were women they'd start wearing skirts and peeing sitting down. *My* game, *my* rules. I chose you because, quite frankly, I thought you were dumb enough to go along with what I wanted just long enough for you to carry the can.

But I was wrong. There's actually a brain at work in that fat head of yours. And frankly, it's getting on my nerves.'

'That's it. I've—'

'That isn't it, Collingwood. Far from it. Things were going so nicely, too. Just remember: do what I say and you'll end up famous.'

'For what?'

'Fucking up at Firefall.'

Del bristled. 'You're setting me up?'

Hartsby tapped him on the forehead. 'At last, light dawns.'

Twenty-three

'We've got to get out of here,' said Entwistle.

'You have a flair for the obvious,' said Maribeth.

'And the impossible,' added Greg. 'There's no way out except through them, and they got guns.'

'Boy's right,' said Rickenbacker.

'Don't call me boy, old man,' said Greg.

Rickenbacker ignored him. 'Soon as we'd been double-crossed we tried to figure a way out, but there's no windows you can break inside a couple of minutes, no vents, and just the one door. You might get a couple of them, but there's more than a dozen men in this building, all of them pros. And even *your* temper won't beat them, Henley.'

Greg stirred but Entwistle shook his head to check him. 'Leave it – for now.'

Rickenbacker raised a bloodied eyebrow.

'We get out of here, Ed,' Entwistle explained, 'I'm gonna stomp you myself, and if the kid wants some of you he's more than welcome.'

'Whatever,' said Rickenbacker, settling back and gripping his side. He had a couple of broken ribs and knew that he wasn't even going to be standing up, let alone getting away.

'OK, suppose we do jump them, get their guns,' said Greg. 'Where's the quickest way out?'

'Way we came in,' said Entwistle. 'The back of the building's best. There's cover there and most'll still be out front.'

'Yes, they all have to line up when someone gets shot . . .' Maribeth suddenly realized she had just pointed out the best moment for them to act.

'We're not waiting that long,' said Entwistle, aware of what she had said. 'Anyone got the right time?'

Three unsteady wrists offered up three watches for his perusal. Entwistle leaned down to check them all.

'Oh, shit,' he said, standing upright.

'What?' said Maribeth.

'They've *all* stopped.' He exchanged a glance with Greg. 'We've got about six minutes,' he estimated.

'So whatever we're gonna do, let's do it soon,' said Greg. 'Nothing personal, but if they decide to kill us in alphabetical order, I ain't arguing!'

This elicited a laugh from the terrified Maribeth, much to her surprise, and Greg was pleased not to have offended, though why such sensibilities should count when they were literally minutes from death he couldn't fathom.

Entwistle pointed at the assembled fools. 'You got us into this shit; you're gonna help us get out of it.'

There was muttering and shaking of heads, Rankin and Schmidt in particular determined to stick it out.

'Hey, perhaps you haven't grasped the full picture. Never mind about spending the rest of your life behind bars – you're already *dead*. Been seen shot, by millions –

and these guys ain't in the resurrection business, as Stick here will testify. Now we need a distraction to catch them off guard.'

He looked around the room at desperate faces. Then Maribeth stepped forward.

'I think I might be able to help,' she said, her voice quavering as she remembered her wilder college days.

Two minutes later Greg was banging on the door, demanding to see 'that fucking Mr 38!' and, as the door was unbolted, he backed away, giving the floor to Maribeth.

The same two men entered, 77 and 52, their machine-guns ready.

'What the fuck—?' Number 52 stopped in mid-sentence, stunned by Maribeth's display, as 77 edged sideways for a look.

Maribeth had stripped to the waist, her breasts exposed, her face set in a come-hither look. 'I'll do anything to get away from these freaks,' she announced.

All could see the momentary indecision of the two gunmen, but just as common sense regained the upper hand Entwistle plunged a metal runner from one of the filing-cabinet drawers into 52's neck, while Greg slammed the drawer into 77's face. Both men dropped instantly – Bacal and Klein crouching on 52's legs to stop him thrashing about noisily as his life spurted away.

Entwistle was in time to pick up 52's machine-gun, but 77's weapon went clattering out into the corridor.

'Brave girl.' He turned to Maribeth.

'They're only breasts,' she said, as she covered herself.

'Yeah, but they ain't bulletproof.' And also damn

cute, he couldn't help thinking. 'OK, Greg and you take the lead, me next, the others when they can. And Ed . . .?'

Rickenbacker shook his head. 'No chance.'

'The time!' hissed Lury.

They heard feet marching along the corridor.

'Oh, fuck,' said Entwistle, motioning everyone over to the right side of the room. 'Turn the desk on its side and get behind it. Use it as a shield!'

He ducked to his left and took up station on one side of the door, next to the four-drawer filing cabinet: Greg was standing across from him. As the approaching feet paused, they heard whispers outside and guns being cocked. Entwistle knew they wouldn't be stupid enough to rush the room, so . . .?

'Grenade!' shouted Rankin.

A grenade bounced off the inside edge of the open door and rolled into the room.

Maribeth screamed.

There was a sick laugh from outside, and the sound of running feet, but everyone in the room froze; there was no way for them to escape.

Entwistle dived at Maribeth, intending to shield her; Greg hurled himself across the room towards the overturned desk, behind which the others were frantically scrambling for cover.

Only Rickenbacker showed no signs of panic. Instead, he leaned over and, clawing at the evil metal egg, finally snagged it and, with a grunt, rolled over on top of it.

The blast shook the room and threw him two feet into the air, then dropped him across the doorway like a fresh side of beef.

Entwistle rushed over, but saw that Rickenbacker was dead, his chest shredded, his face shattered, one arm barely attached.

'You bastard,' he muttered. 'Don't think this absolves you.'

Then, outside, he heard feet again, and swinging the machine-gun in front of him he waited just a fraction of a second before pulling the trigger, and caught a charging black-clad man in the chest.

As blood patterned across the large figure 3, Entwistle knew it would only be seconds before another grenade came flying in. Backing away, he grabbed the still dazed Greg.

'There'll be another one. When it comes in, be ready to grab it.'

'What?'

Maribeth moved up beside them, her eyes betraying total confusion.

'Grab it, then put it on the window sill. It's the only way we'll get out of here.'

'Hey, no way am—'

The next grenade landed on Rickenbacker, and rolled between his twisted legs. As Entwistle moved to pick it up, Maribeth pushed in front and scooped it up. She ran to the window and jammed it in the corner of the frame, then jumped on top of the heap of men behind the desk.

Greg and Entwistle glanced at each other, then hurled themselves either side of the open door as the grenade exploded.

This time the force wasn't contained by two hundred and fifty pounds of flesh and bone, and everyone felt their backs whipped by a hot wind of metal and glass and wood.

Entwistle tried to ignore the searing pain in his shoulders and the back of his head as he forced himself to stand. He glanced over at Greg, who was turning over and clutching his arm, then peered through a cloud of dust at the pile of groaning people behind the splintered desk. Then he squinted through the smoke at the window.

Success! The entire frame had been blasted loose.

At the same time, dazed though he was, Greg scrambled across the room on his hands and knees towards the window, then stood to look outside.

The area behind the Town Hall was still empty, so he leaned over the shredded desk and grabbed at Maribeth's hand and pulled her upright.

'Get yourself out and take cover!' he yelled.

Maribeth stared at him blankly, then nodded. She had no alternative.

Greg leaned down over the upturned table. 'Any of you fuckers want out, now's the time,' he hissed.

Entwistle was still standing by the door, machine-gun at the ready. He wasn't sure what to do next. They would either storm the room or lob in another grenade just to be sure. And there was no way he could close the door without exposing himself. Either way he had to be ready, so as to protect the rest. With his foot he snagged the machine-gun dropped by number 3 and kicked it over to Greg, just as Maribeth clambered over the sill and dropped into the courtyard.

Greg picked up the weapon and climbed up after her, pausing to urge Entwistle to follow. But, hearing activity in the corridor, Entwistle waved Greg out, and saw others follow him. Screw them: this was all their doing.

He guessed someone was about to open fire through

the door. The unseen enemy wouldn't risk showing himself, but he could still point a gun in and sweep a burst of fire across the room.

Two of the hostages were already through the window when the gunfire erupted, catching another two escaping men in the back. Quickly setting the broken file drawer on its end, Entwistle jumped on top of it. Pointing his own gun down at the weapon firing through the door, he pulled the trigger.

There was a scream of pain as the assailant's gun clattered to the floor, and curses filled the air. Entwistle leaped off the collapsing drawer and across the room to the fallen hostages.

Bacal was already dead, from a bullet in the back of his head, while Schmidt was backshot and jerking his last. Entwistle was too desperate now to consider the propriety of his actions so, standing on Bacal's back, he leaped for the open window. Clearing the sill, he landed on his feet outside in the yard, where he executed a perfect roll and ran for the cover of the Caterpillar bulldozer.

Behind him was the sound of more shooting, and Gerry Rankin's voice croaking, 'We surrender.' Then a burst of machine-gun fire. That must take care of those who hadn't escaped, and while it horrified Entwistle to be so close to such violence he could feel little pity for the men who had just died. Lie down with lions and you run the risk of getting eaten.

Ed Rickenbacker's death he did regret, however, even though this had all started with the Sheriff's crazy retirement plan. He had known the man too long to believe he had ever intended it to end so bloodily, despite the apparent brutality of the mock executions. But as Ed himself had said, when there's ten million dollars at stake, no one can be trusted.

Entwistle hunched down behind the red bulldozer, checking that everyone else was OK. All had been peppered with fragments from the grenade explosion, but none dangerously so.

'Fuck, man,' said Greg. 'Why all this? Why all this?' He sounded like a confused teenager.

Aware that the boy could lose it, Entwistle focused on the problems at hand. 'How much ammunition?'

Greg held out his gun as if unaware he had been carrying it. 'What?'

'Ammo? Come on, Greg, stay with us.'

Like an automaton Greg pulled the clip. 'Got bullets,' he confirmed.

Entwistle checked his own machine-gun. Half a clip left, and that was it. A maximum of forty-five shots against an army. The odds hadn't improved.

Two guns suddenly appeared at the base of the blasted window and opened fire, their owners hunched down below the sill. Bullets raked the yard, kicking up debris and zinging off metalwork while the five escapees huddled down behind the Caterpillar. Their only consolation was the fact that such a wide spread of fire indicated their exact location was as yet unknown.

'We've got to get out of here now!' yelled Entwistle.

'Through the drain?' said Greg, his initial shock now receding.

As if in answer, bullets pinged off the discarded manhole cover.

'They'd pick us off easily,' said Maribeth.

'We're fucked,' stammered Lury, shaking uncontrollably.

Entwistle leaned back to survey what he could safely observe of the yard. 'Anyone know how to drive one of these?' he said at last, banging his gun against the track of the bulldozer.

'I do,' said Klein. 'It belongs to me.'

'You're contracted for this construction work? OK, just get up there and drive the fucking thing!'

'What if they start shooting again?'

Entwistle shoved the barrel of his machine-gun into Klein's large gut. 'One bullet wasted won't make much difference to me – but it sure will to you.'

Reluctantly Klein edged up onto the Caterpillar tracks, then slid into the high, exposed seat. Jimmying the bulldozer's starter, he revved the motor till the single exhaust stack on its elongated hood started belching black smoke.

Entwistle then clambered up behind him and, bracing himself against the back of the driving seat, aimed his gun towards the rear of the Town Hall. There were still too many windows for his liking, though many were frosted and most were grimy enough to suggest they might be jammed tight through lack of use.

The bulldozer suddenly juddered forward, almost throwing him off balance, its wide, flat metal tracks grinding stones and debris to dust as it began a slow crawl towards the yard's exit.

Greg and Maribeth and Lury kept pace, out of sight behind it, watching out for anyone trying to sneak round the side of the building. They were halfway out of the yard entrance when a couple of masked men erupted from the rear door of the Town Hall, spraying the lumbering machine with semi-automatic fire. Their shots were wild and posed no threat, and once Entwistle returned a burst they both dived for cover out of sight.

Someone smashed a window on the second floor and loosed off three rapid shots which hit the engine cowling each time, till Entwistle returned fire, missing the marksman but destroying the rest of the window panes. Seconds later the rumbling monster had gained the protective cover of the building's east wing.

'Can't this thing go any faster?' shouted Entwistle above the roaring engine.

Klein shook his head. 'No. It's old. We just couldn't afford—'

'Well, just *drive*!' God, he was sick of these self-pitying whiners.

They crawled on past the side of the building, then out onto Circle One. Here were positioned half a dozen gunmen with weapons trained, who began firing as soon as the bulldozer came into view. Klein took an instant hit in the leg; with a yell he lifted his foot from the gas pedal. Entwistle immediately returned fire, shouting for help from Greg, who darted out in front of the bulldozer's lowered blade to let off a short burst. Two conspirators fell; the rest ran for cover inside the Town Hall.

Entwistle worked his way along the narrow running-board above the caterpillar tracks, and pushed down hard on the knee of Klein's damaged leg to make sure the bulldozer's gas pedal was kept fully depressed. The wounded man howled in pain, but Entwistle had no alternative. They only had a few seconds' grace.

'Take us left. Take us left!'

Even through his pain, Klein couldn't believe this instruction.

'But that's straight towards them!'

'Just do it, damn you!'

Klein gritted his teeth and pulled on his levers. Slowly the bulldozer turned on its axis, grinding up blacktop until it was advancing towards the front entrance of the Town Hall.

'Raise the blade, then get us in reverse!' shouted Entwistle.

At last Klein understood and, despite his injury, did as ordered. In moments the bulldozer was roaring backwards, its giant blade rising three feet off the ground to form a rectangular metal screen between its passengers and the reassembling guns in front of them. They then continued to move backwards along Circle One.

'Greg! You watch Coolidge. I'll do what I can here!'

His voice was suddenly drowned by a fusillade of shots pinging off the Caterpillar's bodywork and blade.

'Fuck!' was all he could manage to say, kneeling down beside Klein. He had maybe only a dozen rounds left, so what the hell were they going to do? Whatever it was, it was going to be *slow*.

Maribeth was fully aware of their predicament and was already trying to work out an answer as she loped ahead of the reversing bulldozer, but whatever protection they were afforded by the blade they were still vulnerable from three other sides, and now, out in the open street, the bulldozer was rapidly becoming redundant to their needs. They had to get away from it and fast – but if they were to make a run for it they would be suddenly even more exposed. *Hellation in trousers!*

Greg was equally aware of their problem. It was only a matter of time until all this gunfire attracted other black-hoods to the scene. He edged back and forth behind the protective width of the looming bulldozer, desperately looking for inspiration but fast coming to believe their luck had finally deserted them.

'Entwistle!' yelled Maribeth suddenly. 'I've got an idea, but you'll have to get off that thing *now*!'

Entwistle braved a glance back down at her. Should he trust her judgement? Then he tapped Klein on the shoulder.

'Can you jam the pedal so as to keep this thing moving?'

Klein was puzzled at first, then understood. 'If you got something long enough to jam under the seat.'

Entwistle glanced about them, found a toolbox on the back of the seat. It was empty. Shit! Then he studied his machine-gun. Oh hell . . .

Holding tight, he leaned out sideways and emptied the remaining bullets in the direction of their opponents, then knelt down and slipped the stock of the gun under the driver's seat, wedging the opposite end against the pedal. Then, grabbing Klein around the waist, he hauled the wounded man out of the seat and edged them both along the running-board towards the rear of the machine, careful to keep their feet well clear of the moving tracks. Reaching the back of the bulldozer he lowered Klein into Greg's arms, then finally jumped down himself.

Maribeth was walking at a crouch ten feet ahead of

the retreating bulldozer, pointing across to a drain cover in the middle of the next intersection.

'Go get it!' Entwistle shouted to the others as he pulled Klein from Greg's arms, looping the man's arm over his shoulders and struggling to maintain his momentum ahead of the unstoppable tonnage of the bulldozer.

Greg and Lury caught up with Maribeth at the drain cover, with thirty seconds to spare before the bulldozer would reach them. Greg snagged the end sight of his weapon under the rim of the manhole cover, which allowed him to lift its heavy weight slightly. Once there was a sufficient gap between metal and lip, Maribeth and Lury slipped their hands underneath the lid and started to haul it away from the hole.

But as Greg stood back again, off guard, Lury snatched hold of his machine-gun and jabbed it threateningly at the pair of them.

'I go first!' he snarled.

Neither had time to argue, so let him indulge his selfishness. But precious seconds were wasted as he floundered halfway inside the manhole, desperately trying to locate a foothold.

'What the fuck's happening?' yelled Entwistle above the bulldozer's roar, diesel fumes obscuring his vision.

Greg and Maribeth merely gaped as he approached them, their eyes telling him just how close the bulldozer was behind. Turning, he realized there was no way they would get down their escape route in time – and if they scattered to either side of the machine, they'd be cut down by gunfire easily.

'Lie down!' Entwistle shouted, pushing Klein to the

ground on the other side of the open drain hole and lying down beside him flat on his back. 'Come on, get down. It's our only chance!'

Greg dived for the tarmac as Maribeth fell to her knees.

'On your back. *On your back!* And grab the tow bar!'

The bulldozer was almost upon them. The long bar welded in a T-shape to its rear fortunately extended to either side of the caterpillar tracks, so offered sufficient purchase. But if one of those tracks slowed or jammed, the monstrous vehicle could easily turn to either side, and ten tons of machinery would squash them like bugs.

The red brute now loomed over them, the space between the moving tracks barely wide enough to span the four of them. The tow bar arrived quicker than expected and a flurry of frantic hands grasped its rusted metal, all yelping in agony as their shoulders were viciously wrenched in their sockets.

Entwistle himself grabbed a firm hold before helping Klein get his other hand up onto the bar. He could see the man's strength was failing, even as the bulldozer ground onwards.

After clinging to the underside of the beast for a full minute, Entwistle glanced along his body and spotted – through the narrow strip beneath the raised blade and the road surface – a group of black-hoods warily approaching the open drain hole.

He watched the men then step back while one lone machine-gunner emptied an entire magazine into it. As smoke drifted up out of the hole, they waited a few seconds, then number 38 gestured for two of his men to venture inside.

They climbed down out of sight as the others stood waiting.

Next 38 waved a man over to the moving bulldozer. He ran forward until level with the driver's seat, which he raked with a vicious burst of gunfire. As the bulldozer continued to crawl along, the man's feet came back into view beneath the blade and Entwistle was relieved to see him trotting back to join his leader.

More black-hoods were ordered down into the sewer, while 38 sent another man in pursuit of the bulldozer, presumably to halt it. Then 38 turned on his heel and led his remaining followers back towards the Town Hall, apparently satisfied that the fugitives were hiding in the drains, so could be hunted down at leisure without interrupting the operations above ground. God above, their strategy had worked!

Thirty seconds later the street was empty bar the single gunman, number 20, who was still trotting after the bulldozer, his gun slung round his back. Entwistle decided he would wait until the man had climbed on board the machine before slipping out to deal with him.

But then Klein finally lost his grip and, with a frantic cry, slumped onto the road. Without thinking, Entwistle released his own hold and let the bulldozer rumble over him, leaving the two of them fully exposed in the middle of the street. Entwistle twisted over to glance back at the machine. Fortunately its blade still hid him from number 20, but he had only seconds left in which to act.

Scrambling up, he ran round to the other side of the bulldozer from the black-hood, then, stepping onto the central guard bar that ran along outside the tracks' guide wheels, he hurled himself onto the driver's seat just as the gunman climbed on board.

A startled face, a hand trying to fend him off, a scream ... and the man tumbled back onto the bulldozer's left caterpillar track.

Entwistle grabbed a lever to pull himself across the seat, trying to catch the man, but he was already travelling on his back along the ribbed track, the strap of his gun snagged between two slats. Entwistle could only watch in horror as the dazed man writhed about like an animal on a slaughterhouse conveyor belt.

Letting out a final cry of terror, 20 fell off the end of the track and the bulldozer ran over him lengthways, his fragile body presenting no obstacle to the monstrous machine. His scream ended as Maribeth's started, his blood jetting all over her face. Both she and Greg let go of the tow bar and found themselves lying exhausted out on the exposed road.

'Did you see? Did you see?' was all she could say. So many awful things had happened so quickly, it had all seemed so unreal. But now she could feel that man's blood on her face – she could *taste* it – and there he lay nearby, a bloody smear on the road, only one arm and a leg retaining a third dimension.

Greg could see from her rolling eyes that she was beginning to lose it, but the time wasn't right for that.

'Come on, Maribeth, gotta move before they see us.'

'Did you see? Did you see?'

'Yeah, I sure as hell did ...'

He squatted, and lifting her under the arms dragged her to the roadside and into the bushes, out of sight. There he collapsed beside her. *Now* was the time for his tears and he didn't give damn who saw them.

Entwistle whirled round to see Greg and Maribeth scrabbling off the road, so he jumped down off the machine and ran towards Klein, dragging the howling man into the bushes. There he found Greg and Maribeth holding on to each other like they had been Superglued together, crying and shaking.

Klein was conscious again, but his leg was a bloody mess, his fall from the bulldozer having increased the damage done by the gunshot. Poking a finger into the hole torn by the bullet in the man's chinos, Entwistle ripped open the trouser leg and studied the wound, still seeping blood. Then he undid the leather belt from his own trousers and slipped it around the man's thigh, tightening it until the flow of blood stopped. He counted to thirty, eased the belt, then tightened it again. He did not know how bad the wound was and it was the best he could do.

Greg had seen Entwistle coming towards him and began trying to extricate himself from Maribeth's stranglehold.

'Maribeth, you're squeezing me to death,' he gasped.

She registered the boy's words, but letting go of him would mean releasing one human being she knew she could rely on in this endless nightmare. So she hugged him harder, hoping his presence would somehow wipe out all the bad things – just like the giant teddy bear she had owned as a child and had always turned to for comfort. But Maribeth knew she faced a stark choice: give in and become a blubbering girlie, curled up in some corner waiting for the cavalry to arrive – or stand up and fight! She knew what she would rather do.

'You OK?' said Entwistle, gently.

'Pretty stupid question,' she muttered; but released her grip.

'Party ain't over yet,' said Entwistle. 'Klein's in bad shape; he needs attention. And we need to get out of sight.'

Entwistle took in their location. The bulldozer was still chugging relentlessly on, but it had now veered off Circle One and was grinding its way through an empty parking lot, heading for a long, low building with a glass frontage.

'Oh shit, no,' he gasped.

'What?' said Maribeth following his gaze.

'Ooh, boy,' said Greg, 'your momma's going to be pissed.'

'Momma?' said Maribeth. 'Is Carol Glass your mother?'

'Yes. And I only hope her insurance is up to date.'

As the sound of smashing glass reached them, all three winced. The bulldozer drove straight on through the glass portico of the Glasshouse restaurant, over a dozen tables, then through the wide window opposite that faced the Hole. It continued across the terrace before finally dropping into the Hole, its animal roar swallowed up in a large plume of water – then all was silent.

Entwistle shook his head, as if to clear from his mind the horrible image of his mother's profitable livelihood destroyed by his very own hand. 'If we get out of this mess, neither of you will *ever* tell her how that happened. Understand?'

There was sudden burst of gunfire, difficult to locate.

'Either they're still chasing that rat Lury, or they're

after shadows,' said Entwistle. 'But as long as they think we're down there below ... Come on, help me get Klein into this house. We might even get time to rest up.'

Five minutes later they were all ensconced in the comfortable lounge of the empty Timmons' home. Entwistle remembered the family was away on its annual vacation. While Klein lay on the sofa, being tended by Maribeth, Greg cleaned up in the bathroom, and Entwistle began searching for some means of contacting the outside world.

The telephone was out, of course, and while the son's room had a CB rig, all its bands were jammed. There wasn't even a cellular phone.

'Find anything?' said Maribeth, as Entwistle returned downstairs.

'No. The CB channels are jammed. That damn kid's got more gear up there than I have: video, TV, phone, computer ...'

'And the clocks?' said Maribeth reluctantly.

'All stopped again, I'm afraid,' said Entwistle.

A small frisson of fear ran through her. 'Hellation, what is going on?'

All Entwistle could offer was a shrug of the shoulders. 'It's damn weird, but to be honest it ain't high on my list of priorities just now.'

Looking at Klein, and their own ragged appearance, Maribeth had to agree.

'You said the boy had a computer? He might be linked to the Internet. Then we could get messages out – and they won't know where they're originating from ... Oh, but he'd need a telephone, wouldn't he? Damn!'

Entwistle ruffled her hair. On an ordinary day it

would have been a beautiful rust-red colour, but right now it was dirty brown and bloody. 'Good thinking.'

'Don't patronize me, Deputy.' Maribeth hated being talked down to, especially if it was by someone she liked.

'I'm not patronizing you – and the name's Entwistle.'

They stared at each other, till Maribeth couldn't help smiling. 'No first name?'

'I got two names. Cedric and Milton. I use Entwistle.'

'I can see why.'

'Thank *you* for not patronizing me.'

'Mind you, Entwistle isn't so hot either.'

'How's Klein doing?' he said, grinning.

'Needs a doctor, but he'll last. Your tourniquet helped. Bullet went straight through, didn't hit an artery.' Maribeth was used to examining wounds because of the animals she helped tend at the shelter.

'Can he talk?'

'Yes,' murmured Klein. 'I can talk.'

'Well, talk, then,' growled Greg, coming back from the downstairs bathroom, wiping his face with a towel.

'Maribeth, you go clean up now,' said Entwistle.

She nodded and left the room, grateful for the chance to wash her face, still sticky with number 20's blood.

As soon as Maribeth had gone, Entwistle leaned over Klein and held up a ballpoint pen in front of his eyes. 'Now the lady's out of the room, you tell me everything you know or I'll put this pen in that hole in your leg and start writing on the inside of your goddam worthless body. Are we clear?'

Twenty-four

Number 38 was unmoved. 'What's your name?' he asked.

Del shifted uncomfortably, aware that everyone else in the comtruck was watching him and listening for his response. Number 38 had been put on a loudspeaker, courtesy of the smiling Hartsby.

'Special Agent Collingwood,' said Del.

'Well, Collingwood, I've warned you about not having the right words—'

'We've got the cash!' butted in Del. 'It's on its way. Ultracom agree to dismantle the rig, and they promise to suspend all exploratory work in the Midwest.'

Hartsby nodded his approval of Del's fiction.

'The hundred million dollars is being dealt with. We're even working on compensating the locals for their lost business. Now will you stop killing the hostages?'

'All I hear from you is "on its way", you "promise to", you're "working on" . . . Now, it's very simple: *I ask – you give – we go – they live.* So far no *give*, so we *stay* – and they *die.* Call me when you're a hundred per cent there, Special Agent Collingwood.'

The line hummed its emptiness.

'Hate to say I told you so . . .' muttered Hartsby.

Del, however, felt pleased. At last he had been able to do everything he could, both as an agent and as a man. He had tried to negotiate with someone who plainly wasn't seeking negotiation, and he had done his duty by Hartsby, and his best by himself. Now was the time to salvage his reputation, if not his career. Ignoring Hartsby, he replaced the receiver and walked calmly out of the comtruck.

Outside he was struck by blinding sunlight. Donning a pair of Ray-Bans, he spotted Calthorpe and beckoned him over, then pulled him round by the cab of the truck.

'I want you to bring me a reporter: CNN, CBS, Sky, anyone. Just make sure they have a live lead.'

Calthorpe was surprised. 'I know what you're thinking—'

'Do it.'

'Yes, sir, but—'

Two of Hartsby's operatives stepped in front of Calthorpe, their expressionless faces interchangeable. Hartsby himself then appeared behind them.

'On your way back to Worthing, Agent Calthorpe?' said Hartsby. 'Urgent family business requiring your attention?'

'Sir?'

Hartsby coughed and the men stood aside. 'Do you know the difference between a job and a career, Calthorpe?'

'No, sir.'

'Your car – get in it and drive away, you've got a career. Do as Collingwood asks and you've got a job – with a very short contract. Clear?'

Calthorpe looked at Del, who nodded.

'Sorry,' said Calthorpe.

'Go "make a difference",' said Hartsby sarcastically.

Calthorpe pulled up short. 'How did . . .'

Del spoke up. 'Mr Hartsby has extremely good hearing.'

'Unlike you, Collingwood,' said Hartsby. 'I thought you were on the team?'

Calthorpe walked away, obviously frightened.

'I'm a home supporter. Seems you're playing away.'

Hartsby laughed and waved the men away, then linked his arm through Del's. 'It seems to me that I'm going to have to play hardball. You game for that?'

'You're in charge.'

'I keep telling you, *you're* the one in charge. I'm just an observer.'

One of the operatives came over with Hartsby's laptop computer and handed it to him.

'Check the time,' said Hartsby.

Del looked at his watch: 9:51 a.m.

'The sixth hostage has just been executed, Collingwood,' said Hartsby. 'His blood is on *your* hands. Now, if you really want to do something, follow me.'

A minute later they were seated in the back of an unmarked police car, the laptop open on Hartsby's knees.

'I want you to watch something. Recognize this place?'

The screen of the computer contained a small square at its centre: a jerky picture that wasn't video but a digital display that was reformatting a couple of times a second.

Del looked at the television screen. The picture was

clear, though the colour was weak, and what he saw made his heart leap. It was too bizarre, too obscene to be true, but there it was, literally in black and white.

He saw his bedroom in Worthing, complete with the small bedside table and its array of pill bottles, the mocking crucifix above the satin headboard, and, in the bed itself, his sleeping wife. Thank God, she wasn't awake to experience this, he thought, his hands shaking, his stomach churning.

A man came into view, dressed in an anonymous suit, his eyes hidden by a pair of reflective sunglasses. He walked to the head of the bed and sat down gently on the empty side that at night would normally be occupied by Del himself. Del watched as the man then adjusted the sheet under his wife's chin, patting her head in a mocking gesture.

'My colleague has something for your wife,' said Hartsby. 'Show Mr Collingwood your present, James.'

James nodded and pulled out a silver automatic, its barrel longer and fatter than it should be. Del gasped when he recognized a silencer, and could only watch with increasing horror as the man on the screen ran the barrel back and forth under Gloria's chin, a sick grin playing on his surprisingly youthful face.

'You see the situation, Collingwood,' explained Hartsby. 'Only you and I and James know of his presence in your bedroom and only we three will know the consequences of your failure to cooperate.

'Item: today's siege in Firefall is going to go wrong. Item: you are going to be blamed. Item: I do not exist.

Accept these facts and your wife lives. Argue with us, she dies.'

'*You've* set all this up? In Firefall?'

'Shall we say my original plans were compromised and I have had to – what? – reschedule.'

'Who the hell *are* you?'

Hartsby looked straight up at Del, his eyes wide and cold like those of a doll. 'I am the man with his finger on the trigger of a gun pointing at your wife's head. Only one thing can save her: just give me the word our mutual friend number 38 wishes you to utter but your God-given duty forbids you to. Just say yes and your wife lives, and you get to do the best you can before it all goes pear-shaped.'

'You're going to kill me?'

'It will look like suicide. But you will die knowing your wife is alive. You have my word.'

'Your word? I couldn't think of anything more worthless on the entire planet just now.'

'I repeat: you have my word. My word that your wife will die if you don't say *yes*; that she will live if you do.'

Del looked at his sleeping wife, for now at peace from the demons consuming her soul. A jolly, loving woman reduced to the status of a frightened infant in a world she could no longer understand. His poor, sweet Gloria. His poor, poor baby.

'Say *yes*, Collingwood.'

Del reached out a shaking hand and stroked the screen of the laptop, tears streaming down his face. He would never see her again, never hold her, never promise her that everything would be all right, never bathe her, mop her brow, hold her hand until she slept, suckle her breasts, never hold her close . . .

Forgive me, Gloria, he thought. Taking an unsteady breath, he finally managed a word.

'No.'

'No?' said Hartsby, plainly surprised. 'You're sure of what you're saying? "No" means your wife *dies*. I'm sorry if I didn't make myself clear.'

'And I said no.'

'Very well. Just let me remind you that I am able to work any number of minor miracles, but bringing your precious wife back from the dead isn't one of them.'

Del could hardly speak, tears streaking his ashen cheeks. 'Kill her, then.'

Hartsby was astounded. 'You can't possibly mean . . . I'm not bluffing.'

Del stared at him. 'Then tell your fucking toad to do it!'

Hartsby shrugged his shoulders. 'You heard the man, James. Kill her.'

James also shrugged, then placed the barrel of his gun to the still sleeping Gloria's temple and pulled the trigger. There was a small noise, nothing dramatic, and his wife whipped in an arc onto the empty half of the bed as a spray of blood stained the pillow and the headboard. The assassin then holstered his gun and walked out of sight. The screen went blank a couple of seconds later.

Del continued to stare at the grey square on the screen, unsure if he was going to faint. He had sentenced his wife to death, quite probably needlessly. She hadn't known that James was in the room; he could have left without her ever knowing he had been there. Of course Del himself would have died – things had gone too far for his fate to be anything else – but now both of them would be dead. Had he been wrong? Thirty-seven years joined at the hip, husband and wife, best friends, lovers, confidants, confessors . . .

'I must say,' said Hartsby, 'that you are a singularly stubborn fellow.'

'No,' said Del, considering his answer, wanting to ensure that Hartsby understood exactly what he had ordered James to do. 'You've just done what I haven't had the nerve to do for the last few weeks.'

'What? Murder your wife?'

'No. *Spare* her. In your haste to co-opt me you may have had access to my files, but you obviously didn't read my wife's medical record. She is . . . she *was* terminally ill. Only months left to live. I could never work up the nerve to do what I knew was right, to spare her the ongoing pain and misery. But you've solved the problem for me, for which I thank you.'

Hartsby let out a snort. 'You're *thanking* me? Incredible. You're right, of course. I should have read the file. I stopped when I saw the word "devoted". Now I know just how much. One up to you, Collingwood.'

For Del it was no victory, as his tears and his uncontrollable shaking bore witness.

Hartsby let out a big sigh, then stepped in front of Del. 'However, we must adapt. I presume you still refuse to cooperate?'

'What the hell do you think?'

'I think,' said Hartsby, drawing his own automatic and levelling it at Del's head, 'that you have become expendable.'

Twenty-five

'I don't know everything,' said Klein. 'You heard what Ed Rickenbacker said back there at the Town Hall. We had this idea that just snowballed the more our businesses went down this summer. Christ, I was set to file for bankruptcy by Christmas, the way things were going. Whether they struck oil or not, the town would be even less popular with tourists next year, and that would just about kill us all. And they'd be bringing in outside contractors. My gear would be just so much junk.'

'So you all came up with this dumb-ass plan.'

'The more we went over it, the more it made sense.'

'But what about everyone else in town? Think of the shit they must be—'

'Not everyone in town is as innocent as you think. Besides, they'll all get to be in the movie.'

'Funny man,' said Greg.

'What do you mean, "not everyone"?' asked Entwistle.

'There are more in it than just those helping out. Why do you think the town's so quiet? We've got people in certain streets who've persuaded the rest in the street to cooperate. We just rounded up those who were going to work with us – and those we knew wouldn't, like the other deputies. Those who know what's happening will have disappeared and put on the same gear you're wearing, so they can help make up the numbers. The rest of the town are like sheep.'

Greg clouted him then, and Entwistle didn't rush to stop him.

'So how were you going to get away?'

'Those who were "shot", like me and Ed and the others, we were going to be bodies in the Town Hall when it blew up – along with the ransom money when it had been delivered. Meanwhile we'd all really be out of town, in hiding – and by the time the dust'd settled, our share of the money'd be sent on to us.'

'So how would the money get itself out?'

'With those hostages who get released. Those of them on our side were going to conceal it in their clothing and walk out under police escort back to their homes where they'd hide it until the fuss died down. Then it would be buried.'

Entwistle now realized what the hole in the cellar of Napier's Farm was for, and couldn't help speculating how many other cellars in Firefall boasted freshly dug holes.

'And the others? The pros?'

'Don't know. They have their own plan – and they take their share with them.'

'Seems like they have other ideas now. They'll still blow you up, and give the authorities their bodies, but they'll have *all* the cash . . . But how will they get out? How were *you* going to get out? The town must be surrounded.'

'It was 38's idea. When the authorities come in,

there'll be police cars, ambulances, fire trucks, God knows what. In all the confusion, we'll take off in a Mary County Hospital ambulance. It's stashed in Taylor Ash's garage. We rendezvous there, using the drains, change our gear, wait till things are really confused, then get out ferrying four serious burn victims with three nurses, a doctor, and a driver, make-up courtesy of Clayton Stick.'

Stick had been not only the town mayor but a doyen of the local amateur theatrical and opera groups, in charge of make-up, which was often the only professional aspect of the shows they regularly staged for the tourists. Ironically, the play running this particular week was Ira Levin's *Death Trap*.

'Except now Stick's dead,' said Greg, remembering the man was shot in the head as the first genuine execution victim.

'So why have so many of your men not even got radios?'

'Patsies. It was Ed's idea. We needed numbers so we hired assholes – let *them* get caught.'

'Some of them might end up getting shot by the FBI?'

The man shrugged. 'They're criminals and morons; goes with the territory.'

Entwistle grabbed him by the collar. 'So what the fuck are you, then?'

The man turned purple. '*Victims!* We're all victims! With that damn oil company coming in here, screwing up our businesses. I've worked here twenty-two years, and in a single year I'm out of business because of those fuckers. No one wants to build here. And does the government care? They gave the licences, overruled the council ... Life or death, Deputy. It's life or death. We ain't hired hands or professional criminals; we're ordinary people trying to survive.'

Entwistle glanced at the recurring message on the TV screen. STAY INSIDE. YOU WILL NOT BE HARMED. OBEY ALL ORDERS. 'Yeah, real *ordinary*.'

Just then the message disappeared, giving way to live coverage from outside the Town Hall. Number 38 appeared, addressing the camera.

'I have now reached the end of my patience. It is already an hour since the deadline passed, and since then seven residents have died needlessly. If the authorities are seeking to call my bluff, they're about to find out that they lack the necessary expertise for that. In ten minutes I shall execute another hostage, and from then on a further hostage every *five* minutes. You have ten minutes to accede to our demands.'

The screen went blank, then the running caption returned.

The man had made no reference to the recent fighting, just offered the outside world the same steely resolve.

Greg spoke up. 'I just wish we'd left you there so's you'd be next.'

'An admirable sentiment, Greg,' said Entwistle. 'Is Bill Napier in on this? I was ambushed out at his farm.'

'Yes. Ed wanted you well out of the way, so he got you sent out there.'

Rickenbacker sent me there, thought Entwistle. *Did he know about that Pendleton guy?* He leaned into Klein, his hand hovering over his thigh, the threat obvious.

'Did you know that an arsonist was going to burn down Napier's Farm with me in it?'

Klein shook his head, his surprise apparently genuine. 'No, no . . . Napier's already left town. Mexico. We were all heading there. He's out making the arrangements.'

'Looks like 38 double-crossed the lot of you.' Whoever had dug that hole in Napier's basement didn't know the house was going to be burned down. 'So who the hell *is* 38?'

Klein shook his head, as Entwistle had expected.

He stood up and stretched. They were hopelessly outnumbered and they had lost the element of surprise. And despite the now real threat to hostages, there was nothing practical the three of them could achieve – any attempted assault would be met with deadly force.

'Who else is involved?' he continued, picking up a piece of paper and fishing in his top pocket for a pen. 'I want names, now. All of them.'

In the bathroom, Maribeth finished rubbing her hair with a towel and leaned back against the door, exhausted. Sunlight reflected off a perfume bottle on the shelf. At first she blinked at its harsh glare, but then she found herself focusing her gaze on it, as if its brilliance triggered something in her mind.

How long she stared at that light, she did not know; like an epileptic experiencing *petit mal*, she was transfixed. Time became irrelevant, her circumstances secondary until, finally, a sound outside attracted her attention and she forced herself to look away from the consuming brightness. In that same moment she felt a desperate sadness: as if the light had meant something *good*.

Maybe she was losing her mind ... but even that gloomy thought could not shake her conviction that such a light would somehow represent safety for her.

She grabbed a hairbrush and made her way back to the main room. As she entered, combing tangles out of her wet hair, she heard Klein reeling off a string of names that had both Entwistle and Greg gasping in surprise. Just about everyone with any influence in the town of Firefall was mentioned.

'What's this?' she asked, hearing the name of her own school principal.

'All the local people who are in on this shit,' explained Greg.

'What?'

Entwistle said, 'They were rounded up, spirited away – then they changed into their goddam uniforms. When this ends, they'll change back, and no one else will be the wiser. All we would ever know is that there were a lot of hooded intruders wearing a lot of different numbers.' He turned back to Klein. 'Is that all of them?'

The man paused for thought, then added, 'No, there's a couple more. Tobe Lillywhite – his wife's dying and he needs the money to take her on one last trip. And there's Bill Hoxteth, Crane Digby, and Hal Campbell.'

'And they're all out there now, dressed up, pretending—?'

Greg interrupted her. 'Hal Campbell? You mean Summer Campbell's dad?'

'Yes. His motel is—'

Greg grabbed the man by the neck as if to throttle him. 'Campbell and his daughter got rounded up, and you mean to say that slime is now out there playing some kinda terrorist? Where the fuck were they taken?'

Klein could scarcely breathe and looked desperately to Entwistle for help. But Entwistle just shrugged. He was too busy absorbing the sheer scale of this conspiracy.

'Where did he take her?' demanded Greg again.

'To the school.'

Greg gave the man's throat an extra squeeze, then dropped him.

'You mean there are people being detained at my school?' said Maribeth, her earlier thoughts confirmed. 'And children too?'

The man gasped a yes.

Greg and Maribeth stared at each other, then at Entwistle.

'Oh no,' said Entwistle. 'No way.'

Twenty-six

'I can't believe I agreed to this,' said Entwistle.

'Well, what else are we going to do? Just sit at home and watch the news?' asked Maribeth.

'Or go raid the Town Hall?' said Greg.

'OK, but what do you plan on *doing* at the school?'

Entwistle was doing the rowing; he sat facing Greg and Maribeth. They had found a small dinghy at the bottom of the Timmons' garden, and Greg had persuaded them both that if they kept inshore they should be able to reach the playing field behind the school without being seen.

'What about men on the rig?' Entwistle had asked, pointing across three hundred yards to the ugly structure rising in the middle of the Hole.

'There are no windows on that hut, look, so anyone who sees us will have to be visible to us, too – and if we have field glasses we'll spot them first.'

And that's exactly what they had done, Greg finding the glasses in Stan Timmons' den. They had then tied up Klein and calmed him with a promise that they would send him medical help as soon as it was safe.

'But what if you get killed and I'm left here unable to move?' he had bleated.

'To be honest,' Entwistle had said, 'I couldn't give a shit. It's your fault you're here, not mine. In fact the only reason you're alive at all is because we risked our asses getting you out, so you sit quiet and be grateful.'

The school lay a quarter of the way around the circumference of the Hole from the Timmons' house, and they were now over halfway there.

'How many people did Klein name to you?' asked Maribeth, still finding it hard to believe so many people she had known and trusted could prove so hugely dishonest.

'About twenty,' said Entwistle between oar strokes. 'But he may have left out some, so call it twenty-five – plus the outsiders. Could be anything up to fifty of them, though only the pros will be a problem.'

'Don't bank on it,' said Greg. 'Campbell's mad enough to start shooting.'

'To get involved with this they must have been desperate,' agreed Maribeth. 'If they get caught, they'll get really long sentences, which means some of them'll have nothing to lose.'

'Corner a dog and he'll turn crazy,' added Greg.

Entwistle thought through that list and assessed how those people might react if they knew they risked spending the rest of their lives in prison. He supposed most of them would in fact surrender, and take their punishment, but unpredictable men like Hal Campbell and Taylor Ash might prefer to shoot it out. He wondered if he could bring himself to shoot them first, if threatened. He looked at Greg and Maribeth in front of him; a kid and a schoolmarm, both of them heading for an unknown situation and motivated by love: the boy for his girl, and Maribeth for her children. His admiration for this woman continued to grow. How he wished they could have met under less trying circumstances – like during a tornado or a flash flood! So yes, by Christ, he would shoot – and also for love. For the love of justice: it was his job.

They were now within sight of the school buildings, their first obstacle being a ten-foot-high chain link fence erected to stop children wandering unsupervised down to the edge of the Hole. They must try to find a way under it, because if they attempted to climb over they would be sitting ducks – never mind them getting across the fifty yards of gently sloping open ground to the rear of the school.

'Maribeth, do you know any other way in, without climbing that fence?'

She shook her head. 'Not unless you go in through the front or via a neighbouring property.'

What lay on this side of the school? Ah yes, Ed Rickenbacker's house. Entwistle guessed there would be conspirators inside. They might as well try gaining access via the Town Hall.

He had stopped rowing. 'We need to think this—'

'You in the boat! Stop!'

Entwistle spun to his right. Two hooded men in black, numbers 44 and 79, stood about eight feet above them on the bank among waist-high reeds, their rifles aiming down at the boat.

'Throw us your line, careful now,' said 79.

Entwistle nodded at Maribeth and she tossed the line to the bank as best she could. It sank into the reeds and 44 stooped down and snagged it, then slowly hauled the dinghy to the side of the lake.

'Get out, all of you: the woman first, the nigger next,' ordered 79.

Entwistle glanced at Greg and saw him getting angry. *Don't try anything stupid, kid,* he thought. *Not now. Wait and see, wait and see . . .*

As Maribeth stood up, the boat started rocking, and she stumbled in trying to find her feet. Then she stepped up onto the stern and stretched out her hand to 44.

'Help me, please.'

Number 44 slung the rifle over his back and took a step down towards her. He grasped her hand and pulled.

Entwistle's eyes locked with Greg's, then shifted down to the field glasses the boy still held in his hand. 'Where are you taking us?' he said.

Number 79 stared at him. 'Wouldn't you like—?'

The field glasses hit him full in the face, just as Maribeth jerked hard on 44's hand and brought him tumbling headlong into the boat, where Entwistle rabbit-punched him on the back of the neck.

Greg clambered quickly out of the boat and up the bank, and started punching at the moaning and no doubt bloodied face of 79. BASTARD BASTARD BASTARD! Entwistle made no attempt to stop him this time.

Instead, pulling the rifle from under the unconscious 44, he helped Maribeth out of the dinghy and onto the shore. By the time they reached Greg, the boy had exhausted himself, and 79 lay very still.

'Is he dead?' asked Maribeth, nervously.

'Let's not find out,' said Entwistle. 'Grab his rifle, and keep low.'

They crept up through the unkempt backyard of Rickenbacker's house until they could see clearly the shaded windows of its upper floor, and below them an open vista of the lounge, with its floor-to-ceiling plate glass. Inside were at least two men in black, but both with their masks off. Greg rolled back down to 79 and retrieved the field glasses, then wormed his way back up to join his two companions.

Focusing them, he identified Vent Collins, the local savings-and-loan manager, and Will Packer, owner of a dry-cleaning franchise. 'Looks like Traitor Central here.'

What now? thought Entwistle. Even if they could break into the school, with its unknown number of guards, they were slap bang next to one of the conspirators' headquarters. At the first sign of trouble, they'd all be out on top of them in seconds – and although the two men they could see were locals, that didn't mean there weren't professionals elsewhere inside the house.

Entwistle glanced across at the boathouse-cum-garage. Rickenbacker had extended his original double garage to incorporate a boathouse with a steep cement slipway down which he would launch his speedboat directly into the Hole. The rear doors facing the lake lay open, which might give them access to first the garage and then the house.

'The boathouse,' he whispered. 'We'll try there first.'

As quietly as they could, all three worked their way

through the grass to the cement slipway and tumbled onto the hard surface, stifling groans of pain. Then they crawled on hands and knees up its steep gradient.

Ahead of them could be seen the blunt rear of a blue speedboat resting on its wheeled trailer, the Mercury outboard motor glinting in the morning sunlight. But beyond that lay darkness, since the garage-type doors at the front of the building were obviously closed.

Having reached the boat, they slumped down to recover their breath, then Entwistle motioned them to stay put while he scouted ahead in the darkened building. He considered it safe to stand up now, being shielded by the open doors from sight of the house, so he walked the length of the speedboat, mockingly named *Laura Norder* (presumably for 'Law and Order'), and on into the rest of the building.

There was a dinghy strung up to the roof at head height, so he had to duck to reach the folding double doors at the rear of the boathouse which divided it from the garage beyond. These doors were constructed to slide on rollers, first to each side and then back around the inside walls of the boathouse, and Entwistle guessed they would be noisy. But if he was to make any progress, he knew he had to risk opening one of them. So, grabbing the handle of the right-hand door, he gently pulled it to one side, and was rewarded by a twelve-inch-wide strip of light running from floor to ceiling – and a rusty shriek.

Ducking back into the darkness, he held his breath as he waited for someone to come and investigate. After several seconds of hearing no voices or footsteps, he decided the garage itself must be empty, so he braved a glance inside – and wished he hadn't.

The front doors of the garage were also closed, and the light he had seen was provided by a neon strip in the ceiling, its harsh white light revealing in all their ugliness a stack of hand-held missile launchers piled beside a green open-top ex-army Jeep.

At first Entwistle couldn't believe his eyes, but he forced himself forward to confirm his initial impression. He didn't know the names or makes, but he knew these green tubes would be capable of downing a helicopter or taking out a car. Surrounding the half-dozen launchers were boxes of ammunition and other heavy firepower – not forgetting the large machine-gun mounted on the back of the Jeep. What on earth were they planning here? And how long had all this stuff been stashed in Rickenbacker's garage? He'd had dinner with the man not three days before, and a fortnight before that – but on neither occasion had he been inside the garage. Could this gear have been here then? How honest had Ed been back in the Town Hall?

One thing now was certain, however: this kind of firepower meant people involved to whom killing would mean nothing – which meant that *no one* in Firefall meant anything to them. Kill one hostage, kill a hundred, the penalty would still be life imprisonment if caught, and each of these people would do anything it took to avoid that. Entwistle wanted to cry out his anger but knew that would be suicide, so instead he steadied his breathing and crept quickly back to Maribeth and Greg.

'They look ready for World War III . . . There's nothing we can do, and if they suspect we're here, they'll come ready to shoot – and not give a damn who else might get in the way.'

'You're saying—'

'I'm saying that so far we've been lucky. From now on we stay out of their way. Innocent people will get hurt if we interfere further.'

'But the schoolchildren . . .?' said Maribeth.

'We go into that school,' said Entwistle, hating himself for sounding so defeatist, 'and they *will* get hurt, never mind what happens to us. It's one thing to want to commit suicide; another entirely to get other people killed in the process.'

Greg and Maribeth stared back at him, indecision and frustration playing on their faces.

'And those two we decked – soon as they're missed, they'll know we've been here, so we gotta leave *now*.'

'But—'

'No buts, Maribeth. As long as we're alive, those kids stay alive, and we might be able to help them in some other way, but trying to get in there now . . .'

'OK.' Greg let out a deep sigh. 'You're the boss. But if anything bad happens to Summer, I swear I'll kill any of those motherfuckers I can find.'

'And I'll join you, but for now—'

Just then they heard another shot, from the direction of the Town Hall.

'Hostage?' said Maribeth, still scarcely believing what was happening.

Entwistle slumped to his knees, feeling completely

powerless, unable to help *anyone* for fear of endangering them. It was a nauseating realization that the best thing for all concerned would be if the three of them just lay down and let events take their course. Then there came a shout from inside the garage. Oh no, he'd left the sliding door open.

There was nowhere to run except down the landing and into the lake but, without thinking, Entwistle sprinted back into the body of the boathouse just as one of the big doors on the right was cranked open, its runners providing noisy resistance.

'Someone's been here. That door was shut,' said a voice.

'OK, OK, just get the damn thing open – give us some light,' said a second.

Entwistle ducked behind the still-closed left-hand door as light flooded the boathouse.

Two shadows were cast across the rear of the *Laura Norder*. He might be able to jump one of them, but not both, and the light would soon reveal Maribeth and Greg, who had nowhere to hide. Of course he could also shoot them – but that would attract reinforcements, and a firefight would mean certain death for all three fugitives.

One man now edged into the boathouse, carrying his machine-gun in front of him, with number 53 on his chest. Entwistle glanced around. Were there any knives? Maybe if he was quick . . .

He spotted a pulley and a rope. His eyes followed the rope up to the ceiling, where another pulley hung over a stowed dinghy. That might work. He grabbed the loose end of the rope, tugged it free, and let go.

The boat was strung up at each end, and luckily

Entwistle had loosened the end nearest to the Hole. The result was that the boat swung suddenly down and hit both numbered men with the impact of a speeding car, sending them crashing back into the garage, where they fell among the weaponry.

Dodging the dinghy as it swung back and forth, Entwistle charged into the garage to check on his victims. One lay on his back cruciform, his head at a strange angle; the other rolled about clutching at his nose, which pumped blood through his fingers like a faucet. Entwistle immediately made things worse for him by smashing the butt of his rifle into the man's hands until he stopped squirming. *Now what?* he thought, his heart hammering so hard he couldn't hold his rifle steady.

He heard more shouting, and looking about he decided he might as well go the whole hog. He grabbed up a couple of the missiles and rushed back through the boathouse.

'Quick! Get in the speedboat!'

Neither Greg nor Maribeth wasted time arguing, even though the boat still rested on its trailer. As they climbed into the *Laura Norder*, Entwistle dumped the two LAW missiles on the rear seat.

'No key,' said Greg.

'Don't tell me *you* can't hot-wire a car!' growled Entwistle, following them on board.

'This is a boat!'

'Same principle, Greg.'

'Oh. Right . . .'

Ten seconds later – and just as several black-hoods exploded out of the house, some into the garage, others into the garden – Greg had the engine gunning, the propeller spinning furiously.

'Need water!' he shouted above the high-pitched whine.

'Get it into reverse and hold on!' shouted Entwistle as he sprawled over the boat's wooden prow and pulled up the brake handle on the trailer. The boat and trailer instantly began to trundle down the steep slipway.

Entwistle had overbalanced and lost his rifle. He was about to right himself when the boat hit the water, and he was thrown over the small windshield and straight into Maribeth.

The boat's propeller grabbed the surface of the lake and finally hauled it off the trailer backwards, water immediately threatening to swamp the vessel: Greg spun the steering wheel to the left, then slammed into forward gear, unbalancing Maribeth and Entwistle once again.

Even above the roar of the motor they could hear the crack of rifles. Entwistle sat upright and found himself facing back towards the garden and boathouse, where he saw four men, all firing, their shots splashing in the water all around the boat and a couple pinging off its rear. He concentrated on finding his own weapons, but as his hand found their other rifle he saw the dinghy he had dropped on the first men come sliding down the ramp and splash into the water. Behind it emerged the Jeep, which reversed to a halt and its driver climbed over his seat to the heavy-duty machine-gun fixed on its rear.

Holy Jesus, if that got them in its sights, they'd be shredded.

'Move it!' he bawled to Greg.

'We're at the max now!' he protested.

The distance between the boat and their pursuers was increasing all the time, but that machine-gun would be able to reach them anywhere on the whole damn lake.

'Head for the rig!' Entwistle shouted.

'But that'll make us sitting targets!' yelled Maribeth.

'They'll not use that gun once we're on the rig. Not with their own men on board there.'

'Their own men – you said it.'

'One crisis at a time, girl!'

But he doubted they would make it there in time, anyway. Already the driver was settling the machine-gun braces on his shoulders and getting a bead on them.

Entwistle looked down at the LAW missiles: their innocent green tubes hid real power. Could he? It was absurd, ludicrous, but it was their last chance.

He grabbed up one of them, tried to remember what they did in the movies, then gave up and read the instructions on the pack itself.

'Weave!' he shouted to Greg. 'Don't let them get a line on us.'

He pulled out the retainer at the end and extended both ends of the tube, then flipped up the top sight.

The men on shore stopped firing to watch their comrade-in-arms let off a burst of machine-gun bullets. They slapped into the water thirty yards away, but Entwistle knew it would find the correct range soon enough.

Fumbling to find the trigger on top of the launcher, he took aim. Greg looked back at him, astonished.

'Make sure you're not directly behind this thing,'

Entwistle warned, but Glen and Maribeth were already leaning to opposite sides of the boat as Entwistle took aim.

'I don't believe I'm fucking doing this . . .'

Bullets now slashed up the water barely a foot from their starboard side as he depressed the trigger. The missile erupted deafeningly, its recoil pushing him back over the front seat so that he couldn't follow its course.

But Maribeth and Greg could see it – and groaned as it passed right over the Jeep and into the boathouse, as the seemingly unfazed machine-gunner sent a line of bullets thunking straight for them.

As there was a sudden muffled explosion, Greg hurled himself at the wheel and the boat turned so sharply they almost fell out of it, more bullets slicing up the water where they should have been. There was another roar, more machine-gun fire, then a huge cracking explosion that boomed across the Hole like thunder.

All three looked back in time to see a fireball surge fifty feet into the air, blowing out all the windows in the house and hurling the four gunmen and the Jeep with its machine-gunner into the lake, followed by a hailstorm of shrapnel peppering everything within a hundred-yard radius – the house, the garden, the lake, and the school.

The sound of breaking glass and the rattle of metal on brickwork was accompanied by the hungry roar of flames as they swarmed over the boathouse and began to devour dry grass in the garden and even the roof of Rickenbacker's house.

Suddenly everything fell quiet bar the odd bang and zing, as the fireball dissipated and all that was left was a large smudge of thick black smoke curling eastwards over the school and out towards the top edge of town.

'Hellation Sunday,' mumbled Maribeth as she watched this destruction, praying that those trapped in the school had been spared. Thankfully there were few windows on that side of the building, but the noise . . .

'That's one for the good guys,' said Greg.

Entwistle could only sit and stare dumbfounded at what his index finger had achieved with a single squeeze. Jesus Christ, what a mess. And what an adrenalin rush!

'Don't think *they'll* be bothering us any more.'

He couldn't see any men surfacing amid the debris still raining down, and he didn't care. Play with fire, you get burned – literally. He turned back to Greg, who was also gaping at the burning boathouse.

Jesus!

Entwistle lunged over the driver's seat to grab the steering wheel and yank it hard left. Greg was surprised by his sudden action, but then realized they were within feet of the rig.

'Kill the motor!' yelled Entwistle, but the force of the turn had thrown Greg too far right, so he lost his grip and tumbled out of the boat.

It was Maribeth instead who reached over to the throttle and slammed it shut, the boat's prow immediately settling, till it began to idle in a circle. But even as Entwistle and Maribeth searched the water for Greg, two guards emerged on the rig thirty feet to their right and took aim. Both were obviously torn between gaping at the explosion and studying the strange speedboat.

'What the fuck happened?' one of them yelled.

For a moment Entwistle couldn't understand why they weren't already shooting, but then he remembered Maribeth's black uniform and that he too was still dressed as one of them, albeit without a hood.

'FBI hit us!'

'FBI? How the—?'

'You're asking *me*? All I know is a dozen guys in blue with FBI written all over them stormed the place! We only just got to the boat in time!'

'Shit! What do we do now?'

'You could give us a hand!'

'Hell, no, you can give us the boat!'

'What?'

'I ain't staying here with the Feds there on shore. Now get out of that goddam boat!'

Entwistle stood up and raised his hands. If they wanted the boat, they could have it. He reached for a line and tossed it to one of them, who grabbed it and hauled them in to the small pontoon on the west side of the rig cabin.

'Now step out!'

'Hey, ain't we coming with you?' said Entwistle.

'Looks like you ain't.'

Entwistle took hold of Maribeth's hand to help her onto the pontoon, but then one of the guards cocked his rifle.

'Ain't been no women on this deal.'

Not again, thought Maribeth.

'Like you know everyone personally?' she snarled. 'Get me off this damn boat!'

Number 34 didn't know how to react, but 97 nudged him and he took Maribeth's hand.

She pulled herself up onto the dock, grunted her thanks, and waited for Entwistle. But then 97 suddenly aimed his rifle.

'I know you. You're a fucking police deputy.'

'Yeah, but when your sheriff's the bossman, who's to argue?'

'I said you didn't know everyone,' said Maribeth.

Entwistle stood up on the pontoon. 'I thought we were all on the same side.'

'Well, there's sides and there's sides,' said 97, still aiming at Entwistle's head.

Entwistle noticed the man's finger pull on the trigger.

Maribeth screamed.

A hand suddenly came up between the planks of the pontoon. It grabbed 97's ankle and tugged him sufficiently off balance so that his shot missed Entwistle's head by twelve precious inches. As the black-hooded man glanced down to see what had happened, Maribeth launched herself at him, head-butting him in the stomach and sending him crashing into the side of the rig cabin.

Number 34 raised his rifle too late to fire at the charging Entwistle. He was knocked off the pontoon into the speedboat, where he cracked his head on the floor and flopped senseless over the seats. Entwistle then turned and grabbed the head of the winded 97 and slammed it repeatedly into the metal wall of the cabin until his body went limp and he fell onto the blood-splattered pontoon.

Maribeth witnessed this pummelling with satisfaction, no longer surprised at her heartless reaction to such violence enacted on her enemies. Then she knelt down and helped the spluttering Greg to gain a purchase on the pontoon, so that he could pull himself out of the water.

Once they had him on the pontoon, Entwistle hauled the boy upright. He then grabbed for 97's rifle – 34's gun unfortunately having fallen into the water.

'We don't know how many are in here,' warned Maribeth.

'Let's secure the boat,' said Entwistle.

But as they examined it, they could see that 97 had holed the *Laura Norder* with his stray shot, which meant it could end up sinking and make them easy pickings for anyone yet to emerge from the cabin.

'Got to deal with this first,' said Entwistle, tapping the cabin wall. 'Just stand back. If I don't come out, do what you can to escape with the boat.'

'We can't leave you!'

'Do as I say. If it's safe in here, we'll decide what to do next, but if it isn't—'

They heard the sudden whine of a motor. Spinning round, they saw another boat heading along the length of the Fun Pier, three men in it, all raising their weapons.

'No choice now,' said Maribeth, approaching the door.

'Do it!' spluttered Greg, dragging himself fully upright as he heard machine-gun fire from the approaching vessel.

Entwistle kicked open the solid metal door and ran inside. He dived to the floor and rolled, then came up onto his knees to find the room empty.

Maribeth entered after him, Greg last, barely managing to slam the door shut before bullets hit metal and thudded along the outside of the cabin. The three of them hunkered away from the door and gasped for breath as they surveyed their new surroundings.

The room was surprisingly narrow, some twenty-five feet long by ten feet wide; the entrance door was set in the middle of its long side. All the surfaces – floor, walls, ceiling – were of metal, and there were no windows. Two of the giant rig's legs descended through the ceiling and straddled the large metal table in the centre of the room. Extending around all sides of the room were control panels and computer consoles, while one wall featured a large chart that looked like a geological survey of the Hole itself. There were also satellite photographs, a couple of red-plastic shell chairs, and smaller tables covered with charts and blueprints. There was even a television and two wall clocks. None of the three new arrivals was surprised to find that both the latter had suddenly stopped.

At the far end of the room there was a second door which Entwistle presumed would belong to the toilet. He wondered if anyone might be hiding there. He strode over and grabbed the handle of the mystery door and pulled it open, stepping aside as the interior was revealed. He cautiously peeked inside.

Maribeth caught the puzzled look on his face and she too braved a look. *Hellation in a nightdress . . .*

Greg caught sight of Maribeth's similar surprise, and all three of them crowded at the door and stared inside.

Whatever they had expected – a toilet, a storeroom, even a kitchen – none of them would have guessed it was an elevator shaft.

Twenty-seven

Collingwood was seated in a helicopter, an FBI MD 500E, its rotor spinning slowly above. Hartsby was by his side, talking into his headset. Two grim-faced agents dressed in black sat opposite them, one clutching a high-powered rifle with a telescopic sight.

'You sure? . . . Jesus, they got away? . . . They what? . . . Missiles? For Christ's sake, man, you're supposed to be a professional. I've seen better . . . Yeah, OK. Where? . . . Who are they? Looks like we'll have to adapt . . . No! I'll do it.'

He tossed the headset aside. 'Got a job for you,' he said without looking up.

Del didn't answer, still numb from the recent murder of his wife – and the subsequent incident with Hartsby's gun. Hartsby had eventually pocketed the revolver, but it seemed plain that he would have easily blown Del's brains out then, had he not had some further use for him.

'Seems there are three troublemakers on the loose,' Hartsby shouted over the roar of the whirring rotor blades. 'The same ones who entered the sewer. They're seriously fucking with the situation, and they're responsible for all those explosions we've been hearing. So I want you to bring them out.'

'What?' Del shouted back.

'You'll take this chopper and these two agents, and you'll rendezvous with those pests and pick them up. Here, I've got their names.'

Hartsby handed Collingwood a sheet of paper containing three names written in large, looping letters.

'Why should I, you bastard?'

'Because you'll be saving those same pests' lives!' Hartsby sneered.

Del didn't much care any longer. 'What about the conspirators?'

'Who the hell do you think I was talking to just now? Number 38 and his team guarantee they won't attack as long as you fly right in, rescue these three morons, and bring them straight out again.'

'Where do we find them?'

'They've got themselves out onto the drilling rig. Now, that rig is wired with explosives and there's a possibility they'll accidentally blow the damn thing up – while 38's men can't make an assault there for fear of doing the same.'

'So it's stalemate.'

'How much patience do you think those hooded guys have? Sooner or later they'll attack that rig, whatever the consequences – and they'll *still* be holding your precious hostages. But it's the rig I'm primarily concerned about. So go get those fuckers out.'

Del stared back defiantly, and Hartsby leaned over to his ear.

'Want me to let you in on a little secret, Collingwood?' he bellowed. 'It's something to do with your so-called career. You remember Coly, Nebraska, five years ago? And Dr Birtles' unfortunate demise?'

'*You* had me taken off that case?' yelled Del in amazement.

'Yes. I doubt you would have turned up anything but I couldn't afford the risk.'

'And my career was—'

'Fucked? All wars have their victims, Collingwood. You got caught in the crossfire. Just like today, in fact.' Hartsby smiled evilly.

'You bastard . . . But why? What was he researching? Something to do with time, wasn't it?'

'He had a big mouth. He made a breakthrough he couldn't keep quiet about. He was meant to be working on a project for me. I had no alternative, really. Just as I have no alternative here.' Hartsby gave a short laugh. 'By the way, who do you think got you assigned here in time to get involved in today's little festivities?'

Del was aghast, unable to respond, suddenly aware that the entire course of his career had been determined by the whims of one evil, scheming little man.

Hartsby turned to the agent with the rifle and tapped him on the knee. 'Time?' he mouthed.

The agent flashed him his wristwatch. Hartsby nodded, stepped down from the helicopter, and waved it away.

As it lifted off, he caught sight of the armed agent shaking his wrist and peering at his wristwatch – as if it had suddenly stopped.

No, it can't be! thought Hartsby. There was no way he himself was going to go out to that rig.

Collingwood? But he knew nothing: couldn't even dream of what was there. There was no need to worry. True, the stopping of clocks and watches was a side effect, but this time it had to be pure coincidence.

And then he remembered his Rolex failing . . . and he realized Collingwood *was* somehow responsible. Damn, damn, damn! He must find a radio and stop him. Collingwood might be in the dark, but the watches themselves didn't lie. Collingwood was obviously much too close to finding the truth.

Up in the helicopter, still ignorant of Hartsby's sudden panic, Del looked out glumly on the Wyoming countryside. They flew on, over the parking lot that had recently been a US highway, and then dived towards the seemingly empty town of Firefall.

He felt totally lost. Whatever else happened, his life was over. Gloria was dead, and he didn't have long left himself – and now the three brave souls who had done their best to save their town were about to be 'rescued' at the behest of the very ones they had been fighting.

Del's duty now was to stay alive, so that he could revenge himself – and all those who had died – on the man he now realized was responsible. Unfortunately, the agents flying with him were about to receive radio orders to jettison Collingwood from the helicopter.

Twenty-eight

It was small – only big enough for three people at most – but it was an elevator none the less.

'What the hell is this doing here? It's meant to be an oil rig, not a department store!' said an astonished Greg.

'They don't have elevators in oil rigs, do they?' added Maribeth, knowing she was stating the obvious.

Outside the firing had stopped – the cabin's metal walls were apparently too strong to be penetrated by bullets – but they could hear the boat's motor getting closer, and soon the rig was going to be boarded.

Entwistle slowly turned and surveyed the main room, which obviously did not take up the whole of the cabin. The point in the floor where the drill-hole and the well-head should be was obviously where this elevator was located. Looking up, he could see that the roof of the cabin must have been fitted after the drilling was completed, thus shielding off inside activities from prying eyes whilst continuing the illusion that this was a regular oil rig. Presumably the original drill-hole had been widened to accommodate the elevator shaft, and its running gear hidden horizontally within the rest of the cabin's structure. But why an elevator? Elevators travelled up or down, but surely always to *some* other place – which meant this elevator must disgorge its passengers into another space somewhere below them. But it sure as hell wasn't basement parking.

They heard a bump outside. The boat had arrived. Entwistle put a finger to his lips.

'Get away from the door, and into the corners.'

As he himself moved towards one corner, he suddenly noticed a hatch in the roof. Locating a metal stepladder clipped to the wall, he set it upright and climbed up to investigate the hatch. Cautiously he cracked it open a couple of inches, lowering it again quickly.

'They've wired the whole place with dynamite,' he announced grimly.

'You mean the rig's rigged,' said Greg, spinning round to examine all four walls.

'Yes, all four struts of the rig are wired.'

Entwistle cursed silently. Their opponents outside would need only to take careful aim from the shore and their troubles would be over. But then again, if their ultimatum included the threat of blowing up the rig, they wouldn't want to jeopardize their position too soon, would they? Very carefully he raised the hatch again and looked out onto the cabin's flat metal roof.

To his immediate right one of the rig's legs soared a hundred feet above him. Attached to it, a couple of feet above roof level, several sticks of dynamite were clearly visible. Entwistle pushed himself further out of the hatch, but lay forward on the roof so he remained out of sight of the men in the boat below.

He squirmed over to the nearby rig leg and reached up towards the dynamite. It was so securely taped to the leg that he would need to cut it free. He rolled back towards the hatch.

'Need a knife,' he hissed, and a few seconds later was handed a penknife.

Lying on his back he carefully sliced the industrial tape and eventually pulled free a bundle of three explosives. He then heard feet start to move about on the pontoon deck below, and realized he needed to distract them. Again he leaned down into the hatch.

'Need me a fuse – anything that'll light. And a rifle too.'

Maribeth handed him their only weapon, aware that this left the rest of them unarmed. Meanwhile Greg was hunting for a fuse, but could not find anything remotely useful. Just as he started to break the bad news, bullets began punishing the lock on the door.

Entwistle rolled back to the nearby strut and cut off a length of the electric fuse that connected the explosives then ran from leg to leg and over one side of the cabin roof. He jammed this in between the three sticks of dynamite, then pulled himself to the very edge of the roof to look down at three armed men pumping bullets into the door. Luckily it was made of reinforced steel, but even that could not hold out much longer.

Rising on his knees, he brandished the dynamite aloft.

'Hey, boys!' he shouted. 'Recognize this stuff?'

He waved the explosive long enough for them to

identify it, then tossed it to the deck between them. All three scattered: one straight into the water, the other two scrambling in opposite directions along the pontoon.

Entwistle stood up and took aim, firing at the fleeing figure on the right just as he reached the corner of the cabin. Caught in the side, the man was spun out onto their half-sunken speedboat, bouncing off it into the water and screaming in agony.

Entwistle then whipped round to fire at the other retreating black-clad gunman, hitting him in the shoulder and sending him crashing onto the pontoon deck.

The man in the water was desperately struggling to stay afloat, plainly no swimmer.

'Asshole,' murmured Entwistle, turning back to the one he had hit in the shoulder, who was number 44.

The wounded man had rolled over onto his back and was now trying to reach the comparative safety of the water. Entwistle let him go unimpeded, then eased himself to the edge of the roof. For a moment he dangled his legs over the side, then dropped himself to the pontoon deck, making straight for the cabin door.

'It's me!' he shouted. 'Entwistle!'

As the door was unbolted he grabbed two of the discarded rifles and stepped inside, slamming the door behind him.

'Got ourselves a breathing space but that's it. Best thing would be to grab their boat and make a break for the shore.'

They lined up behind Entwistle as he checked the situation outside by opening the door a crack. All three terrorists were now thrashing about in the water and hardly posed any threat. Entwistle ducked through the cabin entrance and round to the right; the others followed closely. As they reached the boat – a twenty-foot-long twin-engine yellow model – a helicopter suddenly zoomed overhead from beyond the rig, whipping up the water all about them. Then it turned and hovered side-on, its landing gear only inches from two of the floundering gunmen.

Entwistle didn't know which way to run. He was about to head back to the meagre sanctuary of the control room when a voice boomed out.

'Freeze! This is the FBI. Put down your weapons and face the wall. This is the FBI! Drop your weapons or we fire!'

Entwistle couldn't believe his luck. The government had finally made a move. He stared up at the blue and grey helicopter, recognized the FBI emblem on its nose, observed the marksman training a rifle on him, and gratefully lowered his own rifle to the deck. Raising his hands and backing against the wall, he gestured for the others to do likewise. The FBI might be on their side, but all three of them were still dressed like the masked conspirators, so it was vital to do exactly as ordered.

'Thank Christ,' said Entwistle over and over. The nightmare was finally over – and he had survived.

Greg squinted up at the men in the helicopter, never so happy to see the law arrive, and he could not help raising a smile.

Then the helicopter marksman opened fire.

Twenty-nine

The first shot hit Greg's right hand, the second scored a line across the left side of his head. Luckily the third one missed, as did the fourth. The fifth hit Maribeth's right hand, severing two fingers. The sixth and seventh missed again, but the eighth and ninth struck Entwistle on his right shoulder and ear. All three astonished targets fell to their knees and began to scramble over each other to escape imminent execution.

More shots rang out, embedding themselves in the metal wall just above their heads – and then the firing suddenly stopped. The helicopter's engine roared as it rose sharply into the air, blades clattering furiously. But this strange manoeuvre, and a flurry of activity in its cockpit, signified nothing to those on the pontoon as each, in a private hell of pain, tried desperately to find some way out of the firing line.

First Greg toppled into the lake, then Maribeth dived in after him; but the shock and pain of cold water on raw flesh was so stunning that she flipped over and began swallowing water.

Entwistle forced himself to begin a long crawl towards the nearest corner of the cabin, though this would prove a futile refuge at one flick of the helicopter pilot's wrist.

Then his arm suddenly collapsed, mashing his face against the wet planking. He groaned and rolled over onto his good side, in time to see the helicopter rear up almost vertically and then fall back, its tail rotor chopping up the water of the Hole before flipping over onto one side, its blades whirring towards the rig as it continued to fall.

Entwistle lay frozen by the spectacle, his pain forgotten as he watched the main rotors come closer and closer like the Reaper's scythe. He could feel the wind shear, and hear the air ripped apart above the guttural protests of the helicopter's engine.

Then the mighty blades hit the pontoon's edge, slicing into it like a knife through butter, churning up a storm of splinters and angry white water. Once the monster hit the lake, it immediately started breaking apart and smashing off in all directions. One blade thudded into the deck just a foot from Entwistle's face before becoming embedded in the steel wall of the cabin. The other blades first shot up in the air, then began to fall like giant spears: only one onto the pontoon deck fortunately, the rest into the foaming lake as the helicopter cabin also crumpled into the water, the men inside it frantically waving for help.

There was a sudden silence as the motor drowned, then a deep explosion, more felt than heard . . . and then fifteen feet away the lake erupted, spewing water over Entwistle with almost enough force to wash him off the deck.

Above him he could hear the rig cracking ominously

and thought for a sickening moment that the whole structure was about to crash down on top of him. But then there was just the peaceful creaking of the pontoon as it rode the waves, and frequent splashes as helicopter fragments rained down around them.

Finally Entwistle forced himself to sit up, and he stared around at the scene of disaster. Already the machine itself had almost completely disappeared; all that remained were small pieces of unidentifiable wreckage and a bright, rainbow-coloured slick of aviation fuel. In this filthy flotsam he could see Greg bobbing gently, staring towards him uncomprehending. Entwistle at first feared the boy might be dead, cut off by a whirring blade below the waterline, but then came a cough and Greg spat out a gout of dark water, and he began to kick himself towards the rig.

Of Maribeth there was nothing to be seen.

Jesus Christ, after all this . . .

He was about to drop into the water to search for her, even though his shoulder would hardly take it, when there came a frenzied splashing and a flurry of arms – and not one but *two* heads suddenly surfaced. One of them was Maribeth, her distinctive red hair soaked almost black – and next to her a balding man.

Who the hell was this?

Reaching the pontoon first, Greg managed to pull himself up and lay flat, gasping and coughing. Next the unknown man reached the deck, supporting Maribeth under the chin with one hand while the fumbling fingers of his other struggled to find purchase. Entwistle leaned over and grasped Maribeth under the arms. As he hauled her out of the water, he realized with horror that she was not breathing.

Despite the continuing agony in his shoulder, he managed to roll her over quickly and began to administer artificial respiration. Meanwhile the stranger heaved himself onto the pontoon and remained on his knees, vomiting water.

Finally she coughed, and coughed again, then jerked onto her side and spewed up a gush of lake water and bile.

'Thank God, thank God,' gasped Entwistle, his own pain now irrelevant.

He could hear moaning from behind him and turned to see Greg crawling on hands and knees towards the newcomer, pain and shock and the clear intention of violence distorting his features. Entwistle stared at the mystery man, then felt the same rage come over him. He launched himself at the kneeling stranger in a pathetic flurry of bloodied fists and misdirected kicks, as both he and Greg vented their anger.

The victim of their combined rage remained curled up in the foetal position, perhaps as much from exhaustion as to protect himself, letting them do as they wished. But their energy was as depleted as his own, so their assault was unable to sustain itself for long.

The two aggressors finally slumped to the deck, coughing and groaning pitifully, their anger momentarily masked by pain and exhaustion. Then it was time for the lone survivor of the helicopter to give vent to his fury, as he forced himself onto his knees and bellowed at them.

'Finished now, you fuckers? I just saved your damn lives.'

'What d'you mean *saved*?' screamed Entwistle, almost finding energy to renew the attack. 'You were up in that damned chopper trying to kill us!'

'*They* were trying to kill you,' snarled the other. 'But how come it crashed before they succeeded? Because I clobbered the pilot. That was *me*, you bastard!'

Entwistle sat back and stared. The man was fiftyish with a big build; he was wearing a sodden suit and the only colour in his face was the red of his bloodshot eyes.

'But why?'

'Because they had no right to kill you – and they knew it.'

Greg moved over, wheezing phlegm. The stranger had grabbed his attention, too.

The man continued: 'They knew full well who you were. You are Sheriff's Deputy Entwistle, the lady is Ms Maribeth Hamilton, and this here is Gregory Henley.'

Entwistle said, 'That's right, but if they knew that why did they want to kill us?'

'Because you're *here*.'

Entwistle stared at him, then glanced at Maribeth, who was struggling to sit up.

'You mean here in Firefall?' he said at last.

'No, here on this rig.'

Entwistle stumbled over to Maribeth and helped her to her feet.

'I don't understand,' said Maribeth, trying to focus on what had just been said.

The man fished in his pocket and pulled out a soggy handkerchief. He leaned towards Maribeth and took hold of her damaged hand. She instantly cried out in pain, and Entwistle found himself raising a fist defensively.

'Your fingers . . . I'm sorry,' said the man. 'Look, we'd be better off inside. They'll still be watching us, so inside will be safer.'

The men turned to scan the shoreline, noticing increased activity of men and vehicles, then heard again the distinctive drone of a helicopter somewhere in the distance. They then lamely made their way to the cabin entrance. Once all were safely inside, the stranger slammed the door and bolted it.

'So who are you?' demanded Entwistle.

'Special Agent Del Collingwood, FBI.'

'But that was the FBI who started shooting at us—'

'Just a minute,' interrupted Maribeth, gritting her teeth against the pain. 'You said the FBI knew who we were. But how would they know?'

'Because they've been talking to the conspirators' leaders.'

'You mean to negotiate some kind of settlement?' said Entwistle.

'Or threaten to wipe the motherfuckers out?' added Greg.

'No, not at all,' said Collingwood patiently, as if addressing a kindergarten class. 'As in, those conspirators are working with the government.'

Thirty

'When I say the conspirators, I mean the leader,' said Del.

'Number 38?' said Entwistle.

'Yes. At some point whoever organized this incident contacted a professional mercenary for help; someone who helped him beef up his initial idea into a precision operation. But right from the start that same mercenary was in contact with a superior of mine called Hartsby.'

'Is he FBI?'

'No, he's more important, got more weight. And he knew exactly what was going to happen, right from the beginning.'

'But why? Why on earth let it happen? Why terrorize so many people, get those hostages killed, nearly get *us* killed?' asked Maribeth, the pain in her head growing.

'I don't know. All I do know is that Hartsby's more concerned about this oil rig than about you or the conspirators.'

'But everyone else thought it was about extorting money, even Rickenbacker,' said Entwistle.

'The Sheriff? *He* was in on it too?' said Del.

'And a whole load of locals,' Greg added.

'Well, they were all double-crossed the moment this number 38 became involved.'

'But the FBI are supposed to prevent this kind of thing!' said Entwistle.

'*I* know that, *you* know that, but Hartsby has a different opinion: in fact a different agenda.'

It took a while for everyone to absorb this information. Meanwhile they examined each other's wounds. Every one of them was injured, but most distressing was Maribeth's missing fingers. Though her hand was now tightly wrapped in a handkerchief, the thought was appalling, the pain for her unimaginable.

Del moved round the periphery of the room, checking on the panels and equipment, working out what each item did. Entwistle joined him as he reached the mystery door.

'There's an elevator in there,' he said.

'What?'

'An elevator.'

Entwistle pulled open the door to reveal the small metal room beyond.

'Why on earth . . .?'

A helicopter flew overhead, the roar of its engine slowly circling. They could also hear the sound of speedboat engines in the distance.

'What will they do now?' asked Maribeth, already knowing the answer.

'Storm the place and kill us all. They'll claim we were part of the conspiracy. Those uniforms are enough to convict you, especially when they discover your Sheriff organized it all. And me? I'll just not be found at all.'

'And we've really no chance of defending ourselves?' asked Greg.

'I'm sorry,' said Del. 'It seems I may have only delayed the inevitable.'

'And got yourself killed also.'

'I suspect that was only a matter of time.'

'Not a good pension prospect, the FBI?'

This elicited a bitter laugh from Del.

'What if we surrender now?' said Greg.

'There's no media out there to witness that they abide by the rules.'

Entwistle nodded. 'One thing: they obviously wanted us dead because we were out here on the rig, right? But why? Were they afraid we would destroy it?'

'No. Hartsby, who's in charge, knows you're not conspirators.'

'Right, so there must be something here he doesn't want us to find.'

'And it ain't the fact that the place is about to pump lead-free gas,' said Greg.

All four turned to look towards the mysterious elevator.

'There must be something down below,' said Maribeth finally.

As they stared in thought, renewed machine-gun fire raked the outside of the building.

Del ducked instinctively, but Entwistle clapped his shoulder reassuringly. 'I think the walls are bulletproof. Nothing's penetrated yet.'

'Odd, if it's only a temporary cabin.'

Entwistle shrugged, the pain in his shoulder making

him wince. 'Someone needs to go down in that thing and see what's there,' he said.

'I'll look see,' offered Greg.

'Take Maribeth with you.'

Maribeth didn't protest as Entwistle ushered her into the elevator. 'You're the educated one; so see if what you find down there makes any sense.'

He pushed the DOWN button – the elevator plainly had only one alternative stop – and stepped back as its doorless chamber began to descend.

The machine moved smoothly but slowly. It was clearly no makeshift apparatus but a piece of precision equipment designed to do more than simply transport workmen down to whatever lay below.

Maribeth leaned against one side, cradling her bleeding hand in the other, tears of pain moistening her face. Greg tried to offer sympathy.

As the muted whine of the winding gear slowly receded above them, their descent continued. What seemed to take an age was in fact just forty-five seconds. Eventually the bare cement shaft that slid up past the open side changed to excavated rock as its enclosed funnel broached the bottom of the lake.

The elevator came to a halt with a slight shudder and neon lights flickered into life, plainly triggered by the elevator's arrival. Both Greg and Maribeth found curiosity getting the better of their trepidation as they leaned out to take a better look.

Before them lay a room hewn out of the solid rock. It was about the size of a double garage, its ceiling no more than eight feet high. Illumination was provided by a continuous ring of fluorescent tubes running around the top of the surrounding wall. Near the centre of the room stood a cube, four feet square, of some kind of metal that was smooth and featureless and dull, giving off little reflection despite the brightness of the lights. Apart from this strange object, the room was empty except for a small video camera high up in one corner, pointed into the middle of the room.

'What on earth?' said Maribeth.

'No idea,' answered Greg.

They stepped out of the elevator and skirted the mysterious cube. It looked to be solid, so must be very heavy. A circuit of the room revealed that it was indeed a perfect cube – but nothing else.

Maribeth wanted to touch it but was scared. Her torn fingers were still bleeding onto the floor, but the initial sharp agony had softened to a relentless throbbing that was slightly more bearable. She felt light-headed and wondered if she might be about to faint. So she decided to slump down against a wall, where Greg soon joined her.

'So what *is* it?' said Maribeth.

He shook his head. 'Think we should go back up now?'

'Yes,' agreed Maribeth, but didn't move. She felt so tired.

Greg looked up at the video camera. 'With that thing they should be able to see it for themselves, up there.'

He finally forced himself up, and moved dizzily back to the elevator. Inside there were still just the two buttons, with arrows pointing up and down. Stepping back he noticed a small speaker grille set into the rock, a red button located underneath it.

He pressed it, tentatively.

'Hello? Entwistle? You hear me?'

Up in the control room, Greg's initial, nervous enquiry was drowned out by the racket of the circling helicopter. But his repeated message was noticed by Del, who gestured Entwistle towards a console with a microphone.

'Hello?' said Entwistle, pressing a TRANSMIT button.

'Hey, it's Greg.'

'What did you find down there?'

'Just a metal box about the size of a really big TV set. It's weird-looking. But nothing else. There's a video camera, too. See if you can switch it on.'

As the helicopter continued to circle closer, both Del and Entwistle studied the panel, which contained four video screens labelled separately: DOWN, ROOM, ROOF, SCAN.

'Down?' suggested Del.

Entwistle switched it on, and a black-and-white image of the room at the very base of the rig wobbled into life. It was just as Greg had described. They could also see Maribeth collapsed against a wall.

'Think that thing's a bomb?' asked Del.

'I've no idea. What do you say?' Entwistle turned to Del.

'Don't ask me. I'm as much in the dark as you.'

Entwistle switched on the other cameras in turn and was greeted first with a shot of his own back, next the view towards the smoking Town Hall across the water of the

Hole, and then a panning shot which followed the circling helicopter.

'Camera's moving of its own accord,' said Del. 'It's locked on that chopper.'

Del stared at the screen, recognized the machine. 'That's Hartsby's Huey,' he announced.

'That the guy fucking this all up?' enquired Entwistle.

'The same.'

'Think he's on board?' said Entwistle.

'He'd be a fool if he was.'

'Hey up there!' shouted Greg through the intercom. 'What should we do now?'

'Stay there till I call you,' said Entwistle. If he was honest he hadn't a clue what they should do.

Just then another radio crackled.

'Deputy Entwistle, can you hear me? This is Emile Hartsby, ACA. I think we should talk.'

'Do you think he knows *you're* here?' said Entwistle to Del.

'Maybe not. If he doesn't, that might give us an edge.'

'How?' said Entwistle.

'Because *I* know everything he says is a lie. And now *you* do.'

Entwistle nodded. He located the source of the call, and hit the TRANSMIT button.

'What do you want? And what the hell is ACA?'

'Part of the FBI.'

Del shook his head, negatively.

'We need a face-to-face,' Hartsby continued. 'We've nothing but admiration for the way you guys have been fighting the good fight here . . .'

Del shook his head again.

'... but enough's enough. Negotiations are at a delicate stage. We need to calm things down. Get you out—'

Del started to laugh.

'—and let the pros take over.'

'So what was that shit just then with the FBI chopper?'

'That wasn't the FBI.'

Del strode to the other end of the room and punched the wall.

'What do you mean?'

'One of our helicopters was hijacked by the conspirators. They wanted to take you out of the picture. Seems you took them out instead. Now they just want you *out*.'

'So what do *you* want?'

'I come in. We talk. We leave. You get a rest.'

Entwistle decided to play along. 'Sure as hell could do with some rest.'

'And you deserve it, son.'

Entwistle hated people who called him son. Only one man had ever earned that right. 'So what are you planning to do?'

'Me and my team will winch ourselves down.'

'No team. Just you.'

'Hey, Deputy, it's OK. We're all—'

'Just you.'

'Very well. I'll come down on the east side of the rig, and try to get onto the pontoon.'

The camera followed the helicopter as it swung round and began to hover, its noisy engine drowning out further conversation in the control room.

Del pulled Entwistle towards him and shouted into his ear.

'That piece of shit is here to fuck you. Do not believe a single word he says. Whatever he's peddling, you need to get over there to the state police – not to his people, not even to the FBI. There's too many cops out there for anything to happen to you. Don't trust him, believe me.'

'Should we even let him in?' shouted Entwistle, watching a small figure descend from the helicopter.

'Once he's in here, he becomes *our* hostage!' answered Del.

'You're one devious bastard.'

'That I am – just I learned too late.'

Hartsby finally touched down on the pontoon, released his harness, and waved the helicopter away. The camera swung away to follow the Huey as it flew back across the Hole.

Del stabbed a finger at the monitor. 'See? He knew the camera would do that. Now we can't see him outside at all. Remember those boats we heard earlier?'

'So when we open the door . . .?'

Del shrugged, his face creased with the pain.

'Shit,' said Entwistle, lowering his voice as the sound of the helicopter continued to recede. 'So what do we do?'

Del spoke up. 'Surprise the weasel.'

Seconds later, Hartsby knocked on the door.

'Deputy Entwistle? It's Emile Hartsby,' he shouted, his voice muffled by the solid metal. 'It's rather inconvenient talking through reinforced steel . . .'

'You alone?'

'Very alone – and very exposed. I've no guarantees

that the terrorists will keep their word, and I'm out here in plain sight.'

'OK, I'm opening the door now.'

Entwistle unlocked it, slid back the bolts, and grabbed the handle.

'You sure?' he asked Del.

Del nodded.

Entwistle suddenly pulled back the door, raising his rifle to point five feet above the ground, as recommended by Del. Refocusing, he saw Hartsby's face in his sights, the man's expression a treasure as Del stood out in clear view next to Entwistle.

'Get in here, you fucker,' snarled Del. 'You've got one second, then . . .'

Hartsby lurched forward and into the control room, the shock still obvious on his face.

As Entwistle slammed the door shut, he caught sight of two other men outside, lying on the pontoon with rifles trained on the door. What he did not register was the frogman in the water, harpoon gun in hand, and three other men in a speedboat, weapons also aimed at the door.

Entwistle spun Hartsby round and thrust the rifle into his chest.

'You armed?'

'Only with the truth.'

'I've had enough smart-ass answers for one day.' He lashed the rifle round and hit the man across the temple.

Hartsby staggered back against the table.

'Deputy, what do you—' he gasped.

'Don't waste your breath.' Del snatched the rifle from

Entwistle and fired it into Hartsby's knee, then handed the gun back.

'That's for Gloria,' he growled, then returned to the video monitors.

Hartsby collapsed, gasping in pain, both hands clutching his shattered joint, blood welling over his fingers.

'Who's Gloria?' said Entwistle, aghast, staring at Del's back.

'Someone else who got shafted by this vicious piece of work – like he shafts everyone. Just ask yourself one question, Deputy Entwistle. How the hell does he know your name?'

Good point, thought Entwistle.

'He shot me! He fucking shot me!' squealed Hartsby.

'Very observant,' said Entwistle, bending over him. 'And I'll shoot your other fucking knee if you don't give me some answers quickly. We've come too far now to be fobbed off by some short-ass motherfucker in a suit. So start explaining.'

'For pity's sake, I can't. My knee—'

Entwistle jabbed the rifle barrel hard against the man's undamaged knee. 'Then use your fucking mouth. Now talk.'

'About what?' gasped Hartsby.

'For a start, what's so damn important about *that*?' Del pointed at the screen showing Greg and Maribeth and the mysterious metal cube.

'You wouldn't understand. Highly classified.'

'You've one last chance to answer the man,' growled Entwistle.

Hartsby locked eyes with Entwistle.

'Now talk.' Entwistle glared into the man's dark eyes. He didn't know if Del was telling the truth, but there was something about this one he didn't like. And after all that had gone down, he wasn't about to be outstared by some Fed dwarf who shouldn't actually know his name. For once he let his emotions rule his head: he pulled the trigger, and the man's other knee disintegrated.

Hartsby fell onto his back, a strange hiss issuing from his mouth, his hands in mid-air and shaking frantically, as if he couldn't bear to touch his bloody wounds. Then he collapsed unconscious.

'What's happening up there?' yelled Greg through the intercom.

Entwistle examined his rifle. 'No more ammunition.' He turned to Del. 'What now?'

'Wake him up. Get him to talk.'

'What if he won't?'

'He will.'

'Why?'

'He'll admire your ruthlessness.'

'What?'

'Trust me. He has no reason now not to talk. None of us is getting out of here alive, so he's got nothing to lose except his own life. He'll talk.'

'Hey! What's going on up there?' repeated Greg loudly enough to be heard up the elevator shaft.

Del switched on the microphone. 'Nothing to worry about. We're trying to find out what that thing is down there with you.'

Greg walked back to Maribeth. 'Think we should stay down here?'

Maribeth was too tired to care, in deep pain, her mind buzzing, her eyes starting to fail. The cube in front of her seemed to glow slightly, as if lit from inside. She blinked and the illusion vanished. *Oh, hellation! I'm starting to hallucinate again.*

Up in the control room, Del and Entwistle lifted Hartsby onto the table and laid him on his back. Del began slapping him across the face until he roused, his moans soon turning to cries of agony.

Entwistle leaned down towards him.

'Your last chance. The doctors you can afford might get you to walk again. But I doubt you know any can fix up your dick once I blow it off.' He prodded the man's groin. 'So talk, you motherfucker.'

'What – what do you want to know?' Hartsby's face was bathed in sweat, his eyes clenching every couple of seconds as new waves of pain washed over him.

'What's that thing down below?' said Entwistle. 'Is it some kind of bomb?'

Hartsby swivelled his head to follow the pointing finger, then he recognized the cube on the screen.

'You could say that.'

'Is it a bomb?' repeated Entwistle.

'Oh, hell, I should have . . .' said Del. 'He's ACA, so he's got total control.'

'What's ACA?'

'It's a weapons research group. So the rig, the takeover of the town, setting me up . . . It's all a cover, am I right?'

'Yes.'

Del mused out loud. 'So what would make the

government go to all this trouble? What's so important they'd need such an elaborate cover-up – and at such a cost in lives?'

Greg piped up from below via the intercom. 'It ain't a UFO, is it?'

Del snorted. 'Grow up, kid. But I think I do know what it is now.'

'Oh?' said Hartsby, grimacing.

'It's a broken arrow: a nuclear weapon. Got dropped here in the lake sometime in the past, and all this shit is a cover while they haul the thing up. It could be leaking. That's it, isn't it?'

'There used to be an Air Force base near here,' added Greg. 'It closed in the early seventies. My dad used to clean there. About ten, fifteen miles east: Rabley, Ribley, something like that. You mean they had nuclear weapons out there – and they lost one? Accidentally dropped it in the Hole years back?'

'Sure as hell would account for how dishonest all this business is,' said Del. 'Anything nuclear, the shutters come down – we might as well be in Russia. Nothing comes more secret – or more ruthless.'

Hartsby attempted to laugh, a wet gurgle that sounded as if a child's squeezy toy was stuck in his throat.

Entwistle grabbed him by the neck. 'Is that it, then? A nuclear weapon you're trying to recover. But why all this shit? Why not just clear the town legally? Why not—?'

'Hey, hey!' came Greg's frantic voice on the intercom. 'Do you lot up there see what I see?'

All three men turned to the monitor.

The cube was beginning to glow.

Thirty-one

'What the hell is this?' shouted Entwistle as he watched the cube brighten. 'Maribeth, Greg, get out of there!'

He saw the two figures move out of shot towards the elevator.

'I can stop it,' croaked Hartsby. 'But I need someone to work the computer.' He pointed at a console to the right of the video monitors.

'Collingwood, get over there,' said Entwistle.

'The elevator won't work!' he heard Greg's voice shouting.

'What's going on?'

'Safety shutdown,' said Hartsby. 'Don't panic. Just do what *I* say.'

Del reached the computer. He never had felt at home with the damn things; still couldn't get his video to record Letterman. 'OK, what do I do?'

'The keyboard ... to the right ... red switch. Press it.'

A small computer screen on the panel bloomed into blue life.

'Now type in what I say.'

Del did his best to keep up with the string of

commands gasped out by Hartsby, and it was after a couple of errors and a full ninety seconds before he completed the coded sequence. Hartsby let out a little gasp of satisfaction.

'Good. You did well, Collingwood. Knew I chose right.'

Entwistle stared over at the monitor showing the room containing the mysterious cube. 'It's still glowing.'

'Too damn right it's still fucking glowing!' yelled Greg through the intercom.

Maribeth stood beside him facing the cube, utterly transfixed. Despite her terror and her pain, it seemed to her a beautiful sight. Although clearly made of metal, it looked as if it was transforming into some kind of glass lit from the inside. It was also getting warmer. She now realized the odd visions she had been experiencing were all somehow linked to this strange object. Whether they had been premonitions or warnings she did not know, but she *did* know she had been destined somehow to be standing here now. But why?

'What the fuck is that?' said Entwistle, breaking into her thoughts.

Del stared at the focus of the Deputy's anguish. Above the console a green digital display was counting down.

11:41

11:40

11:39

'What the hell is that?' Del echoed.

'Countdown,' said Hartsby.

'Countdown to what?' said Entwistle.

'Explosion.'

'But you said you could stop that thing.'

'And I have. In eleven minutes it will stop glowing because the bomb you've just programmed will go off and destroy it – and also every living soul in Firefall.'

'That thing down there *isn't* a bomb?'

'No.'

'So where's the bomb? You mean the dynamite?' said Del.

'That will go up, but it's not that, no.'

'So where is it, you motherfucker?'

Hartsby raised his hand to point at the ceiling, then he even managed a chuckle. Entwistle bent over and punched him in the mouth, so he stopped with a little scream.

'The roof?' Entwistle wondered, while eyeing the timer.

10:44

No, not the roof . . .

10:43

He pictured the rig in his mind, the bulbous shape at its apex.

10:42

'The top of the rig?'

Hartsby spat out a bloody affirmative. 'Fuel-air bomb. Most powerful explosive device after a nuclear bomb. Firefall will *disappear*.'

'And I've just set it going?' said Del.

'You were dumb enough to do exactly what I told you, again.'

Del marched over and grabbed Hartsby and dragged him off the table. He hauled the squealing man on his broken knees to the computer console.

'Stop the thing!'

'Can't . . .' gasped Hartsby. 'I coded in a non-reversal command. It can't be defused.'

Entwistle pushed him aside and knelt down underneath the desk. 'Maybe if we disconnect the computer from the—'

Hartsby hawked more blood onto the floor. 'Message's been received in the bomb. Can't be countermanded. So unless you can airlift that half-ton beauty five miles away inside ten minutes . . . boom!'

'But why?' said Entwistle. 'Why kill us all? Why blow up Firefall? *Why all this!*'

'There's no harm in telling you now. You won't be able to understand anyway, but I have to admire your tenacity, Deputy Entwistle. In another life you might have . . . in another life . . .' and he started spluttering again.

'What's going on?' yelled Greg from below. 'It's starting to heat up down here.'

'That *is* a bomb down there, isn't it, you lying fuck?' snarled Entwistle.

'No, it's not. But it's essential that it's destroyed if I couldn't salvage it.'

'Salvage?' said Del, ignoring the man's previous denials. 'So the Air Force drops a nuclear weapon. You manage to trace it years after the event, but don't want to make a show of recovering it? So why didn't you invent some routine cover story? Why all this? And why destroy the town? That's as bad as letting that thing downstairs go off anyway.'

'Will you get it into your thick, hick heads, that device down there is not a bomb! And all this elaborate charade, the terrorism, the environmental crap, the ransom – all of it was a cover to enable me to remove that device *without* the government finding out it was ever there, or where it had gone.'

'But if it's not a nuclear weapon, what the hell is it?'

After his outburst Hartsby coughed some more, his face now white with pain. Twin trickles of scarlet ran from the corners of his mouth and down either side of his jaw. Combined with his high raspy voice and inability to move, as he lay slumped against the desk, with his bloody, broken legs in front of him, he looked like a discarded ventriloquist's dummy, which made his words sound all the more insane.

'What is it?' demanded Del, again.

'*What is it?*' screamed Greg, the open microphone having allowed him to hear everything just said.

'It's a TRD.'

'What the fuck is that?' demanded Entwistle.

'A Temporal Repeatment Device.'

'A what?'

'In plain English, it's a time machine.'

Thirty-two

Both men stared at Hartsby in silence, seeking some trace of humour in his grimacing features.

'You don't believe me – as I expected.'

Del knelt down beside Hartsby, his hand slowly wrapping the man's bloody tie around his knuckles so that it formed an effective garrotte.

'Seems that if we're going to die, we deserve more than silly jokes.'

'No joke.'

'A time machine?'

Hartsby tried to nod, but he was choking.

'So why's it glowing?'

'Because it knows the bomb's about to go off.'

Entwistle shook his head. 'But it was glowing even before you tricked us into triggering the bomb.'

'Because it already knew what was going to happen.'

Del gave the tie another twist and Hartsby began to gasp, his grey face gradually turning red.

'No,' intervened Entwistle. 'Let him tell us.'

'Tell us what?' said Del, eager to choke the life out of the little sonofabitch. He glanced up at the clock. It read **7:58**.

'If we're going to die in less than eight minutes, at least I want to know why. He owes us that.'

Del loosened his grip.

'I don't owe you anything,' croaked Hartsby defiantly, 'but I'll tell you anyway.'

Del sat back on his haunches. 'Tell away.'

From the intercom came Greg's plea. 'Will someone tell me what's happening up there?'

Entwistle went over to the microphone. 'You want the truth?'

'Oh, shit, is it bad?'

'I'm sorry, but Hartsby tricked us into triggering the timer of some bomb. A big bomb. It goes off in seven minutes, forty seconds. We've no hope of getting away. Is Maribeth there?'

'Yes,' came her voice.

'I'm sorry. I did all—'

'Not your fault. Not your fault.'

She stepped back from the microphone and turned to face the cube. It was glowing white now and, although giving off increasing amounts of heat, it was not dangerously hot. Its warmth was actually soothing, helping to ease the pain that had seemed to penetrate every nerve of her body. She thought of it being like a sunlamp – although she had never used one of those because of her very fair complexion. Now, if she stepped nearer to it, maybe the pain would diminish even further. For some inexplicable reason she was no longer frightened of this strange object. Had she finally lost her sanity?

'Hey, what you doing?'

Greg suddenly grabbed her arm. 'That thing might be radioactive.'

'You heard Entwistle. It doesn't make much difference now.'

Greg could not argue with her logic, and certainly could not deny the pleasing warmth with which the glowing cube now imbued the room. For some reason he reached for Maribeth's good hand and held it. She glanced at him and gave a squeeze; the fear on his face was plain to see. However tough he might act, he was still just a boy.

'Maybe they'll figure a way out?' she offered.

'You're a bad liar.'

'Sorry.'

He squeezed her hand again by way of a thank-you.

Up in the control room, Entwistle had sat Hartsby upright.

7:18

'Time machine?' Entwistle prodded.

'ACA checks weapons for the government once they're in use. It's in combat and on the ground that performance matters. We collate data on every weapon purchased by government and the state authorities. In the late eighties there was a spate of accidents on military bases: bombs dropped, fires . . .'

He paused and coughed, his face creased with pain. 'We analysed all data, including satellite passes before, during, and after these disasters, in case of sabotage. And we detected an anomaly, a pinprick of energy near the site of each disaster, but which disappeared after the event. In '92 a hangar containing eight fighter aircraft caught fire, killing fourteen aircrew. In '93 a missile plant blew up, killing forty-two. In both cases this identical energy signature was found near the plant, but its position was such that it couldn't have been destroyed by the explosion. It had simply disappeared. Then we detected two other energy sources – and a couple of days later there was an unpublicized nuclear mishap at Erie Wells, Utah, and a chemical explosion in Waipeg, Minnesota.'

'Waipeg. I've heard of that.'

'Two hundred and eight workers killed, a billion dollars' worth of plant wrecked. Using my contacts in various corporations, I amassed aerial and satellite data to find other energy pinpoints. I found four: two of them too late, but two others we found in time. The first was near Conniston, Kentucky. Yes, the mining disaster – eighty-four men gassed or crushed underground. We were excavating this object – identical to that thing below – and it began to glow at almost the same moment that the mine collapse started. I was trapped in the shaft with it, and it was then I realized the device itself wasn't causing the accidents. All it was transmitting was its own energy field. As the gas and the wall of flame approached me I touched the cube . . . and woke up four years previously.'

Simultaneously, Del and Entwistle snorted their disbelief.

Hartsby looked offended. 'You have six minutes to live. I've no need to—'

'Get on with it.'

'I woke up as myself four years prior to that incident, fully aware of everything that was due to happen to me over the next four years. Naturally, at first I thought I was delusional, but as events began to repeat themselves I took action to correct my mistakes from the first time round: to eliminate rivals, strengthen my position – and extend my research into these energy points. I found four further devices, but each was destroyed in our attempts to analyse them – and each subsequently proved to be at the site of an incipient disaster, including one of our own making when we screwed up. How these things work, who put them here, why – all I've surmised is that they've been seeded from some time in the future as beacons designed to warn us of impending disasters, which are almost always man-made. Floods, tornadoes, earthquakes, these are uncontrollable, but the disasters I've linked with these devices are all avoidable if foreknowledge is available.'

'This is the biggest load of shit!'

Hartsby ignored Del. 'They glow whenever a disaster is imminent. And since this whole town is about to be destroyed, that thing below is glowing.'

'But it was glowing *before* we set off the bomb,' argued Del.

'Precisely.'

'So that's a self-fulfilling prophecy!' said Entwistle. 'But why blow up the rig, anyway?'

'There are others who'd like to get their hands on my research, and I needed to remove this device and study it at my leisure, away from circumstances where it might be destroyed through clumsy experimentation. If these devices remain where they are, they disappear. But I myself am being watched by certain people eager to step in and take over. My plan was to shut down the town to all except those I controlled through Collingwood and number 38, next remove the device in a helicopter carrying released hostages, then fake a foul-up so that the rig and any eyewitnesses were vaporized. And then I'd lay the blame on Collingwood, who would conveniently commit suicide. There would thus be no trace of the device or of my involvement. Already all my links with Ultracom have been severed, any key personnel there succumbing to unfortunate accidents.'

'So you get hold of the device, whatever it is—'

'It's a time machine!' Hartsby hacked more blood onto his chest and looked down at it in disgust. 'At some point in a benevolent future, people send these back to us as warnings.'

'But what if you did act on one of these warnings? Wouldn't that change the future?' said Entwistle.

'And if you changed the future, you might even stop the people who sent these back from being born? Or maybe preclude the invention of the device?' added Del.

'If you believe that time is linear, a straight road with present actions having direct consequences ahead, then yes. But a theory I now believe to be true, because I've lived it, is that of time-streams. If you go back, you can only go back as yourself – you cannot go back beyond your own existence. And if in that existence you do something that alters future time, a new time-stream is created, but the time-stream you were in originally carries on unaltered.'

'So what's the point? By that logic all the disasters will *still* happen in their own time-stream.'

Del stared at Entwistle, amazed that the man was able to follow Hartsby's reasoning – or even wanted to. The timer clock read **4:23**.

'True benevolence. They are creating alternative time-streams in which people survive who otherwise would die. And if each beacon is acted upon, more and more people survive.'

'This is crap,' said Del.

'Then die ignorant!' Hartsby hissed.

The little man seemed pleased to be able to tell other people about his work. No doubt it was helping to concentrate his mind and keep it off his pain, but Entwistle knew, from his own experience of dealing with stoolies, that the burden a secret creates is the desire to share it. Commit the perfect crime, who's to know how perfect it is unless you tell someone? Now Hartsby had the ideal opportunity to share his secret because his audience wouldn't be able to tell it to anyone else.

'So if you used that device down there, you'd go back in time?' said Entwistle. 'And thus be able to stop this happening? But in *another* time-stream?'

Hartsby didn't answer.

'Oh, don't go quiet on us now,' snapped Entwistle.

'Who cares?' said Del, unable or unwilling to understand any of the gibberish the man had been spouting.

Hartsby refused to say more. Entwistle watched him try to move his legs, but the pain seemed too great. He glanced over at the monitor, and saw Maribeth and Greg down below, staring at the cube.

'But *you're* not interested in preventing disasters, are you?' continued Entwistle.

Hartsby still refused to answer, so Entwistle tried another tack. 'What happened to the other you: the one you took over?'

'What?' said Hartsby, holding his breath against his pain.

'What happened to the other *you* when you went back?'

'I . . . I entered his mind. My thoughts and knowledge became his.'

'You took him over.'

'Yes.'

'You *killed* him.'

'What?'

'*He* stopped existing in his time-stream because you took over. You killed this other you,' said Entwistle.

'Yes, if you want to put it that way.'

'Now *that's* ruthless,' said Del.

'So what? I am me. I am me in every time-stream. Every event that changes history creates a new time-stream with everyone in it. An infinite number of parallel universes. Those in the future can't alter their past but they can change my future. In their past, Waipeg blew up, killed hundreds. If the machine had been used in time, it wouldn't have happened, and they'd know that in an alternative time-stream all those who perished would have survived and each could play a part in altering their time-stream's course.'

'Including not inventing the device—'

'Cretin, don't you understand? Once the device is used you *create* another time-stream from the point at which you arrive. This one happens, but you create a second and in *that* one they hope you will manage to avert the disaster.'

'How will they know if you succeed?'

'They won't! They act from true benevolence – the fools.'

Entwistle remained staring at the video monitor. Of course what Hartsby had said sounded garbage. Yet what was the point of his spinning a fairy tale so close to death for all of them? They say confession's good for the soul – though he doubted this particular bastard possessed one. So perhaps Hartsby *was* telling the truth. Then, again, maybe he was simply mad.

Del glanced at the two wall clocks. Both were frozen at the same second. Pointing at one, he turned to Hartsby. 'This something to do with—?'

Hartsby spluttered with amusement. 'That's one of the effects it has on anyone who ends up this . . .' he paused, as if searching for the word, 'this *close* to the device. It's as if it senses their inevitable approach.'

'But what about all those clocks in your trailer?' said Del. 'They weren't affected, and both of us were there.'

'Their time is beamed in by satellite, just so it will always be one hundred per cent accurate. The central timepiece is actually fifteen thousand miles out in space!'

'Yet all four of us here were stopping clocks . . .' Entwistle mumbled to himself. 'Which would imply that . . .'

What was it he had been saying to Hartsby when the man had clammed up earlier? It was something about, if he were to use the device, he could go back in time and so stop the explosion. And yet it had been glowing even before the bomb exploded, so there was obviously no stopping it. But what else had he just intimated: that anyone who gets *close* to the device is automatically affected? Now why had he chosen that particular word so carefully? Entwistle needed to find out if the man was still hiding something.

'I'm going down there,' he announced.

'No!' rasped Hartsby.

Entwistle spun round. 'Why not?'

'It – it's pointless. Too late. You have less than three minutes.'

'What I do with my last three minutes on earth is my business.'

Hartsby began struggling as if to get up. 'No, it's pointless, believe me.'

Entwistle pulled the man's head back by his hair. 'I don't know whether I believe you or not, but *you* certainly do, otherwise you wouldn't want to stop me going down there. There's still time for that device to work, isn't there? Time for me to use it, and go back and prevent all this.'

'But you can't. The future mustn't be altered. All you'd be doing . . .'

Entwistle let go his hair. 'Jesus Christ Almighty . . .'

'What?' said Del.

'He is serious,' said Entwistle, his mind reeling at the possibility.

'What do you mean?' said Del, his heart now racing.

2:57

'If we go down and use that device, we'll go back in time.'

'Crap,' protested Del.

Entwistle stared down at Hartsby, who avoided his gaze. 'Whatever it all means, he's been telling the truth – and he doesn't want us using that thing.'

'But why not?'

'Because we'll then create a new time-stream, and stop his plans.'

Hartsby chuckled croakily.

'This is so unreal,' said Del, holding his head in his hands.

But suddenly it was all so clear to Entwistle. He always found logic came best to him under pressure.

'Whoever goes back changes the time-stream. That means in every time-stream *this* is happening. In every time-stream Firefall's being taken, Hartsby's using that as a cover to recover this same device, and the town is then blown up. Unless someone changes things around, and then a different outcome's possible. Whoever goes back creates their own time-stream.'

'It's nonsense,' protested Del, again.

'No, Del, it ain't! Look at him, at us, at that fucking clock, at that thing down there. He couldn't make this up, not now, not here, not with the clock ticking. Which means . . .'

'What?' said Del.

'We've got two and a half minutes to get down below.'

He ran over to the elevator, pressed the call button. It began to rise, its safety cut-out obviously overridable from up top.

'Greg, did you hear any of that?'

'All of it, and didn't understand a word.'

'Trust me. Did Maribeth hear us?'

'Yes,' said Greg, 'she's nodding.'

'Does she believe it?'

He spun and looked at the monitor. Maribeth was

still staring at the cube bathed now in a glow so bright that the camera was starting to flare.

'What?' he heard Greg asking her over the intercom. 'What d'you say, Maribeth?'

'What?' said Entwistle, the elevator not yet halfway up.

'She says it's true.'

'How would she . . .?' Then he stared at her image.

The light seemed to be reaching around her, as if embracing her. In the instant that analogy occurred to him, he realized everything Hartsby had said was indeed true. The device was *talking* to Maribeth. Its purpose was to save people, and it was now saving her. He only hoped it could save the rest of them, too.

Greg stepped over to Maribeth. 'What do you mean, it's true?'

The light from the cube was extremely bright, yet not so dazzling that he could not look at it directly. It was not harsh, but a warming, nourishing diffusion.

'It's a time machine. I just know it.'

Even as Maribeth said that, she did not understand *how* she knew. Those semi-visions she had been experiencing now made sense. Whether they were intended as warnings or as instructions, she could not know. All that counted now was that she believed. And if she *touched* it . . . Touch was all it required. Touch and be transported. Touch and . . .

. . . *live.*

Thirty-three

The clock timer said only ninety-five seconds remained, and the elevator hadn't arrived. Del shouted something about looking, and on the ROOF monitor Entwistle saw armed men in full SWAT gear. They were obviously planning an assault, and the roof hatch offered the most vulnerable entry point. Knowing Hartsby was captive in the control room, they would most likely lob in stun grenades first then use gas – already they were beginning to pull on their masks. Such action would wreck any hopes Entwistle had of getting down to the time machine.

The elevator finally arrived.

1:24

'Collingwood, get into the elevator,' said Entwistle, grabbing up the intercom microphone. 'Greg, we're coming down now. Don't touch that thing till we're all there.'

'Who's going to touch the fucking thing, anyway?' shouted Greg.

I will, I will, thought Maribeth, edging closer to the glowing cube.

Entwistle turned to Hartsby. 'For once in your life do something for someone else. Tell us how it works.'

Hartsby glared up at Entwistle with contempt. 'Go fuck yourself.'

1:16

Entwistle glanced at the monitor showing all the activity on the roof. He could hear footfalls, suggesting they were about to attack. He grabbed Hartsby under the arms and pulled him across the floor to the corner of the room directly underneath the roof hatch, a bloody smear marking his progress.

'Say hi to your buddies for me,' said Entwistle, balling up the man's tie and stuffing it hard into his mouth.

'Go down, now!' he shouted, and Del hit the button. Entwistle was about to run over to join him when something else caught his eye: a box welded to the side of one of the consoles. He snapped it open, pocketed its contents, then dashed across to the elevator.

1:05

At that precise moment the hatch was ripped open. Two small objects shaped like hockey pucks dropped onto Hartsby's chest. He tried to scream but the stun grenades exploded, taking away his face, eyes, and hearing. Then four armed men jumped into the room and landed on his stomach and chest, crushing the life out of him. Two primed gas bombs were tossed to opposite corners of the room, just as Entwistle dived for the open door of the elevator shaft.

How far the cage had travelled he didn't know, but his sudden impact with its roof made it judder, and knocked the wind from him. Above, he heard shouting amid short bursts of automatic fire. He fumbled in his pocket, aware that at any second a gun could spray him, and Del beneath him in the elevator car, with deadly fire.

A flashlight beam lanced into the black tube of the shaft above him and a masked face peered down. Entwistle grabbed one of the cables holding the car, to steady himself, then took out his find. He raised his arm just as a machine-gun tilted down to fix him in its sights.

He only had one chance.

He pulled the trigger of the flare gun – and the mini-rocket shot up to embed itself in the perspex of the gunman's gas mask. The man whipped back, shrieking in agony, his face on fire, releasing his weapon to clatter onto the elevator car roof beside Entwistle.

Dropping the spent flare gun, he picked up the compact machine-gun. It would not be long before another one braved a burst of fire down the shaft, or tossed in a hand grenade – or the bomb above them all finally exploded. Whichever happened first, there seemed no hope.

'Del! Is there a safety hatch in the roof?'

'Yes,' came the muffled reply.

A small hatch popped up instantly, barely wide enough for a man to slide through.

'We gotta get down faster. Brace yourself.'

'What?' said Del, puzzled.

Entwistle held the snub barrel of the Uzi against the guide cables holding the elevator car. He realized elevators mostly had automatic brakes to halt a sudden drop, and prayed this didn't have one. As he fired at the cable the flashes were blinding, the noise deafening; his chest, face and hands caught splinters of hot metal. With a sharp snap the elevator juddered, stalled, then suddenly began to plummet, a roaring following it from above.

And then it hit the basement floor, and its roof collapsed inwards. Entwistle plunged through it, down onto Del. Heavy cable snaked down after him, coiling about the two of them like angry snakes. And then the counterweight followed, smashing through the side of the car and bending its flimsy metal wall in two.

Amid the dust and debris Greg reached in and hauled Entwistle clear.

'Collingwood ... Get Collingwood...' wheezed Entwistle, only able to crawl, his right leg numb.

As Greg pulled Del out by the collar, the man screamed, 'My hand, my hand!'

Greg swatted away the dust and realized that the man's wrist had been speared by a piece of cable, which was pinning it to the floor as effectively as if it had been nail-gunned. Maribeth hurried across and with her one good hand helped Entwistle out of the way while Greg struggled to free him.

Entwistle tried to take command. 'Got only seconds ... got to use this device...'

'But how?' said a frantic Greg, almost unable to look at Del's ruptured hand as he tried to pull it free.

'Touch it,' said Maribeth.

'What?' said Entwistle.

He saw the light from the cube reflecting in her eyes: she looked possessed.

'Touch it,' she repeated.

'Get Del over here,' said Entwistle.

'He's stuck!'

'Well, unstick him. Only got seconds—'

Up above, they heard more machine-gun fire, bullets dancing amid the debris of the wrecked elevator, one cutting a slice from Del's thigh.

'Help me!' he screamed, unable to dodge the ricochets.

'It's his hand!' explained Greg. There was nothing he could do.

The device was glowing white now, the entire basement as bright as the control room upstairs.

Entwistle remembered the Uzi he had used to sever the elevator cables. He pointed to it, lying beside Greg's foot.

'Shoot him. Shoot Del!'

Greg stared at him. 'You mean kill him?'

Del turned to Entwistle. 'Yes, save yourselves. Use the device!'

More gunfire.

'No, wait,' said Entwistle. 'Maribeth?'

She glanced down at him, nodded, then picked up the gun and aimed it down at Del.

'Get hold of him, Greg, and pull. Now!'

Terrified, Greg did as ordered. He tugged as Maribeth fired a blast through Del's forearm until he came free. His right hand remained pinned to the floor, his severed wrist now spurting blood all over Greg's shins as he hauled him clear.

Del was screaming in agony, Greg cursing and sobbing.

Maribeth dropped the Uzi and helped Entwistle stand upright on his one good leg.

'We must all touch it at the same time,' she explained.

No one argued. But as they advanced on the glowing cube, there came a shaking and a deep rumble, and then the world above pressed down on them and heat and light roared out of the elevator shaft.

Each was flung forward onto the strange device, their yells of terror and pain cut short as Firefall – and everyone in it, guilty or innocent – was blasted off the face of the earth.

Thursday 4 September
Yesterday
5:00 a.m.

One

Del woke up screaming. Raising his bulky frame, he sat bolt upright in the bed, the sheets cast aside, his left hand clasping his right wrist.

He had seen his own hand cut off – the bullets slicing through flesh and sinew and bone! And as the pain exploded in his arm he had been dragged aside, and he had seen his twitching hand still skewered to the floor. There *on the floor*, severed and bloody. And so he now stared at this same hand, unable to believe its fingers were still a part of him.

Sweat ran down his face and back and he couldn't stop shaking. Lying beside him, Gloria had been disturbed by his sudden movement and was beginning to cry with a frightened childish sound that told him her addled mind would not be easily placated.

He swung his legs out of bed, found his feet thrumming in agitation on the floor, his nerves completely shot. Had that ever been a nightmare . . .

Ignoring Gloria, he lurched to the bathroom and threw up into the toilet bowl, the vile smell rising around him. After a couple of minutes he splashed cold water over his face and, glancing in the mirror, saw his pale reflection, looking more scared than he could ever remember. It had only been a damn dream, and yet it was so vivid, so detailed . . . and he could remember *all* of it.

The siege in the town, Hartsby, his own impotence, the flight on the helicopter, the bomb . . .

The time machine.

He felt faint and had to grasp the sides of the washbasin, his mind filled with conflicting emotions. Oh God, it had seemed so real, so real . . .

He walked back into the bedroom and did his best to pacify Gloria, but it was a hopeless task. If she was upset by something during her waking hours – and who was to know what was at the root of any of her terrors – she would rock back and forth and repeat the same phrases, but was generally quiet. But if she was woken suddenly, or heard a loud inexplicable noise, or she saw blood, then her hysterics would become loud and enduring and she would remain as inconsolable and shrill as a baby with colic.

Del tried to embrace her, to gently stroke her hair, but she kept pulling away from him. When she fell into one of these moods – when the maggots in her head bit through the cords of reason – any attempt at helping her would be interpreted as a further threat, and her panic would increase accordingly. And he also knew from sad experience that now only exhaustion would stall her hysteria, a process that could take anything from fifteen minutes to a couple of hours. Given that she had managed a quiet night's sleep, he suspected she might continue in this agitated state for quite some time.

Eventually he left her and sought refuge in the kitchen, leaving the door to their bedroom slightly ajar. He made himself some coffee and sat at the table composing his thoughts. On an impulse he grabbed at his wristwatch. It was working! The second hand was moving for every two beats of his hammering heart. Thank God, thank God! It *must* have been a dream. *It must have been* . . . The very notion of a time machine – that he was now reliving the same day over again – was such Hollywood-style nonsense. He had obviously experienced a real doozy of a nightmare, but soon it would dissolve from his memory like a Polaroid photograph in reverse, perhaps becoming just a vague memory like his drowning dream or his falling dream.

He rubbed his unmarked wrist, but couldn't help recalling the image of it being shot off by that woman. The thought made him shiver; he wondered if he should see a doctor. Perhaps he was overstressed; *of course* he was stressed, coping with Gloria and his fears about retirement. Yes, that was it. He'd ring Dr Bell from the office, arrange an appointment this afternoon – and endure the man's barbed comments about Del's weight.

He sipped his coffee, trying to blot out Gloria's weeping. At least her screaming had now turned to sobbing, and as long as he kept the right tone of voice when he re-entered the bedroom, he wouldn't exacerbate the problem. He might even get her back to sleep by the time Nurse Bentley arrived.

He cast an eye over his paperwork, couldn't suppress a nauseating burst of déjà vu, and decided he would run through it at work instead.

It was as he poked his head into the bedroom and was preparing his, 'There, there, it's only Del,' that the telephone rang. Damn, even its hushed tone could set her off again. He rushed back across the kitchen, his bare feet slapping on the tiles.

'Yes?' he hissed as soon as he had picked it up.

Two minutes later he knew for certain it had not been a nightmare.

Greg jerked spastically, opened his eyes, and saw white. And then he heard choking. Swinging his head down, his vision swimming, his head buzzing, he found Summer naked on her knees in front of him, coughing. As he knelt down beside her, he realized he too was naked. He tilted her head up, solicitously.

'You nearly choked me!' she gasped.

'What?'

She slapped at his hard-on. 'With that thing, you stupid prick!'

He stared at his swinging erection, still wet with her saliva, its firmness already diminishing as his mind flooded with images of another time, of murder and explosions and . . .

He staggered back, gripped at the drapes, but, tripping, ripped them away from their rail.

'Greg!' gasped Summer, horrified.

But Greg wasn't now concerned about Summer's reaction, or the damage to her bedroom. He was gaping at the clock, remembering the last time he had been here at this same hour, and what had happened after . . .

He heard her father's shout from downstairs.

Summer stared at him, then down at herself, and dived for the bed to retrieve what clothes she could find.

Greg *knew* that he should now climb out of the window, there to hang precariously out of sight, as Hal Campbell bellowed at his only daughter. And then he would fall ... and hide himself in a tree house ... and then ...

Confusion confounded his movements and despite Summer's urging he remained motionless on the floor, legs akimbo, his mind running through an impossible scenario.

Then Hal Campbell burst into the room, saw his daughter in only a blouse and no underwear, saw Greg naked, his legs open as if awaiting a medical examination. And Hal's face went white, then red, and in one swift movement he dived on the boy, his hands twisting round his throat.

Greg screamed, but his cry of pain was lost amid the man's obscenities as Hal Campbell began to lash out at him, his eyes wild with betrayal.

Greg tried to shield himself, but the man was everywhere, as were his fists and head and knees. Greg heard Summer shrieking for her father to stop.

'You little nigger fuck!' screamed Campbell. 'You psycho nigger bastard! Touch my baby, would you?'

Greg's world was so full of pain and confusion that there wasn't room for anger, just an acceptance that this was where his life might end. Greg knew he was likely to be killed.

Then the punches and kicks ceased just as suddenly as they had started, and Greg felt a dead weight pressing on top of him. He opened one weeping eye and saw

Summer standing over the two of them, a heavy lamp in her hand.

'Daddy? Daddy?' she squealed.

Greg heaved the man off him, and registered the bloody gash where Summer must have clouted the side of the man's head. He sat up, gulping in breath, scarcely able to believe he had survived. Dropping the lamp, Summer fell to her knees and began pawing at her father's back.

'I didn't kill him, did I? He isn't dead?'

'No,' gasped Greg, not that he cared. 'He's breathing. Thanks. You saved me.'

But Summer was still more concerned for her father.

Greg dragged his leg out from under the man's heavy weight, then crawled across the room to the bed. God, but he hurt . . . It took him a while to gather his thoughts but underneath them, like a low hum on a hi-fi, stayed the recurring memory of fighting men dressed all in black. How on earth could he have dreamed all that while he was making love? It was like he'd been taking part in an action movie!

He finally hauled himself upright and started to get dressed. The noise they had made would mean the police were bound to arrive eventually and if he still had a chance of running he'd better take it. It was as he was pulling on his trainers that Hal Campbell stirred.

Oh, shit!

Greg realized he should stay and face the music – not least because Summer was now in trouble – but he also knew that everyone in Firefall would be on Hal Campbell's side, so this time it wouldn't be a hospital for him but jail. He wanted to say something reassuring to Summer but her hands were cradling her father's head, Greg being now the least of her worries.

So he rolled over to the other side of the bed and headed for the stairs. But halfway along the landing he suddenly felt his legs being kicked to one side, and found himself staring down the wide, varnished wooden staircase.

Turning round, he saw Hal Campbell raising his fist for a knockout blow. The man's face was twisted with venom.

Greg had only a split second to act. As he grabbed Hal's wrist, he raised his knees to knock the man sideways – and to his horror watched him crash through the banisters and down to the hall floor fifteen feet below. His head cracked audibly on the white tiling.

Greg forced himself up and ran down the stairs, intent on getting past him to the front door. But when he saw Hal staring up at him through unblinking eyes, even though he had landed on his front, he realized he had just killed Summer's father.

He glanced up to see her standing at the top of the stairs, her eyes wide and uncomprehending. He started back up to her, but she ignored him and stumbled on down towards her father. Greg watched her kneel by the corpse and start talking to it, caressing her father's hands and hair and urging him to wake up. And then, as realization sank in, she fell forward and sobbed like a child, her long blond hair fanning over his face like a shroud.

Greg didn't know what to do next. He really only had one option, but where could he run? And for how long? No one would believe the truth; he would be seen as just another black kid taking it out on respectable white folk.

He glanced around towards Hal Campbell's bedroom. Perhaps he would find a weapon there. He knew Hal kept guns racked up in his den, but to reach there he would have to get past Summer and he couldn't face that yet.

Campbell's bedroom was surprisingly feminine, all pinks and yellows; it must have been decorated by his late wife. Greg started ransacking all the drawers, hoping to come upon a hidden revolver kept for bedside protection.

But eight drawers emptied of underwear and socks and toiletries and he was no further on. Worse, he could hear a siren in the distance; some neighbour had obviously reported a disturbance at the Campbell house. He ferreted quickly under the bed. Nothing but damned dust there. He wondered if he really wanted a gun; the last thing he needed was an armed confrontation with the law. But what other option did he have?

He scrabbled through the wardrobe, his mind frantic with fear, the siren moving ever closer. Suits, jackets, trousers, workshirts ... but nothing remotely useful as a weapon. Even the hangers were made of plastic. He stood on tiptoe to run his hand through the clothes folded on the top shelf, then, losing his temper, he started to toss them over his shoulder onto the bed.

Moments later the shelves were empty, apart from some porno magazines. So that was it. He slammed the wardrobe door shut and slumped back against it. He hadn't a chance. Just like everyone had warned him over the last few years, he had gone too far and killed a man. It didn't matter who was really to blame, with Greg's record he was doomed.

He suddenly began to cry. He knew that was pathetic, but he couldn't help himself. And *still* his mind kept hounding him over that fucking dream. He balled his fists and ground them into his temples. He was beginning to lose it, and soon the police would burst in and find him here, a soggy heap, but he didn't care. The siren was now only a block away. He banged his head back against the wardrobe. FUCK IT FUCK IT! Surrender was the best thing.

He began to walk out onto the landing, then stopped mid-step. Something on the bed had drawn his eye.

Oh my God . . .

A minute later he was running down the stairs. He moved past the weeping Summer to the front door and pulled it open.

A police car stood there, its door open, lights whirling, engine running.

No, not now, not—

'*Freeze!*'

A gun barrel was jabbed into his ear.

Three

Sheriff's Deputy Entwistle had never been prone to fantasy. His favourite reading was outdoor pursuit, motorbike, and gun magazines, his favourite movies were Westerns. So when he woke up face-down in a bed of straw, his mind alive to a scenario of conspirators and murder and time machines, he paused to consider.

He knew that instead he should be thrashing about desperately to loosen his bonds and escape this cloying atmosphere of throat-tickling dust, but instead he kept himself calm and took stock.

He had dreamed a complicated tale involving Greg Henley, Maribeth Hamilton, some FBI guy called Collingwood ... and Ed Rickenbacker had been involved: a traitor to his town and his team of men. Think it through. *Think it through* ...

He had been sent out here to Napier's Farm by Rickenbacker. He would escape eventually, only to run into an arsonist and accidentally kill him. He would then sneak around town, trying to prevent hooded men from ...

A time machine? Come on ...

Entwistle rolled himself upright, aware that in his dream he had fallen through the trapdoor, and carefully eased himself down the wide ladder to the barn floor ... where he found his cruiser with its doors locked and its radio smashed, just as he had dreamed it.

He went straight over to the hole in the barn wall, and shoulder-charged his way out. And then he began to relive his dream, finding the farm empty of people, but instead of hunting through the building he went straight down into the cellar and cut his bonds on the rusted pit-saw he knew in advance would be there, even though he had never entered Napier's cellar in his life. Hell, he had only set foot in the man's kitchen just once, yet he somehow knew the layout of the house intimately ... even, no doubt, to that goddam model in the attic.

But a *time machine*?

It did nothing to steady his nerves when he found that the clocks had stopped again, though at an earlier time – which reflected his earlier arrival in the house this time round.

Confirming that the telephone was indeed out of order, and with a sick feeling growing in his stomach, he tried to remember from his dream what time the arsonist had turned up. Judging by the short cuts he had already taken in a familiar train of events, that would be a good twenty minutes off yet. And if any of this crap was true, he could not afford to wait around. Which meant ...?

Which meant the arsonist would get to torch the farm this time, but no one would be killed. OK, let him do it (if he even existed).

Entwistle broke into his cruiser, reversed up, and drove straight through the barn doors. Relieved not to find a black Sunfire drawing up outside, he headed straight on to the highway leading to Firefall.

Three minutes later he was killing his flashers and letting the car drift to a halt just out of sight of the Hummer which was blocking the highway. He stepped out quietly and studied the other vehicle from some concealing foliage, then returned to his cruiser. Whatever was going on, it looked bad. Even if it was just some kind of prescience – as if somehow he'd had a vision of what was about to befall Firefall – the detail of it all was so uncannily accurate. And, worse, he obviously had no control over what would be unfolding.

But was that necessarily true? He forced himself to remember the events of his 'dream' in sequence, right up to the final fatal moment when the bomb had exploded, and they had all been thrown onto the glowing cube, and they had . . .

Died?

Maybe he *was* dead. He glanced at his white face in the mirror, startling himself. He sure as hell looked like a ghost. No, there had to be a logical explanation.

He knew Ed Rickenbacker was one of the leaders – at least until he was double-crossed, that is. *Christ, listen to yourself, Entwistle. You're actually believing this weird shit!* But he had been accurate in his predictions up until now, hadn't he? And he knew there were two guys wearing black sweatshirts with numbers on guard over there on the Hummer. There was no reason why his previous ruse should not work again . . . but he did not have time to mess around.

He climbed back into his Contour and headed straight for the Hummer, only switching on his lights and siren at the last moment.

As expected, the amateurs panicked, and he was out of the car and covering them with his .38 before they knew what hit them.

'Drop your weapons – or I drop *you*!'

Number 11 dropped his gun immediately, still the coward; the other raised his rifle slightly. Entwistle shot 32 in the shin, watched him scream and tumble off the Hummer into the ditch. He then climbed back into his cruiser and edged his way past the Hummer, satisfied that they had no means of communicating with their gang, nor the resolve to come after him.

Staying on Taft, he reached Circle Six within three minutes, and slowed to a stop at the intersection. So where would Ed be at this time? As Entwistle's car radio was smashed, he had to find another way to contact Rickenbacker. So he wheeled the car along Circle Six and took a quiet route back to his mother's house.

Carol was still fast asleep, and he didn't disturb her. Instead he went straight to a desk in the corner of the lounge and pulled out his CB rig, and found the police channel. So what to say?

'Sheriff Rickenbacker, this is Deputy Entwistle. Come back.'

No response.

'Ed, this is Entwistle. If you're listening, come back.'

He sat back, waiting, his heart racing. It all hinged on the other man's response. Even if some of that stuff he had dreamed was nonsense – a *time machine*, for Chrissakes? – Ed had still sent him out to Napier's Farm.

'Ed, if you can hear me, respond. This is Entwistle.'

There was another long pause, then a hiss and a voice replied. 'This is Rickenbacker. What is it, Entwistle?'

Entwistle recognized the voice and for a moment was frozen, unable to answer, his mind a blur of images like a movie on fast-forward ... until the action slowed and paused, then held on the still image of a man in black with a number on his shirt and a smoking revolver in his hand.

'This isn't Ed,' said Entwistle.

'So who is it?' replied the calm voice.

'Number 38.'

The radio went dead.

Holy shit. It was all true.

Four

Maribeth stared at the bag of school books on the chair by the motel bed. The smell of sex still lingered on the sheets, even though she had showered. And before that she had been having the weirdest dream . . .

She glanced over at the television, trying to recall whether it had been showing a film that could have inspired such a violent and fantastical tale. But then she remembered the set was broken.

Maribeth rolled over and sat up. She had a headache. She then crossed to the window and pulled aside the drapes, looking out into the night. She caught sight of her reflection: a pale face, her red hair still dark from the shower. She didn't usually suffer from nightmares, and was finding it difficult to come down from this one.

Releasing the window catch, she pushed open the upper frame, drinking in the cool air, and feeling the perspiration on her face turn cold. *Hellation*, what a dream . . .

But then she remembered why she was here, about Ben Angelis, and the dilemma it posed of getting back into town undetected . . . just like it did in the dream. And thinking back to the people in her dream, she found herself wishing it was Deputy Entwistle she had been sharing her bed with, rather than Ben Angelis. Now all the horrors of her nightmare were slowly coming back to her in vivid and bloody detail.

She began to get dressed, an awful feeling of déjà vu accompanying every movement. Then she picked up the schoolbag and slipped out of the cabin. Outside the motel's office she debated whether to call a cab, and had decided against it again when a sudden impulse made her knock on the door. If it *had been* a dream, why should she repeat her actions?

A minute later the bleary-eyed owner – a fat man called Fitzroy, wearing a stained grey dressing gown – pulled open the door and glared at her accusingly.

'Waddisit? You know the goddam time, babe?'

'I need to use the phone.'

'Emergency?'

'Can I use it, please?'

He grunted, then held open the door. Through a cloud of whiskey fumes, Maribeth made her way behind the reception desk to reach the telephone.

'Lock up after yourself,' said Fitzroy as he lumbered his way to the back room and slammed the door behind him, the sound of video sex providing a muted reminder of why she was here at all.

She picked up the receiver. She should ring a cab, and damn the rumours, but it had all seemed so *real* – and then she remembered getting her fingers shot off!

She stared at her hand: her long, slender digits were a perfect match for her physical build. She could now remember the armed assault on the rig pontoon as plain as

... as plain as if it had happened. She was grateful that the human mind couldn't recreate the pain of it, for the loss of her fingers would have been horrendous.

She flexed them with relief, and ran on through her dream: the killings, the violence, the explosions ... so *real.* She hated war movies, abhorred violence, and yet she had just written a Schwarzenegger blockbuster in her head – and thrown in a sinister government conspiracy to boot. No, it was all preposterous. But the other characters, the Deputy and the black boy, they had seemed so *real,* too, though she didn't know either of them ...

Then she checked her watch, and her heart skipped a beat. The watch had stopped – as had the clock on the reception desk.

On an impulse she grabbed the directory and looked up a number for C. M. Entwistle. No listing. Well, he was a deputy, he might have an unlisted number. Who had his mother been? Carol Glass. How on earth did she know *that*? Still, she checked for a number, but found only the Glasshouse Restaurant. Why did she want to talk to them anyway? *'Excuse me, but you were in this stupid dream ...'* Oh, hellation! Well, if she was going to make a fool of herself she would at least make sure there was no comeback.

She tossed the phone book aside and rang Information and was given a number. Dialled it up. Waited. After six rings a man answered.

'Yes?'

Maribeth paused. This was going to be *so* embarrassing.

'Were you there when the bomb went off?'

'Who is this?'

'Please answer the question.' *Please don't, please don't,* she silently begged.

There was a long, agonizing silence, eventually broken by the man's quiet, halting response.

'Yes, I was, Miss Hamilton . . . but I suspect, like me, you didn't want to know that.'

Oh, no . . . 'S-so it's all true? Everything?'

'Yes, unfortunately.'

'*Hellation!*' she said, dropping the phone.

She felt faint and sat down in the tatty leather chair behind the reception desk and stared out into the motel parking area. But all she could see was her own image staring back at her like a woman from another world. Or another time.

A small tinny voice broke into her reverie. She reached for the receiver and put it to her ear.

'Hello, hello . . . Miss Hamilton?'

'Yes,' she said hoarsely. 'What are you going to do?'

Del listened to the sound of his wife weeping from down the hall, his mind stubbornly refusing to accept this appalling conundrum. But unless he was *still* dreaming . . .

'I'll stop Hartsby,' he finally decided. 'It's too late to stop Firefall being taken over, but with him out of the picture the situation might be resolved without loss of life.'

'But if number 38 is in charge, people will be killed eventually.'

'Not necessarily. Hartsby appears to have been in contact with him throughout. Without Hartsby to give him orders, he may be more reasonable.'

'Perhaps . . .'

'Where are you now?' he asked.

'In a motel outside Firefall. Yesterday I . . . well, whatever day it was, I walked into town and eventually met up with Deputy Entwistle and Greg Henley, after I . . . killed one of their men.'

'Well, there'll be none of that this time. I want you to stay out of town. Stay in your motel room, watch the news, see what happens – and be grateful you got a second chance.'

'Not if what Hartsby said was true. Then we *died*,' she said, the full horror of her words suddenly hitting her as badly as any period cramp. She gripped her side, the pain intense, a cold sweat sprouting on her brow, and she had to bend double and breathe in deeply.

Del's Christianity had often been tested in the past, both by what he had to witness as an agent and what his job required of him, but he was having to dig really deep to find anything positive in their current experience.

'I prefer to think we were given another chance.'

'To get it right?' she said through gritted teeth.

'Yes,' said Del, steeling himself for the task he had just set himself.

Maribeth took some comfort in this idea, not least because when they had died the first time round the entire town would have been killed as well. She had heard some of Hartsby's explanation over the intercom, but she had also formed some kind of mental link with the glowing cube – and that strange intimacy still lingered, if she would but admit it, prompting her thoughts and guiding her actions, like cue cards being held up for a TV host.

'Now, promise me you won't try anything,' Del said, disturbing her train of thought.

'I don't see what I *can* do.'

'Good. As long as you stay out of Firefall you'll be safe. That's an order from the FBI, ma'am.' It was an attempt at humour that failed

There was a long silence.

'Good luck,' Maribeth said finally.

'And you.'

The phone went dead. She slowly replaced the receiver, her hands shaking as the truth overwhelmed her. *Hellation in a high hat!* If Agent Collingwood succeeded, then he could well be right, especially if Hartsby had been directing the operation all along. But then another thought occurred.

What if he *failed* to stop Hartsby? What if Hartsby remained in control? And then she thought of the children and their families in town, of the fear they would soon be experiencing: the uncertainty, the threats, and that final explosion designed to wipe the town off the map. All those innocent people . . . and Deputy Entwistle.

The image of his bloodied face, as he dragged himself from the wreckage of the elevator towards the cube, brought a lump to her throat. But then she also recalled the ease with which she had obeyed his order to shoot off Collingwood's hand. His *hand*. Oh, hellation! And she hadn't even apologized! She began laughing – a desperate, toneless sound, one that an insane person might make – and it was some moments before she understood just how close she was to surrendering her sanity.

She forced herself to rise from the chair and hammer

on the rear office door. When Fitzroy answered she demanded the keys to his car. As he protested she grabbed the greasy lapel of his dressing gown.

'I want your car, and I want it now. Just give me one hour' – she fished in her bag – 'and you can run up any tab you like on my Visa.'

The man's dopey eyes lit up, his finger already itching to switch to the Shopping Channel. He grabbed for the card.

'The keys?' she insisted.

He pulled them off a hook. 'Blue Honda,' he said.

She took them, ignoring the key fob shaped like an erect penis. 'One other thing.'

'What?' he said, taking the card.

'Do you have a gun?'

Five

How long Del sat in his kitchen, his mind going over and over his plan, he didn't know. In fact it was only the expected phone call from Hartsby that roused him, again. Having answered it as naturally as he could, he then dressed quickly, making sure to put on his best suit. He would need to do some bluffing and, as his long career had taught him, looking smart was the first step to being believable. (The public, colleagues, superiors, they all respected a well-pressed suit and a good haircut, rounded off with politeness and punctuality.)

He then went back into the bedroom and sat by his darling Gloria, taking her fretting hands and clutching them on her lap.

She stared up at him, still burbling quietly, not recognizing him, but some small part of her dying mind telling her that she was safe with this big man. He tilted her head up and kissed her on the lips. Her breath was stale but he didn't mind. He stroked her hair, speaking softly.

'I'm sorry I could never give you children, Gloria. I know you wanted kids . . . *I* wanted kids . . . And then there was all the crap I put you through with the Bureau. How you stuck by me all those years, all the home moves, all the let-downs, I'll never know. All I do know, my dearest, is that no man ever loved a better, kinder woman, and that if there's a God then He's a mean bastard for making you suffer this way.'

Despite his faith, the last eighteen months had tested him to the limit. And this madness that had apparently engulfed him and the town of Firefall seemed to be the final straw. And yet . . . and yet it was *so* big, *so* inexplicable, that he had to believe what he had said to Miss Hamilton: it was a test and they were now being given a chance to make amends.

He kissed Gloria on the forehead, and felt her shiver slightly, as if in recognition, but then she resumed her meanderings.

'I love you, Gloria. I love you enough to die for. Thank you for all you gave me and all the good times we had, and I'm so, so sorry for everything we never did.'

He took a pillow from behind her head and placed it over her face, then leaned onto it, pressing one hand tight to it and waiting until her skittering hands stalled and her frail form relaxed. Then he tenderly lifted the pillow and eased it back behind her head, and arranged the bed covers, crossing her small hands over the sheets and closing her eyes. Again he kissed her, the last warm touch he would ever feel from his wife of thirty-four years, and then, weeping quietly, he walked into the kitchen, dialled 911 and asked for paramedics to see to his wife.

Then he checked his revolver and his ID, did up his jacket, and walked down to the waiting car. He knew he was now damned, but knew he was as right as he had ever been in a life dedicated to right.

Entwistle didn't have many choices. Sheriff Rickenbacker had sent him out to Napier's Farm, and was apparently the originator of the conspiracy; and events were already so under way that locating Ed now wouldn't stop it. Besides, the guy was probably already in the Town Hall and Entwistle knew that place was unbreachable.

The other police deputies? But who could he trust? However well he thought he knew people, they could just as easily be working along with Rickenbacker. Even if he found any of them at home, there was no guarantee that they didn't have a sweatshirt somewhere in their attic which marked them out as a team player. And even if he did find someone he could rely on, how to convince them of what he himself knew? *Because he had used a time machine?* Get real.

He filled a glass with water and swilled it down, gasping at its coldness. The clock told him he was probably too late anyway; whatever he did now would only leave him exposed outside, a plain target on the streets. So what about the other three who had also used that machine?

The FBI guy, Collingwood? He would be miles away. Maribeth Hamilton? No idea where she'd be, though he wished he could find her. He admired a woman of character and she had certainly proved to be determined. (She was also attractive, even if that was just a bonus.)

And the black kid? The only place he knew where Greg Henley might be was where he first bumped into him on the junction of Circle Five and Elm. But if any of the others had made it – and if this wasn't all some seriously fucked-up nightmare – they wouldn't likely repeat their actions anyway! Each of them was as alone as they had originally been this morning, or yesterday, or whenever it had all damned happened.

He drained another glass of water. So what should he do? Slip out of town with Carol? Contact the authorities outside? Except most of those authorities were under the command of Hartsby, weren't they? He turned on his police scanner in the hope that he might pick up some clue as to the loyalties of his fellow deputies. Nothing was said for a couple of minutes, and he had almost convinced himself that the scanner was faulty, when a message came over.

'Unit Two, Unit Two, report of disturbance Gibson Road. Can you handle?'

'Unit Two proceeding.'

That sounded like Gil Brackhouse responding to Rob Pilcher the dispatcher. That could mean neither of them knew what was going on – but it could also be that both were just maintaining an illusion of normality. Of all the deputies, Entwistle considered Brackhouse the most trustworthy, but he was also a gambler, and a share of five million dollars would provide a mighty temptation. Maybe

Entwistle could intercept him, put a gun to his head and find out the truth . . . Gibson Road? He knew that address. Of course! The Campbells' house.

He beat Brackhouse to the house by thirty seconds and had his gun to Greg Henley's head as he tried to exit. A bundle in the boy's hand was clamped tight to his chest.

Brackhouse ran over from his cruiser, his gun ready.

'Hi, Entwistle, where you been?'

'Radio's busted.'

Entwistle studied his fellow deputy, who didn't seem surprised at Entwistle being there – which meant he didn't know of the set-up at Napier's Farm. But that still didn't mean Brackhouse wasn't involved in the big picture. What was it Klein had said: 'Not everyone knows everyone else . . .'?

'So what's the story?' said Brackhouse, peering into the hallway.

You tell me, thought Entwistle, barely able to think straight.

'I'm about to ask Henley here the same question. You check inside.'

As soon as Brackhouse had entered the house, Entwistle turned to Greg. 'You anything to say, boy?'

His face shining with sweat, Greg lifted quivering arms.

Entwistle stepped back. 'Easy . . .'

The boy's bundle unfurled itself to reveal a large white number 59 on a black sweatshirt.

'True,' was all Greg could manage. '*True!*'

Entwistle exhaled sharply. 'Oh my God . . .'

His oath was echoed from inside the hall. 'Looks like Campbell's bought it. Musta come off the landing. Broken neck.'

Entwistle stared at Greg.

'Accident. Honest. It—'

Entwistle grabbed Greg's arm and, pulling him behind him, walked them both into the hallway.

There he saw Brackhouse kneeling by the twisted body of Hal Campbell, checking for a pulse. Summer Campbell was sitting on a chair, her hands in her lap, her wide eyes staring at her dead father like a disbelieving infant. She turned to look at Entwistle and the pain and loss in her eyes was heart-wrenching.

'Looks like that kid finally went too far—'

Entwistle smashed Brackhouse across the head with his revolver and curtailed his verdict.

'Sorry, Gil,' Entwistle said, honestly.

The Deputy slumped to the floor. Greg picked up the man's dropped .38 and walked over to Summer, but Entwistle grabbed his arm, aware that the poor girl was a fraction away from total hysteria.

'Leave her, please, for all our sakes . . .'

Greg stared at Summer, her scared eyes boring into his. It was plain that at that moment she didn't recognize who he was or why he was there; all she knew was that her father, her only parent, was lying dead on the floor in front of her.

Entwistle slowly pulled Greg back to the front door.

'I'm sorry, Summer,' he said. 'You'll never understand. I'm sorry for all of this.'

Stepping outside, Entwistle sucked in cool air and

tried to steady the shaking in his legs. Shock was catching up with him.

'What now?' mumbled Greg, the Deputy's gun seeming a dead weight in his hand.

'More like "What then?"' said Entwistle, without any humour.

Seven

Maribeth pulled the rattly Honda Civic up to the kerb outside her home: one of four small apartments in a bland two-storey building near the corner of Hoover and Circle Six. Her original encounter on Nancy Road would have taken place an hour from now, so she was theoretically ahead of the game, but did it matter? She could try contacting the outside world, but who would believe her? So she had to presume that Special Agent Collingwood would already be doing his best to avert the coming disaster, though there were no guarantees. And even if Entwistle and Greg were also in town, they might not succeed in improving on their previous performance – which meant that if all three of the others failed, then the fate of the town could rest on her own shoulders.

She walked into her apartment and closed the door behind her, and began to cry. When she saw how the clocks instantly stopped on her entry, the temptation to just twist the locks and slide the bolts and curl up in a ball behind the sofa and wish the horror away was almost irresistible. But then she bumped into her desk, and the computer that she must have left on from the previous evening flickered into life, its screensaver presenting a white screen populated by a couple of small cartoon cats chasing butterflies.

Almost immediately this square of white light arrested Maribeth's attention. As she gradually defocused, her world became a friendlier, safer place. Oh, hellation, she just wanted to stay here, to touch that screen and feel its secure warmth course through her fingers and into her body and then . . . and then . . .

She slapped at the mouse and a personal finances spreadsheet appeared instead, all grey on blue, and the spell was broken.

Let others worry about the damn conspirators; let others do the negotiating or fighting or whatever it took. This time it might turn out differently. She was a schoolteacher, an ordinary woman; she wasn't meant to be a heroine.

Then her mind began to relive the nightmare of the time before: the man she had shot, the violence, the gunfire, the explosions . . . and the death of the town. For that bomb had exploded and destroyed Firefall, killing everyone she knew, everything she cared about. All her pupils . . . Oh, hellation!

But this time she did not run to the bathroom. Much to her surprise the memories had a different effect. The more she recalled the horrors the more she was determined that the outcome would now be different and that she would do her best to help avert disaster. This time she would be prepared. This time she wouldn't take unnecessary risks or cause needless bloodshed.

Wiping the tears from her face she judged the odds. But what did it matter? Everyone she knew or cared about in Firefall was already locked into a pattern leading to their deaths when that bomb exploded. She could run around the streets screaming or she could skulk in backyards and urge people to sneak away, but ultimately ninety-nine per cent of the town – the old, the young, the families, the visitors, the good, the bad ... oh, Lord help me, *the children* – all would be blown to pieces. It was her duty as a caring citizen privy to horrible pre-knowledge to do all she could to help change events. Why else had they been given a second chance? But if she was to make a difference this time she needed to select her target very carefully and plan her strategy in detail – and the one place she must avoid was the Town Hall.

On shaking legs she went into her kitchen and made herself a strong black coffee – she had been up most of the night, after all. As she sipped it, she got out a map of the town, spread it on her breakfast bar, and studied it with the new-found eye of a military strategist. She would have no allies and no fall-back position: once she was out on the streets there was no turning back, only the possibility of hiding and waiting for the eventual explosion. She would also need some effective weapon other than the hideous and thoroughly unreliable Saturday night special the motel owner had foisted on her. Ten minutes later she had a plan – and the thought of what she intended finally had her trotting to the bathroom.

Another ten minutes and she was dressed in black jeans, dark blue sweatshirt, and trainers, her hair tied back, the key she needed retrieved from her desk. Looking at the telephone she wondered if she should call her parents, but didn't know what she could say to them. It wasn't as if any explanation for the early-morning call would make sense; the only thing that would make sense would be if she packed her bags and headed out of town. But she couldn't do that; run now and she would be for ever haunted by the knowledge that she might have been able to effect something, however small, to help change the course of ... go on, say it: *history*.

So instead of running or hiding, she slipped out of her apartment building and drove over to the animal rescue shelter. There she used her key to let herself into the surgery, where lay her weapon of choice.

Del Collingwood knew that Hartsby would be calling him soon so he instructed Calthorpe, his driver, to pull over at a public telephone. There he called up Fuller at Quantico.

'Hi, Del. Long time.'

You have no idea, thought Del. 'Whatever I say, just do it, OK?'

'You in trouble?'

'Sort of. I need to know the whereabouts of Emile Hartsby.'

'*The* Emile Hartsby?'

'He's got me working for him. Believe me, I know he's a piece of work, but I need a face-to-face with him. All I've got now is him calling me.'

'And you want to surprise him?'

'You could say that.'

'I'll do what I can. I'll use Red Route, that should shake him out.'

'Thanks for taking the risk.'

'I know you, Del. And that's unusual these days, the way the Bureau's been politicized.'

'Appreciate it. Oh, and *I'll* call *you*.'

Del got back into the car and ordered the puzzled Calthorpe to drive on.

Red Route was a term used when information was needed in a hurry and employing the usual channels would slow it down. Red Route meant it was a request from the President or one of his top advisers. If Fuller was caught in his lie, he would get in big trouble – there's no point having a short cut if everyone starts using it – but Fuller and Del went back a long way.

As he watched the world pass by, Del remembered the good times with Gloria. That brought a smile to his face, despite what he had just done. He had no doubts he had done the right thing, it was just the fact that he'd needed to do it at all. Gloria was only fifty-three, two months away from her next birthday.

They had been driving for almost thirty minutes, lights and siren full on, and he had just heard the first recording of the terrorists' demands patched through to the television in the car when, right on cue, Hartsby's call came in to him.

'Special Agent Collingwood, my name is Hartsby, ACA,' said the voice on Del's car phone. 'I will be in charge of this operation, but you will be my liaison on the ground. People will take orders from you, understand? Hostage Rescue are tied up with a hijacking at Dulles and the siege in Sacramento, and Cheyenne SWAT were shot to pieces in a botched bank robbery in Laramie two days ago. You are the highest-ranking agent I can get for the next two hours and if those bastards hold true to their noon deadline, no one will be able to get here from Washington in time to assume on-site control.'

Del wasn't sure how to reply. The last time he had called Fuller, and he didn't want to waste time doing that, but would that arouse Hartsby's suspicions? The man knew Del's record after all – and Del knew why he had been chosen as the sacrificial lamb.

'Mr Hartsby, if you're in charge, why aren't you giving the orders direct?'

'Let's say my presence isn't necessary. There is a lot more at stake than the fate of an oil rig and some Treasury dollars, but for now you needn't concern yourself with that. Suffice to say I work for a branch of government that gives me jurisdiction over yours. You may check with your immediate superiors if you wish.'

'There's no need for that. Judging by their broadcast, they mean business and we haven't got much time.'

'I like your attitude, Collingwood. I'll get back to you once you're on the scene.'

Del put the phone down and tapped Calthorpe on the shoulder.

'Stop the car at the first payphone you see.'

'But the—'

'Just do it!' Del shouted over the whine of the siren.

Five minutes later he was in a truck stop, yelling above the din of breakfast and diesel engines.

'Where is he?'

'Wyoming.'

'I know that! Sorry, I need an exact location.'

'He's mobile. In a Double A Mobile Communications Centre, to be exact. A comtruck.'

The bastard. He must be planning to stop sometime and get the helicopter out to Firefall.

'You got a fix on the truck?'

'Route 26, heading west. I can get a satellite fix—'

'Do it.'

A minute later Del had the location accurate to within a hundred yards from one minute before.

'Thanks, Elmore. And forget this conversation ever happened.'

'What conversation?'

Del trotted back to the car. 'Get us out onto 26.'

'But Firefall's only ten miles—'

'Will you ever do what you're told, Agent Calthorpe? I thought you believed in obeying orders?'

'Pardon, sir?'

'Never mind. Just drive.'

Fifteen minutes later they intersected with 26, and travelling at ninety miles per hour caught up with the truck as it left Pagabee.

'I want you to get round that truck, and get it to stop.'

'Hey, that's a comtruck. I try and—'

Del put his gun to Calthorpe's neck. 'What did I tell you about obeying orders?'

A thoroughly confused Calthorpe accelerated and pulled alongside the truck, then pulled in front of it, causing the truck to brake sharply.

'Now, just ease on down and slow it,' said Del, aware that if they stopped side-on the truck would more than likely just drive over them.

Despite the truck's blaring horn and flashing lights, both vehicles were soon reduced to a twenty miles per hour crawl, Calthorpe and Del waving the vehicle down through their respective windows.

Much to Calthorpe's surprise and relief, the truck did eventually stop, pulling over to the side of the road in a cloud of dust, its air brakes hissing impatiently. (No doubt their car's licence plate had been confirmed as belonging to a Bureau vehicle.) Del stepped out, his gun hidden in his jacket pocket, and walked back towards the truck, his FBI warrant card held high in his right hand.

The door in the side of the trailer slid open, the steps dropped down, and out walked two shirtsleeved operatives. Both wore sunglasses, and both had their hands conspicuously placed on their shoulder holsters.

Del walked straight up to them. 'Collingwood, FBI. I need to speak to Hartsby.'

'Who?' said one of them, totally unfazed by Del's unusual entrance.

'Don't fuck me around. Hartsby's in there. I need to speak to him. Now!'

The other man held up his hands. 'Don't care who you are, if we say Mr Hartsby's not in the truck, then he's—'

'If you don't know who he is, how come he's a Mister all of a sudden?' said Del.

The two men shifted uneasily.

'Hold it!' shouted a voice from behind the two men.

Del looked past the grim-faced duo and saw Hartsby appearing at the top of the steps, putting on his own sunglasses.

'Collingwood, what on earth are you doing here? You should be at Firefall by now.'

Del eased between the two men and walked towards the trailer.

'*Now*? That's an interesting word. I have to speak to you.'

'They've invented the phone for that,' said Hartsby descending the steps and moving into Del's path, as if to stop him seeing into the trailer.

'Don't worry,' said Del, leaning down to the shorter man. 'I've already seen inside.'

'How could you?'

Del smiled. 'Ever had that feeling of déjà vu?'

A shock of recognition came into Hartsby's eyes, and he stepped back as Del pulled his revolver and pointed it. 'Maybe this time the town'll make it.'

He fired at the man's heart but before he could pull the trigger a second time, six bullets ripped into his back and spine, dropping him instantly, all control gone from his body.

Hartsby was whipped back by the impact of Del's shot, but grabbing the step rail he managed to remain standing, albeit bent over and coughing.

Del lay face-down, his only sight the man's shoes. *Fall, you bastard, fall.*

Then the feet moved – towards him. And Hartsby leaned down into Del's range of vision, his face white and twisted with pain, but most definitely not that of a dying man.

'Tell me, not-so-Special Agent Collingwood, did the town go boom that time?'

'Yes . . .' croaked Del, his body strangely painless despite his wounds. 'And so did you.'

'Well, I'll have to be more careful this time around.'

Hartsby stood up again, out of Del's sight. Next Del

saw the man's dark grey jacket and white shirt fall to the ground, followed by a white bulletproof vest, and then, as the man walked back into the trailer, bare from the waist up and rubbing his chest, Del heard '. . . *ruined a perfectly good suit* . . .' and felt a gun barrel touch the back of his head.

He wanted to say Gloria's name, to whisper his love for her, but his time had finally run out.

Nine

Entwistle pulled his cruiser into an alley and slewed to a halt.

'We gotta have a plan.'

Greg nodded, but his face showed he still wasn't with it yet.

Entwistle shook him. 'Look, kid, there's just us now. We can't depend on anyone else. We don't know where the others are or what they're doing, or even if they made it. Only us two can do anything to stop Firefall being blown away. Now are you ready?'

'Ready for what?'

'I don't know ... but look at the alternatives. You just killed Hal Campbell.'

'He fell!'

'You are you, Hal Campbell was Hal Campbell, now who they gonna believe? The little black psycho who hated Hal Campbell or the Hal Campbell who begged that you be put away for the sake of his daughter? If he was to rise from his grave and point his finger at you in open court you couldn't seem more guilty! Now, add to that me whacking Brackhouse and leaving the murder scene and I'm in deep shit too. But on top of all that we know what's happening in this damn town – and no one's going to believe us!'

'Ever thought of being a public defender?'

'It gets worse, kid. They'll have taken KFLL by now, the telephone exchange, the Town Hall. Getting a message out isn't the problem, it's stopping what's going to happen from happening.'

'We tried that before.'

'No, we didn't. What we did was try and *survive.* This time we've got to *attack.*'

'Attack?' Greg looked at the two of them. 'Can't you see the flaw in this plan, man?'

'Yeah, the flaw is we probably die . . .'

Greg stared at Entwistle, then pushed open his door and walked to the side of the alley and pressed his forehead against cool brickwork. 'No way, no way . . .'

Entwistle climbed out after him and leaned back against the wall, next to Greg.

'Did you notice how the clocks are stopping again?'

'They're what?'

'The clocks out at Napier's Farm, Deputy Brackhouse's wristwatch – they all just stopped.'

'Meaning?'

Entwistle sighed. 'I don't know. Hartsby said some stuff about you getting close to the time machine makes you affect clocks like that. And I suppose it's now telling us that we're going to get near it *again* – whether we like it or not.'

Greg kicked angrily at a piece of garbage.

'Come noon, everyone dies anyway, kid. Including

Summer.' He tried not to think of the same fate befalling Maribeth Hamilton.

'Don't call me kid.'

'OK, sorry. Look, forget it's us, right. We're back making movies . . .'

Greg turned and offered a bitter smile, which Entwistle ignored.

'We're making a movie. You've seen the plot, how it ends. How do we stop that bomb going off on the rig?'

Greg let out a deep sigh. The bastard was playing dirty. 'We can't defuse it, or wish it away?'

'No, it's up there in the open. And we can't get to it for the same reason.'

'So we have to stop whoever's going to detonate it.'

'And that would be Hartsby.'

'Except we don't know where he comes from, when he arrives – nothing.'

'OK. Work backwards,' said Entwistle, glad to be able to apply logic at last. '*He* set it off, so how do we make sure the guy doesn't get here?'

'Not give him a reason to come?'

'Yes, but we're too late for that. Firefall's taken.'

'So?'

'So we take out the leaders. Most of those assholes are amateurs. Once they see it's all falling apart, they'll most likely run or surrender. Even the pros will want out. We can then let the world know what's been happening – or at least make sure Hartsby doesn't detonate the bomb.'

'Makes sense.' Greg laughed at his words. 'But how do we take out number 38?'

'Full-frontal assault. Catch them off guard. So far, they have no idea there's any resistance in town. Go for the throat and they may not be ready yet.'

'Uh-oh, here comes the bad news: how do you plan to do that?'

'I've got an idea but it'll mean getting bloody.'

'Surprise, surprise. Our blood or theirs?'

'Hopefully theirs.'

'The plan's getting better. So what do we use?' he said, looking down at Brackhouse's revolver which he hadn't realized was in his hand.

'I've got stuff at my mother's house.'

'Yeah, but that's just guns.'

'What do you want? A tank?'

'No, we want an edge. Something that'll blow their socks off. Something . . .'

They looked at each other.

'Rickenbacker's house!'

Five minutes later they were slowing down on Circle One as they approached the Sheriff's house.

'Best way is to bold this out,' said Entwistle. 'Don't be afraid to shoot. They may have done nothing yet but we know what they're *going* to do.'

Greg nodded, though he didn't seem convinced.

Entwistle grabbed him by the shoulders and stared the frightened teenager in the eye. 'What have you got to lose, anyway? You're wanted for murder, your girlfriend won't have anything to do with you now her daddy's dead, and you're trapped in a town full of conspirators which you know is going to be blown to pieces. Of course, you could always go watch MTV . . .'

'Shut up, or I'll forget you're on my side.'

Entwistle offered Greg his hand and the boy took it.

'And no doubts,' said Entwistle. 'We are right; they are wrong.'

'We are right; they are wrong,' echoed Greg.

'Now, let's do it.'

Entwistle drove the cruiser onto Rickenbacker's short driveway and stepped out and walked purposefully to the door. As he was about to knock, a black-clad but unhooded man answered, gun aimed at Entwistle.

'Easy, boy,' said Entwistle. 'Got a message from 38.'

He could see this had thrown the man – what was a cop doing delivering messages? Entwistle pressed home his advantage.

'Wants a couple of us deputies in uniform acting like we're concerned for the people. You know, everything'll be all right as long as you cooperate.'

'Yeah. Makes sense.'

'No, it doesn't, you asshole,' said Entwistle, punching the man hard in the face, and giving him two more sharp jabs before he hit the ground.

Taking his gun, he signalled to Greg, who ran from behind the cruiser and followed Entwistle into the house. In the lounge they found two men, both unmasked, watching TV and eating cereal.

'Getting plenty of fibre, boys?' asked Entwistle.

The two men turned to find a sheriff's deputy holding a revolver on them.

'One move out of either of you and Mr Kellogg loses a couple of customers.'

One of them lunged for a gun on the table beside

him, and Entwistle shot him in the knee. The man screamed and fell onto the floor and rolled about, blood running between his hands, patterning the powder-blue carpet. Greg walked over to the other man and smashed him across the back of the head with his pistol butt.

'Shut him up,' said Entwistle, pointing his gun at the shrieking man. Greg smacked him upside his head, so he too fell silent.

'Whoever else is about will be here real soon after hearing that shot. Take cover.'

Greg ran for the wide patio window and peered out into the overgrown garden. Two men were bounding towards the house, rifles at the ready. Shit! He dived out of the way.

Entwistle hunched up behind the door through which they had entered the lounge, and waited for someone else who was running downstairs. Unfortunately, even though Greg had moved to the side of the window, he would still be in the line of sight of whoever entered the room from the hall. And Entwistle could also see that the two men in the garden were heading straight for the window rather than the side door, and so would spot him soon. Damn!

Timing was going to be tight. Grabbing the door handle, Entwistle chose his moment and slammed it shut. The door made solid contact, and he heard a gasp and a groan. Then he yanked open the door, jumped into the entrance space, and aimed his gun at a man who stood there holding his face.

'Should always knock,' said Entwistle, before kicking him in the balls and slamming his head against the door jamb.

He heard shouting from outside, and turned to see both men in the garden aiming their rifles at him through the wide windows. He had no way to escape.

Suddenly Greg stepped out in front of the window. The men in the garden, standing six feet apart, had their rifles trained on Entwistle hovering at the back of the room, inside the door. Greg was exactly midway between them and before either could take new aim he shot through the window at the man on the left, hitting him in the stomach.

As the other man shifted his aim, Entwistle took him out through the showering glass of the still disintegrating window, hitting him twice: in the shoulder and head.

He slowly lowered his gun and walked across the lounge to Greg, who stood shaking and staring at the writhing man he had just shot. Entwistle stood next to the boy, his own victim dead.

'You OK?'

'He's not.'

'But that could have been you.'

The man outside jerked then lay very still, blood smearing the grass around him.

'I killed him.'

'You killed others yesterday.'

Greg looked at him. 'Yesterday? You could call it that. Don't make it feel any better.'

'No, it doesn't. But remember: *we are right; they are wrong*. Now let's go get some more weapons.'

But despite his self-enforced righteousness, Entwistle vowed never to remove any of the conspirators' masks in case he discovered he had killed someone he knew.

They hurried through to the garage and examined the stockpile of weapons they knew they would find there.

'What do we take?'

Entwistle shook his head. 'Wish I knew. Let's be logical. It's a matter of tactics. We need explosives, machine-guns – go for quantity, not quality. Couple of rocket launchers, grenades, Uzis.'

They found a case of dynamite, complete with a reel of fuse and a battery-powered detonator.

'How long do you reckon that wire is?'

Greg held up the roll by its handle.

'Says a thousand metres.'

'I just got me a plan.'

It took two trips outside to get everything they needed loaded into the cruiser, by which time they could hear an approaching vehicle screeching round a turn, a block or so away, obviously in a hurry to find out why there had been shooting.

'What do we do?' asked Greg, slamming shut the cruiser's trunk.

'We take them out. Get behind those bushes on the lawn. First clear shot you get, plug them.'

'Just like that?'

'*Just* like that. You think they're going to invite you in for coffee and doughnuts when they find their friends are dead?'

Greg rolled across the lawn to the large hydrangea bush and hunkered low, while Entwistle knelt down beside the cruiser's hood.

A black BMW 525 slid to a halt outside the next

house, and three men leaped out of it and ran for cover. Entwistle recognized one of the numbers, 77, but couldn't place it. Damn, three opponents could be tricky, and if they didn't get out of here fast there would be others arriving. Entwistle also realized that if the terrorists had any proper training, they would soon guess where he and Greg were hiding.

The three men were crouched down behind a four-foot-high wall that bordered Rickenbacker's lawn. Chances were they would be making their way towards the house before braving a look over it. Entwistle checked around for inspiration but all he could see was a flower bed with scattered rocks to his rear. What to do, what to do?

They had come here in such a hurry not just because of the gunshots, but because they knew the place contained a lot of their arms and ammunition. If someone had breached their security, they could have stolen those weapons. Therefore they must assume ... Entwistle picked up a rock, feeling its weight. *Yes.* He stood up and hurled it across the lawn and over the wall.

'Grenade!' he shouted.

As it landed in undergrowth, the three men suddenly leaped over the wall, desperate to escape what they hadn't time to check. Entwistle stood up straight, grasping his revolver in both hands, and picked off two of them. The third fell to a single shot from Greg, who was now lying on his back facing the wall.

This time there were no regrets, no inquests between them. They both got into the Contour and Entwistle drove east along Circle One, away from the Town Hall, then hung a left on Coolidge and headed up to Circle Three, where he pulled into the 7-Eleven parking lot and drew the car up at its rear, out of sight.

Greg fell out of the cruiser and threw up into a dumpster, his body awash with adrenalin and refusing to respond normally. Entwistle pushed open his own door and sucked in the stench of ripe garbage. He had shot at men before – twice, in fact, in San Francisco – but neither time had he killed them. In both cases he had been in the right and felt no guilt, knowing in both situations that his failure to fire could well have ended with himself being shot. And it was the same here in Firefall, though that didn't make it any less unpleasant.

Then a thought began to nag at him.

What if by changing the way things had happened that first time round they now precipitated a different disaster? If Hartsby found out his plan wasn't working, he might move his schedule up, and instead set an 11:00 a.m. deadline. Worse: outbreaks of fighting in the town would provide an even better cover for Hartsby's story; he could then claim the bomb was accidentally set off by those among the population foolhardy enough to take on the invaders. After all, he had insisted he would rather see the device destroyed than taken by others. In other words, Entwistle and Greg might just have sealed the fate of Firefall for a second time.

'Greg, stop your puking, start working,' said Entwistle. If they were to avoid his new worries becoming fact, they needed to move fast.

'What you gonna do?'

'Take out the Town Hall.'

'Oh, is that all.'

Ten

Tall as she was, and fit as she was, Maribeth had never had much strength in her legs. Naturally slim and possessing only a small appetite, she had never seen the need, nor indeed the attraction, of concerted bouts of aerobics or exhausting workouts in sweat-sodden gyms. Consequently anything involving a long run or an uphill trek was doomed to failure. However, her upper body was unusually strong. Again she made no special effort to exploit it, but this had proven useful during games of volleyball – and more recently when she had been dragged under the bulldozer. And now it was coming into play again.

After arming herself at the animal shelter, and wrapping her weapons up in a plastic bin liner, she had made her way on foot along Circle Six, keeping out of sight of any approaching vehicles, until she was able to turn onto Roosevelt. Halfway down, she spotted a truck pulling up on the corner of Circle Four and half a dozen black-clad men getting out. It was with some shock she realized this was the first proof that events really were about to repeat themselves. Ducking down on a nearby veranda, she waited as the men dispersed, then made her way round the back of the house and pressed on by crossing garden walls and fences until she reached Circle One.

There was no traffic about and checking her watch she realized the first demand messages would have been broadcast to the town by now. No turning back.

Maribeth dashed across the road, her heart pounding, her ears tuned for any warning shout, and then she was running down a narrow pathway between two souvenir shops, one of them, ironically, Herman Lury's Firefall Heaven. Coming out by the water's edge, she found herself at the back of a low building that was home to Rankin's Rowboats.

Knowing Gerry Rankin was in on the conspiracy and was to be publicly carted away and later 'executed', she realized his premises would be empty. She took the risk of smashing a small pane of glass on a door to let herself in. Once inside, she hid motionlessly out of sight for five minutes in case anyone came to investigate the noise of her break-in. Satisfied she hadn't been heard, she found the labelled keys that would give her access to the boats, and then she went into the boathouse itself.

There was a selection of boats, several of them covered in dust and plainly unused for some time. No wonder the man was worried about his business failing, but that was no excuse for his activities. No excuse whatsoever.

She found a small dark blue dinghy, complete with plastic paddles, and using all her strength, dragged this surprisingly heavy craft down the shallow cement ramp to the water's edge. There she pointed it in the right direction and gently eased it into the water. She knew her journey would be a lot quicker using a boat with an engine, but the noise of it would attract attention. Besides, small dinghies and rowing boats were forever working themselves loose and floating about the Hole, neighbours often retrieving them unbidden. It was all part of community life on a lake. Now she hoped that fact would provide her with cover.

She stepped into the fibreglass craft barely big enough for two – hellation, it was wobbly – and therefore all the less detectable to the casual eye, and began to row her way towards the Ultracom rig.

It was a long journey, the paddles being clearly designed for 'messing about' rather than for the hard graft of serious rowing. Every so often she would stop, lie low in the boat, and scan the horizon, looking for any tell-tale signs of her presence being detected: the flash of field glasses, sudden shouts, men standing on the bank, or, worst of all, a speedboat grinding its way across the lake towards her.

Her stop-start method, and the pathetic propulsion provided by the plastic paddles – so short they barely dipped their ends in the water – meant her journey stretched out to a good half-hour and by the time she was within swimming distance of the rig she was hot, tired, frightened, and convinced she had made a big, big mistake.

And then she heard a boat heading towards the rig from the opposite side of the Hole. If they spotted her sitting in the dinghy they wouldn't waste any time asking questions.

So she checked that her bundle was still airtight in its plastic bag, then slipped over the side of the boat, resisting the temptation to cry out as cold water saturated her clothing. *Hellation on skates!*

Keeping the plastic bag as much out of the water as

possible, she carefully kicked her way the thirty remaining yards to the cabin, silently praying that the approaching speedboat would dock itself on the other side of the rig. Thankfully it did, and she could hear voices as men jumped onto the pontoon and entered the building. Then the door slammed shut metallically, and quiet returned to the lake.

She pushed her bundle up onto the pontoon, then heaved herself up onto the wooden planking, where she spent a couple of shivering minutes catching her breath and wishing she was somewhere else. She checked the Town Hall clock. 8:51. Only a few minutes now until the first mock execution. Again there was nothing she could do to prevent that, or the genuine killings that would follow, but her present concern was for the awesomely powerful bomb perched a hundred feet above her, atop the fake drilling rig. All she had on her side was surprise. True, she was armed, but her choice of weapons – although they had been selected with care – might fail to perform satisfactorily. Hellation, why was she so squeamish?

She stood up, unwrapped the bundle, checked her equipment was ready, then edged round the pontoon until she could see the closed door of the rig cabin. She still had time to chicken out, but because as yet everything would have gone right for the conspirators they might easily be caught off guard. So she walked to the door, rapped on it hard, and stepped back.

A man opened it, number 97, clearly unprepared for the sight of a soggy redhead armed with two large pistols.

'What the—?'

Maribeth fired the gun in her right hand, the man immediately clutching at his chest and giving her a pained and puzzled look. He tried to speak, but suddenly fell to his knees, and then forwards, landing face-down at her feet.

'Who is it?' came a voice from inside.

Maribeth kept her cool and waited for the second man to reach the door, at which point she fired her other gun, catching him in the shoulder. Again there was pain and surprise followed by quick collapse.

Stepping over the two fallen men, she reloaded her air pistols with another pair of drugged darts and scanned the cabin's interior. It was exactly as she remembered it, but fortunately empty of other people. It still made her shiver.

She placed her guns on the table, then dragged the two unconscious men inside and shut the door. Checking their pulses, she found them slow and steady and guessed they would both be out of it for several hours. After all, she had used enough sedative on them to knock out a pony. Why she had chosen to be so humane with potential murderers she didn't know, but it gave her a small glow of satisfaction that she had accomplished the first part of her mission so effectively.

Now for the tricky part: disabling the bomb – or rather disconnecting it from the console that controlled it. But which console? She had been down below with the time machine when Hartsby had tricked Collingwood into setting off the bomb's timer.

It was as she reached the first console, praying there would be some clue, but doubting there would be a sign announcing BOMB CONTROL, that she noticed the stepladder was unfolded and standing underneath the roof hatch. The *open* roof hatch.

Never taking her eyes off the hole in the ceiling, she stepped back to the table and picked up one of her pistols. Too late, a man swung through, his head and shoulders upside down, his revolver pointing straight at her.

'Don't you move.'

Maribeth began to raise her pistol towards him. Hellation, why hadn't she anticipated that there could be more than two of them?

'Another inch and I'll blow your head off, babe.'

Maribeth froze.

'Better still, shoot yourself, bitch.'

'What?' she managed.

'That dart gun – use it on yourself. Or I'll use these bullets.'

She looked down at the air pistol and its dart. She couldn't shoot herself with it. She didn't know how much anaesthetic she could stand. Besides, once she was unconscious it would all be over. How long would she remain asleep? What would this man do to her then? He could shoot her, rape her . . .

'Fire that damn dart into your thigh now or I'll shoot.' He cocked his revolver for emphasis.

Maribeth looked down at her still wet thigh, aimed the pistol downwards, and after a moment's terrified hesitation, pulled the trigger.

The pain was intense and she instinctively reached for the dart's feathered tail and pulled it out, but even as it came loose, so did her mind. The room swam, her legs ceased to work, and she fell sideways onto the floor with a thud she never even felt.

Eleven

The problem wasn't the momentum – the hill would cater for that – and it wasn't the volume of explosives. By no means an expert, Entwistle knew that thirty-six sticks of dynamite would pack *some* kind of punch. No, the problem was steering.

Although Harding ran down to the Town Hall, it contained a slight curve and, more to the point, the entrance to the Town Hall was offset at the junction. If the Contour carried on straight it would miss the main building altogether and simply take out the construction site behind.

'Well, we're all set,' said Greg, walking back from the car and letting the fuse unreel. They were parked on Circle Six, well out of sight.

'The car hits,' said Entwistle, 'you grab the wire, cut it, attach it to the terminals, press the plunger. Kaboom!'

'I like the kaboom part, but the rest . . .'

'Can't risk connecting the terminals yet. If it gets ripped out . . .'

'OK, but what about the steering?'

'That's the sixty-four-thousand-dollar question.'

'How fast does the car need to be going?'

'As long as it gets to knock on the front doors, any

speed'll do. In fact, slow might be best. That way we're sure the fuse won't come loose.'

'OK, I'll do it, then,' said Greg, getting into the driver's seat.

'Hey, no way, kid. If anyone—'

'There's *you*, a sheriff's deputy with the law behind you, and there's *me*, a psycho murderer. However this comes out my ass is grass. This way I get to stick it to the mothers who fucked up my life: Hal Campbell's buddies.'

Entwistle could see the boy's point, not least that he himself would be better prepared than Greg to deal with anything that happened afterwards. The only doubt was whether Greg could get clear away before the vehicle blew up.

'Where you going to jump out of the car?' asked Entwistle.

'We need to be accurate, so I figure on stopping at the intersection with Circle Two. Set the car's aim true, tie the wheel, let her roll.'

'No. If they shoot out the tyres, it'll stop. It's got to have momentum so it keeps going.'

'OK, I'll sort it. Let's just get on with it before I change my mind.'

Five minutes later Entwistle stepped out of the car on Circle Three and Harding, taking with him two of the LAW missiles, an Uzi, and clips of ammunition. He knew their intended actions were probably going to kill the hostages-cum-conspirators, including Ed Rickenbacker, but with the entire town of Firefall at stake it was a cost that would have to be borne, however painful it might be.

'Just get away from the place, kid. Run like shit.'

'You can bet on that.'

He popped the trunk, pulled out the reel of fuse wire, and closed the lid gently, ensuring that the wire in the trunk had sufficient slack.

'OK, drive it slow at first, but once you got the Town Hall in your sights, bail out and take cover. Soon as she hits, I'm setting her off.'

'See you in a couple of minutes,' said Greg.

'Just make sure it ain't in a couple of pieces.'

Greg dropped the clutch and slowly the car drove down Harding towards Circle Two, the wire unrolling rapidly. Entwistle was pleased to see that it didn't snap. He pulled out his penknife, ready to grab it as soon as the car had stopped.

Greg reached Circle Two, the Contour already doing twenty miles per hour. Slowing slightly he adjusted the steering until he was heading straight for the Town Hall steps, above which loomed the double wooden doors of the Town Hall entrance. Then he switched off the engine, which locked the steering wheel in place, opened the door, and, without worrying about the consequences, dived out of the moving vehicle. Landing on his shoulder, he yelled in agony, but he let himself roll and bounce fully thirty yards down the hill behind the cruiser.

Only as he came to a halt, and was able to think of anything other than his pain, did he catch sight of the still accelerating cruiser as its pace easily carried it up the Town Hall steps, where it soared into the air and landed square against the doors, knocking them off their hinges, its radiator exploding and sending up a shower of scalding steam. Greg turned and looked back up the hill, to spot

Entwistle kneeling down with the detonator in front of him.

The wire cut, Entwistle flayed the two ends, slipped one under the left contact and spun the nut shut, then followed suit with the second bared wire. Then he pulled up the handle to prime the electrical charge, and rammed it home.

Nothing happened.

He checked the connections. They were solid. He pulled up the handle, primed it, pushed down. Again it failed to respond. The impact must have dislodged something. All those bastards would have to do would be unload the damn stuff! Even from this distance he could see the trunk lid had been thrown open. What a waste . . .

Then he heard a shout. It was Greg.

'The missile! Use the rocket!' Greg yelled, also guessing what had happened.

Entwistle frowned, then came realization. The LAW!

He picked one up, popped the tube end, extended it, pulled up the sight, and scanned through it for the wraith of steam now enveloping the Town Hall doors. But as his finger reached the trigger, he heard another voice, this time closer.

'Put that down or I'll blow your fucking spine out.'

Entwistle's heart skipped a beat. *Oh God no, so close . . .*

He could see black-clad figures swarming like ants over the cruiser, some already staring into the open trunk. Maybe he should fire anyway, do his duty – but he would probably miss.

'I'll give you just two seconds . . .'

Entwistle slowly lowered the missile launcher from his shoulder, letting it point at the ground, then he carefully turned around until he could see the man standing twenty feet away up the hill. He had a number 67 on his chest.

'Put it down real' fuckin' slow,' repeated the man, his rifle aimed unswervingly at Entwistle's chest.

'It's armed,' warned Entwistle. 'I'll have to be real careful or we'll both go.'

He suddenly recognized the man's number: he was the bastard who Maribeth had shot because he was going to rape her. Entwistle's anger surged.

The man watched as he slowly lowered the launcher to the ground.

'Now stand the fuck away—'

As it touched the road surface and rolled over because of its bottom-mounted handle, Entwistle pressed the trigger and it fired, and a second later the hooded man was up in the air minus a leg, the missile itself exploding in a parked pick-up behind him.

Entwistle dived for the second missile launcher, opened it, sighted on the Town Hall doors, and fired – and watched in satisfaction as it coursed a white trail down the hill, past Greg, and on to the rear of the Contour. Some of the men began to scatter, but it was too late.

The explosion was huge: the front two floors of the building ripped open, debris flung a hundred yards in every direction, men torn apart or thrown in one piece right across Circle One. All the windows within a three-block radius imploded, car alarms went off, and as the boom rolled across the Hole and the sounds of collapsing masonry and steel and glass filled the air there came screams of pain and terror.

Entwistle charged down towards Greg, but fell to his knees as bricks and metal fragments rained down on him, clipping him on the back and legs like God was ticking him off. And as the chaos in the air calmed, the chaos on the ground increased, with men running in all directions, mostly away from the building, but others towards it to see if they could help.

Entwistle stumbled on until at last he found Greg and dragged him clumsily onto the lawn of a nearby house, its immaculate green swath now transformed into a rockery as chunks of stone and smoking debris embedded themselves in the soft ground like a meteorite shower.

Greg was shaking his head. 'Jesus, man, we did it. We fucking did it!'

A breathless Entwistle watched the pandemonium at the bottom of the hill, then shook his head. 'No, we just started it. If 38 wasn't killed there, we may just have pissed him off.'

'Now he tells me.'

'Got to make sure.'

'Meaning?'

He handed Greg an Uzi.

'Meaning we go in there and finish it off.'

He helped Greg up, but as they were about to set off he spotted a man staring at him from the door of the house nearby. Entwistle beckoned him outside and the man reluctantly complied.

'It's Bill Farthing, isn't it?' said Entwistle.

'Yes, it is, Deputy.'

'We need your car.'

'To do what?'

'To go for a fucking picnic!' snarled Greg.

'Don't ask. Just give me the keys. Please.'

The man stared at them without reacting.

'Where the hell are they?' shouted Greg, rushing towards the house.

'Hall table,' said the man.

Greg burst through the front door, spotted the keys on the table, and grabbed at them – and then noticed a clock on the wall, its second hand sweeping past the figure 10. Holy shit, the clock was working!

As he tossed the keys to Entwistle, he shouted, 'Entwistle! The clock's working! His clock's working!'

Entwistle paused, trying to understand this information. Then he turned and stared into the Uno's interior. The car's clock had stopped.

'Get in,' he urged. 'No time!'

'You'll bring it back?' asked the owner.

'Want us to fucking valet it?' shouted Greg.

They got into the car, reversed out onto the street, then, in a cloud of burning rubber, headed for the Town Hall.

Greg was ecstatic. '*His* clock was working! That means we don't get close to that time machine! Oh, shit . . .' The possibilities hit Greg suddenly: the fact that the clock was working could just mean that they were going to *die.*

Understanding the boy's fears, Entwistle pointed at the car clock. '*This* one has stopped, so don't give up yet!'

This knowledge didn't cheer Greg. So what if

Entwistle could still stop clocks? Greg himself couldn't – which looked like bad news for Greg.

'You see a number 38, you aim for the circles of the 8 and cut the mother down!' shouted Entwistle.

'Where you going to be stopping?'

'Round back. If they want to get out of that building they got to do it through the back. Best place to corner the bastards.'

At which point Entwistle swung the car left and yomped it over the sidewalk onto the gravel space beside the Town Hall, scattering a couple of men and clipping two others, one of whom bounced over the hood and through the windshield, his bloodied face coming to rest on Greg's lap.

Despite the man's legs obscuring his vision, Entwistle managed to get the Uno round the side of the building and into the rear compound. However, the explosion had ruptured a fire hydrant and already the yard was inches deep in water from a fat jet shooting out from the corner of the main building. Brakes suddenly proving useless, Entwistle shouted a warning as the vehicle slammed sideways into the crawler crane of the piledriver, trapping him.

Greg kicked open his own door, then hauled their unwanted passenger in through the windshield and out through the same door, before leaning in and helping Entwistle to extricate himself from the now-broken side of the Fiat.

Shots suddenly rang out and Greg hit the ground, allowing Entwistle to fire with his Uzi from inside the car, and bring down the gunman who was firing from an entrance. There followed shouting and the crash of falling masonry, but no more shots.

Crouched over the dead terrorist, whose black mask was sodden with blood, they surveyed the back of the Town Hall through the heavy shower from the burst pipe.

'We going in?' said Greg.

'No, wait for them to come out.'

They were now up to their ankles in water, the compound having a central dip that served to pool the water.

'We need some advantage, while they're still confused!' Entwistle shouted above the hissing roar from the hydrant.

'Like what?' said Greg.

'Like height. If we're up high, they won't expect that, so we can pick them off.'

They both looked around. The piledriver.

'Oh, shit, you've got to be joking.'

Entwistle glanced up at the rear of the Town Hall. There was smoke beginning to rise above it.

'Building's on fire. They're gonna have to evacuate soon. It's our only chance. But unless we take out number 38, they can soon regroup and all this has been for nothing.'

Greg thought back over the last few hours, and the *today* that was *yesterday*. All for nothing . . . fuck it! He swung the Uzi over his shoulder, clambered over the trunk of the Uno onto the caterpillar tracks of the crane, then worked his way round the cab until he was out of view of the Town Hall.

The crane was huge, its arm fully one hundred and

fifty feet high and pointing upwards. He found footholds on the doorframe and the windows of the cab and, grunting with the effort, hauled himself up onto its roof. Pausing to gain his breath, he looked down to see Entwistle running across the compound through the pooling water until he hugged brickwork, his eyes trained on the corner nearest to the rear entrance. From his vantage point Greg could see three men running down the alley to the right of the main building. He might be able to shoot them one by one, but then he would be giving his position away. He just hoped Entwistle could deal with them.

He shifted his gaze up to the metal framework of the crane that soared above him like a robotic spider's web. Heading for the first crossbar, he began hauling himself upwards.

He had been climbing for over a minute when he heard gunfire. Looking down, he spotted Entwistle lying flat on the ground, but up to his neck in muddy water, firing at the hooded men as they tentatively crept around the corner of the building, each of them falling in turn as they failed to discern where the shots were coming from. *Thank God for that*, thought Greg. Now maybe he would be able to get up further – oh shit! There came shouting from the rear door of the Town Hall – the same entrance they had been taken through that time before, when they had been captured – as three more men came out to investigate.

Greg continued climbing, the going easier than he had expected. The framework of the structure was as easy to scale as a ladder, though, fuelled as he was by adrenalin, he was moving instinctively before he could think. He only hoped no one would spot him, since there was only one way to get down a ladder quickly. He was already seventy-five feet up in the air, and beginning to remember his natural dislike of heights, when there came more firing.

Entwistle stared up at Greg. Good, the boy was in the perfect position, whereas he himself was lying on his back in the ever-growing puddle, muddy water lapping round his chin. Another couple of minutes and this deputy might just drown. He noticed movement across the compound as men barged their way through the rear door, smoke and dust following as they coughed and gasped into the open air – and all wearing black with white numbers, like some criminal football team.

Entwistle took aim between his feet, confident he would be able to take them out, and quickly, because soon they would get their bearings. He squeezed the trigger, intending just a warning burst before standing up and demanding their surrender – they were so plainly disorientated it might just work. But his gun clicked impotently. *Oh, hell!* He shook it, and tried again. It was jammed.

Then one of the men spotted him, and shouted to the others. Entwistle hadn't a hope.

So he stood up anyway and shouted: 'Freeze, you mothers! Any one of you moves I blow away the lot of you!'

The men stopped, all of them eventually spotting him through the thin smoke that drifted from the burning building to their rear.

Greg stared down at the bizarre scene. Eight heavily armed terrorists and one lone deputy of police. For now the stand-off might work, but it was going nowhere.

Entwistle didn't have any back-up; as soon as he fired, all eight of them would return fire. The man was doomed. He could hear Entwistle ordering them to lose their weapons. None of them, of course, moved.

'Drop those guns, or so help me I'll fire!'

One or two began to falter – even if they killed him eventually, he could still damage most of them with one sweep of the Uzi – but the majority simply stared him down. Greg had to act now, even if it meant exposing himself. He was two-thirds of the way up the piledriver crane arm, maybe a hundred feet up, and that was what he had come up for anyway.

'You heard the man!' he shouted. 'Drop your guns!'

All eight men looked up, spotted Greg – and three immediately dropped their weapons. The others, however, resolutely refused, so he fired a short burst at the Town Hall wall above their heads.

'Next time I shoot *you*!'

All but one lowered their weapons and dropped them into the six-inch-deep water. But the last man, number 30, kept his gun trained on Entwistle.

'You shoot, he dies!' he shouted.

Entwistle shouted back, 'You shoot, you die!'

The man laughed. 'Then we're *all* gonna fucking die!'

This was no amateur. Greg didn't have any options. 'Drop your gun or I fire!' he repeated.

'Like I said—'

Greg then shot him, and he fell back with a splash.

The others scattered, Entwistle meanwhile backing away to the corner of the building. But Greg noticed new movement and shouted a warning. Entwistle dived into the water as bullets pinged into the wall behind him. Greg fired towards the corner, bringing both gunmen down.

Entwistle struggled through the deepening water, floundering like a drowning man, until, spluttering and hacking, he broke free of it and grabbed a machine-gun from the corpse of one of the two newcomers Greg had just shot down. He was about to turn back into the rear compound, in search of those who had taken flight, when someone else fired from the side alley leading to Circle One, and instead he had to hug the wall.

Greg was in trouble. He only had about half a clip of ammunition left, he was in plain view, the enemy had him surrounded. Soon one of them would find a weapon and blast him off his perch. Even if the shot didn't kill him, the fall sure as hell would. He looked around to see if there was any way out for him.

To his rear, beyond the compound, there was a stretch of lawn that ran down to the Hole. In front stood the Town Hall, and on either side the compound itself, which because of the flooding now looked like a sea with islands of machinery and lumber and bricks. No soft landings there, even in the water. To make it worse there were temporary power lines running from the Town Hall along the side of the compound and on down to a substation near the edge of the Hole. Land on any of those and he would be fried.

He heard urgent shouting and noticed movement: men trying to keep out of sight as they regrouped and found a way to bring him down. He also caught sight of

Entwistle running across the width of the alley, bullets kicking up dirt and water behind him. At least *he* might have a chance of getting out of this mess.

Greg felt his temper rising, not only with the situation and with the men who were trying to kill him, but also with himself for being so stupid as to volunteer to get his ass blown off – and for what? A town that had kicked him out on his rear nine months ago; that had banded together to get shot of its nigger troublemaker. Even his goddam mother had moved away while he was stuck in hospital – and she had not left an address. So why was he doing this? WHY WAS HE SO FUCKING STUPID?

Gunfire zinging about the metalwork interrupted his anger, and in his shock he slipped ... and for an awful, heart-stopping moment he felt himself beginning to fly. But his free hand caught hold of metal, and he swung in an arc and slammed into metal, the wind knocked out of him, his feet treading air until they found a perch. OH GOD OH GOD OH GOD.

Above his own shouting, he heard yelling, splashes caused by running feet, more gunfire.

Looking about, he saw sky ... the Town Hall ... the Hole. Then, forcing himself to look down, he saw four men, all staring up at him from the flooding water. Two of them raised their weapons – and fired.

Bullets whizzed past him, ricocheted off the metalwork, hot sparks of metal stabbing at his hands and face. He couldn't hold on much longer. BASTARDS, BASTARDS.

He swung his gun around but it was stuck on the

wrong side of the crane arm, his own body blocking its movement. He couldn't even fire back.

'YOU MOTHERFUCKING BASTARDS!' he screamed – hearing laughter in response.

He looked about him. He couldn't jump. He was going to die. *He was going to die.*

A bullet sliced along the outside of his thigh, grazing it for six inches, the pain intense. He nearly lost his grip. Not long, not long . . . FUCKERS, FUCKERS!

Glancing down, he saw six of the men taking up a position to shoot him off the crane. He tried to turn but he was stuck, the heels of his trainers caught on a rung so that his left hand, still holding on, was twisted up behind him, while his right hand, although free, was aiming his Uzi in the wrong direction. He might as well have been tied to a post and be awaiting a firing squad. Except he was innocent, and they were guilty, and in the movies the good guys always won.

He looked over his shoulder as the firing began. The piledriver arm was almost vertical, held up by cables that ascended its length to pulleys at the top and by a jib that diverted the cables into the winding gear at the bottom behind the cab. *He could try leaping?* – forget it.

A bullet hit his left shoe, just missing his toes but ripping out the front of his Nike trainer. Another inch and that would have gone up his leg or up his ass. He was fucked. He only wished he could take some of them with him. Just to get off one good burst – blow some of them out of the water. *Water?* He looked over his shoulder. Power lines? He looked down. Metal caterpillar tracks, metal frame, metal arm. If he was going to die, he wasn't going out on his own.

'FUCK YOU, YOU BASTARDS!' he yelled as he took aim with the Uzi and fired into the air in front of him, the burst achieving its suicidal task.

Instantly the crane arm began to move as the cables restraining it snapped and whipped away, slicing into nearby trees like chainsaws. The weight of the arm immediately set it crashing back to earth. As Greg screamed and the hundred-and-fifty-foot-long arm plunged through the air, he clung on like a bronco rider. Tortured and ruptured metal howled and the flooded compound rushed up to meet him. Then the crane arm fell onto the power lines, and thousands of volts of electricity instantly zapped their way through the entire metal framework of the arm, through its cab and platform, and down through the tracks into the water below.

Greg felt the electricity punch him like he had been hit by a Kenworth, saw a huge blue flash and tasted charcoal, then felt himself flying through the air, catapulted from the crane arm, his mind already shutting down, his hands and feet burning.

Eight men immediately began to dance, their guns firing off in all directions, their screams stolen as electricity froze their muscles and began to cook them.

Entwistle heard the crash and the screams and glancing back saw the cab of the crane lifted into the air as its arm pulled down the power lines and hit the ground with sufficient force to dislodge the stacked bricks about him.

Up ahead, at the top of the alley, a lone gunman was still keeping him pinned down. But realizing that the crane's disintegration meant Greg's certain death, Entwistle lost his temper and stood up from behind the dumpster and fired six shots at the remaining gunman.

The man panicked and ran, Entwistle clicking off empty rounds at his retreating form. It was some moments before he stopped firing, and tossed his dead weapon aside.

Dashing back to the compound, he slewed to a halt as he saw the water sparkling and heard the frizzing of electricity. Peering over the area he saw the crane arm settling, power lines sparking like fireworks and several men jerking and juddering in the water like stranded fish.

Jesus Christ Almighty!

Of Greg there was no sign, and because the water was live, Entwistle couldn't get over to the wreckage of the crane to check on him. But he couldn't have survived anyway, the poor bastard. So Entwistle turned and ran back up the side alley.

At the top of the alley there was chaos: injured men lying on the ground, others walking in a daze. Few seemed concerned now about his presence. A black helicopter suddenly clattered overhead, hovering over the scene, whipping up dust, and driving away those who cared to seek shelter from its downdraught.

Entwistle stared up at it, shielding his eyes. The last time round it had been an FBI helicopter carrying snipers and Del Collingwood. But this wasn't an FBI helicopter; in fact it was completely unmarked. And he *had* seen it before . . .

He watched as the anonymous Huey circled the devastated Town Hall, then followed Circle One to the west where it descended out of sight. It was landing, probably in the War Memorial Gardens, but *who* was on board?

Looking around he found an overturned motorcycle, a yellow Honda 250, and beside it lay an injured black-hood, blood staining both his legs. The key was still in the bike's ignition. Turning it on, Entwistle got on board, dropped it into gear, and roared off across the road – weaving in and out of the burning debris and the dazed survivors, and on along Circle One.

Two minutes brought him to a sliding halt outside the Memorial Gardens, the statue of an armed marine on top of the squat plinth at its centre seemingly mocking the town's impotence. The Huey had indeed landed on the other side of the memorial, and Entwistle could see several men running down to the side of the Hole, one of them distinctly shorter than the others.

Hartsby! Now he remembered this chopper: the same one that had dropped Hartsby onto the rig.

He watched as Hartsby stepped into a speedboat on his own, then sped off across the lake, his course set to take him straight to the oil rig. Just through the trees that surrounded the gardens, Entwistle could see the rig itself gleaming in the sunlight, the ominous box positioned at its top looking all the more terrifying now he knew what it really was. *He had to stop the man.* But how?

He wheeled the motorcycle back onto the road and accelerated. He needed to get himself out to the rig before Hartsby could set the bomb off, for surely that was what he intended. The man had already demonstrated an ego so large that he could now die safe in the knowledge that his other selves might succeed – and with that kind of mindset there was no reasoning. But Entwistle couldn't think of anywhere he would find a boat guaranteed to get him out to the rig in time. Hartsby was going to win. After all this, he was going to win again – and this time there would be no second chance to make amends.

Twelve

Entwistle sped along Circle One, the boat in his sights already a good third of its way towards the rig. Soon it would pass Uncle Art's Fun Pier and be out of sight.

Entwistle noticed a man in black in the road ahead, staring towards the smoke rising from the Town Hall and thus too confused to react to Entwistle's arrival. Lashing out with his foot, Entwistle sent the masked man spinning before turning sharp left towards the Pier entrance. It was a slim chance, but it would have to do. The Fun Pier gates were open, but the Pier itself would be empty.

Kicking in as much speed as he could, Entwistle raced the length of its boardwalk. Concession stands, game stalls, and video machines whizzed past him in a colourful blur. He saw that the double glass doors of the arcade were still closed, but he didn't brake. Instead he aimed himself straight for the left-hand door and – head down, shoulders hunched – he let the Honda suffer the impact as he crashed through it.

Fighting to keep his balance amid the shower of shattered glass, he steered the motorbike through the carpeted foyer and on into the arcade proper. Luckily, as the shape of the Pier dictated, the arcade offered a straight run for its length and, apart from clipping a table-hockey game, Entwistle quickly reached the rear emergency exit: another set of glass doors.

Twisting his throttle all the way, he felt the bike begin a wheelie, then smash through the glass panels to grab the last few yards of planking, before launching itself out over the water of the Hole, Hartsby's speedboat dead ahead.

The motorbike flew on eighty feet, before it and Entwistle parted company, the Honda landing with a large splash just ahead of the speedboat and its lone, startled occupant. Entwistle himself hit the boat's starboard side, and winded and disorientated, he grabbed for anything he could.

Hartsby turned to face his attacker, his expression a mixture of surprise and fear. 'Who the fuck . . .!'

Keeping hold of the steering wheel with one hand, he lashed out at Entwistle with his fist, but didn't quite find the reach.

However Entwistle's grip on the wet seat-back was quickly lost, and as he began to slip he fumbled for a line that trailed in the water from the boat's prow and grabbing it, wrapped it around his wrist just as he fell overboard.

The boat was nearing the rig and as Hartsby killed the motor he turned it so that it would hit the pontoon sideways on, crushing Entwistle in between.

Looking over his shoulder Entwistle spotted the imminent danger, but the rope he had wrapped around his wrist wouldn't loosen, and he found himself being dragged under the boat.

On seeing Entwistle disappear, Hartsby put on the power again, the twin propellers biting deep into the water, their blades like giant razors – Entwistle being doomed to meet them as the boat slid over his head.

Kicking at the water, Entwistle managed to unfurl the rope around his wrist and let the propellers drag it into reach, where it was sliced and diced and chewed until it finally choked both motors. The boat lurched into a slow drift. Hartsby was flung against the wheel.

Entwistle kicked himself up into the open air and surfaced, gasping and coughing, his lungs desperate for replenishment. But even as he drew in precious oxygen he saw Hartsby leaping from the boat across the three feet to the pontoon. The bastard had made it.

Entwistle then dragged up unknown reserves of energy in swimming his way to the pontoon. He scrambled up the side in time to see Hartsby kick his way into the cabin office.

Too late, I'm too damn late, Entwistle thought, even as he crawled onto the pontoon's wet surface and forced himself towards the cabin door.

As he reached it, another man in black ran out, pistol in hand. Entwistle grabbed his extended wrist and spun the man round until his back faced the Hole. He then punched him as hard as he could in the face and knocked him into the water. His gun flew up into the air, and Entwistle made a vain bid to grab it before it too fell into the lake.

Angered by the sudden attack, he let out an animal howl and, bursting into the cabin, he succeeded only in crashing into the table which occupied the centre of the room. Rolling over, he saw Hartsby standing at the computer console that controlled the functioning of the bomb.

'Don't!' shouted Entwistle.

Hartsby punched another key with a flourish then turned round, his face red and his breath obviously difficult to capture.

'Too late ... It's done. Countdown now ... can't be stopped.'

Entwistle stared at the green digital counter: 4:55. Then threw himself at the little man, bringing him to the ground before pummelling his smiling face.

'You lose again!' Hartsby managed. 'In just five minutes, no town ... no you.'

'And no you, either.'

'Like I care?'

Entwistle was kneeling on the man's chest. 'Is there any way to stop it?' he rasped.

'No. Clock is ... ticking.'

Entwistle punched him then in the nose, felt bone break and the man fall limp. He didn't know whether he had killed him, and didn't care. Then he pulled himself up and studied the console. Lots of buttons and lights that meant nothing to him, but there, in the top right-hand corner, that damned digital display repeating its deadly story.

4:34

4:33

4:32

Thirteen

The elevator started to rise from the lower level. Entwistle felt near to exhaustion, too weak to venture across the room to hide, so instead he searched Hartsby for a gun.

He quickly found a Sig Sauer .45, fully loaded, and leaning back against a table leg, cocked the pistol and aimed it as steadily as he could at the door opening of the small elevator. He wasn't even going to wait to see who his new opponent was; he was just going to blow the fucker away, because whoever it was they were between him and his only hope of survival: which was the device at the bottom of the shaft.

As the winding gear slowly whirred its load upwards, Entwistle couldn't help speculating what would happen if he now got down to the device only to find that it didn't work any more. But what if it still *did* work? What if he jumped back again, and had to start all over again? Oh, Christ, this would be impossible. And could he stand knowing that Firefall and its people had been blasted apart and incinerated for a second time? Entwistle doubted it, doubted it very much, his sanity already riding the ragged edge of the abyss.

After thirty long seconds, the elevator cage stopped

and the door opened outwards. A figure emerged and Entwistle squeezed the trigger – but at the last moment he pulled his gun to the right, his shot embedding itself in the wall.

Maribeth screamed and crashed back into the elevator, the door slamming shut behind her.

'Maribeth! It's OK. It's me, Entwistle! I'm sorry!'

Maribeth slowly pushed open the door and stared at him. Then she saw Hartsby – then turned to glance at the bomb console.

'Oh, hellation . . .'

She came over to Entwistle and helped him up, and they immediately hugged each other, both shivering with relief. Maribeth was ecstatic at finding him alive, but the anaesthetic lingering in her system still fudged her mind. Even the green numbers flashing their downwards count at the corner of her vision failed to dislodge her from the comforting solidity of Entwistle's tight embrace.

For his part, Entwistle couldn't describe how happy he felt to find she was alive, but reality quickly stomped on his heart and he reluctantly pushed her away and slumped down in a chair, rubbing his face.

3:51

'It's running again?' she asked at last.

'Yes. And it can't be stopped.'

'What do we do?'

'Is the time machine down there still?'

'Yes.'

'We can use it again.'

He almost wished the bomb would go off prematurely and end it all now so he didn't have to think or act.

But too many lives were at stake, not least Maribeth's – nor did he want Greg's death to have been in vain.

'Yes,' said Maribeth. 'But what about the town?'

'In the next time-stream we'll—'

'And the next and the next . . .?' Maribeth sounded equally defeatist. 'What about *this* one? We've seen everyone die in Firefall once. I don't want it to happen again now.'

Entwistle was angry. 'Neither do I, but what can we do?'

Maribeth kicked at the table. 'How does that bomb work?'

'Hell if I know. Except it mixes fuel and oxygen in a vapour that ignites and spreads over a wide area, burning everything in between. It's like a nuclear explosion without the radiation.'

'What if it went off underground?'

'The bomb? I don't know. You mean down there? It would evaporate most of the Hole I suppose, but as for the town . . . But how the hell would we get it down there? In just three minutes?'

For the first time he caught sight of the two men lying in one corner. 'What happened to them?'

'I shot them with some anaesthetic darts, but the third one made me shoot myself. Where is he, anyway?'

'Swimming.'

'I woke up down below. I doubt he knew what that machine's for, otherwise he wouldn't have left me alone with it.'

'Was it glowing?'

'Yes,' she said.

'Which means we *can't* stop this damn bomb.'

'The legs of the rig are dynamited,' Maribeth offered.

'So?'

'So blow up the rig, and the bomb might fall into the Hole.'

Unless an explosion set the bomb off . . . but what other option was there? Remembering his last visit here, Entwistle hauled out the stepladder, and with a glance at the clock – **2:58** – he climbed up to the roof hatch. There he pulled himself out onto the flat metal surface and slithered over to one of the struts, grabbed the wire running from the sticks of dynamite, and followed it to the next leg, and then onto the third strut, where he found the wire running off the roof and down the side of the building. Easing his legs over the side, he dropped onto the pontoon and followed the course of the wire to a freshly drilled hole a foot above the pontoon on the side facing away from the Fun Pier.

Rushing round the cabin, he re-entered the room and, hurling chairs aside, knelt down and found a reel of electric fuse wire and a plunger hidden under the console. Judging by the length of fuse wire, they had probably intended to run it all the way to the shore. Entwistle wondered why they didn't just use a radio transmitter, but there was probably then the chance of an accident, or having their signal jammed. After all, the town of Firefall would be completely surrounded by now.

'How much time?' he shouted, pulling out the reel and the plunger.

'Two minutes, two seconds . . .'

He unspooled a length of wire.

'Get into the elevator. Set it going.'

'What about you?'

'I'll be fine.' He grabbed her hand and squeezed it. 'I promise.'

He looked around for a penknife, and found the same one he had been handed by Greg the first time round. 'I'll come down on the elevator roof. When we're at the bottom, I'll set this up and blow the rig. With a bit of luck the bomb will fall into the water and do less damage. And if they see the rig going up, some might take cover.'

Maribeth did as she was ordered, pumping the DOWN button until the elevator started to descend. Tossing the reel of wire onto the roof of the elevator cage, Entwistle grabbed the plunger and quickly stepped onto it too. He wouldn't be able to strip the wires and set the detonator until they were safely at the bottom.

The elevator ride was agonizingly long. He shouted down to Maribeth.

'How long have we got?'

'Maybe ninety seconds. How long do you need?'

He didn't dare answer – nor did he want to tell her that the last time he had tried this same trick, he had failed. And still the elevator continued descending into darkness. He looked up but could see only a dim light from the cabin above.

Finally the elevator shuddered to a halt and he heard Maribeth step out and shout up to him.

'You need to open the hatch.'

'I will, I will. Just let me set this . . .'

He picked up the wire, though barely able to see, and, using the penknife, cut it in half. Then he took the ends of the copper core wire and stripped an inch off each, cutting his fingers in the process, but not feeling the pain.

As he twisted the first wire around the detonator cap, his very limited light was blotted out. *What the . . .?*

'You'll not make it, Deputy!' shouted Hartsby. 'Not with a chair on your head!'

Entwistle looked up to see the man leaning over the rim of the shaft a hundred and fifty feet above him, and saw him struggling to push a chair through the narrow entrance. Reaching into his waistband, Entwistle pulled out the other man's own automatic and taking aim at the vague figure above him, fired it twice.

Movement stopped, there was a guttural gasp, and then Hartsby fell forward into the shaft.

The wires suspending the elevator cage rattled suddenly, a zithering noise running the length of the narrow metal shaft. Entwistle couldn't see what had happened, but he didn't have time to worry. He tightened the screw on the positive lead, then threaded the negative and twisted it tight. Then he pulled up the plunger and was about to press it when there was a scream from above and he looked up to see the dying Hartsby losing his grip on the cables and falling towards him, his eyes white in the darkness, his scream following him.

Entwistle pushed himself back against the wall of the shaft and watched in horror as the man slammed head first onto the cage roof, his shoulder depressing the plunger, his weight then taking out the roof of the elevator and causing both of them to fall into the cage in a shower of debris and dust.

High above there sounded a muffled boom, and as

Entwistle tried to get his bearings and force the corpse of Hartsby off his twisted legs there was a shaking and a huge cracking explosion, and then light flared bright above him and he saw the sky for a split second, and then it turned fiery yellow and seemed to fall into the shaft like molten lead.

Maribeth grabbed his hand and began to drag him clear of the wrecked cage, the questing tongue of flame from above roaring down the shaft to consume him.

He had only just got his legs clear as the flames poured down onto Hartsby's body like a billion vulpine firebugs, his body fats exploding as the metal turned red, then white hot, and the flames bounded into the heart of the small lower room.

Entwistle caught fire first, his trousers and shoes bursting into flame, even though they were soaking wet. The entire room was suddenly ablaze, a hellish inferno that guaranteed no survival. He managed to dive for the glowing cube at the same time as Maribeth: a supposed fire escape in the heart of what was now a crematorium, flames scorching their legs, setting ablaze their clothing, and charcoaling their hair.

Like a roaring beast the flames explored every inch of the underground chamber but even as they succeeded in touching the time machine they saw it only through bubbling eyes and felt it with fingers that had started to steam and blacken.

Fourteen

Greg was hot but he felt biting cold, and there was a tremendous pain in his chest. He opened his eyes, saw murkiness surrounding him; opened his mouth to shout, and found it filled with water. Soon his lungs were also full of water, his breathing halted, and a pain was arcing through his torso that forced him to kick and jerk. But even as his eyes began to see light, they began to dim.

No! I will not die. Not after all this.

He kicked some more, waved his hands, felt a million icy fingers trying to drag him away from the light – from life itself – but he stubbornly resisted.

Suddenly he was in the air, and he was spewing water from his mouth and his nose. Hacking and hawing, he floundered in the Hole, desperate to keep his mouth out of the water. It was hard, hard work. He kept wanting to sink, as if his feet were attached to a bungee rope and the elastic was at its very limit and he was about to be dragged back under. But somehow he managed to keep afloat, his arms working, his feet kicking, until his lungs were empty of water and filling with precious oxygen. His head boomed, his chest ached, his hands were on fire, but he was *alive.* How he had survived the jolt of electricity and his flight from the crane into the Hole he didn't know but it didn't matter. *He had survived.*

Looking about him, he seemed quite a way from the shore – it must have been one heck of a shock – and the rig was to his back. He wondered briefly what had happened to Entwistle, but didn't have the strength to worry about him. He needed all his concentration for his own slog back to the shore.

Focusing on the burning remains of the Town Hall – all three floors were now well alight – and the crippled piledriver that lay broken and twisted like so much blue-painted matchwood, he struggled through the water towards the edge of the Hole. He could hear occasional explosions and bangs but didn't care what they meant or what was causing them. All he wanted was to get to land and lie down and hope he didn't die in the meantime.

It took him several long minutes, the shore like an illusive mirage that never seemed to get nearer, no matter how much he splashed and kicked. And then his hand touched something solid and delved into wet leaves, and his knees scraped on mud, and he was soon crawling his way up the bank until his feet were clear of lake water, and then he rolled over and coughed and praised the Lord in the blue sky above.

How long he lay there burbling his new-found faith he didn't know and cared less, but then he heard a massive explosion and, craning his neck up, he saw the oil rig flying apart, its legs disintegrating and the hundred-foot-high tower first slumping down on itself, then toppling to one side, the large covered box at its apex plunging into the

Hole with a heavy splash. Fire instantly consumed the cabin at its base, flames ripping up from underneath the walls, and with a deep *whumph* the building was lifted bodily into the air before it too settled back into the Hole.

And then all went quiet; only the splashing of debris and the hiss of drowning flames disturbed the placid surface of the Hole.

Greg vaguely remembered hearing something about an explosion big enough to destroy Firefall, and was relieved that this hadn't been so. But then there came a deep bass rumble like an earthquake, the ground vibrated under him, and the surface of the Hole became instantly as choppy as a gale-lashed sea.

Then there followed an incredible boom that shook every building nearby and set off a shrilling chorus of burglar and car alarms. A huge, hundred-foot-wide plume of water then exploded into the air, and in seconds it had dwarfed the town, its topmost spume rising higher than the rim of the surrounding valley. The entire centre of the Hole, including what was left of the rig, rose hundreds of feet into the air, the remainder of the lake instantly dropping by four feet or so to reveal struggling fish stranded amid tangled weeds as if some ogre had sucked the water up with a giant straw.

Steam then followed the plume, and a whiplash shockwave roared across the lake surface like an invisible wall, slamming into Greg and tumbling him head over heels into bushes, leaving him battered but unable to tear his eyes away from the nightmare vision of the Hole emptying itself skywards in a storm of steam and froth.

The water level dropped even further, revealing the sharp edge of the shelf of rock that ringed the very centre of the Hole.

And then the water came down again.

It crashed back into the emptied lake, countless millions of gallons as solid as rock, causing a circular tidal wave that spread outwards and rose and grew at astonishing speed until Greg found himself watching a wall of water fully twenty feet high now racing towards him.

He screamed but the air was sucked from his mouth as the wave rode towards him, surging higher and higher until it blotted out his view of the sky, its horizon-wide surface a raging white maelstrom.

And then the angry, roaring white wall fell on top of him.

Fifteen

Greg had been conscious for three days now, although he had been in the hospital for the best part of a week. His left leg was suspended from some pulleys, as was his left arm, while both his hands were wrapped in slimy plastic to protect his burns from the electric voltage. Both eyes were puffed up and he found it difficult to hear or speak, but he didn't care. He was alive. Not only had he come through the chases and the gunfights and his electrocution, but he had also survived the fuel-air bomb explosion and its nightmarish tidal wave.

According to the doctor he had been found in a tree, about fifteen feet up, hanging like a broken doll. At first they had assumed he was as dead as all those who had been caught in and around the Town Hall when the wave had demolished its already weakened structure, but luckily someone had heard his moans and he was quickly helicoptered out to the hospital in Penniston.

Firefall had suffered a lot of broken windows from the initial blast, and everywhere up to Circle Two had been swamped with water, some buildings – such as the Town Hall and the Pier and the Glasshouse – being completely washed away. Others, like the school and the telephone exchange, had survived because of their sturdier structure. Casualties had been comparatively light, only a dozen or so falling victim to the wave itself, all the rest, including most of the conspirators and all the Town Hall hostages, having been killed by gunfire or explosion.

Of Deputy Entwistle, Maribeth Hamilton, and the rig there was no trace. Greg could only hope that in some way they had got to the mysterious device in time, but he would never know. However, newspapers had carried reports about the bravery of a government agent called Emile Hartsby who had made his way out to the rig to try and defuse the bomb but had perished in the attempt.

It was on the afternoon of his third day of consciousness that Deputy Brackhouse called with a visitor.

'Got someone here to see you,' he said. 'She's given us a statement about her father's death. How he attacked you but fell off the landing. Don't know whether I believe her or not, but there doesn't seem any point in pursuing it, not least with all the other shit that's gone on in town. I'm Acting Sheriff now because Rickenbacker and Entwistle are both dead. When you're up to it, I'd like to take a full statement of what you two got up to at the Town Hall – and why.'

'Why?'

'Hey, no disrespect, kid, but you weren't exactly Firefall Citizen of the Year.'

'It was Entwistle. He . . . he asked me to help.'

'He asked you?'

'Said he couldn't trust anyone else. Didn't know who-all was in on it. But me, he knew I'd been out of town for a while.'

'And you just said yes?'

'Was Rickenbacker involved?'

'Yes. We found—'

'I rest my case.'

'OK, point taken. I'd better get back. Town's a mess – TV crews still crawling all over it like it was the Second Coming. I'll send your visitor in now.'

Brackhouse walked out, and a moment later Summer Campbell entered. Dressed in a white and yellow summer frock, she looked beautiful. Greg was lost for words and there was a long, embarrassed silence, until she took hold of his good arm and squeezed it.

'What you did was very brave.'

'About your dad—'

'I miss him. I loved him. But he was wrong to attack you like that, and it was an accident. I don't blame you for it.'

'Thanks.'

There came another long pause.

'So what now?' said Greg, enjoying the smell of her perfume as she sat down on the bed beside him.

'*You* get better. Decide if you want to make some money.'

'Money?'

'There's about a hundred reporters trying to get in here to see you. Seems they heard all about what you and Entwistle did. There's even been Hollywood producers on. Looks like you could get rich from this.'

'Should I?' said Greg, scarcely able to believe he had developed a conscience.

'What else you gonna do?'

'Get a job.'

Summer stared at him. 'You sure you didn't suffer brain damage?'

Greg laughed, even though it hurt his ribs. 'No, no, I'm fine. Just had a lesson in responsibility. Cost a lot of lives . . .'

He thought back to the first time round, and couldn't help the tears. So many lives, including Summer's. 'I . . . I got a second chance. So I aim to make it right . . . this time.'

Summer pecked him on his cut lips and wiped his tears. He stroked her face with the back of his bandaged hand.

'*This* time,' he repeated.

Thursday 10 July
Two months ago

One

It was something Rickenbacker had mentioned the first time round, when they were held captive in the Town Hall. He'd explained how the idea for the conspiracy had started when he had picked up a drunken rig worker on 4 July. Given a precise date and an event, it was easy enough for Entwistle to check out the Department's records a week later, and locate the address of the same rig worker.

He was staying at a motel, the Three Lions, some fifteen miles out of town, which was odd in itself. Why so far? And why a motel, when work on the rig was going to continue for months? The motel room had been registered to a John Hershall, who, according to the manager, kept himself to himself, paid his rent promptly, and left his room neat.

'So neat it looks like he ain't there sometimes, but what do I care?' grumbled Runyon the manager. 'Makes a change from the usual assholes I gets to clean after.'

'When was the last time you saw him?' interrupted Entwistle as he and Maribeth stood in the man's stuffy office, the noonday sun high and hot outside, Runyon's deodorant no longer performing its allotted task.

'Coupla days back. Tuesday. Looked smart. Suit 'n'

all. I waved to him, but he seemed to have things on his mind.'

'Got a spare key?'

'Sure.'

The room was plain and simple, and exceptionally tidy. There were clothes in the wardrobe and drawers, toiletries in the bathroom, a suitcase under the bed. Once the motel manager had left, Entwistle asked Maribeth's opinion.

'He's supposed to be a rig worker, yet there are no work clothes here. It's all suits and sweaters. Good labels. And his toilet articles are expensive. Paco Rabanne. Rembrandt toothpaste.'

'Suitcase is a brand-new Antler. Not a scuff mark on it.'

'And there's nothing else apart from clothes. No books, magazines, not even a *TV Guide*.'

'No booze, no food wrappers. This must be the cleanest, most prissy, most health-conscious, most *boring* oil worker on the entire planet.'

'Meaning?'

Entwistle didn't offer an answer, knowing full well that Maribeth knew what he was thinking. He also knew they had no alternative but to stake out the motel – and wait.

'Best thing is if we hide up here. It's gonna cost some, but there's a lot more at stake than our wallets. This is cabin 12, so we'll take 11.'

An hour later they were ensconced and waiting in the next room, Entwistle having drilled a hole in the skirting and secreted a small microphone linked up to a voice-activated recorder. He had taken three days' leave and intended spending those days in this room, to be joined by Maribeth in the evenings after she had finished with school. Talk was sparse between the two of them, the gravity of their present task far outweighing casual conversation or even assessing what had happened between them since they had jumped back in time on a second occasion.

After they had used the glowing device again, their minds paralysed with the terror of being burned alive, they had both woken up in strange places.

Entwistle had seemingly been involved in a car chase, doing about eighty miles per hour, when he had experienced a sudden blinding flash, and a pain so sharp it made him slam on the Contour's brakes, slewing the cruiser two hundred yards into a ditch.

It was ten terrifying minutes before he could adjust to his new situation. He checked a copy of the *Firefall Comet* lying on the passenger seat for proof of the date before falling out of the car, weeping like a baby.

Entwistle eventually managed to call a tow truck, then sat leaning up against the broken wheel of his vehicle, trying to control his shaking. His mind kept running over his dramatic memories: the double dose of bloody battles and fiery endings. This time round he was able to accept more readily what had happened, but that didn't make it any easier to live with.

After he had been transported back into town, he had not needed to feign an injured knee and he had slipped back to his mother's house, where he rapidly sank the best part of a fifth of bourbon. Only then did he get up the courage to phone Maribeth Hamilton.

There was no answer to the first seven rings, and he didn't know whether her absence from home augured well or ill. He desperately wanted to know if she had made it safely but, like a frightened child, he accepted that no news was good news and, rather than go out looking for her, he entrusted his worries to a tumbler with ice and its continual warming top-ups of Jim Beam. His mother Carol was out at work, lording it over the patrons of the Glasshouse, so he had her house all to himself. Yet the last thing he wanted was to be alone ... so merciful release arrived when both the shock and the alcohol took their tolls and he collapsed unconscious on the couch.

At around 9:30 p.m. there came a knocking at the door. Finally roused from his drunken stupor, Entwistle stumbled to answer it, to encounter Maribeth, equally drunk and distraught.

They instantly fell into each other's arms, hands fumbling, lips sliding, slurred expressions of joy mingling incoherently. Never had either of them experienced such sweet relief.

Within minutes they were on Entwistle's bed, clothing scattered about the room, their desperation for each other translated into the groping and kissing of blessedly unscarred flesh. However, despite their urgent need for physical intimacy, the excessive amounts of alcohol both had imbibed over the last few hours conspired to ensure that their lustful intentions were frustrated. Ten minutes later, breathless, half-naked and sheathed in sweat, they were content to be wrapped in each other's arms, as Maribeth told *her* story.

She had collapsed suddenly while teaching class, her

mind suddenly blown out by a surge of vivid memories of their experiences in a different time-stream. Noticing the day's date on the blackboard, she had fainted away and spent the next few hours in the clinic – before discharging herself in order to prescribe a different kind of medicine from the nearest liquor store.

It wasn't lust that had brought them together in Entwistle's bed, though anyone witnessing their frantic tumbling could well have believed so, but rather a need to get as close as possible to the one other person they had shared so many nightmares with – and, horror upon horror, were surely destined to share them with again. For both realized that unless they now acted effectively, Firefall could be destroyed for a *third* time. And so the two of them hugged each other frantically, oblivious to the passing of time, though trying desperately to think of a way out of this destructive loop.

Until a little after midnight, when Carol Glass came home and found her son in bed with that nice schoolteacher. *Perhaps now he will move out,* she thought, closing the door on the sleeping pair, *and stop worrying about me.*

When Maribeth and Entwistle awoke the next morning, they had sobered up and calmed down, and were keen to complete what they had started unsuccessfully the night before. Their resultant lovemaking was the tenderest and most satisfying either had experienced, and though they knew that they couldn't be in love so quickly, both knew it was inevitable – which lent even greater urgency to their task of stopping the catastrophe happening all over again.

It was after Entwistle returned to duty that same afternoon – and found himself avoiding Sheriff Rickenbacker – that a new idea occurred to him. That evening he shared it with Maribeth, and after much discussion she reluctantly agreed to help him in his plan.

All of which had subsequently found them in the Three Lions Motel for the third day now, the bed still unused, their clothing resolutely intact. It was about 6:00 p.m. and the doubts, at least for Maribeth, had begun to set in. What was all this for if it turned out Entwistle was wrong in his suspicions? She looked up from an exercise book she was marking, Chris Becker's arithmetic every bit a match for his poor grammar. (She couldn't help reflecting that she hadn't yet set the class that essay on 'My Home Town', though she already knew what their individual marks would be.)

'What if he *never* comes back?' she argued. 'Are you still so sure it's him?'

'Has to be,' said Entwistle. 'All this mess had to get started somewhere, and we don't know for sure if we stopped it the second time around. This time we'll make sure we get it right by stopping it before it even starts. I know Ed Rickenbacker's already making plans, so there'll be no stopping it soon – and when the pros eventually get involved, they'll really stop us from stopping them.'

'Very astute,' said a voice from behind him. 'And to think there was a time when you didn't believe me.'

Entwistle whirled round to find Hartsby in the doorway, holding the same Sig Sauer .45 he'd used on the rig, but this time fitted with a silencer.

'So it *was* you!' cried Maribeth.

'Yes,' said Hartsby, walking further into the room. 'As I already told you, the TRD in the mine sent me back four years. Curious fact, isn't it: the more people who use it, the shorter time you travel back? Four years, then . . . and thus armed with all that knowledge of the years to come. So, with that advantage, I worked myself into a position of power that would ensure no one could take the device away from me once it was uncovered by Ultracom's drilling – drilling that was done at my behest, naturally – after a satellite picked up the device's energy source lying under the lake.'

'But why destroy Firefall?' said Maribeth. 'Why kill all those people? You'd have got what you wanted anyway.'

'Just making sure. After all, you must have gone and spoiled it for me, or you wouldn't be here now, would you? As for all those people,' he sneered, 'who cares about them? Come the moment, you obviously did *your* bit to survive. So did I. And so *will* I.'

Maribeth was appalled. 'You really intend for the same thing to happen again?'

'Yes, if necessary. Of course, with you two out of the way I should be able to rescue the TRD without interference this time.'

'But you'll still destroy the town?'

'Oh, yes. No loose ends.'

'And then what?' interrupted Entwistle.

'Power. I'll feed the subsequent government investigation sufficient information to let them think that the rig uncovered something of scientific interest before those bumbling "terrorists" blew it up – and then persuade them to let me head up all future investigations. And they will, they will! You blow up a whole town, people take notice.'

Entwistle edged towards him, but Hartsby jerked the gun up into his face.

'Don't be stupid. Think of it: you die now, the both of you, you solve my problem for me!'

'You're going to kill us anyway. So what about Agent Collingwood?'

'You *are* well informed. He's working away like the obedient little time-server he is. When the time comes I'll call him in, he'll screw up badly and get killed, and finally take the blame.'

'Leaving you to do what, exactly?'

'To find more of those time devices – and use them.' He grinned mockingly. 'To keep jumping, keep healthy – and always moving into a younger body.'

'And the disasters these same beacons are sent to warn us about?'

'Who gives a damn?'

Maribeth threw her school book at him in disgust.

'Temper, temper,' he sneered.

'So what's all this?' asked Entwistle, gesturing around the room.

'As you correctly guessed, I took time off from my government work to masquerade part-time as a rig worker and encourage certain local morons in a certain direction. Really, those folks from the future aren't nearly as bright as they think. If they hadn't planted their device, Firefall wouldn't have been disturbed or harmed. Ultracom wouldn't even be drilling for oil.'

'So if you've been here for four years already, why haven't you taken us out before now?' said Entwistle.

'Because eliminating you would alter the time-stream. I've no idea what you counted for here before you began to interfere. For example, if your gullible Sheriff – my key player in getting support for this plan from people in Firefall – if he was to lose a valuable deputy in the run-up to his little conspiracy, who knows how he might react? Heavens, he might even suffer a fit of conscience and not go through with it.'

'But killing us *now* is OK?' asked Maribeth.

'You've pre-empted my plans, so I have to take the risk that your disappearance won't spoil things. And even if it does, one trip out to the rig and, *shazam*, four years back and we start again. But this time you two and the nigger won't pop up to spoil things for me. Why do you think I sent a man to burn down that building with you inside it, Entwistle?'

'But how could you know about my being out at the farm that day?' said Entwistle.

'Because in *another* time-stream *you* failed to get to the device and *I* succeeded! I've jumped back *twice*, but this time I'm ready for you.'

'And you still haven't got it right?'

'Oh, I think *this* time my plan's dead on the nail.'

'Dead is right. I hate to argue with you, Shorty,' said Entwistle, nodding over Hartsby's shoulder, 'but it looks like you fucked up again.'

'Don't try that old—'

'Reckon I've heard enough,' said the imposing voice of Ed Rickenbacker.

Hartsby swung round and was obviously startled to see Firefall's Sheriff standing framed in the doorway.

'This time our town makes it, you bastard,' continued

Rickenbacker, firing twice. His own silenced automatic felled Hartsby instantly with two short coughs.

Maribeth let out a wail of horror but quickly stifled it, as Entwistle knelt down and checked for Hartsby's pulse. Satisfied the man was dead, he removed the pistol from the corpse's hand and pocketed it. Rickenbacker sat down heavily on the bed.

'When you told me about all this last night, I didn't believe a goddam word. Fairy tales, I thought. *Twilight* fucking *Zone.* But hearing him crowing about it all just now . . . Christ Almighty . . .'

He slowly holstered his gun and wiped his sweating face. 'But I *still* don't understand it at all.'

'Me neither, Ed.' Entwistle closed the cabin door. 'But you understand *why* he had to die. There was no way of stopping him, not with his official power, and no way of bringing him to justice. Hell, the man hasn't even committed a crime.'

'Yet,' said Maribeth.

'Yeah, *yet,*' echoed Entwistle, walking over and hugging her. 'What are we going to do with the body?'

'I'll lose it, don't worry. No need for you to know.'

'And you? You OK with this, Ed?'

'What, murdering some Fed with an overactive imagination? Fine, just fine . . .'

'Really?' said Maribeth, worried by the man's callous tone.

Rickenbacker sighed and patted her hand. 'I've been Sheriff for thirty-three years, Miss Hamilton. In that time I've never shot anyone, even in self-defence, but I've put away four murderers, two rapists, six child molesters, four wife beaters, two bank robbers, and a couple of dozen hold-up artists. And all of them rolled up together weren't a tenth as bad as this here vicious piece of shit. Your story sounded to me as big a crock as I ever heard, Entwistle, but to hear this bastard casually boasting about blowing up Firefall like it meant no more than blowing his goddam nose . . .' He tapped the body with the toe of his boot. 'He's just lucky he died so quick.'

'You sure?' said Entwistle.

'Are you?' replied Rickenbacker.

'Yes.'

'Then so am I. You see, he was right about all that eco-terrorism. Last night I was all set to make a call to that guy he'd recommended, when you called round and gave me pause to think – hell, it gave me pause to drink! You were talking such loony garbage, it sounded to me. But I trust you, and I never trusted him, and that's what made the difference. Loony or not, I had to get here and check it out for myself.'

'Why did you never trust him?' asked Maribeth.

'He said he worked for an oil company.'

Two

The room was spartan, its only colour provided by a couple of posters of rap stars on the doors and considerable amounts of Magic Marker graffiti on the walls, most of it creatively obscene. Maybe this was a mistake, thought Entwistle, studying a cartoon of a black robot stomping on a white police car. But then again, considering this boy's circumstances . . .

'There's two ways to do this, Greg,' continued Entwistle. 'There's the hard way and there's my way.'

'You sound like a goddam movie.'

'Well, if'n I do, it's *The Sound of Music*, boy. Now get off that bed and get outside and talk to your girlfriend.'

Greg Henley glared up at the Deputy, hate blazing in his eyes, then he rose slowly and pulled on his jeans, the muscles rippling in his arms.

'Why you doing this? In this place you got me locked up safe and out of the way.'

'Let's say I've had a change of heart.'

'If you'd got one.'

Suddenly Entwistle grabbed the boy by the collar and slammed him against the door, Ice-T leering over his shoulder from one of the posters there.

'I've seen some good in you, Greg, hard as that might be to imagine. You've got a bitch of a temper, but deep down you're decent. Now, I know you were planning on escaping, so I've decided to save you the trouble. The Sheriff and I have also had a word with your girl's father, Hal Campbell, and he's prepared to give you a chance to prove yourself. It's up to you, boy. Either you come good, or you're screwed – and there won't be no soft-hearted Sheriff's Deputy coming to rescue you. You follow me?'

'Yes, sir,' said Greg, though plainly confused. 'The Sheriff and you? I . . . appreciate it.'

Entwistle stared into the boy's eyes, which seemed sincere.

'This time, get it right, Greg.'

'What do you mean, this time?'

'Private joke, kid. Private joke.'

Entwistle followed Greg down the long, echoing corridor to the hospital lobby, and as Greg and Summer hugged each other, he proceeded on out to his cruiser.

Maribeth was sitting in the front passenger seat. 'How'd he take it?' she asked.

'Surprised. Let's just hope.'

Maribeth nodded. 'And he'll never know why.'

Entwistle took her hand and squeezed it. 'Lucky bastard.'

She smiled and pecked him on the cheek.

'How'd your mother take the news that you were moving into my apartment?'

Now it was Entwistle's turn to laugh. 'She'd half packed for me already! Couldn't see the back of me sooner.

And there all the time I thought I was doing her a favour, by helping her get over Frank's death.'

'I think taking over the running of the Glasshouse did that for her,' observed Maribeth.

'You've been talking to her, haven't you?'

'Now and again. She's a heck of a lady.'

'What worries me, she's been having gentlemen callers, and I still think she needs protecting from that flock of goddam vultures.'

'Hey, she's entitled to get her life back on track. It's been five months since Frank died.'

'Oh, that part I don't mind. Hell, it's none of my business. But it *is* my business when those callers include Stefano Bacal and Wolfgang Klein.'

'No!' gasped Maribeth, remembering her encounter with those same men in the Town Hall.

'Now, we know all that shit ain't going to happen any more, but we also know most of the men in town who would be only too happy to join in if some other smart-ass pulled a similar stunt. And we know their motive: money, plain and simple. As you know, Mom's quite a wealthy woman now, with the business and Frank's life insurance, to say nothing of inheriting his house and all the art collection in it. And here we have a succession of Firefall's finest calling to pay their respects just as their own businesses start failing! Good looker my mom may be, but I bet they find her bank balance looks a whole lot cuter. It's as plain as day.'

'The rig's now being dismantled,' she argued. 'Their businesses should pick up as a result.'

'True, but the real damage may have been done already, particularly to Klein's construction company. So there's no harm in making sure there's a wife with money nearby, in case your finances take a tumble.'

'But how can you explain to her about them? I mean, you're not known as a clairvoyant, are you?'

He laughed. 'You know I can't say anything. Luckily, my mom's sharp. Sharper, it seems, than I gave her credit for. She already sent both of them packing! Remember, her business is keeping people satisfied, and you can only do that if you know what people want. But that still leaves Sheriff Ed.'

'Ed Rickenbacker? No!'

'Oh, yes. And it ain't him who's doing the running! Mum's already got her eyes fixed on him.'

'What does Ed say about it?'

'Ed's scared I'll sneak up behind and shoot him.'

Maribeth studied Entwistle. Was he being serious?

'And would you?'

'Only if he hurt Mom. Besides, I'm after his job, and his support would clinch it.'

'So he's giving it up?'

'Yeah, heart's not in it any more. He told me this morning.'

'Because he killed Hartsby?'

'No, no. Ed's no wuss. What he did then was right, and he knows it. All three of us know it. No, it's guilt. He knows what he *nearly* did, selling out his town and his principles and all – and he knows what it would have cost Firefall if he'd gone ahead with it. Pretty hard to uphold the law when you know what you yourself are capable of deep down. No, he's – what? – lost his way? Yeah . . . lost his way.'

Deep down, thought Maribeth, remembering the man she had killed in a different time-stream, it seemed everyone was capable of things they might not consider in normal circumstances.

Gloom had descended on the car, and in trying to rekindle their conversation Entwistle failed to improve matters by asking if she felt all right.

'Course I'm not all right, Entwistle. Remember, I'm a schoolteacher, not a green beret!'

'Sorry. It'll heal, given time,' he said, knowing his answer was pathetic. But how could it heal something neither of them had the medicine for?

Then, desperate for something to cheer her up, he mentioned an invitation he and his mother had received from an old friend.

'It's a party down in San Francisco. Before what happened to us happened, I was planning on taking Carol, to show her a good time. But now I reckon *we* deserve the good time, and anyway Ed can take care of Carol. So, do you fancy a trip to California? Maybe even make it a honeymoon?' he mumbled.

'I presume that's a proposal.'

'Can't go the whole hog, Maribeth. Got my bad knee to consider.'

She had known a proposal was inevitable, given their growing love and their active love life, but it still came as a bit of a shock. (Hell, it was still a couple of months before Ben Angelis was due to abandon her out at that damn seedy motel.)

'I'll think about it,' she answered simply.

Entwistle didn't press the matter further. He had already waited this long for the right woman; a few days longer wouldn't be too much to bear.

A contented silence fell as they stared out at the sunny afternoon.

'Did you have another nightmare last night?' Maribeth finally asked, thinking back to his quiet whimpering.

'Yes,' said Entwistle. 'Same one, too, when I keep killing myself. I know it's because we jumped into ourselves and ended the *us* in this time-stream, but it's still unnerving.'

He didn't need to add that if Hartsby was accurate then those other time-streams would still be carrying on without them.

Maribeth stared at her hands, noticing the occasional tremor. 'At least we know that in *this* time-stream we've saved all those other people's lives.'

'Third time lucky,' he added bitterly. Then, turning to her, anger flared in his eyes. 'You know what the worst thing of all is? Wondering who number 38 was – who he *is*. Because that bastard's still out there somewhere.'

Maribeth, too, found it a depressing thought that someone so ruthless and evil was still loose in the world – someone willing to wreak havoc on so many innocent victims.

Just then Greg and Summer walked out of the hospital together, giggling, and climbed into the back of the cruiser.

'Greg, promise me one thing,' remarked Entwistle as they set off down the wooded drive.

'What?'

'That this'll be the last time you ever take a ride in the back of a cop car.'

Greg turned and hugged Summer Campbell, still unable to believe his luck. 'This is the last time, Deputy Entwistle. I promise, the last time.'

Entwistle and Maribeth exchanged glances, aware of the little shiver that Greg's final words had provoked in them. Still, thought Entwistle, it looked like today would be a good day – and there had been several 'todays' recently that had been anything but good!

Unfortunately, as they reached the top of the hospital drive, Sheriff Rickenbacker's cruiser slewed to a stop in front of them, forcing Entwistle to slam on his brakes and slide to a halt in a cloud of dust.

'What the hell?' Entwistle shouted, his cop instincts making him reach for his .38 even as he kicked open the door.

By the time he exited his Contour, he was already too late.

Blood running from a gash on the side of his head, Ed Rickenbacker stumbled out of the driver's side, as an unknown man climbed out of the passenger door, aiming an automatic pistol at Entwistle.

'Lose the gun, Deputy!' barked the stranger.

He was tall and well built, his hair short and dark, his face tight, his plain features sheened in sweat.

For any policeman the cardinal rule is *Never lose your weapon*, but Entwistle could sense from the man's unwavering aim, and the steely determination in his flinty eyes, that this was no time for arguing.

Sheriff Rickenbacker hastily concurred. 'Do it, Entwistle. He won't shoot so long as you do what he says.'

'Who the hell are you?' Entwistle asked the gunman.

'Doesn't matter, Deputy. Just drop the weapon.'

Entwistle wondered if he should brave a shot, then reluctantly lowered his gun and let it drop with a clatter onto the driveway.

'Kick it over here!'

Entwistle complied, his weapon sliding into the man's foot. The stranger flicked it into the undergrowth behind him.

'Right, everyone else out!' he commanded.

As the other three climbed out of Entwistle's car, the gunman moved around the front of Rickenbacker's cruiser and motioned for the Sheriff to join the small group of prisoners.

'I ain't about to waste my time arguing with you. If I don't get a straight answer, I shoot these two women. End of story.'

'What do—?' Entwistle started.

Without a flicker the man aimed a shot at Summer's left leg. She screamed and dropped to the ground, Greg immediately diving down beside her.

'You bastard!' he yelled in fury.

'Not another word,' growled the stranger. 'I ask, and you answer. Where's the money?'

'What money?' said Entwistle, puzzled.

Again the man took aim at Summer. She lay weeping and shaking on the ground, while Greg tried to staunch the flow of blood from just above her knee.

'No!' shouted Rickenbacker. 'I know where it is.'

'What?' Entwistle was totally mystified.

'Well, in that case I don't need the rest of them, do I?' The man was now taking aim at Maribeth.

As Rickenbacker stepped towards him, he instantly switched his aim to the Sheriff's head.

'You shoot anyone else here, I'll not tell you a word,' said the Sheriff.

The stranger stared at Rickenbacker for a couple of seconds, then he slowly nodded.

'OK. Where is it?'

'On a farm about five miles out from here.'

'OK, we leave the girl and the nigger. You take your car and lead the way, Sheriff. The Deputy and the redhead get back in their own car, I sit in the back.'

There was no argument: he was in complete control.

Before he stepped into Entwistle's Contour, he pointed his pistol back where Greg was kneeling.

'Any cops follow us, these three will die. Then I come looking for you and the bitch.'

Greg merely nodded, his eyes blazing hatred.

Rickenbacker steered his cruiser out onto the highway. Entwistle followed. Maribeth was beside him in the front; the gunman sat directly behind Entwistle, the automatic pressed to the Deputy's ear.

'He takes one wrong turn or tries to speed off, you die instantly. Now get him on the radio.'

Patched through to Rickenbacker's car, he repeated these warnings to the Sheriff, then handed the microphone back to Entwistle.

But instead of placing the instrument back in its holder, Entwistle pressed SPEAK.

'Ed, what is this shit? *What* money?'

Before Rickenbacker could reply, the microphone was slapped out of Entwistle's hand and the pistol jabbed deep into his ear.

'Listen up, Deputy. I don't know if you're as ignorant as you make out, but you and this bitch were there when Hartsby was shot. He arrived with money for me – and now it's gone. So I reckon one of you fucks has got it, and I aim to make it mine.'

'We don't know anything about any money,' interrupted Maribeth, finally finding her voice.

'Well, either your Sheriff's mighty casual with other people's lives, or he's a deceitful sonofabitch. Either way, if there's no money found at this farm we're heading to, you're all dead. Every one of you.'

'We're all dead anyway. It's not like you're going to let us live to testify,' murmured Entwistle to himself, finally understanding who the stranger was.

For the gunman sitting behind them had to be number 38.

It took them just ten minutes to reach Napier's Farm. Napier himself heard them arrive and was standing on his porch when number 38 stepped out of Entwistle's cruiser and ordered everyone into the farmhouse. Once inside, Rickenbacker led them all downstairs to the cellar.

The large, dank room looked just as Entwistle remembered it – even to the digging of a hole in the ground, although this time it had been filled in again. That was a puzzle in itself, for the attack on Firefall wasn't due to take place for another six weeks, yet the hole had already been prepared.

'So where is it, Sheriff?' demanded 38.

'Buried down there.' Rickenbacker nodded towards the darker patch of earth in the grey dirt floor. 'Along with Hartsby.'

'Better get digging, then. You lot too,' said 38, gesturing to Entwistle and the nervous farmer.

'Fetch some shovels,' said Rickenbacker, turning to Napier. 'Let's get this over with.'

'But he's going to kill us,' protested Napier, suddenly more angry than frightened.

'You want to die right now?' said Rickenbacker. 'I'm

not keen on shovelling dirt either, but at least we're still alive while we're doing it. Now get those damn shovels!'

Napier fetched three long-handled shovels and the digging progressed quickly.

'Is there really money down here?' whispered Entwistle, tossing a shovelful to the side of the rapidly growing pit.

Rickenbacker grunted, 'Yes.'

'Where from?'

'Shut up and dig,' ordered 38.

After a while Entwistle paused, sweat stinging his eyes. He glanced at Maribeth, who had been instructed to sit cross-legged over to one side of the room, her hands on her head in full view. She must be suffering cramp in her arms, but her face remained impassive except for the occasional glare at number 38.

'Hey, if I'm gonna die because Ed here stole your money,' began Entwistle, 'I want to hear how he did it, because *we* saw no damn money. So where'd you find it, Ed?'

Rickenbacker looked warily up at 38, then started to explain.

'After you left the motel, I waited till dark, then loaded Hartsby's body into the trunk of his car. I was in a bit of a hurry, so didn't look carefully, but when Napier and I came to unload his corpse in the yard outside, we found a briefcase wedged behind. Inside of it there was about three hundred grand. A scary amount of money, but I remembered how much Hartsby had been promising me, so I figured it was seed money for this guy here.'

Number 38 did not contradict; he was leaning back

against a workbench, his gun moving regularly to cover his prisoners in turn.

'We had us all a little plan,' said 38 suddenly after a silence. 'Looks like it won't work out now but that's no reason to kiss off the cash – not least with Hartsby himself gone.'

Entwistle turned to Rickenbacker. 'So what the hell were *you* going to do with it?'

'You know my financial situation,' said Rickenbacker.

'For God's sake, I trusted you, Ed.'

'Aw, for Chrissakes, Entwistle, the man was dead. The money was going spare, and who was to know?'

'No one but me,' said 38. 'I was due to meet him at that motel. And just as I get there, you two come out, so I bide my time to see who else is there. Lo and behold, out comes our crooked Sheriff carrying some suspiciously heavy-looking bedding.'

Just then Napier let out an oath. All eyes turned to look at his discovery. It was a man's hand.

Number 38 nodded approvingly. 'One out of two. Now find me the cash.'

Between them, the three diggers proceeded to uncover the rest of Hartsby, who was lying face-down and fully clothed. They then pulled his body to one side of the pit and, under Rickenbacker's directions, began digging at the spot where the corpse's feet had lain.

'We buried the money first,' explained Rickenbacker. 'Figured on leaving it here a couple months just in case anyone came snooping around.'

Suddenly number 38 fired a shot into the ceiling, startling them all.

'Getting bored with your chat. Just find the money!'

They resumed their digging, but Entwistle was curious to know more about 38 himself, so he persevered.

'Your little plan would never have worked,' he challenged.

'And how the fuck would you know?'

Rickenbacker answered for his deputy. 'Oh, he knows, believe me. It wouldn't have worked.'

'Not least because this shithead here was planning a double-cross.' Entwistle pointed at Hartsby's corpse.

Number 38's face showed surprise. 'And just how the fuck—?'

'You and Hartsby were planning to recruit a gang of local malcontents to hold the town to ransom. But then you were going to double-cross the gullible idiots and keep the whole ten million for yourselves.'

'I'm impressed,' sneered 38. 'Did you torture this out of Hartsby before you killed him?'

Entwistle saw no point in arguing. 'Sort of, yes. What's more, he told us how he intended double-crossing you as well.'

'What do you mean?'

'Have you scouted out the town yet? Have you inspected that rig?'

'Sure. That thing was the excuse for it all.'

'Noticed that box on top, then?'

'Yeah, so what?'

'Well, you might not know that contains a bomb. And Hartsby was going to use it to blow the town and you all to hell.'

'Well, that I don't believe. So just keep digging.'

Rickenbacker and Napier continued shovelling but Entwistle wanted to drive home his advantage. 'To put such trust in that vicious bastard, you must have worked with Hartsby before. Some sort of covert ops, I'd guess?'

'Whooh, you been watching too much of *The X-Files*. Yeah, we go a long way back. I did some business for him. I'm good. The best.'

So he liked to brag, but now he was talking.

'Not if you couldn't spot what that weasel was planning, you ain't.'

The man considered this, then smiled grimly. 'Seems you can't trust *nobody* these days, Deputy. But there's still this cash to soothe my injured pride.'

Just then Napier announced he had found something else.

Rickenbacker got down on his knees and began scraping soil off a tan briefcase. Uncovering the handle, he yanked the case free, tossing it at 38's feet.

'You open it,' said 38, nodding at Entwistle.

Entwistle stepped out of the three-foot pit and kneeled to flick the catches on the briefcase. Lifting its lid, he found it crammed tight with neat stacks of used hundred-dollar bills.

'Well, seems I could trust Hartsby enough to deliver the cash like he promised,' said 38. 'Maybe all that other stuff you're spouting is just so much bullshit.'

'Oh, yes?' said Maribeth, rising suddenly, and attracting the aim of 38's automatic. 'So how come we know your personal code name for this operation?'

'Code name?'

'Number 38, isn't it?' said Entwistle.

The man looked genuinely surprised. 'Well, well, well, the little shit . . . he obviously *did* do some confessing. Which means you three are pretty determined – all the more reason for me to eliminate you.'

'Why don't you just take the money?' said Entwistle, slowly standing upright while scanning the cellar for some weapon he could use. 'If we three murdered Hartsby, we can't exactly go running to the cops, can we? Hell, we are the damn cops!'

'Maybe so, but you can still come looking for me.'

Despite feeling scared, Maribeth managed to add, 'But if you're the best, do you honestly think we'd ever find you? We don't even know your name.'

'Let's cut the crap!' yelled Rickenbacker suddenly, trying to scramble out of the pit. 'Just get it over with, or so help me I'll—'

Number 38's first bullet hit him in the chest. The Sheriff fell backwards, slumping against the side of the pit.

Napier threw himself down behind the fallen Sheriff, but 38's next shot followed him down, striking him in the shoulder. Yelling in agony, Napier thrashed over onto his back – as 38 took aim again at the farmer's head.

Moving swiftly from behind, Maribeth hurled herself at the gunman, crashing against his hip and making him stagger sideways.

'Bitch!' he yelled, twisting round to shoot.

Entwistle now saw his chance. He leaped headlong across the cellar to collide with 38's other side, then landed heavily against the wall. Raising his hand, he grasped hold of a familiar object.

As he yanked it away from the wall, and out into the middle of the cellar, he yelled aloud: 'Hey, you fucker!'

Number 38 whipped round, saw Entwistle huddled at the base of the wall, and raised his automatic for the kill.

But then another movement caught his eye. Looking up, his face registered puzzlement, then horror, and then . . .

Blood.

The eight-foot pit-saw – the same one Entwistle had used to free himself of his bonds twice before – descended heavily in an arc and slammed into the crown of 38's head. Half a dozen of its two-inch-long teeth buried themselves into the fragile shell of his skull, the sheer weight of the saw driving him to his knees. There he came to rest, his arms limp at his side, the vicious implement holding him grotesquely erect from the waist up. His dead eyes were frozen wide in disbelief, but quickly filling with the dark blood that rilled from the punctures in his face and head.

Thank God I've been here before, thought Entwistle. He turned away to check on Maribeth, who was quaking with fear and adrenalin but otherwise unhurt. He then switched his attention to Rickenbacker.

The Sheriff was lying on his back, his eyes wide open, his face deathly white.

'Ed! Come on, Ed, you bastard! You damned hypocrite, you're not going to get out of this mess by playing the hero and martyr again! Hold on . . . hold on!' Entwistle was leaning over his boss and shouting into his face.

Rickenbacker suddenly blinked, his face creasing up with pain.

'Oh Jesus, sweet Jesus,' he gasped. 'Get off me, will ya . . .'

Entwistle stumbled back as Rickenbacker thrashed himself into a sitting position. The Sheriff ripped open his uniform shirt to reveal a bulletproof vest beneath.

'Thank God,' moaned Maribeth, dissolving into tears.

'I live. She cries,' gasped Rickenbacker. 'Go figure.'

'But why? You never wore one of those before.'

Rickenbacker offered Entwistle and Maribeth both hands, and together they helped him out of the pit. They next tried to help Napier, but he cursed them all and insisted on hauling himself out onto the cellar floor. They could see he had merely a flesh wound.

Between groans of pain, Rickenbacker started to explain. 'When I was driving Hartsby's car out here, with the bastard's body in the trunk, I began to reckon I was being followed. So I took a few back roads and lost him. Couple of days later Brackhouse reported some guy watching my house and we checked his licence plate. It was registered to a rental from Laramie. Before Gil got to talk to this guy, he'd disappeared, so we checked his rental ID, and it was faked. I've been keeping my eyes open ever since, and thought I'd better wear this thing in the meantime. I guess he decided to wait for his opportunity – then you lot turned up. Sorry I had to drop you in it.'

'Thanks a whole bunch, you bastard,' said Napier.

'Hey, you weren't objecting to spending the money.'

Napier fell quiet and began to shamble up the stairs, gently clutching his bleeding shoulder.

The three others studied the dead man, still sitting upright like some grotesque sculpture.

'And what about him?' asked Maribeth.

'Looks like he got us to dig his own grave,' said Rickenbacker. 'Whoever he was.'

'I don't think Bill Napier'll thank you for burying him in his cellar,' commented Entwistle.

'Bill Napier can go screw himself. I know enough dirt about Mr Out-Of-State Dirty-Deeds Napier to keep him in line.'

'What about all this money?' said Maribeth. 'I can't pretend I'm not disappointed in you, Sheriff. After what we told you ... and all that stuff you gave us about being so grateful for a second chance.'

Rickenbacker shook his head. 'But I also told you how I had no pension. What would *you* have done? Entwistle knows I'm courting his mom and he also knows I'm broke. That's a lousy situation for a man, but if I had access to some funds of my own, well ... ain't like the IRS are going to be after it.'

'Still a dirty trick,' said Entwistle, pulling a look of disgust as he struggled to extricate the rusted pit-saw from number 38's bloodstained head.

'It's a dirty world, Entwistle,' replied Rickenbacker. 'As you'll find when you become the Sheriff.'

'What if I don't want the job?'

'Oh, you want it all right, and you'll enjoy it. Not least because it'll be easier now you know the men in this town who are capable of turning bad. Wouldn't be surprised if we don't get ourselves a new sheriff's office pretty soon, too.'

'And now they're pulling that oil rig out, the town should be back to normal next year,' said Maribeth.

'But there's still people here going out of business. Look at Gerry Rankin. Look at all of them – you heard them that time in the Town Hall.'

'When?' said Rickenbacker, looking puzzled.

'Just before you took the—' Entwistle stopped himself in time. It wouldn't do to describe to a man how he had died.

'Took what?'

'Never mind that,' interrupted Maribeth, her queasy stomach taking another lurch as she remembered Rickenbacker's mutilated body. 'I think we've found a use for the money.'

'Uh-oh,' said Rickenbacker, rubbing his bruised chest.

'What?' said Entwistle, stepping back as the pit-saw and number 38 finally parted company and the corpse rolled into the pit to join his erstwhile employer.

'A hardship fund,' explained Maribeth. 'Interest-free loans to those who need them to get over the bad times.'

'Good idea,' said Entwistle.

'What about those of us who don't run businesses?' Rickenbacker addressed Maribeth with an ingratiating grin.

She smiled back. 'Oh, I think we can make a small allowance here and there.'

'Yeah, and Mom might make one as well, as long as you're honest.'

The two men stared at each other, then burst out laughing.

'Hell, what's a couple of murders in this day and age!' said Rickenbacker.

'Two too many,' Maribeth interrupted their joviality. 'Now, if you'll excuse me, I'm going upstairs to throw up.'

'Well, don't do it over the money.'

Entwistle closed the briefcase and handed it to her.

As Maribeth carefully hauled herself up the steep wooden stairs to the kitchen, Rickenbacker and Entwistle returned their gaze to number 38.

'And we've absolutely no idea who he is?' said Entwistle.

'Maybe we could take his fingerprints and check them out?'

They stared down at the man's hands, one lying across his chest, the other over his bloodied face.

'They'd probably want to know why we were asking, and that could start a whole new pile of shit. I think maybe we'll just let it rest.'

They skirted the pit, and its two incumbents, and headed up the stairs.

'We'll sort this out later,' said Rickenbacker. 'Right now I need a drink.'

He paused at the top step. 'One thing, Entwistle, where do we say the money came from – for this goddam hardship fund of Maribeth's?'

'An anonymous benefactor. Maybe someone who'd had such a hot time in Firefall, he wanted to show us his appreciation.'

'A hot time?'

'You ever seen a fuel-air bomb explode?'

Or felt it, thought Entwistle, staring at his soiled hands. He made his way over to the sink and held his hands under the cold water for much longer than was necessary to rinse away the cellar dirt.

'I'd better call in about Summer Campbell,' said Rickenbacker, making his way out to his car. 'Good thing that happened outside the hospital. He missed the artery, so she should be OK.'

'Yeah, but she might still have a busted knee,' said Entwistle, thinking of how the cold weather always made his own bad knee play up.

'Better than being dead, anyway.'

That was also true. Entwistle looked at Maribeth sitting by the kitchen table. She was still shivering.

His heart ached to see someone he realized he loved looking so scared. He could imagine that Greg was now feeling just the same. He went over and sat down next to her and held her cold hands, brushing his lips across the salty tracks of tears on her cheek.

Shock had clearly caught up with Maribeth. It was all she could manage to squeeze his fingers, while praying that, at last, it was all over.

Entwistle silently vowed, then and there, that he *would* become Sheriff – and would use his privileged insight into the varying characters of the town's leading citizens to ensure they acted for the good of Firefall, and not for their own personal aggrandizement. And, if ever he should find himself hesitating in this, all he needed to do was remember the horrific sight of his beloved Maribeth on fire – as they leaped together towards that glowing cube.

WORTHING TRIBUNE 13 October

DEATHS

COLLINGWOOD (Gloria Marie) – Passed away peacefully 11 October at home, aged 54 years. The dearly loved wife of Del, the much loved sister of Harriet and Mark, a loving aunt to Clarice, Fiona, Eloise and Daniel. She will be very sadly missed by all friends and relatives. Family flowers only. Donations to FBI Benevolent Fund or the Alzheimer's Research Foundation. Funeral service at St Mark's Chapel, Alden Road at 10 A.M., Wednesday 15 October.

All enquiries to P. Epperdine Funeral Services.

All Pan Books are available at your local bookshop or newsagent, or can be ordered direct from the publisher. Indicate the number of copies required and fill in the form below.

Send to: Macmillan General Books C.S.
Book Service By Post
PO Box 29, Douglas I-O-M
IM99 1BQ

or phone: 01624 675137, quoting title, author and credit card number.

or fax: 01624 670923, quoting title, author, and credit card number.

or Internet: http://www.bookpost.co.uk

Please enclose a remittance* to the value of the cover price plus 75 pence per book for post and packing. Overseas customers please allow £1.00 per copy for post and packing.

*Payment may be made in sterling by UK personal cheque, Eurocheque, postal order, sterling draft or international money order, made payable to Book Service By Post.

Alternatively by Access/Visa/MasterCard

Card No. | | | | | | | | | | | | | | | | |

Expiry Date | | | | | | | | | | | | | | | | |

Signature ______________________________

Applicable only in the UK and BFPO addresses.

While every effort is made to keep prices low, it is sometimes necessary to increase prices at short notice. Pan Books reserve the right to show on covers and charge new retail prices which may differ from those advertised in the text or elsewhere.

NAME AND ADDRESS IN BLOCK CAPITAL LETTERS PLEASE

Name ______________________________

Address ______________________________

____

____

____

8/95

Please allow 28 days for delivery.
Please tick box if you do not wish to receive any additional information. ☐